KU-038-594

TURTLE RECALL: THE DISCWORLD COMPANION . . . SO FAR
(with Stephen Briggs)

NANNY OGG'S COOKBOOK
(with Stephen Briggs, Tina Hannan and Paul Kidby)

THE PRATCHETT PORTFOLIO
(with Paul Kidby)

THE DISCWORLD ALMANAK
(with Bernard Pearson)

THE UNSEEN UNIVERSITY CUT-OUT BOOK
(with Alan Batley and Bernard Pearson)

WHERE'S MY COW?
(illustrated by Melvyn Grant)

THE ART OF DISCWORLD
(with Paul Kidby)

THE WIT AND WISDOM OF DISCWORLD
(compiled by Stephen Briggs)

THE FOLKLORE OF DISCWORLD
(with Jacqueline Simpson)

THE WORLD OF POO
(with the Discworld Emporium)

MRS BRADSHAW'S HANDBOOK
(with the Discworld Emporium)

THE COMPLEAT ANKH-MORPORK
(with the Discworld Emporium)

THE STREETS OF ANKH-MORPORK
(with Stephen Briggs, painted by Stephen Player)

THE DISCWORLD MAPP
(with Stephen Briggs, painted by Stephen Player)

A TOURIST GUIDE TO LANCRE – A DISCWORLD MAPP
(with Stephen Briggs, illustrated by Paul Kidby)

DEATH'S DOMAIN (with Paul Kidby)

THE DISCWORLD ATLAS
(with the Discworld Emporium)

Non-Discworld books

THE DARK SIDE OF THE SUN

STRATA

THE UNADULTERATED CAT (illustrated by Gray Jolliffe)

GOOD OMENS (with Neil Gaiman)

Shorter Writing

A BLINK OF THE SCREEN

A SLIP OF THE KEYBOARD

SHAKING HANDS WITH DEATH

With Stephen Baxter

THE LONG EARTH

THE LONG WAR

THE LONG MARS

THE LONG UTOPIA

THE LONG COSMOS

Non-Discworld books for young adults

THE CARPET PEOPLE

TRUCKERS

DIGGERS

WINGS

ONLY YOU CAN SAVE MANKIND

JOHNNY AND THE DEAD

JOHNNY AND THE BOMB

NATION

DODGER

JACK DODGER'S GUIDE TO LONDON

DRAGONS AT CRUMBLING CASTLE

THE WITCH'S VACUUM CLEANER

FATHER CHRISTMAS'S FAKE BEARD

A complete list of Terry Pratchett ebooks and audio books as well as other books based on the Discworld series – illustrated screenplays, graphic novels, comics and plays – can be found on **www.terrypratchett.co.uk**

MEN AT ARMS

A Discworld® Novel

Terry Pratchett

CORGI BOOKS

TRANSWORLD PUBLISHERS
61-63 Uxbridge Road, London W5 5SA
A Random House Group Company
www.transworldbooks.co.uk

MEN AT ARMS
A CORGI BOOK: 9780552167536

First published in Great Britain
in 1993 by Victor Gollancz Ltd
Corgi edition published 1994
Corgi edition reissued 2005
Corgi edition reissued 2013

Addresses for Random House Group Ltd companies outside the UK
can be found at: www.randomhouse.co.uk
The Random House Group Ltd Reg. No. 954009.

The Random House Group Limited supports The Forest Stewardship
Council® (FSC®), the leading international forest-certification organisation.
Our books carrying the FSC label are printed on FSC®-certified paper. FSC is
the only forest-certification scheme supported by the leading environmental
organisations, including Greenpeace. Our paper procurement policy can be
found at www.randomhouse.co.uk/environment

Typeset in Minion by Kestrel Data, Exeter, Devon.

Printed and bound in Great Britain by Clays Ltd, Elcograf S.p.A.

15

MEN AT ARMS

CORPORAL CARROT, ANKH-MORPORK CITY GUARD (Night Watch), sat down in his nightshirt, took up his pencil, sucked the end for a moment, and then wrote:

'Dearest Mume and Dad,
'Well here is another fine Turnup for the Books, for I have been made Corporal!! It means another Five Dollars a month plus also I have a new jerkin with, two stripes upon it as well. And a new copper badge! It is a Great responsibility!! This is all because we have got new recruits because the Patrician who, as I have formerly vouchsafed is the ruler of the city, has agreed the Watch must reflect the ethnic makeup of the City—'

Carrot paused for a moment and stared out of the small dusty bedroom window at the early evening sunlight sidling across the river. Then he bent over the paper again.

'—which I do not Fulley understand but must have something to do with the dwarf Grabpot

Thundergust's Cosmetic Factory. Also, Captain Vimes of who I have often written to you of is, leaving the Watch to get married and Become a Fine Gentleman and, I'm sure we wish him All the Best, he taught me All I Know apart, from the things I taught myself. We are clubbing together to get him a Surprise Present, I thought one of those new Watches that don't need demons to make them go and we could inscribe on the back something like "A Watch from, your Old Freinds in the Watch", this is a pune or Play on Words. We do not know who will be the new Captain, Sgt Colon says he will Resign if it's him, Cpl Nobbs—'

Carrot stared out of the window again. His big honest forehead wrinkled with effort as he tried to think of something positive to say about Corporal Nobbs.

'—is more suited in his current Roll, and I have not been in the Watch long enough. So we shall just have to wait and See—'

It began, as many things do, with a death. And a burial, on a spring morning, with mist on the ground so thick that it poured into the grave and the coffin was lowered into cloud.

A small greyish mongrel, host to so many assorted doggy diseases that it was surrounded by a cloud of dust, watched impassively from the mound of earth.

Various elderly female relatives cried. But Edward d'Eath didn't cry, for three reasons. He was the eldest son, the thirty-seventh Lord d'Eath, and it was Not Done for a d'Eath to cry; he was – just, the diploma still had the crackle in it – an Assassin, and Assassins didn't cry at a death, otherwise they'd never be stopping; and he was angry. In fact, he was enraged.

Enraged at having to borrow money for this poor funeral. Enraged at the weather, at this common cemetery, at the way the background noise of the city didn't change in any way, even on such an occasion as this. Enraged at history. It was never meant to be like this.

It shouldn't have *been* like this.

He looked across the river to the brooding bulk of the Palace, and his anger screwed itself up and became a lens.

Edward had been sent to the Assassins' Guild because they had the best school for those whose social rank is rather higher than their intelligence. If he'd been trained as a Fool, he'd have invented satire and made dangerous jokes about the Patrician. If he'd been trained as a Thief,* he'd have broken into the Palace and stolen something very valuable from the Patrician.

However . . . he'd been sent to the Assassins . . .

That afternoon he sold what remained of the d'Eath estates, and enrolled again at the Guild school.

---

*But no *gentleman* would *dream* of being trained as a Thief.

For the post-graduate course.

He got full marks, the first person in the history of the Guild ever to do so. His seniors described him as a man to watch – and, because there was something about him that made even Assassins uneasy, preferably from a long way away.

In the cemetery the solitary gravedigger filled in the hole that was the last resting place of d'Eath senior.

He became aware of what seemed to be thoughts in his head. They went something like this:

Any chance of a bone? No, no, sorry, bad taste there, forget I mentioned it. You've got beef sandwiches in your wossname, lunchbox thingy, though. Why not give one to the nice little doggy over there?

The man leaned on his shovel and looked around.

The grey mongrel was watching him intently.

It said, 'Woof?'

It took Edward d'Eath five months to find what he was looking for. The search was hampered by the fact that he did not *know* what he was looking for, only that he'd know it when he found it. Edward was a great believer in Destiny. Such people often are.

The Guild library was one of the largest in the city. In certain specialized areas it was *the* largest. These areas mainly had to do with the regrettable brevity of human life and the means of bringing it about.

Edward spent a lot of time there, often at the top of a ladder, often surrounded by dust.

He read every known work on armaments. He didn't know what he was looking for and he found it in a note in the margin of an otherwise very dull and inaccurate treatise on the ballistics of crossbows. He copied it out, carefully.

Edward spent a lot of time among history books as well. The Assassins' Guild was an association of gentlemen of breeding, and people like that regard the whole of recorded history as a kind of stock book. There were a great many books in the Guild library, and a whole portrait gallery of kings and queens,* and Edward d'Eath came to know their aristocratic faces better than he did his own. He spent his lunch hours there.

It was said later that he came under bad influences at this stage. But the secret of the history of Edward d'Eath was that he came under no outside influences at all, unless you count all those dead kings. He just came under the influence of himself.

That's where people get it wrong. Individuals aren't naturally paid-up members of the human race, except biologically. They need to be bounced around by the Brownian motion of society, which is a mechanism by which human beings constantly remind one another that they are . . . well . . . human beings. He was also spiralling inwards, as tends to happen in cases like this.

He'd had no plan. He'd just retreated, as people

---

*Often with discreet plaques under them modestly recording the name of the person who'd killed them. This was the *Assassins'* portrait gallery, after all.

do when they feel under attack, to a more defensible position, i.e. the past, and then something happened which had the same effect on Edward as finding a plesiosaur in his goldfish pond would on a student of ancient reptiles.

He'd stepped out blinking in the sunlight one hot afternoon, after a day spent in the company of departed glory, and had seen the face of the past strolling by, nodding amiably to people.

He hadn't been able to control himself. He'd said, 'Hey, you! Who are y-ou?'

The past had said, 'Corporal Carrot, sir. Night Watch. Mr d'Eath, isn't it? Can I help you?'

'What? No! No. Be about your b-usiness!'

The past nodded and smiled at him, and strolled on, into the future.

Carrot stopped staring at the wall.

'I have expended three dollars on an iconograph box which, is a thing with a brownei inside that paints pictures of thing's, this is all the Rage these days. Please find enclosed pictures of my room and my freinds in the Watch, Nobby is the one making the Humerous Gesture but he is a Rough Diamond and a good soul deep down.'

He stopped again. Carrot wrote home at least once a week. Dwarfs generally did. Carrot was two metres tall but he'd been brought up as a dwarf, and then further up as a human. Literary endeavour did not come easily to him, but he persevered.

'The weather,' he wrote, very slowly and carefully, 'continues Very Hot . . .'

Edward could not believe it. He checked the records. He double-checked. He asked questions and, because they were innocent enough questions, people gave him answers. And finally he took a holiday in the Ramtops, where careful questioning led him to the dwarf mines around Copperhead, and thence to an otherwise unremarkable glade in a beech wood where, sure enough, a few minutes of patient digging unearthed traces of charcoal.

He spent the whole day there. When he'd finished, carefully replacing the leafmould as the sun went down, he was quite certain.

Ankh-Morpork had a king again.

And this was *right*. And it was *fate* that had let Edward recognize this *just* when he'd got his Plan. And it was *right* that it was *Fate*, and the city would be *Saved* from its ignoble present by its *glorious* past. He had the *Means*, and he had the *end*. And so on . . . Edward's thoughts often ran like this.

He could think in *italics*. Such people need watching.

Preferably from a safe distance.

'I was Interested in your letter where you said people have been coming and asking about me, this is Amazing, I have been here hardly Five Minutes and already I am Famus.

'I was very pleased to hear about the opening of #7 shaft. I don't mind Telling You that although,

I am very happy here I miss the Good Times back Home. Sometimes on my day Off I go and, sit in the Cellar and hit my head with an axe handle but, it is Not the Same.

   'Hoping this finds you in Good Health,
     Yrs faithfully,
          'Your loving son, adopted,
               Carrot.'

He folded the letter up, inserted the iconographs, sealed it with a blob of candle wax pressed into place with his thumb, and put it in his pants pocket. Dwarf mail to the Ramtops was quite reliable. More and more dwarfs were coming to work in the city, and because dwarfs are very conscientious many of them sent money home. This made dwarf mail just about as safe as anything, since their mail was closely guarded. Dwarfs are very attached to gold. Any highwayman demanding 'Your money or your life' had better bring a folding chair and packed lunch and a book to read while the debate goes on.

Then Carrot washed his face, donned his leather shirt and trousers and chainmail, buckled on his breastplate and, with his helmet under his arm, stepped out cheerfully, ready to face whatever the future would bring.

This was another room, somewhere else.

It was a poky room, the plaster walls crumbling, the ceilings sagging like the underside of a fat man's bed. And it was made even more crowded by the furniture.

It was old, good furniture, but this wasn't the place for it. It belonged in high echoing halls. Here, it was crammed. There were dark oak chairs. There were long sideboards. There was even a suit of armour. There was barely room for the half dozen or so people who sat at the huge table. There was barely room for the table.

A clock ticked in the shadows.

The heavy velvet curtains were drawn, even though there was still plenty of daylight left in the sky. The air was stifling, both from the heat of the day and the candles in the magic lantern.

The only illumination was from the screen which, at that moment, was portraying a very good profile of Corporal Carrot Ironfoundersson.

The small but very select audience watched it with the carefully blank expressions of people who are half convinced that their host is several cards short of a full deck but are putting up with it because they've just eaten a meal and it would be rude to leave too soon.

'Well?' said one of them. 'I think I've seen him walking around the city. So? He's just a watchman, Edward.'

'Of course. It is essential that he should be. A humble station in life. It all fits the classic p-attern.' Edward d'Eath gave a signal. There was a click as another glass slide was slotted in. '*This* one was not p-ainted from life. King P-paragore. Taken from an old p-ainting. This one' – *click!* – 'is King Veltrick III. From another p-portrait. This one is Queen Alguinna IV . . . note the line of the chin? This one' –

click! – 'is a sevenpenny p-iece from the reign of Webblethorpe the Unconscious, note again the detail of the chin and general b-bone structure, and this' – *click!* – 'is . . . an upside d-own picture of a vase of flowers. D-elphiniums, I believe. Why is this?'

'Er, sorry, Mr Edward, I 'ad a few glass plates left and the demons weren't tired and—'

'Next slide, please. And then you may leave us.'

'Yes, Mr Edward.'

'Report to the d-uty torturer.'

'Yes, Mr Edward.'

Click!

'And this is a rather good – well done, Bl-enkin – image of the bust of Queen Coanna.'

'Thank you, Mr Edward.'

'More of her face would have enabled us to be certain of the likeness, however. There is sufficient, I believe. You may go, Bl-enkin.'

'Yes, Mr Edward.'

'A little something off the ears, I th-ink.'

'Yes, Mr Edward.'

The servant respectfully shut the door behind him, and then went down to the kitchen shaking his head sadly. The d'Eaths hadn't been able to afford a family torturer for years. For the boy's sake he'd just have to do the best he could with a kitchen knife.

The visitors waited for the host to speak, but he didn't seem about to do so, although it was sometimes hard to tell with Edward. When he was excited, he suffered not so much from a speech impediment as from misplaced pauses, as if his brain were temporarily putting his mouth on hold.

Eventually, one of the audience said: 'Very well. So what is your point?'

'You've seen the likeness. Isn't it ob-vious?'

'Oh, come now—'

Edward d'Eath pulled a leather case towards him and began undoing the thongs.

'But, but the boy was adopted by Discworld dwarfs. They found him as a baby in the forests of the Ramtop mountains. There were some b-urning wagons, corpses, that sort of thing. B-andit attack, apparently. The dwarfs found a sword in the wreckage. He has it now. A very *old* sword. And it's always sharp.'

'So? The world is full of old swords. *And* grind-stones.'

'This one had been very well hidden in one of the carts, which had broken up. Strange. One would expect it to be ready to hand, yes? To be used? In b-andit country? And then the boy grows up and, and . . . Fate . . . conspires that he and his sword come to Ankh-Morpork, where he is currently a watchman in the Night Watch. I couldn't believe it!'

'That's still not—'

Edward raised his hand a moment, and then pulled out a package from the case.

'I made careful enq-uiries, you know, and was able to find the place where the attack occurred. A most careful search of the ground revealed old cart n-ails, a few copper coins and, in some charcoal . . . this.'

They craned to see.

'Looks like a ring.'

'Yes. It's, it's, it's superficially d-iscoloured, of course, otherwise someone would have spot-ted it. Probably secreted somewhere on a cart. I've had it p-artly cleaned. You can just read the inscription. Now, *here* is an ill-ustrated inventory of the royal jewellery of Ankh done in AM 907, in the reign of King Tyrril. May I, please, may I draw your a-ttention to the small wedding ring in the b-ottom left-hand corner of the page? You will see that the artist has hel-pfully drawn the inscription.'

It took several minutes for everyone to examine it. They were naturally suspicious people. They were all descendants of people for whom suspicion and paranoia had been prime survival traits.

Because they were all aristocrats. Not one among them did not know the name of his or her great-great-great-grandfather and what embarrassing disease he'd died of.

They had just eaten a not-very-good meal which had, however, included some ancient and worthwhile wines. They'd attended because they'd all known Edward's father, and the d'Eaths were a fine old family, if now in very reduced circumstances.

'So you see,' said Edward proudly, 'the evidence is overwhelming. We have a king!'

His audience tried to avoid looking at one another's faces.

'I thought you'd be pl-eased,' said Edward.

Finally, Lord Rust voiced the unspoken consensus. There was no room in those true-blue eyes for pity, which was not a survival trait, but sometimes it was possible to risk a little kindness.

'Edward,' he said, 'the last king of Ankh-Morpork died centuries ago.'

'Executed by t-raitors!'

'Even if a descendant could still be found, the royal blood would be somewhat watered down by now, don't you think?'

'The royal b-lood *cannot* be wa-tered down!'

Ah, thought Lord Rust. So he's *that* kind. Young Edward thinks the touch of a king can cure scrofula, as if royalty was the equivalent of a sulphur ointment. Young Edward thinks that there is no lake of blood too big to wade through to put a rightful king on a throne, no deed too base in defence of a crown. A romantic, in fact.

Lord Rust was not a romantic. The Rusts had adapted well to Ankh-Morpork's post-monarchy centuries by buying and selling and renting and making contacts and doing what aristocrats have always done, which is trim sails and survive.

'Well, maybe,' he conceded, in the gentle tones of someone trying to talk someone else off a ledge, 'but we must ask ourselves: does Ankh-Morpork, at this point in time, *require* a king?'

Edward looked at him as though he were mad.

'Need? *Need?* While our fair city languishes under the heel of the ty-rant?'

'Oh. You mean Vetinari.'

'Can't you see what he's done to this city?'

'He is a very unpleasant, jumped-up little man,' said Lady Selachii, 'but I would not say he actually *terrorizes* much. Not as such.'

'You have to hand it to him,' said Viscount

Skater, 'the city operates. More or less. Fellas and whatnot do things.'

'The streets are safer than they used to be under Mad Lord Snapcase,' said Lady Selachii.

'Sa-fer? Vetinari set up the Thieves' Guild!' shouted Edward.

'Yes, yes, of course, very reprehensible, certainly. On the other hand, a modest annual payment and one walks in safety . . .'

'He always says,' said Lord Rust, 'that if you're going to have crime, it might as well be organized crime.'

'Seems to me,' said Viscount Skater, 'that all the Guild chappies put up with him because anyone else would be worse, yes? We've certainly had some . . . difficult ones. Anyone remember Homicidal Lord Winder?'

'Deranged Lord Harmoni,' said Lord Monflathers.

'Laughing Lord Scapula,' said Lady Selachii. 'A man with a *very* pointed sense of humour.'

'Mind you, Vetinari . . . there's something not entirely . . .' Lord Rust began.

'I know what you mean,' said Viscount Skater. 'I don't like the way he always knows what you're thinking before you think it.'

'Everyone knows the Assassins have set *his* fee at a million dollars,' said Lady Selachii. 'That's how much it would cost to have him killed.'

'One can't help feeling,' said Lord Rust, 'that it would cost a lot more than that to make sure he stayed dead.'

'Ye gods! What happened to pride? What happened to honour?'

They perceptibly jumped as the last Lord d'Eath thrust himself out of his chair.

'Will you listen to yourselves? Please? Look at you. What man among you has not seen his family name degraded since the days of the kings? Can't you remember the men your forefathers were?' He strode rapidly around the table, so that they had to turn to watch him. He pointed an angry finger.

'You, Lord Rust! Your ancestor was cr-eated a Baron after single-handedly killing thirty-seven Klatchians while armed with nothing more than a p-in, isn't that so?'

'Yes, but—'

'You, sir . . . Lord Monflathers! The first Duke led six hundred men to a glorious and epic de-feat at the Battle of Quirm! Does that mean n-othing? And you, Lord Venturii, and you, Sir George . . . sitting in Ankh in your old houses with your old names and your old money, while Guilds – *Guilds*! Ragtags of tradesmen and merchants! – Guilds, I say, have a voice in the r-unning of the city!'

He reached a bookshelf in two strides and threw a huge leather-bound book on the table, where it upset Lord Rust's glass.

'*Twurp's P-eerage*,' he shouted. 'We all have pages in there! We *own* it. But this man has you mesmerized! I assure you he is flesh and blood, a mere mortal! No one dares remove him because they th-ink it will make things a little worse for themselves! Ye g-ods!'

23

His audience looked glum. It was all true, of course . . . if you put it that way. And it didn't sound any better coming from a wild-eyed, pompous young man.

'Yes, yes, the good old days. Towerin' spires and pennants and chivalry and all that,' said Viscount Skater. 'Ladies in pointy hats. Chappies in armour bashin' one another and whatnot. But, y'know, we have to move with the times—'

'It was a golden age,' said Edward.

My god, thought Lord Rust. He actually *does* believe it.

'You see, dear boy,' said Lady Selachii, 'a few chance likenesses and a piece of jewellery – that doesn't really add up to much, does it?'

'My nurse told me,' said Viscount Skater, 'that a *true* king could pull a sword from a stone.'

'Hah, yes, and cure dandruff,' said Lord Rust. 'That's just a legend. That's not *real*. Anyway, I've always been a bit puzzled about that story. What's so hard about pulling a sword out of a stone? The real work's already been done. You ought to make yourself useful and find the man who put the sword in the stone in the first place, eh?'

There was a sort of relieved laughter. That's what Edward remembered. It all ended up in laughter. Not exactly at *him*, but he was the type of person who always takes laughter personally.

Ten minutes later, Edward d'Eath was alone.

They're being so *nice* about it. Moving with the times! He'd expected more than that of them. A lot more. He'd dared to hope that they might be inspired by his lead. He'd pictured himself at the head of an army—

Blenkin came in at a respectful shuffle.

'I saw 'em all off, Mr Edward,' he said.

'Thank you, Blenkin. You may clear the table.'

'Yes, Mr Edward.'

'Whatever happened to honour, Blenkin?'

'Dunno, sir. I never took it.'

'They didn't want to listen.'

'No, sir.'

'They didn't want to l-isten.'

Edward sat by the dying fire, with a dog-eared copy of Thighbiter's *The Ankh-Morpork Succesſion* open on his lap. Dead kings and queens looked at him reproachfully.

And there it might have ended. In fact it did end there, in millions of universes. Edward d'Eath grew older and obsession turned to a sort of bookish insanity of the gloves-with-the-fingers-cut-out and carpet slippers variety, and became an expert on royalty although no one ever knew this because he seldom left his rooms. Corporal Carrot became Sergeant Carrot and, in the fullness of time, died in uniform aged seventy in an unlikely accident involving an anteater.

In a million universes, Lance-Constables Cuddy and Detritus didn't fall through the hole. In a million universes, Vimes didn't find the pipes. (In one strange but theoretically possible universe the Watch House was redecorated in pastel colours by a freak whirlwind, which also repaired the door latch and did a few other odd jobs around the place.) In a million universes, the Watch failed.

In a million universes, this was a very short book.

Edward dozed off with the book on his knees and had a dream. He dreamed of glorious struggle. Glorious was another important word in his personal vocabulary, like honour.

If traitors and dishonourable men would not see the truth then he, Edward d'Eath, was the finger of Destiny.

The problem with Destiny, of course, is that she is often not careful where she puts her finger.

Captain Sam Vimes, Ankh-Morpork City Guard (Night Watch), sat in the draughty anteroom to the Patrician's audience chamber with his best cloak on and his breastplate polished and his helmet on his knees.

He stared woodenly at the wall.

He ought to be happy, he told himself. And he was. In a way. Definitely. Happy as anything.

He was going to get married in a few days.

He was going to stop being a guard.

He was going to be a gentleman of leisure.

He took off his copper badge and buffed it absent-mindedly on the edge of his cloak. Then he held it up so that the light glinted off the patina'd surface. AMCW No.177. He sometimes wondered how many other guards had had the badge before him.

Well, now someone was going to have it after him.

* * *

This is Ankh-Morpork, Citie of One Thousand Surprises (according to the Guild of Merchants' guidebook). What more need be said? A sprawling place, home to a million people, greatest of cities on the Discworld, located on either side of the river Ankh, a waterway so muddy that it looks as if it is flowing upside down.

And visitors say: how does such a big city exist? What keeps it going? Since it's got a river you can chew, where does the drinking water come from? What is, in fact, the basis of its civic economy? How come it, against all probability, *works*?

Actually, visitors don't often say this. They usually say things like 'Which way to the, you know, the . . . er . . . you know, the young ladies, right?'

But if they started thinking with their brains for a little while, that's what they'd be thinking.

The Patrician of Ankh-Morpork sat back on his austere chair with the sudden bright smile of a very busy person at the end of a crowded day who's suddenly found in his schedule a reminder saying: 7.00-7.05, Be Cheerful and Relaxed and a People Person.

'Well, of course I was very saddened to receive your letter, captain . . .'

'Yes, sir,' said Vimes, still as wooden as a furniture warehouse.

'*Please* sit down, captain.'

'Yes, sir.' Vimes remained standing. It was a matter of pride.

'But of course I quite understand. The Ramkin

country estates are very extensive, I believe. I'm sure
Lady Ramkin will appreciate your strong right hand.'

'Sir?' Captain Vimes, while in the presence of the
ruler of the city, always concentrated his gaze on a
point one foot above and six inches to the left of the
man's head.

'And of course you will be quite a rich man,
captain.'

'Yes, sir.'

'I hope you have thought about that. You will
have new responsibilities.'

'Yes, sir.'

It dawned on the Patrician that he was working
on both ends of this conversation. He shuffled
through the papers on his desk.

'And of course I shall have to promote a new
chief officer for the Night Watch,' said the Patrician.
'Have you any suggestions, captain?'

Vimes appeared to descend from whatever cloud
his mind had been occupying. This was *guard work*.

'Well, not Fred Colon . . . He's one of Nature's
sergeants . . .'

Sergeant Colon, Ankh-Morpork City Guard (Night
Watch) surveyed the bright faces of the new recruits.

He sighed. He remembered his first day. Old
Sergeant Wimbler. What a tartar! Tongue like a
whiplash! If the old boy had lived to see *this* . . .

What was it called? Oh, yeah. Affirmative action
hirin' procedure, or something. Silicon Anti-
Defamation League had been going on at the
Patrician, and now—

'Try it one more time, Lance-Constable Detritus,'
he said. 'The trick is, you stops your hand just above
your ear. Now, just get up off the floor and try
salutin' one more time. Now, then . . . Lance-
Constable Cuddy?'

'Here!'

'Where?'

'In front of you, sergeant.'

Colon looked down and took a step back. The
swelling curve of his more than adequate stomach
moved aside to reveal the upturned face of Lance-
Constable Cuddy, with its helpful intelligent
expression and one glass eye.

'Oh. Right.'

'I'm taller than I look.'

Oh, gods, thought Sergeant Colon wearily. Add
'em up and divide by two and you've got two normal
men, except normal men don't join the Guard. A
troll and a dwarf. And that ain't the worst of it—

Vimes drummed his fingers on the desk.

'Not Colon, then,' he said. 'He's not as young as
he was. Time he stayed in the Watch House, keeping
up on the paperwork. Besides, he's got a lot on his
plate.'

'Sergeant Colon has always had a lot on his plate,
I should say,' said the Patrician.

'With the new recruits, I mean,' said Vimes,
meaningfully. 'You remember, sir?'

The ones you told me I had to have? he added in
the privacy of his head. They weren't to go in the
Day Watch, of course. And those bastards in

the Palace Guard wouldn't take them, either. Oh, no. Put 'em in the Night Watch, because it's a joke anyway and no one'll really see 'em. No one important, anyway.

Vimes had only given in because he knew it wouldn't be his problem for long.

It wasn't as if he was speciesist, he told himself. But the Watch was a job for men.

'How about Corporal Nobbs?' said the Patrician.

'Nobby?'

They shared a mental picture of Corporal Nobbs.

'No.'

'No.'

'Then of course there is,' the Patrician smiled, 'Corporal Carrot. A fine young man. Already making a name for himself, I gather.'

'That's . . . true,' said Vimes.

'A further promotion opportunity, perhaps? I would value your advice.'

Vimes formed a mental picture of Corporal Carrot—

'This,' said Corporal Carrot, 'is the Hubwards Gate. To the whole city. Which is what we guard.'

'What from?' said Lance-Constable Angua, the last of the new recruits.

'Oh, you know. Barbarian hordes, warring tribesmen, bandit armies . . . that sort of thing.'

'What? Just *us*?'

'Us? Oh, no!' Carrot laughed. 'That'd be silly, wouldn't it? No, if you see anything like that, you just ring your bell as hard as you like.'

'What happens then?'

'Sergeant Colon and Nobby and the rest of 'em will come running along just as soon as they can.'

Lance-Constable Angua scanned the hazy horizon.

She smiled.

Carrot blushed.

Constable Angua had mastered saluting first go. She wouldn't have a full uniform yet, not until someone had taken a, well, let's face it, a *breastplate* along to old Remitt the armourer and told him to beat it out really well *here* and *here,* and no helmet in the world would cover all that mass of ash-blond hair but, it occurred to Carrot, Constable Angua wouldn't need any of that stuff really. People would be queuing up to get arrested.

'So what do we do now?' she said.

'Proceed back to the Watch House, I suppose,' said Carrot. 'Sergeant Colon'll be reading out the evening report, I expect.'

She'd mastered 'proceeding', too. It's a special walk devised by beat officers throughout the multiverse – a gentle lifting of the instep, a careful swing of the leg, a walking pace that can be kept up hour after hour, street after street. Lance-Constable Detritus wasn't going to be ready to learn 'proceeding' for some time, or at least until he stopped knocking himself out every time he saluted.

'Sergeant Colon,' said Angua. 'He was the fat one, yes?'

'That's right.'

'Why has he got a pet monkey?'

'Ah,' said Carrot. 'I think it is Corporal Nobbs to whom you refer . . .'

'It's human? He's got a face like a join-the-dots puzzle!'

'He does have a very good collection of boils, poor man. He does tricks with them. Just never get between him and a mirror.'

Not many people were on the streets. It was too hot, even for an Ankh-Morpork summer. Heat radiated from every surface. The river slunk sullenly in the bottom of its bed, like a student around 11 a.m. People with no pressing business out of doors lurked in cellars and only came out at night.

Carrot moved through the baking streets with a proprietorial air and a slight patina of honest sweat, occasionally exchanging a greeting. Everyone knew Carrot. He was easily recognizable. No one else was about two metres tall with flame-red hair. Besides, he walked as if he owned the city.

'Who was that man with the granite face I saw in the Watch House?' said Angua, as they proceeded along Broad Way.

'That was Detritus the troll,' said Carrot. 'He used to be a bit of a criminal, but now he's courting Ruby she says he's got to—'

'No, that *man*,' said Angua, learning as had so many others that Carrot tended to have a bit of trouble with metaphors. 'Face like thu—face like someone very disgruntled.'

'Oh, that was Captain Vimes. But he's never *been* gruntled, I think. He's retiring at the end of the week, and getting married.'

'Doesn't look very happy about it,' said Angua.

'Couldn't say.'

'I don't think he likes the new recruits.'

The other thing about Constable Carrot was that he was incapable of lying.

'Well, he doesn't like trolls much,' he said. 'We couldn't get a word out of him all day when he heard we had to advertise for a troll recruit. And then we had to have a dwarf, otherwise they'd be trouble. I'm a dwarf, too, but the dwarfs here don't believe it.'

'You don't say?' said Angua, looking up at him.

'My mother had me by adoption.'

'Oh. Yes, but I'm not a troll *or* a dwarf,' said Angua sweetly.

'No, but you're a w—'

Angua stopped. 'That's it, is it? Good grief! This is the Century of the Fruitbat, you know. Ye gods, does he really think like that?'

'He's a bit set in his ways.'

'Congealed, I should think.'

'The Patrician said we had to have a bit of representation from the minority groups,' said Carrot.

'Minority groups!'

'Sorry. Anyway, he's only got a few more days—'

There was a splintering noise across the street. They turned as a figure sprinted out of a tavern and hared away up the street, closely followed – at least for a few steps – by a fat man in an apron.

'Stop! Stop! Unlicensed thief!'

'Ah,' said Carrot. He crossed the road, with Angua padding along behind him, as the fat man slowed to a waddle.

''Morning, Mr Flannel,' he said. 'Bit of trouble?'

'He took seven dollars and I never saw no Thief Licence!' said Mr Flannel. 'What you going to do about it? I pay my taxes!'

'We shall be hotly in pursuit any moment,' said Carrot calmly, taking out his notebook. 'Seven dollars, was it?'

'At least fourteen.'

Mr Flannel looked Angua up and down. Men seldom missed the opportunity.

'Why's she got a helmet on?' he said.

'She's a new recruit, Mr Flannel.'

Angua gave Mr Flannel a smile. He stepped back.

'But she's a—'

'Got to move with the times, Mr Flannel,' said Carrot, putting his notebook away.

Mr Flannel drew his mind back to business.

'In the meantime, there's eighteen dollars of mine that I won't see again,' he said sharply.

'Oh, *nil desperandum*, Mr Flannel, *nil desperandum*,' said Carrot cheerfully. 'Come, Constable Angua. Let us proceed upon our inquiries.'

He proceeded off, with Flannel staring at them with his mouth open.

'Don't forget my twenty-five dollars,' he shouted.

'Aren't you going to *chase* the man?' said Angua, running to keep up.

'No point,' said Carrot, stepping sideways into an alley that was so narrow as to be barely visible. He strolled between the damp, moss-grown walls, in deep shadow.

'Interesting thing,' he said. 'I bet there's not

many people know that you can get to Zephire Street from Broad Way. You ask anyone. They'll say you can't get out of the other end of Shirt Alley. But you can because, all you do, you go up Mormius Street, and then you can squeeze between these bollards *here* into Borborygmic Lane – good, aren't they, very good iron – and here we are in Whilom Alley—'

He wandered to the end of the alley and stood listening for a while.

'What are we waiting for?' said Angua.

There was the sound of running feet. Carrot leaned against the wall, and stuck out one arm into Zephire Street. There was a thud. Carrot's arm didn't move an inch. It must have been like running into a girder.

They looked down at the unconscious figure. Silver dollars rolled across the cobbles.

'Oh dear, oh dear, oh dear,' said Carrot. 'Poor old Here'n'now. He *promised* me he was going to give it up, too. Oh well . . .'

He picked up a leg.

'How much money?' he said.

'Looks like three dollars,' said Angua.

'Well done. The exact amount.'

'No, the shopkeeper said—'

'Come on. Back to the Watch House. Come on, Here'n'now. It's your lucky day.'

'Why is it his lucky day?' said Angua. 'He was *caught*, wasn't he?'

'Yes. By us. Thieves' Guild didn't get him first. They aren't so kind as us.'

Here'n'now's head bounced from cobblestone to cobblestone.

'Pinching three dollars and then trotting straight home,' sighed Carrot. 'That's Here'n'now. Worst thief in the world.'

'But you said Thieves' Guild—'

'When you've been here a while, you'll understand how it all works,' said Carrot. Here'n'now's head banged on the kerb. 'Eventually,' Carrot added. 'But it all does work. You'd be amazed. It all works. I wish it didn't. But it does.'

While Here'n'now was being mildly concussed on the way to the safety of the Watch's jail, a clown was being killed.

He was ambling along an alley with the assurance of one who is fully paid up this year with the Thieves' Guild when a hooded figure stepped out in front of him.

'Beano?'

'Oh, hello . . . it's Edward, right?'

The figure hesitated.

'I was just going back to the Guild,' said Beano.

The hooded figure nodded.

'Are you OK?' said Beano.

'I'm sorry about th-is,' it said. 'But it is for the good of the city. It is nothing p-ersonal.'

He stepped behind the clown. Beano felt a crunch, and then his own personal internal universe switched off.

Then he sat up.

'Ow,' he said, 'that hur—'

But it didn't.

Edward d'Eath was looking down at him with a horrified expression.

'Oh . . . I didn't mean to hit you that hard! I only wanted you out of the way!'

'Why'd you have to hit me at all?'

And then the feeling stole over Beano that Edward wasn't exactly looking at him, and certainly wasn't talking to him.

He glanced at the ground, and experienced that peculiar sensation known only to the recently dead – horror at what you see lying in front of you, followed by the nagging question: so who's doing the looking?

KNOCK KNOCK.

He looked up. 'Who's there?'

DEATH.

'Death who?'

There was a chill in the air. Beano waited. Edward was frantically patting his face . . . well, what until recently had been his face.

I WONDER . . . CAN WE START AGAIN? I DON'T SEEM TO HAVE THE HANG OF THIS.

'Sorry?' said Beano.

'I'm s-orry!' moaned Edward, 'I meant it for the best!'

Beano watched his murderer drag his . . . *the* . . . body away.

'Nothing personal, he says,' he said. 'I'm glad it wasn't anything personal. I should hate to think I've just been killed because it was *personal*.'

IT'S JUST THAT IT HAS BEEN SUGGESTED THAT I SHOULD BE MORE OF A PEOPLE PERSON.

'I mean, *why?* I thought we were getting on really well. It's very hard to make friends in my job. In your job too, I suppose.'

BREAK IT TO THEM GENTLY, AS IT WERE.

'One minute walking along, the next minute dead. Why?'

THINK OF IT MORE AS BEING . . . DIMENSIONALLY DISADVANTAGED.

The shade of Beano the clown turned to Death.

'What *are* you talking about?'

YOU'RE DEAD.

'Yes. I know.' Beano relaxed, and stopped wondering too much about events in an increasingly irrelevant world. Death found that people often did, after the initial confusion. After all, the worst had already happened. At least . . . with any luck.

IF YOU WOULD CARE TO FOLLOW ME . . .

'Will there be custard pies? Red noses? *Juggling?* Are there likely to be baggy trousers?'

NO.

Beano had spent almost all his short life as a clown. He smiled grimly, under his make-up.

'I *like* it.'

Vimes' meeting with the Patrician ended as all such meetings did, with the guest going away in possession of an unfocused yet nagging suspicion that he'd only just escaped with his life.

Vimes trudged on to see his bride-to-be. He knew where she would be found.

The sign scrawled across the big double gates in Morphic Street said: Here be Dragns.

The brass plaque *beside* the gates said: The Ankh-Morpork Sunshine Sanctuary for Sick Dragons.

There was a small and hollow and pathetic dragon made out of papier-mâché and holding a collection box, chained very heavily to the wall, and bearing the sign: Don't Let My Flame Go Out.

This was where Lady Sybil Ramkin spent most of her days.

She was, Vimes had been told, the richest woman in Ankh-Morpork. In fact she was richer than all the other women in Ankh-Morpork rolled, if that were possible, into one.

It was going to be a strange wedding, people said. Vimes treated his social superiors with barely concealed distaste, because the women made his head ache and the men made his fists itch. And Sybil Ramkin was the last survivor of one of the oldest families in Ankh. But they'd been thrown together like twigs in a whirlpool, and had yielded to the inevitable . . .

When he was a little boy, Sam Vimes had thought that the very rich ate off gold plates and lived in marble houses.

He'd learned something new: the very *very* rich could afford to be poor. Sybil Ramkin lived in the kind of poverty that was only available to the very rich, a poverty approached from the other side. Women who were merely well-off saved up and bought dresses made of silk edged with lace and pearls, but Lady Ramkin was so rich she could afford to stomp around the place in rubber boots and a tweed skirt that had belonged to her mother. She was so rich she could afford to live on biscuits and cheese sandwiches. She was so rich she lived in three rooms in a thirty-four-roomed mansion; the rest of them were full of very expensive and very *old* furniture, covered in dust sheets.

The reason that the rich were so rich, Vimes reasoned, was because they managed to spend less money.

Take boots, for example. He earned thirty-eight dollars a month plus allowances. A really good pair of leather boots cost fifty dollars. But an *affordable* pair of boots, which were sort of okay for a season or two and then leaked like hell when the cardboard gave out, cost about ten dollars. Those were the kind of boots Vimes always bought, and wore until the soles were so thin that he could tell where he was in Ankh-Morpork on a foggy night by the feel of the cobbles.

But the thing was that *good* boots lasted for years and years. A man who could afford fifty dollars had a pair of boots that'd still be keeping his feet dry in ten years' time, while a poor man who could only afford cheap boots would have spent a hundred dollars on boots in the same time *and would still have wet feet*.

This was the Captain Samuel Vimes 'Boots' theory of socio-economic unfairness.

The point was that Sybil Ramkin hardly ever had to buy anything. The mansion was full of this big, solid furniture, bought by her ancestors. It never wore out. She had whole boxes full of jewellery which just seemed to have accumulated over the centuries. Vimes had seen a wine cellar that a regiment of speleologists could get so happily drunk in that they wouldn't mind that they'd got lost without trace.

Lady Sybil Ramkin lived quite comfortably from day to day by spending, Vimes estimated, about half as much as he did. But she spent a lot more on dragons.

The Sunshine Sanctuary for Sick Dragons was built with very, very thick walls and a very, very lightweight roof, an idiosyncrasy of architecture normally only found elsewhere in firework factories.

And *this* is because the natural condition of the common swamp dragon is to be chronically ill, and the natural state of an unhealthy dragon is to be laminated across the walls, floor and ceiling of whatever room it is in. A swamp dragon is a badly run, dangerously unstable chemical factory one step from disaster. One quite small step.

It has been speculated that its habit of exploding violently when angry, excited, frightened or merely plain bored is a developed survival trait* to discourage predators. Eat dragons, it proclaims, and you'll have a case of indigestion to which the term 'blast radius' will be appropriate.

Vimes therefore pushed the door open carefully. The smell of dragons engulfed him. It was an unusual smell, even by Ankh-Morpork standards – it put Vimes in mind of a pond that had been used to

---

*From the point of view of the species as a whole. Not from the point of view of the dragon now landing in small pieces around the landscape.

dump alchemical waste for several years and then drained.

Small dragons whistled and yammered at him from pens on either side of the path. Several excited gusts of flame sizzled the hair on his bare shins.

He found Sybil Ramkin with a couple of the miscellaneous young women in breeches who helped run the Sanctuary; they were generally called Sara or Emma, and all looked exactly the same to Vimes. They were struggling with what seemed to be an irate sack. She looked up as he approached.

'Ah, here's Sam,' she said. 'Hold this, there's a lamb.'

The sack was thrust into his arms. At the same moment a talon ripped out of the bottom of the sack and scraped down his breastplate in a spirited attempt to disembowel him. A spiky-eared head thrust its way out of the other end, two glowing red eyes focused on him briefly, a tooth-serrated mouth gaped open and a gush of evil-smelling vapour washed over him.

Lady Ramkin grabbed the lower jaw triumphantly, and thrust the other arm up to the elbow down the little dragon's throat.

'Got you!' She turned to Vimes, who was still rigid with shock. 'Little devil wouldn't take his lime-stone tablet. Swallow. *Swallow!* there! Who's a good boy then? You can let him go now.'

The sack slipped from Vimes' arms.

'Bad case of Flameless Gripe,' said Lady Ramkin. 'Hope we've got it in time—'

The dragon ripped its way out of the sack and

looked around for something to incinerate. Everyone tried to get out of the way.

Then its eyes crossed, and it hiccuped.

The limestone tablet *pinged* off the opposite wall.

'*Everybody down!*'

They leapt for such cover as was provided by a watertrough and a pile of clinkers.

The dragon hiccuped again, and looked puzzled.

Then it exploded.

They stuck their heads up when the smoke had cleared and looked down at the sad little crater.

Lady Ramkin took a handkerchief out of a pocket of her leather overall and blew her nose.

'Silly little bugger,' she said. 'Oh, well. How are you, Sam? Did you go to see Havelock?'

Vimes nodded. Never in his life, he thought, would he get used to the idea of the Patrician of Ankh-Morpork having a first name, or that anyone could ever know him well enough to call him by it.

'I've been thinking about this dinner tomorrow night,' he said desperately. 'You know, I really don't think I can—'

'Don't be silly,' said Lady Ramkin. 'You'll enjoy it. It's time you met the Right People. You know that.'

He nodded mournfully.

'We shall expect you up at the house at eight o'clock, then,' she said. 'And don't look like that. It'll help you *tremendously*. You're far too good a man to spend his nights traipsing around dark wet streets. It's time you got on in the world.'

Vimes wanted to say that he *liked* traipsing around dark wet streets, but it would be no use. He *didn't* like it much. It was just what he'd always done. He thought about his badge in the same way he thought about his nose. He didn't love it or hate it. It was just his badge.

'So just you run along. It'll be terrific fun. Have you got a handkerchief?'

Vimes panicked.

'What?'

'Give it to me.' She held it close to his mouth. 'Spit . . .' she commanded.

She dabbed at a smudge on his cheek. One of the Interchangeable Emmas gave a giggle that was just audible. Lady Ramkin ignored it.

'There,' she said. 'That's better. Now off you go and keep the streets safe for all of us. And if you want to do something *really* useful, you could find Chubby.'

'Chubby?'

'He got out of his pen last night.'

'A dragon?'

Vimes groaned, and pulled a cheap cigar out of his pocket. Swamp dragons were becoming a minor nuisance in the city. Lady Ramkin got very angry about it.

People would buy them when they were six inches long and a cute way of lighting fires and then, when they were burning the furniture and leaving corrosive holes in the carpet, the floor and the cellar ceiling underneath it, they'd be shoved out to fend for themselves.

'We rescued him from a blacksmith in Easy Street,' said Lady Ramkin. 'I said, "My good man, you can use a forge like everyone else". Poor little thing.'

'Chubby,' said Vimes. 'Got a light?'

'He's got a blue collar,' said Lady Ramkin.

'Right, yes.'

'He'll follow you like a lamb if he thinks you've got a charcoal biscuit.'

'Right.' Vimes patted his pockets.

'They're a little bit over-excited in this heat.'

Vimes reached down into a pen of hatchlings and picked up a small one, which flapped its stubby wings excitedly. It spurted a brief jet of blue flame. Vimes inhaled quickly.

'Sam, I really wish you wouldn't do that.'

'Sorry.'

'So if you could get young Carrot and that *nice* Corporal Nobbs to keep an eye out for—'

'No problem.'

For some reason Lady Sybil, keen of eye in every other respect, persisted in thinking of Corporal Nobbs as a cheeky, lovable rascal. It had always puzzled Sam Vimes. It must be the attraction of opposites. The Ramkins were more highly bred than a hilltop bakery, whereas Corporal Nobbs had been disqualified from the human race for shoving.

As he walked down the street in his old leather and rusty mail, with his helmet screwed on his head, and the feel of the cobbles through the worn soles of his boots telling him he was in Acre Alley, no one would have believed that they were looking at a man who was very soon going to marry the richest woman in Ankh-Morpork.

Chubby was not a happy dragon.

He missed the forge. He'd quite liked it in the forge. He got all the coal he could eat and the blacksmith hadn't been a particularly unkind man. Chubby had not demanded much out of life, and had got it.

Then this large woman had taken him away and put him in a pen. There had been other dragons around. Chubby didn't particularly like other dragons. And people'd given him unfamiliar coal.

He'd been quite pleased when someone had taken him out of the pen in the middle of the night. He'd thought he was going back to the blacksmith.

Now it was dawning on him that this was not happening. He was in a box, he was being bumped around, and now he was getting angry . . .

Sergeant Colon fanned himself with his clipboard, and then glared at the assembled guards.

He coughed.

'Right then, people,' he said. 'Settle down.'

'We are settled down, Fred,' said Corporal Nobbs.

'That's Sergeant to you, Nobby,' said Sergeant Colon.

'What do we have to sit down for anyway? We didn't used to do all this. I feel a right berk, sitting down listenin' to you goin' on about—'

'We got to do it proper, now there's more of

us,' said Sergeant Colon. 'Right! Ahem. Right. Okay. We welcome to the guard today Lance-Constable Detritus – *don't salute!* – and Lance-Constable Cuddy, also Lance-Constable Angua. We hope you will have a long and – what's that you've got there, Cuddy?'

'What?' said Cuddy, innocently.

'I can't help noticing that you still has got there what appears to be a double-headed throwing axe, lance-constable, despite what I vouchsafed to you earlier re Guard rules.'

'Cultural weapon, sergeant?' said Cuddy hopefully.

'You can leave it in your locker. Guards carry one sword, short, and one truncheon.'

With the exception of Detritus, he added mentally. Firstly, because even the longest sword nestled in the troll's huge hand like a toothpick, and secondly, because until they'd got this saluting business sorted out he wasn't about to see a member of the Watch nail his own hand to his own ear. He'd have a truncheon, and like it. Even then, he'd probably beat himself to death.

Trolls and dwarfs! Dwarfs and trolls! He didn't deserve it, not at his time of life. And that wasn't the worst of it.

He coughed again. When he read from his clipboard, it was in the sing-song voice of someone who learned his public speaking at school.

'Right,' he said again, a little uncertainly. 'So. Says here—'

'Sergeant?'

'Now wh – Oh, it's you, Corporal Carrot. Yes?'

'Aren't you forgetting something, sergeant?' said Carrot.

'I dunno,' said Colon cautiously. 'Am I?'

'About the recruits, sarge. Something they've got to take?' Carrot prompted.

Sergeant Colon rubbed his nose. Let's see . . . they had, as per standing orders, taken and signed for one shirt (mail, chain) one helmet, iron and copper, one breastplate, iron (except in the case of Lance-Constable Angua, who'd need to be fitted special, and Lance-Constable Detritus, who'd signed for a hastily adapted piece of armour which had once belonged to a war elephant), one truncheon, oak, one emergency pike or halberd, one crossbow, one hourglass, one short sword (except for Lance-Constable Detritus) and one badge, office of, Night Watchman's, copper.

'I think they've got the lot, Carrot,' he said. 'All signed for. Even Detritus got someone to make an X for him.'

'They've got to take the oath, sarge.'

'Oh. Er. Have they?'

'Yes, sarge. It's the law.'

Sergeant Colon looked embarrassed. It probably was the law, at that. Carrot was much better at this sort of thing. He knew the laws of Ankh-Morpork by heart. He was the only person who did. All Colon knew was that *he'd* never taken an oath when he joined, and as for Nobby, the best he'd ever get to an oath was something like 'bugger this for a game of soldiers'.

'All right, then,' he said. 'You've all, er, got to take the oath . . . eh . . . and Corporal Carrot will show you how. Did you take the, er, oath when you joined us, Carrot?'

'Oh, yes, sarge. Only no one asked me, so I gave it to myself, quiet like.'

'Oh? Right. Carry on, then.'

Carrot stood up and removed his helmet. He smoothed down his hair. Then he raised his right hand.

'Raise your right hands, too,' he said. 'Er . . . that's the one nearest Lance-Constable Angua, Lance-Constable Detritus. And repeat after me . . .' He closed his eyes and his lips moved for a moment, as though he was reading something off the inside of his skull.

'"I comma square bracket recruit's name square bracket comma" . . .'

He nodded at them. 'You say it.'

They chorused a reply. Angua tried not to laugh.

'". . . do solemnly swear by square bracket recruit's deity of choice square bracket . . ."'

Angua couldn't trust herself to look at Carrot's face.

'". . . to uphold the Laws and Ordinances of the city of Ankh-Morpork, serve the public truſt comma and defend the ſubjects of His ſtroke Her bracket delete whichever is inappropriate bracket Majeſty bracket name of reigning monarch bracket . . ."'

Angua tried to look at a point behind Carrot's ear. On top of everything else, Detritus' patient monotone was already several dozen words behind everyone else.

"'. . . without fear comma favour comma or thought of perſonal ſafety semi-colon to purſue evil-doers and protect the innocent comma laying down my life if neceſsary in the cauſe of said duty comma so help me bracket aforeſaid deity bracket full stop Gods Save the King stroke Queen bracket delete whichever is inappropriate bracket full stop.'"

Angua subsided gratefully, and then *did* see Carrot's face. There were unmistakable tears trickling down his cheek.

'Er . . . right . . . that's it, then, thank you,' said Sergeant Colon, after a while.

'—*pro-tect the in-no-cent com-ma—*'

'In your own time, Lance-Constable Detritus.'

The sergeant cleared his throat and consulted the clipboard again.

'Now, Grabber Hoskins has been let out of jail again, so be on the look out, you know what he's like when he's had his celebratory drink, and bloody Coalface the troll beat up four men last night—'

'—*in the cauſe of said du-ty com-ma—*'

'Where's Captain Vimes?' demanded Nobby. 'He should be doing this.'

'Captain Vimes is . . . sorting things out,' said Sergeant Colon. ''S'not easy, learning civilianing. Right.' He glanced at his clipboard again, and back to the guardsmen. Men . . . hah.

His lips moved as he counted. There, sitting between Nobby and Constable Cuddy, was a very small, raggedy man, whose beard and hair were so overgrown and matted together that he looked like a ferret peering out of a bush.

'—me brack-et af-ore-said de-it-y brack-et full stop.'

'Oh, no,' he said. 'What're you doing here, Here'n'now? Thank you, Detritus – *don't salute* – you can sit down now.'

'Mr Carrot brings me in,' said Here'n'now.

'Protective custody, sarge,' said Carrot.

'*Again?*' Colon unhooked the cell keys from their nail over the desk and tossed them to the thief. 'All right. Cell Three. Take the keys in with you, we'll holler if we need 'em back.'

'You're a toff, Mr Colon,' said Here'n'now, wandering down the steps to the cells.

Colon shook his head.

'Worst thief in the world,' he said.

'He doesn't look that good,' said Angua.

'No, I mean the *worst*,' said Colon. 'As in "not good at it".'

'Remember when he was going to go all the way up to Dunmanifestin to steal the Secret of Fire from the gods?' said Nobby.

'And I said "but we've *got* it, Here'n'now, we've had it for thousands of years,"' said Carrot. 'And *he* said, "that's right, so it has antique value".'*

'Poor old chap,' said Sergeant Colon. 'Okay. What else have we got . . . yes, Carrot?'

'Now, they've got to take the King's Shilling,' said Carrot.

---

*Fingers-Mazda, the first thief in the world, stole fire from the gods. But he was unable to fence it. It was too hot.†
†He got really burned on that deal.

'Right. Yes. Okay.' Colon fished in his pocket, and took out three sequin-sized Ankh-Morpork dollars, which had about the gold content of seawater. He tossed them one at a time to the recruits.

'This is called the King's Shilling,' he said, glancing at Carrot. 'Dunno why. You gotta get give it when you join. Regulations, see. Shows you've joined.' He looked embarrassed for a moment, and then coughed. 'Right. Oh, yeah. Loada roc—some trolls,' he corrected himself, 'got some kind of march down Short Street. Lance-Constable Detritus – *don't let him salute!* Right. What's this about, then?'

'It Troll New Year,' said Detritus.

'Is it? S'pose we got to learn about this sort of thing now. And says here there's this gritsuc— this dwarf rally or something—'

'Battle of Koom Valley Day,' said Constable Cuddy. 'Famous victory over the trolls.' He looked smug, insofar as anything could be seen behind the beard.

'Yeah? From ambush,' grunted Detritus, glowering at the dwarf.

'What? It was the trolls—' Cuddy began.

'Shut up,' said Colon. 'Look, it says here . . . says here they're marching . . . says here they're marching *up* Short Street.' He turned the paper over. 'Is this right?'

'Trolls going one way, dwarfs going the other?' said Carrot.

'Now *there's* a parade you don't want to miss,' said Nobby.

'What's wrong?' said Angua.

Carrot waved his hands vaguely in the air. 'Oh, dear. It's going to be dreadful. We must do something.'

'Dwarfs and trolls get along like a house on fire,' said Nobby. 'Ever been in a burning house, miss?'

Sergeant Colon's normally red face had gone pale pink. He buckled on his sword belt and picked up his truncheon.

'Remember,' he said, 'let's be careful out there.'

'Yeah,' said Nobby, 'let's be careful to stay in here.'

To understand why dwarfs and trolls don't like each other you have to go back a long way.

They get along like chalk and cheese. Very like chalk and cheese, really. One is organic, the other isn't, and also smells a bit cheesy. Dwarfs make a living by smashing up rocks with valuable minerals in them and the silicon-based lifeform known as trolls are, basically, rocks with valuable minerals in them. In the wild they also spend most of the daylight hours dormant, and that's not a situation a rock containing valuable minerals needs to be in when there are dwarfs around. And dwarfs hate trolls because, after you've just found an interesting seam of valuable minerals, you don't like rocks that suddenly stand up and tear your arm off because you've just stuck a pick-axe in their ear.

It was a state of permanent inter-species vendetta and, like all good vendettas, didn't really need a reason any more. It was enough that it had always existed.* Dwarfs hated trolls because trolls hated dwarfs, and vice versa.

The Watch lurked in Three Lamps Alley, which was about halfway down Short Street. There was a distant crackle of fireworks. Dwarfs let them off to drive away evil mine spirits. Trolls let them off because they tasted nice.

'Don't see why we can't let 'em fight it out amongst themselves and then arrest the losers,' said Corporal Nobbs. 'That's what we always used to do.'

'The Patrician gets really shirty about ethnic trouble,' said Sergeant Colon moodily. 'He gets really sarcastic about it.'

A thought struck him. He brightened up a little bit.

'Got any ideas, Carrot?' he said.

A second thought struck him. Carrot was a simple lad.

'Corporal Carrot?'

'Sarge?'

'Sort this lot out, will you?'

Carrot peered around the corner at the advancing walls of trolls and dwarfs. They'd already seen each other.

'Right you are, sergeant,' he said. 'Lance-Constables Cuddy and Detritus – *don't salute!* – you come with me.'

'You can't let him go out there!' said Angua. 'It's certain death!'

---

*The Battle of Koom Valley is the only one known to history where both sides ambushed each other.

'Got a real sense o'duty, that boy,' said Corporal Nobbs. He took a minute length of dog-end from behind his ear and struck a match on the sole of his boot.

'Don't worry, miss,' said Colon. 'He—'

'Lance-Constable,' said Angua.

'What?'

'Lance-Constable,' she repeated. 'Not miss. Carrot says I don't have any sex while I'm on duty.'

To the background of Nobby's frantic coughing, Colon said, very quickly, 'What I mean *is*, lance-constable, young Carrot's got krisma. Bags of krisma.'

'Krisma?'

'Bags of it.'

The jolting had stopped. Chubby was really annoyed now. Really, really annoyed.

There was a rustling noise. A piece of sacking moved aside and there, staring at Chubby, was another male dragon.

It looked annoyed.

Chubby reacted in the only way he knew how.

Carrot stood in the middle of the street, arms folded, while the two new recruits stood just behind him, trying to keep an eye on both approaching marches at the same time.

Colon thought Carrot was simple. Carrot often struck people as simple. And he was.

Where people went wrong was thinking that simple meant the same thing as stupid.

Carrot was not stupid. He was direct, and honest, and good-natured and honourable in all his dealings. In Ankh-Morpork this would normally have added up to 'stupid' in any case and would have given him the survival quotient of a jellyfish in a blast furnace, but there were a couple of other factors. One was a punch that even trolls had learned to respect. The other was that Carrot was genuinely, almost supernaturally, likeable. He got on well with people, even while arresting them. He had an exceptional memory for names.

For most of his young life he'd lived in a small dwarf colony where there were hardly any other people to know. Then, suddenly, he was in a huge city, and it was as if a talent had been waiting to unfold. And was still unfolding.

He waved cheerfully at the approaching dwarfs.

''Morning Mr Cumblethigh! 'Morning, Mr Stronginthearm!'

Then he turned and waved at the leading troll. There was a muffled 'pop' as a firework went off.

''Morning, Mr Bauxite!'

He cupped his hands.

'If you could all just stop and listen to me—' he bellowed.

The two marches *did* stop, with some hesitation and a general piling up of the people in the back. It was that or walk over Carrot.

If Carrot did have a minor fault, it lay in not paying attention to small details around him when his mind was on other things. So the whispered conversation behind his back was currently escaping him.

'—*hah! It was too an ambush! And your mother was an ore*—'

'Now then, gentlemen,' said Carrot, in a reasoned and amiable voice, 'I'm sure there's no need for this belligerent manner—'

'—*you ambush us too! my great-great-grandfather he at Koom Valley, he tell me!*'

'—in our fair city on such a lovely day. I must ask you as good citizens of Ankh-Morpork—'

'—*yeah? you even know who your father is, do you?*'

'—that, while you must certainly celebrate your proud ethnic folkways, to profit by the example of my fellow officers here, who have sunk their ancient differences—'

'—*I smash you head, you roguesome dwarfs!*'

'—for the greater benefit of—'

'—*I could take you with one hand tied behind my back!*'

'—the city, whose badge they are—'

'—*you get opportunity! I tie BOTH hands behind you back!*'

'—proud and privileged to wear.'

'Aargh!'

'Ooow!'

It dawned on Carrot that hardly anyone was paying any attention to him. He turned.

Lance-Constable Cuddy was upside down, because Lance-Constable Detritus was trying to bounce him on the cobbles by his helmet, although Lance-Constable

Cuddy was putting the position to good effect by gripping Lance-Constable Detritus around the knee and trying to sink his teeth into Lance-Constable Detritus' ankle.

The opposing marchers watched in fascination.

'We should do something!' said Angua, from the guards' hiding place in the alley.

'Weeell,' said Sergeant Colon, slowly, 'it's always very tricky, ethnic.'

'Can put a foot wrong very easily,' said Nobby. 'Very thin-skinned, your basic ethnic.'

'Thin-skinned? They're trying to *kill* one another!'

'It's cultural,' said Sergeant Colon, miserably. 'No sense us tryin' to force our culture on 'em, is there? That's speciesist.'

Out in the street, Corporal Carrot had gone very red in the face.

'If he lays a finger on either of 'em, with all their friends watching,' said Nobby, 'the plan is, we run away like hell—'

Veins stood out on Carrot's mighty neck. He stuck his hands on his waist and bellowed:

'*Lance-Constable Detritus! Salute!*'

They'd spent hours trying to teach him. Detritus' brain took some time to latch on to an idea, but once it was there, it didn't fade away fast.

He saluted.

His hand was full of dwarf.

So he saluted while holding Lance-Constable Cuddy, swinging him up and over like a small angry club.

The sound of their helmets meeting echoed off

the buildings, and it was followed a moment later by the crash of them both hitting the ground.

Carrot prodded them with the toe of his sandal.

Then he turned and strode towards the dwarf marchers, shaking with anger.

In the alleyway, Sergeant Colon started to suck the rim of his helmet out of terror.

'You've got *weapons*, haven't you?' snarled Carrot at a hundred dwarfs. 'Own up! If the dwarfs who've got weapons don't drop them right this minute the entire parade, and I mean the *entire* parade, will be put in the cells! I'm serious about this!'

The dwarfs in the front row took a step backwards. There was a desultory tinkle of metallic objects hitting the ground.

'*All* of them,' said Carrot menacingly. 'That includes you with the black beard trying to hide behind Mr Hamslinger! I can *see* you, Mr Stronginthearm! Put it *down*. No one's amused!'

'He's going to die, isn't he,' said Angua, quietly.

'Funny, that,' said Nobby. 'If *we* was to try it, we'd be little bits of mince. But it seems to work for him.'

'Krisma,' said Sergeant Colon, who was having to lean on the wall.

'Do you mean charisma?' said Angua.

'Yeah. One of them things. Yeah.'

'How does he manage it?'

'Dunno,' said Nobby. 'S'pose he's an easy lad to like?'

Carrot had turned on the trolls, who were smirking at the dwarfs' discomfiture.

'And as for you,' he said, 'I shall definitely be patrolling around Quarry Lane tonight, and I won't be seeing any trouble. Will I?'

There was a shuffling of huge oversized feet, and a general muttering.

Carrot cupped his hand to his ear.

'I couldn't quite hear,' he said.

There was a louder mutter, a sort of toccata scored for one hundred reluctant voices on the theme of 'No, Corporal Carrot.'

'Right. Now off you go. And let's have no more of this nonsense, there's good chaps.'

Carrot brushed the dust off his hands and smiled at everyone. The trolls looked puzzled. In theory, Carrot was a thin film of grease on the street. But somehow it just didn't seem to be happening . . .

Angua said, 'He just called a hundred trolls "good chaps". Some of them are just down off the mountains! Some of them have got *lichen* on them!'

'Smartest thing on a troll,' said Sergeant Colon.

And then the world exploded.

The Watch had left before Captain Vimes got back to Pseudopolis Yard. He plodded up the stairs to his office, and sat down in the sticky leather chair. He gazed blankly at the wall.

He *wanted* to leave the Guard. Of course he did.

It wasn't what you could call a way of life. Not *life*.

Unsocial hours. Never being certain from one day to the next what the Law actually was, in this pragmatic city. No home life, to speak of. Bad food, eaten when you could; he'd even eaten some of Cut-Me-Own-Throat Dibbler's sausages-in-a-bun before now. It always seemed to be raining or baking hot. No friends, except for the rest of the squad, because they were the only people who lived in *your* world.

Whereas in a few days he would, as Sergeant Colon had said, be on the gravy boat. Nothing to do all day but eat his meals and ride around on a big horse shouting orders at people.

At times like this the image of old Sergeant Kepple floated across his memory. He'd been head of the Watch when Vimes was a recruit. And, soon afterwards, he retired. They'd all clubbed together and bought him a cheap watch, one of those that'd keep going for a few years until the demon inside it evaporated.

Bloody stupid idea, Vimes thought moodily, staring at the wall. Bloke leaves work, hands in his badge and hourglass and bell, and what'd we get him? A watch.

But he'd still come in to work the next day, with his new watch. To show everyone the ropes, he said; to tidy up a few loose ends, haha. See you youngsters don't get into trouble, haha. A month later he was bringing the coal in and sweeping the floor and running errands and helping people write reports. He was still there five years later. He was still there six years later, when one of the Watch got in early and found him lying on the floor . . .

And it emerged that no one, *no one*, knew where he lived, or even if there was a Mrs Kepple. They had a whip-round to bury him, Vimes remembered. There were just guards at the funeral . . .

Come to think of it, there were always just guards at a guard's funeral.

Of course it wasn't like that now. Sergeant Colon had been happily married for years, perhaps because he and his wife arranged their working lives so that they only met occasionally, normally on the door-step. But she left him decent meals in the oven, and there was clearly something there; they'd got grand-children, even, so obviously there had been times when they'd been unable to avoid each other. Young Carrot had to fight young women off with a stick. And Corporal Nobbs . . . well, he probably made his own arrangements. He was said to have the body of a twenty-five year old, although no one knew where he kept it.

The point was that everyone else had someone, even if in Nobby's case it was probably against their will.

So, Captain Vimes, what is it really? Do you care for her? Don't worry too much about love, that's a dicey word for the over-forties. Or are you just afraid of becoming some old man dying in the groove of his life and buried out of pity by a bunch of youngsters who never knew you as anything other than some old fart who always seemed to be around the place and got sent out to bring back the coffee and hot figgins and was laughed at behind his back?

He'd wanted to avoid that. And now Fate was handing him a fairy tale.

Of course he'd known she was rich. But he hadn't expected the summons to Mr Morecombe's office.

Mr Morecombe had been the Ramkins' family solicitor for a long time. Centuries, in fact. He was a vampire.

Vimes disliked vampires. Dwarfs were law-abiding little buggers when they were sober, and even trolls were all right if you kept them where you could see them. But all the undead made his neck itch. Live and let live was all very well, but there was a problem right there, when you thought about it logically . . .

Mr Morecombe was scrawny, like a tortoise, and very pale. It had taken him ages to come to the point, and when it came the point nailed Vimes to his chair.

'*How* much?'

'Er. I believe I am right in saying the estate, including the farms, the areas of urban development, and the small area of unreal estate near the University, are together worth approximately . . . seven million dollars a year. Yes. Seven million at current valuation, I would say.'

'It's all *mine*?'

'From the hour of your wedding to Lady Sybil. Although she instructs me in this letter that you are to have access to all her accounts as of the present moment.'

The pearly dead eyes had watched Vimes carefully.

'Lady Sybil,' he said, 'owns approximately one-tenth of Ankh, and extensive properties in Morpork, plus of course considerable farm lands in—'

'But . . . but . . . we'll own them together . . .'

'Lady Sybil is very specific. She is deeding all the property to you as her husband. She has a somewhat . . . old-fashioned approach.' He pushed a folded paper across the table. Vimes took it, unfolded it, and stared.

'Should you predecease her, of course,' Mr Morecombe droned on, 'it will revert to her by common right of marriage. Or to any fruit of the union, of course.'

Vimes hadn't even said anything at that point. He'd just felt his mouth drop open and small areas of his brain fuse together.

'Lady Sybil,' said the lawyer, the words coming from far away, 'while not as young as she was, is a fine healthy woman and there is no reason why—'

Vimes had got through the rest of the interview on automatic.

He could hardly think about it now. When he tried, his thoughts kept skidding away. And, just as always happened when the world got too much for him, they skidded somewhere else.

He pulled open the bottom drawer of his desk and stared at the shiny bottle of Bearhugger's Very Fine Whiskey. He wasn't sure how it had got there. Somehow he'd never got around to throwing it out.

Start that again and you won't even *see* retirement. Stick to cigars.

He shut the drawer and leaned back, taking a half-smoked cigar from his pocket.

Maybe the guards weren't so good now anyway. Politics. Hah! Watchmen like old Kepple would turn in their graves if they knew that the Watch had taken on a w—

And the world exploded.

The window blew in, peppering the wall behind Vimes' desk with fragments and cutting one of his ears.

He threw himself to the floor and rolled under the desk.

Right, that did it! The alchemists had blown up their Guild House for the last time, if Vimes had anything to do with it . . .

But when he peered over the window sill he saw, across the river, the column of dust rising over the Assassins' Guild . . .

The rest of the Watch came trotting along Filigree Street as Vimes reached the Guild entrance. A couple of black-clad Assassins barred his way, in a polite manner which nevertheless indicated that impoliteness was a future option. There were sounds of hurrying feet behind the gates.

'You see this badge? You see it?' Vimes demanded.

'Nevertheless, this is Guild property,' said an Assassin.

'Let us in, in the name of the law!' bellowed Vimes.

The Assassin smiled nervously at him. 'The law is that *Guild* law prevails inside Guild walls,' he said.

Vimes glared at him. But it was true. The laws of the city, such as they were, stopped outside the Guild

Houses. The Guilds had their own laws. The Guild owned the . . .

He stopped.

Behind him, Lance-Constable Angua reached down and picked up a fragment of glass.

Then she stirred the debris with her foot.

And then her gaze met that of a small, non-descript mongrel dog watching her very intently from under a cart. In fact non-descript was not what it was. It was very easy to descript. It looked like halitosis with a wet nose.

'Woof, woof,' said the dog, in a bored way. 'Woof, woof, woof, and growl, growl.'

The dog trotted into the mouth of an alleyway. Angua glanced around, and followed it. The rest of the squad were gathered around Vimes, who'd gone very quiet.

'Fetch me the Master of Assassins,' he said. 'Now!'

The young Assassin tried to sneer.

'Hah! Your uniform doesn't scare *me*,' he said.

Vimes looked down at his battered breastplate and worn mail.

'You're right,' he said. 'This is not a scary uniform. I'm sorry. Forward, Corporal Carrot and Lance-Constable Detritus.'

The Assassin was suddenly aware of the sunlight being blocked out.

'Now *these*, I think you'll agree,' said Vimes, from somewhere behind the eclipse, 'are scary uniforms.'

The Assassin nodded slowly. He hadn't asked for this. Usually there were never any guards outside the

Guild. What would be the point? He had, tucked away in his exquisitely tailored black clothes, at least eighteen devices for killing people, but he was becoming aware that Lance-Constable Detritus had one on the end of each of his arms. Closer, as it were, to hand.

'I'll, er, I'll go and get the Master, then, shall I?' he said.

Carrot leaned down.

'Thank you for your co-operation,' he said gravely.

Angua watched the dog. The dog watched her.

She squatted on her haunches as it sat down and scratched an ear furiously.

Looking around carefully to make sure that no one could see them, she barked an inquiry.

'Don't bovver,' said the dog.

'You can *talk?*'

'Huh. *That* don't take much intelligence,' said the dog. 'And it don't take much intelligence to spot what *you* are, neither.'

Angua looked panicky.

'Where does it show?'

'It's the *smell*, girl. Din't you learn nuffin? Smelled you a mile orf. I thought, oh-ho, what's one of *them* doing in the Watch, eh?'

Angua waved a finger wildly.

'If you tell anyone—!'

The dog looked more pained than normal.

'No one'd listen,' it said.

'Why not?'

''cos everyone knows dogs can't talk. They *hear* me, see, but unless things are really *tough* they just think they're thinking to 'emselves.' The little dog sighed. 'Trust me. I know what I'm talking about. I've read books. Well . . . chewed books.'

It scratched an ear again. 'Seems to me,' it said, 'we could help each other . . .'

'In what way?'

'Well, you could put me in the way of a pound of steak. That does wonders for my memory, steak. Makes it go clean away.'

Angua frowned.

'People don't like the word "blackmail",' she said.

'It ain't the only word they don't like,' said the dog. 'Take my case, now. I've got chronic intelligence. Is that any use to a dog? Did I ask for it? Not me. I just finds a cushy spot to spend my nights along at the High Energy Magic building at the University, no one told *me* about all this bloody magic leaking out the whole time, next thing I know I open me eyes, head starts fizzing like a dose of salts, oh-oh, thinks I, here we go again, hello abstract conceptualizing, intellectual development here we come . . . What bloody use is that to me? Larst time it happened, I ended up savin' the world from horrible wossnames from the Dungeon Dimensions, and did anyone say fanks? Wot a Good Dog, Give Him A Bone? Har har.' It held up a threadbare paw. 'My name's Gaspode. Something like this happens to me just about every week. Apart from that, I'm just a dog.'

Angua gave up. She grasped the moth-eaten limb and shook it.

'My name's Angua. You know what I am.'

'Forgotten it already,' said Gaspode.

Captain Vimes looked at the debris scattered across the courtyard from a hole in one of the ground-floor rooms. All the surrounding windows had broken, and there was a lot of glass underfoot. Mirror glass. Of course, assassins were notoriously vain, but mirrors would be in rooms, wouldn't they? You wouldn't expect a lot of glass outside. Glass got blown in, not out.

He saw Lance-Constable Cuddy bend down and pick up a couple of pulleys attached to a piece of rope, which was burned at one end.

There was a rectangle of card in the debris.

The hairs on the back of Vimes' hand prickled.

He sniffed rankness in the air.

Vimes would be the first to admit that he wasn't a good copper, but he'd probably be spared the chore because lots of other people would happily admit it for him. There was a certain core of stubborn bloody-mindedness there which upset important people, and anyone who upsets important people is automatically not a good copper. But he'd developed instincts. You couldn't live on the streets of a city all your life without them. In the same way that the whole jungle subtly changes at the distant approach of the hunter, there was an alteration in the feel of the city.

There was something happening here, something

wrong, and he couldn't quite see what it was. He started to reach down—

'What is the meaning of this?'

Vimes straightened up. He did not turn around.

'Sergeant Colon, I want you to go back to the Watch House with Nobby and Detritus,' he said. 'Corporal Carrot and Lance-Constable Cuddy, you stay with me.'

'Yes, *sah*!' said Sergeant Colon, stamping heavily and ripping off a smart salute to annoy the Assassins. Vimes acknowledged it.

Then he turned around.

'Ah, Dr Cruces,' he said.

The Master of Assassins was white with rage, contrasting nicely with the extreme black of his clothing.

'No one sent for you!' he said. 'What gives you the right to be here, mister policeman? Walking around as if you own the place?'

Vimes paused, his heart singing. He savoured the moment. He'd like to take this moment and press it carefully in a big book, so that when he was old he could take it out occasionally and remember it.

He reached into his breastplate and pulled out the lawyer's letter.

'Well, if you would like the most fundamental reason,' he said, 'it is because I rather think I do.'

A man can be defined by the things he hates. There were quite a lot of things that Captain Vimes hated. Assassins were near the top of the list, just after kings and the undead.

He had to allow, though, that Dr Cruces recovered

very quickly. He didn't explode when he read the letter, or argue, or claim it was a forgery. He simply folded it up, handed it back, and said, coldly, 'I see. The freehold, at least.'

'Quite so. Could you tell me what has been happening, please?'

He was aware of other senior Assassins entering the courtyard through the hole in the wall. They were very carefully looking at the debris.

Dr Cruces hesitated for a moment.

'Fireworks,' he said.

'What happened,' said Gaspode, 'was that someone put a dragon in a box right up against the wall inside the courtyard, right, and then they went and hid behind one of the statues and pulled a string and next minute – bang!'

'Bang?'

''S'right. Then our friend nips into the hole for a few seconds, right, comes out again, trots around the courtyard and next minute there's Assassins everywhere and he's among 'em. What the hell. Another man in black. No one notices, see?'

'You mean he's still in there?'

'How do I know? Hoods and cloaks, everyone in black . . .'

'How come you were able to see this?'

'Oh, I always nip into the Assassins' Guild on a Wednesday night. Mixed grill night, see?' Gaspode sighed at Angua's blank expression. 'The cook always does a mixed grill of a Wednesday night. No one ever eats the black pudding. So it's round the kitchens, see, woof woof, beg beg, who's a good boy then, look at the little bugger, he looks as though he understands every word I'm sayin', let's see what we've got here for a good doggy . . .'

He looked embarrassed for a moment.

'Pride is all very well, but a sausage is a sausage,' he said.

'Fireworks?' said Vimes.

Dr Cruces looked like a man grasping a floating log in a choppy sea.

'Yes. Fireworks. Yes. For Founder's Day. Unfortunately someone threw away a lighted match which ignited the box.' Dr Cruces suddenly smiled. 'My dear Captain Vimes,' he said, clapping his hands, 'much as I appreciate your concern, I really—'

'They were stored in that room over there?' said Vimes.

'Yes, but that's of no account—'

Vimes crossed to the hole in the wall and peered inside. A couple of Assassins glanced at Dr Cruces and reached nonchalantly towards various areas of their clothing. He shook his head. His caution might have had something to do with the way Carrot put his hand on the hilt of his sword, but it could also have been because Assassins did have a certain code, after all. It was dishonourable to kill someone if you weren't being paid.

'It seems to be some kind of . . . museum,' said Vimes. 'Guild memorabilia, that sort of thing?'

'Yes, exactly. Odd and ends. You know how they mount up over the years.'

'Oh. Well, that all seems in order,' said Vimes. 'Sorry to have troubled you, doctor. I will be going. I hope I have not inconvenienced you in any way.'

'Of course not! Glad to have been able to put your mind at rest.'

They were ushered gently yet firmly towards the gateway.

'I should clean up this glass,' said Captain Vimes, glancing at the debris again. 'Someone could hurt themselves, all this glass lying around. Wouldn't like to see one of your people get hurt.'

'We shall be doing it right this minute, captain,' said Dr Cruces.

'Good. Good. Thank you very much.' Captain Vimes paused at the doorway, and then thumped the palm of his hand on his forehead. 'Sorry, excuse me – mind like a sieve these days – what was it you said was stolen?'

Not a muscle, not a sinew moved on Dr Cruces' face.

'I didn't say anything was stolen, Captain Vimes.'

Vimes gaped at him for a moment.

'Right! Sorry! Of course, you didn't . . . Apologies . . . Work getting on top of me, I expect. I'll be going, then.'

The door slammed in his face.

'Right,' said Vimes.

'Captain, why—?' Carrot began. Vimes held up a hand.

'That wraps it up, then,' he said, slightly louder than necessary. 'Nothing to worry about. Let's get back to the Yard. Where's Lance-Constable Whats-hername?'

'Here, captain,' said Angua, stepping out of the alley.

'Hiding, eh? And what's *that*?'

'Woof woof whine whine.'

'It's a little dog, captain.'

'Good grief.'

The clang of the big corroded Inhumation Bell echoed through the Assassins' Guild. Black-clad figures came running from all directions, pushing and shoving in their haste to get to the courtyard.

The Guild council assembled hurriedly outside Dr Cruces' office. His deputy, Mr Downey, knocked tentatively at the door.

'Come.'

The council filed in.

Cruces' office was the biggest room in the building. It always seemed wrong to visitors that the Assassins' Guild had such light, airy, well-designed premises, more like the premises of a gentlemen's club than a building where death was plotted on a daily basis.

Cheery sporting prints lined the walls, although the quarry was not, when you looked closely, stags or foxes. There were also group etchings – and, more recently, new-fangled iconographs – of the Guild, rows of smiling faces on black-clad bodies and the youngest members sitting cross-legged in front, one of them making a face.*

---

*There's always one.

Down one side of the room was the big mahogany table where the elders of the Guild sat in weekly session. The other side of the room held Cruces' private library, and a small workbench. Above the bench was an apothecary cabinet, made up of hundreds of little drawers. The names on the drawer labels were in Assassins' code, but visitors from outside the Guild were generally sufficiently unnerved not to accept a drink.

Four pillars of black granite held up the ceiling. They had been carved with the names of noted Assassins from history. Cruces had his desk four-square between them. He was standing behind it, his expression almost as wooden as the desk.

'I want a roll-call,' he snapped. 'Has anyone left the Guild?'

'No, sir.'

'How can you be so sure?'

'The guards on the roofs in Filigree Street say no one came in or went out, sir.'

'And who's watching *them*?'

'They're watching one another, sir.'

'Very well. Listen carefully. I want the mess cleaned up. If anyone needs to go outside the building, I want everyone watched. And then the Guild is going to be searched from top to bottom, do you understand?'

'What for, doctor?' said a junior lecturer in poisons.

'For . . . anything that is hidden. If you find anything and you don't know what it is, send for a council member immediately. And don't touch it.'

'But doctor, all sorts of things are hidden—'

'This will be different, do you understand?'

'No, sir.'

'Good. And no one is to speak to the wretched Watch about this. You, boy . . . bring me my hat.' Dr Cruces sighed. 'I suppose I shall have to go and tell the Patrician.'

'Hard luck, sir.'

The captain didn't say anything until they were crossing the Brass Bridge.

'Now then. Corporal Carrot,' he said, 'you know how I've always told you how observation is important?'

'Yes, captain. I have always paid careful attention to your remarks on the subject.'

'So what did you observe?'

'Someone'd smashed a mirror. Everyone knows Assassins like mirrors. But if it was a museum, why was there a mirror there?'

'Please, sir?'

'Who said that?'

'Down here, sir. Lance-Constable Cuddy.'

'Oh, yes. Yes?'

'I know a bit about fireworks, sir. There's a smell you get after fireworks. Didn't smell it, sir. Smelled something else.'

'Well . . . smelled, Cuddy.'

'And there were bits of burned rope and pulleys.'

'I smelled dragon,' said Vimes.

'Sure, captain?'

'Trust me.' Vimes grimaced. If you spent any

time in Lady Ramkin's company, you soon found out what dragons smelled like. If something put its head in your lap while you were dining, you said nothing, you just kept passing it titbits and hoped like hell it didn't hiccup.

'There was a glass case in that room,' he said. 'It was smashed open. Hah! Something was stolen. There was a bit of card in the dust, but someone must have pinched it while old Cruces was talking to me. I'd give a hundred dollars to know what it said.'

'Why, captain?' said Corporal Carrot.

'Because that bastard Cruces doesn't want me to know.'

'I know what could have blown the hole open,' said Angua.

'What?'

'An exploding dragon.'

They walked in stunned silence.

'That could do it, sir,' said Carrot loyally. 'The little devils go bang at the drop of a helmet.'

'Dragon,' muttered Vimes. 'What makes you think it was a dragon, Lance-Constable Angua?'

Angua hesitated. 'Because a dog told me' was not, she judged, a career-advancing thing to say at this point.

'Woman's intuition?' she suggested.

'I *suppose*,' said Vimes, 'you wouldn't hazard an intuitive guess as to what was stolen?'

Angua shrugged. Carrot noticed how interestingly her chest moved.

'Something the Assassins wanted to keep where they could look at it?' she said.

'Oh, *yes*,' said Vimes. 'I suppose next you'll tell me this dog saw it all?'

'Woof?'

Edward d'Eath drew the curtains, bolted the door and leaned on it. It had been so easy!

He'd put the bundle on the table. It was thin, and about four feet long.

He unwrapped it carefully, and there . . . it . . . was.

It looked pretty much like the drawing. Typical of the man – a whole page full of meticulous drawings of crossbows, and this in the margin, as though it hardly mattered.

It was so simple! Why hide it away? Probably because people were afraid. People were always afraid of power. It made them nervous.

Edward picked it up, cradled it for a while, and found that it seemed to fit his arm and shoulder very snugly.

You're mine.

And that, more or less, was the end of Edward d'Eath. Something continued for a while, but what it was, and how it thought, wasn't entirely human.

It was nearly noon. Sergeant Colon had taken the new recruits down to the archery butts in Butts Treat.

Vimes went on patrol with Carrot.

He felt something inside him bubbling over. Something was brushing the tips of his corroded but nevertheless still-active instincts, trying to draw attention to itself. He had to be on the move. It was all that Carrot could do to keep up.

There were trainee Assassins in the streets around the Guild, still sweeping up debris.

'Assassins in daylight,' snarled Vimes. 'I'm amazed they don't turn to dust.'

'That's vampires, sir,' said Carrot.

'Hah! You're right. Assassins and licensed thieves and bloody vampires! You know, this was a great old city once, lad.'

Unconsciously, they fell into step . . . proceeding.

'When we had kings, sir?'

'Kings? Kings? Hell, no!'

A couple of Assassins looked around in surprise.

'I'll tell you,' said Vimes. 'A monarch's an absolute ruler, right? The head honcho—'

'Unless he's a queen,' said Carrot.

Vimes glared at him, and then nodded.

'Okay, or the head honchette—'

'No, that'd only apply if she was a young woman. Queens tend to be older. She'd have to be a . . . a honcharina? No, that's for very young princesses. No. Um. A honchesa, I think.'

Vimes paused. There's something in the air in this city, he thought. If the Creator had said, 'Let there be light' in Ankh-Morpork, he'd have got no further because of all the people saying 'What colour?'

'The supreme ruler, okay,' he said, starting to stroll forward again.

'Okay.'

'But that's not right, see? One man with the power of life and death.'

'But if he's a good man—' Carrot began.

'What? *What?* Okay. Okay. Let's believe he's a good man. But his second-in-command – is he a good man too? You'd better hope so. Because *he's* the supreme ruler, too, in the name of the king. And the rest of the court . . . they've got to be good men. Because if just one of them's a bad man the result is bribery and patronage.'

'The Patrician's a supreme ruler,' Carrot pointed out. He nodded at a passing troll. 'G'day, Mr Carbuncle.'

'But he doesn't wear a crown or sit on a throne and he doesn't tell you it's *right* that he should rule,' said Vimes. 'I hate the bastard. But he's honest. Honest like a corkscrew.'

'Even so, a good man as king—'

'Yes? And then what? Royalty pollutes people's minds, boy. Honest men start bowing and bobbing just because someone's grandad was a bigger murdering bastard than theirs was. Listen! We probably had good kings, once! But kings breed other kings! And blood tells, and you end up with a bunch of arrogant, murdering bastards! Chopping off queens' heads and fighting their cousins every five minutes! And we had centuries of that! And then one day a man said "No more kings!" and we rose up and we fought the bloody nobles and we dragged the king off his throne and we dragged him into Sator Square and we chopped his bloody head off! Job well done!'

'Wow,' said Carrot. 'Who was he?'

'Who?'

'The man who said "No More Kings".'

People were staring. Vimes' face went from the red of anger to the red of embarrassment. There was little difference in the shading, however.

'Oh . . . he was Commander of the City Guard in those days,' he mumbled. 'They called him Old Stoneface.'

'Never heard of him,' said Carrot.

'He, er, doesn't appear much in the history books,' said Vimes. 'Sometimes there has to be a civil war, and sometimes, afterwards, it's best to pretend something didn't happen. Sometimes people have to do a job, and then they have to be forgotten. He wielded the axe, you know. No one else'd do it. It was a king's neck, after all. Kings are,' he spat the word, '*special*. Even after they'd seen the . . . private rooms, and cleaned up the . . . bits. Even then. No one'd clean up the world. But he took the axe and cursed them all and did it.'

'What king was it?' said Carrot.

'Lorenzo the Kind,' said Vimes, distantly.

'I've seen his picture in the palace museum,' said Carrot. 'A fat old man. Surrounded by lots of children.'

'Oh yes,' said Vimes, carefully. 'He was very fond of children.'

Carrot waved at a couple of dwarfs.

'I didn't know this,' he said. 'I thought there was just some wicked rebellion or something.'

Vimes shrugged. 'It's in the history books, if you know where to look.'

'And that was the end of the kings of Ankh-Morpork.'

'Oh, there was a surviving son, I think. And a few mad relatives. They were banished. That's supposed to be a terrible fate, for royalty. I can't see it myself.'

'I think I can. And *you* like the city, sir.'

'Well, yes. But if it was a choice between banishment and having my head chopped off, just help me down with this suitcase. No, we're well rid of kings. But, I mean . . . the *city* used to work.'

'Still does,' said Carrot.

They passed the Assassins' Guild and drew level with the high, forbidding walls of the Fools' Guild, which occupied the other corner of the block.

'No, it just keeps going. I mean, look up there.'

Carrot obediently raised his gaze.

There was a familiar building on the junction of Broad Way and Alchemists. The façade was ornate, but covered in grime. Gargoyles had colonized it.

The corroded motto over the portico said 'NEITHER RAIN NOR SNOW NOR GLOM OF NIT CAN STAY THESE MEßENGERS ABOT THIER DUTY' and in more spacious days that may have been the case, but recently someone had found it necessary to nail up an addendum which read:

> DONT ARSK US ABOUT:
> rocks
> troll's with sticks
> All sorts of dragons
> Mrs Cake
> Huje green things with teeth

Any kinds of black dogs with orange eyebrows
Rains of spaniel's.
fog.
Mrs Cake

'Oh,' he said. 'The Royal Mail.'

'The Post Office,' corrected Vimes. 'My granddad said that once you could post a letter there and it'd be delivered within a month, without fail. You didn't have to give it to a passing dwarf and hope the little bugger wouldn't eat it before . . .'

His voice trailed off.

'Uh. Sorry. No offence meant.'

'None taken,' said Carrot cheerfully.

'It's not that I've got anything against dwarfs. I've always said you'd have to look very hard before you'd find a, a better bunch of highly skilled, law-abiding, hard-working—'

'—little buggers?'

'Yes. No!'

They proceeded.

'That Mrs Cake,' said Carrot, 'definitely a strong-minded woman, eh?'

'Too true,' said Vimes.

Something crunched under Carrot's enormous sandal.

'More glass,' he said. 'It went a long way, didn't it.'

'Exploding dragons! What an imagination the girl has.'

'Woof woof,' said a voice behind them.

'That damn dog's been following us,' said Vimes.

'It's barking at something on the wall,' said Carrot.

Gaspode eyed them coldly.

'Woof woof, bloody whine whine,' he said. 'Are you bloody blind or what?'

It was true that normal people couldn't hear Gaspode speak, because dogs *don't* speak. It's a well-known fact. It's well known at the organic level, like a lot of other well-known facts which overrule the observations of the senses. This is because if people went around noticing everything that was going on all the time, no one would ever get anything done.* Besides, almost all dogs don't talk. Ones that do are merely a statistical error, and can therefore be ignored.

However, Gaspode had found he did tend to get heard on a subconscious level. Only the previous day someone had absent-mindedly kicked him into the gutter and had gone a few steps before they suddenly thought: I'm a bastard, what am I?

'There is something up there,' said Carrot. 'Look . . . something blue, hanging off that gargoyle.'

'Woof woof, *woof*! Would you *credit* it?'

Vimes stood on Carrot's shoulders and walked his hand up the wall, but the little blue strip was still out of reach.

The gargoyle rolled a stony eye towards him.

'Do you mind?' said Vimes. 'It's hanging on your ear . . .'

With a grinding of stone on stone, the gargoyle

---

*This is *another* survival trait.

reached up a hand and unhooked the intrusive material.

'Thank you.'

''on't ent-on it.'

Vimes climbed down again.

'You like gargoyles, don't you, captain,' said Carrot, as they strolled away.

'Yep. They may only be a kind of troll but they keep themselves to themselves and seldom go below the first floor and don't commit crimes anyone ever finds out about. My type of people.'

He unfolded the strip.

It was a collar or, at least, what remained of a collar – it was burnt at both ends. The word 'Chubby' was just readable through the soot.

'The devils!' said Vimes. 'They *did* blow up a dragon!'

The most dangerous man in the world should be introduced.

He has never, in his entire life, harmed a living creature. He has dissected a few, but only after they were dead,* and had marvelled at how well they'd been put together considering it had been done by unskilled labour. For several years he hadn't moved outside a large, airy room, but this was okay, because

---

*Because he was an early form of free-thinking scientist, and did not believe that human beings had been created by some sort of divine being. Dissecting people when they were still alive tended to be a priestly preoccupation; they thought mankind *had* been created by some sort of divine being and wanted to have a closer look at His handiwork.

he spent most of his time inside his own head in any case. There's a certain type of person it's very hard to imprison.

He had, however, surmised that an hour's exercise every day was essential for a healthy appetite and proper bowel movements, and was currently sitting on a machine of his own invention.

It consisted of a saddle above a pair of treadles which turned, by means of a chain, a large wooden wheel currently held off the ground on a metal stand. Another, freewheeling, wooden wheel was positioned in front of the saddle and could be turned by means of a tiller arrangement. He'd fitted the extra wheel and tiller so that he could wheel the entire thing over to the wall when he'd finished taking his exercise and, besides, it gave the whole thing a pleasing symmetry.

He called it 'the-turning-the-wheel-with-pedals-and-another-wheel-machine'.

Lord Vetinari was also at work.

Normally, he was in the Oblong Office or seated in his plain wooden chair at the foot of the steps in the palace of Ankh-Morpork; there was an ornate throne at the top of the steps, covered with dust. It was the throne of Ankh-Morpork and was, indeed, made of gold. He'd never dreamed of sitting on it.

But it was a nice day, so he was working in the garden.

Visitors to Ankh-Morpork were often surprised to find that there were some interesting gardens attached to the Patrician's Palace.

The Patrician was not a gardens kind of person. But some of his predecessors had been, and Lord Vetinari never changed or destroyed anything if there was no logical reason to do so. He maintained the little zoo, and the racehorse stable, and even recognized that the gardens themselves were of extreme historic interest because this was so obviously the case.

They had been laid out by Bloody Stupid Johnson.

Many great landscape gardeners have gone down in history and been remembered in a very solid way by the magnificent parks and gardens that they designed with almost god-like power and foresight, thinking nothing of making lakes and shifting hills and planting woodlands to enable future generations to appreciate the sublime beauty of wild Nature transformed by Man. There have been Capability Brown, Sagacity Smith, Intuition De Vere Slade-Gore . . .

In Ankh-Morpork, there was Bloody Stupid Johnson.

Bloody Stupid 'It Might Look A Bit Messy Now But Just You Come Back In Five Hundred Years' Time' Johnson. Bloody Stupid 'Look, The Plans Were The Right Way Round When I Drew Them' Johnson. Bloody Stupid Johnson, who had 2,000 tons of earth built into an artificial hillock in front of Quirm Manor because 'It'd drive me mad to have to look at a bunch of trees and mountains all day long, how about you?'

The Ankh-Morpork palace grounds were considered the high spot, if such it could be called, of his career. For example, they contained the ornamental trout lake, one hundred and fifty yards long and, because of one of those trifling errors of notation that were such a distinctive feature of Bloody Stupid's designs, one inch wide. It was the home of one trout, which was quite comfortable provided it didn't try to turn around, and had once featured an ornate fountain which, when first switched on, did nothing but groan ominously for five minutes and then fire a small stone cherub a thousand feet into the air.

It contained the hoho, which was like a haha only deeper. A haha is a concealed ditch and wall designed to allow landowners to look out across rolling vistas without getting cattle and inconvenient poor people wandering across the lawns. Under Bloody Stupid's errant pencil it was dug fifty feet deep and had claimed three gardeners already.

The maze was so small that people got lost looking *for* it.

But the Patrician rather liked the gardens, in a quiet kind of way. He had certain views about the mentality of most of mankind, and the gardens made him feel fully justified.

Piles of paper were stacked on the lawn around the chair. Clerks renewed them or took them away periodically. They were different clerks. All sorts and types of information flowed into the Palace, but there was only one place where it all came together, very much like strands of gossamer coming together in the centre of a web.

A great many rulers, good and bad and quite

often dead, know what happened; a rare few actually manage, by dint of much effort, to know what's happening. Lord Vetinari considered both types to lack ambition.

'Yes, Dr Cruces,' he said, without looking up.

How the *hell* does he do it? Cruces wondered. I *know* I didn't make any noise . . .

'Ah, Havelock—' he began.

'You have something to tell me, doctor?'

'It's been . . . mislaid.'

'Yes. And no doubt you are anxiously seeking it. Very well. Good day.'

The Patrician hadn't moved his head the whole time. He hadn't even bothered to ask what It was. He bloody well knows, thought Cruces. How is it you can never tell him anything he doesn't know?

Lord Vetinari put down a piece of paper on one of the piles, and picked up another.

'You are still here, Dr Cruces.'

'I can assure you, m'Lord, that—'

'I'm sure you can. I'm sure you can. There is one question that intrigues me, however.'

'M'Lord?'

'Why was it in your Guild House to be stolen? I had been given to understand it had been destroyed. I'm quite sure I gave orders.'

This was the question the Assassin had been hoping would not be asked. But the Patrician was good at that game.

'Er. We – that is, my *predecessor* – thought it should serve as a warning and an example.'

The Patrician looked up and smiled brightly.

'Capital!' he said. 'I have always had a *great* belief in the effectiveness of examples. So I am sure you'll be able to sort this out with minimum inconvenience all round.'

'Certainly, m'Lord,' said the Assassin, glumly. 'But—'

Noon began.

Noon in Ankh-Morpork took some time, since twelve o'clock was established by consensus. Generally, the first bell to start was that one in the Teachers' Guild, in response to the universal prayers of its members. Then the water clock on the Temple of Small Gods would trigger the big bronze gong. The black bell in the Temple of Fate struck once, unexpectedly, but by then the silver pedal-driven carillon in the Fools' Guild would be tinkling, the gongs, bells and chimes of all the Guilds and temples would be in full swing, and it was impossible to tell them apart, except for the tongueless and magical octiron bell of Old Tom in the Unseen University clock tower, whose twelve measured silences temporarily overruled the din.

And finally, several strokes behind all the others, was the bell of the Assassins' Guild, which was always last.

Beside the Patrician, the ornamental sundial chimed twice and fell over.

'You were saying?' said the Patrician mildly.

'Captain Vimes,' said Dr Cruces. 'He's taking an interest.'

'Dear me. But it is his job.'

'Really? I must demand that you call him off!'

The words echoed around the garden. Several pigeons flew away.

'Demand?' said the Patrician, sweetly.

Dr Cruces backed and filled desperately. 'He is a servant after all,' he said. 'I see no reason why he should be allowed to involve himself in affairs that don't concern him.'

'I rather believe he thinks he's a servant of the law,' said the Patrician.

'He's a jack-in-office and an insolent upstart!'

'Dear me. I did not appreciate your strength of feeling. But since you demand it, I will bring him to heel without delay.'

'Thank you.'

'Don't mention it. Do not let me keep you.'

Dr Cruces wandered off in the direction of the Patrician's idle gesture.

Lord Vetinari bent over his paperwork again, and did not even look up when there was a distant, muffled cry. Instead, he reached down and rang a small silver bell.

A clerk hurried up.

'Go and fetch the ladder, will you, Drumknott?' he said. 'Dr Cruces seems to have fallen in the hoho.'

The back door to the dwarf Bjorn Hammerhock's workshop lifted off the latch and creaked open. He went to see if there was anyone there, and shivered.

He shut the door.

'Bit of a chilly breeze,' he said, to the room's other occupant. 'Still, we could do with it.'

The ceiling of the workshop was only about five

feet above the floor. That was more than tall enough for a dwarf.

Ow, said a voice that no one heard.

Hammerhock looked at the thing clamped in the vice, and picked up a screwdriver.

Ow.

'Amazing,' he said. 'I *think* that moving this tube down the barrel forces the, er, six chambers to slide along, presenting a new one to the, er, firing hole. That seems clear enough. The triggering mechanism is really just a tinderbox device. The spring . . . *here* . . . has rusted through. I can easily replace that. You know,' he said, looking up, 'this is a very interesting device. With the chemicals in the tubes and all. Such a *simple* idea. Is it a clown thing? Some kind of automatic slap-stick?'

He sorted through a bin of metal offcuts to find a piece of steel, and then selected a file.

'I'd like to make a few sketches afterwards,' he said.

About thirty seconds later there was a *pop* and a cloud of smoke.

Bjorn Hammerhock picked himself up, shaking his head.

'That was lucky!' he said. 'Could have been a nasty accident there.'

He tried to fan some of the smoke away, and then reached for the file again.

His hand went through it.

AHEM.

Bjorn tried again.

The file was as insubstantial as the smoke.

'What?'

AHEM.

The owner of the strange device was staring in horror at something on the floor. Bjorn followed his gaze.

'Oh,' he said. Realization, which had been hovering on the edge of Bjorn's consciousness, finally dawned. That was the thing about death. When it happened to you, you were among the first to know.

His visitor grabbed the device from the bench and rammed it into a cloth bag. Then he looked around wildly, picked up the corpse of Mr Hammerhock, and dragged it through the door towards the river.

There was a distant splash, or as close to a splash as you could get from the Ankh.

'Oh dear,' said Bjorn. 'And I can't swim, either.'

THAT WILL NOT, OF COURSE, BE A PROBLEM, said Death.

Bjorn looked at him.

'You're a lot shorter than I thought you'd be,' he said.

THIS IS BECAUSE I'M KNEELING DOWN, MR HAMMERHOCK.

'That damn thing *killed* me!'

YES.

'That's the first time anything like that has *ever* happened to me.'

TO ANYONE. BUT NOT, I SUSPECT, THE LAST TIME.

Death stood up. There was a clicking of knee joints. He no longer cracked his skull on the ceiling.

There wasn't a ceiling any more. The room had gently faded away.

There were such things as dwarf gods. Dwarfs were not a naturally religious species, but in a world where pit props could crack without warning and pockets of fire damp could suddenly explode they'd seen the need for gods as the sort of supernatural equivalent of a hard hat. Besides, when you hit your thumb with an eight-pound hammer it's nice to be able to blaspheme. It takes a very special and strong-minded kind of atheist to jump up and down with their hand clasped under their other armpit and shout, 'Oh, random-fluctuations-in-the-space-time-continuum!' or 'Aaargh, primitive-and-out-moded-concept on a crutch!'

Bjorn didn't waste time asking questions. A lot of things become a shade urgent when you're dead.

'I believe in reincarnation,' he said.

I KNOW.

'I tried to live a good life. Does that help?'

THAT IS NOT UP TO ME. Death coughed. OF COURSE . . . SINCE YOU BELIEVE IN REINCARNATION . . . YOU'LL BE BJORN AGAIN.

He waited.

'Yes. That's right,' said Bjorn. Dwarfs are known for their sense of humour, in a way. People point them out and say: 'Those little devils haven't *got* a sense of humour.'

UM. WAS THERE ANYTHING AMUSING IN THE STATEMENT I JUST MADE?

'Uh. No. No . . . I don't think so.'

IT WAS A PUN, OR PLAY ON WORDS. BJORN AGAIN.

'Yes?'

DID YOU NOTICE IT?

'I can't say I did.'

OH.

'Sorry.'

I'VE BEEN TOLD I SHOULD TRY TO MAKE THE OCCASION A LITTLE MORE ENJOYABLE.

'Bjorn again.'

YES.

'I'll think about it.'

THANK YOU.

'Hright,' said Sergeant Colon, 'this, men, is your truncheon, also nomenclatured your night stick or baton of office.' He paused while he tried to remember his army days, and brightened up.

'*Hand* you will look *after* hit,' he shouted. 'You will eat with hit, you will sleep with hit, you—'

''Scuse me.'

'Who said that?'

'Down here. It's me, Lance-Constable Cuddy.'

'Yes, pilgrim?'

'How do we eat with it, sergeant?'

Sergeant Colon's wound-up machismo wound down. He was suspicious of Lance-Constable Cuddy. He strongly suspected Lance-Constable Cuddy was a trouble-maker.

'What?'

'Well, do we use it as a knife or a fork or cut in half for chopsticks or what?'

'What are you talking about?'

'Excuse me, sergeant?'

'What *is* it, Lance-Constable Angua?'

'How exactly do we sleep with it, sir?'

'Well, I . . . I meant . . . *Corporal Nobbs, stop that sniggering right now!*' Colon adjusted his breastplate and decided to strike out in a new direction.

'Now, hwat we have 'ere is a puppet, mommet or heffigy' – indicating a vaguely humanoid shape made of leather and stuffed with straw, mounted on a stake – 'called by the hnickname of Harthur, weapons training, for the use hof. Forward, Lance-Constable Angua. Tell me, Lance-Constable, do you think you could kill a man?'

'How long will I have?'

There was a pause while they picked up Corporal Nobbs and patted him on the back until he settled down.

'Very well,' said Sergeant Colon, 'what you must do now is take your truncheon like *so*, and on the command one, proceed smartly to Harthur and on the command two, tap him smartly upon the bonce. Hwun . . . two . . .'

The truncheon bounced off Arthur's helmet.

'Very good, only one thing wrong. Anyone tell me what it was?'

They shook their heads.

'From *behind*,' said Sergeant Colon. 'You hit 'em from *behind*. No sense in risking trouble, is there? Now you have a go, Lance-Constable Cuddy.'

'But sarge—'

'Do it.'

They watched.

'Perhaps we could fetch him a chair?' said Angua, after an embarrassing fifteen seconds.

Detritus sniggered.

'Him too *little* to be a guard,' he said.

Lance-Constable Cuddy stopped jumping up and down.

'Sorry, sergeant,' he said, 'this isn't how dwarfs do it, see?'

'It's how *guards* do it,' said Sergeant Colon. 'All right, Lance-Constable Detritus – *don't salute* – you give it a try.'

Detritus held the truncheon between what must technically be called thumb and forefinger, and smashed it over Arthur's helmet. He stared reflectively at the truncheon's stump. Then he bunched up his, for want of a better word, fist, and hammered Arthur over what was briefly its head until the stake was driven three feet into the ground.

'Now the dwarf, he can have a go,' he said.

There was another embarrassed five seconds. Sergeant Colon cleared his throat.

'Well, yes, I think we can consider him thoroughly apprehended,' he said. 'Make a note, Corporal Nobbs. Lance-Constable Detritus – *don't salute!* – deducted one dollar for loss of truncheon. And you're supposed to be able to ask 'em questions afterwards.'

He looked at the remains of Arthur.

'I think around about now is a good time to demonstrate the fine points of harchery,' he said.

* * *

Lady Sybil Ramkin looked at the sad strip of leather that was all that remained of the late Chubby.

'Who'd do something like this to a poor little dragon?' she said.

'We're trying to find out,' said Vimes. 'We . . . we think maybe he was tied up next to a wall and exploded.'

Carrot leaned over the wall of a pen.

'Coochee-coochee-coo?' he said. A friendly flame took his eyebrows off.

'I mean, he was as tame as anything,' said Lady Ramkin. 'Wouldn't hurt a fly, poor little thing.'

'How could someone make a dragon blow up?' said Vimes. 'Could you do it by giving it a kick?'

'Oh, yes,' said Sybil. 'You'd lose your leg, mind you.'

'Then it wasn't that. Any other way? So you wouldn't get hurt?'

'Not really. It'd be easier to make it blow itself up. Really, Sam, I don't like talking about—'

'I have to know.'

'Well . . . at this time of year the males fight. Make themselves look big, you know? That's why I always keep them apart.'

Vimes shook his head. 'There was only one dragon,' he said.

Behind them, Carrot leaned over the next pen, where a pear-shaped male dragon opened one eye and glared at him.

'Whosagoodboyden?' murmured Carrot. 'I'm sure I've got a bit of coal somewhere—'

The dragon opened the other eye, blinked, and then was fully awake and rearing up. Its ears flattened. Its nostrils flared. Its wings unfurled. It breathed in. From its stomach came the gurgle of rushing acids as sluices and valves were opened. Its feet left the floor. Its chest expanded—

Vimes hit Carrot at waist height, bearing him to the ground.

In its pen the dragon blinked. The enemy had mysteriously gone. Scared off!

It subsided, blowing off a huge flame.

Vimes unclasped his hands from his head and rolled over.

'What'd you do that for, captain?' said Carrot. 'I wasn't—'

'It was attacking a dragon!' shouted Vimes. 'One that wouldn't back down!'

He pulled himself to his knees and tapped Carrot's breast-plate.

'You polish that up real bright!' he said. 'You can see yourself in it. So can anything else!'

'Oh, yes, of course there's *that*,' said Lady Sybil. 'Everyone knows you should keep dragons away from mirrors—'

'Mirrors,' said Carrot. 'Hey, there were bits of—'

'Yes. He showed Chubby a mirror,' said Vimes.

'The poor little thing must have been trying to make himself bigger than himself,' said Carrot.

'We're dealing here,' said Vimes, 'with a twisted mind.'

'Oh, no! You think so?'

'Yes.'

'But . . . no . . . you can't be right. Because Nobby was with us all the time.'

'*Not* Nobby,' said Vimes testily. 'Whatever he might do to a dragon, I doubt if he'd make it explode. There's stranger people in this world than Corporal Nobbs, my lad.'

Carrot's expression slid into a rictus of intrigued horror.

'Gosh,' he said.

Sergeant Colon surveyed the butts. Then he removed his helmet and wiped his forehead.

'I think perhaps Lance-Constable Angua shouldn't have another go with the longbow until we've worked out how to stop her . . . her getting in the way.'

'Sorry, sergeant.'

They turned to Detritus, who was standing sheepishly behind a heap of broken longbows. Crossbows were out of the question. They sat in his massive hands like a hairpin. In theory the longbow would be a deadly weapon in his hands, just as soon as he mastered the art of when to let go.

Detritus shrugged.

'Sorry, mister,' he said. 'Bows aren't troll weapon.'

'Ha!' said Colon. 'As for you, Lance-Constable Cuddy—'

'Just can't get the hang of aiming, sergeant.'

'I thought dwarfs were famous for their skills in battle!'

'Yeah, but . . . not these skills,' said Cuddy.

'Ambush,' murmured Detritus.

Since he was a troll, the murmur bounced off distant buildings. Cuddy's beard bristled.

'You devious troll, I get my—'

'Well now,' said Sergeant Colon quickly, 'I think we'll stop training. You'll have to . . . sort of pick it up as you go along, all right?'

He sighed. He was not a cruel man, but he'd been either a soldier or a guard all his life, and he was feeling put-upon. Otherwise he wouldn't have said what he said next.

'I don't know, I really don't. Fighting among yourselves, smashing your own weapons . . . I mean, who do we think we're fooling? Now, it's nearly noon, you take a few hours off, we'll see you again tonight. If you think it's worth turning up.'

There was a *spang!* noise. Cuddy's crossbow had gone off in his hand. The bolt whiffled past Corporal Nobbs' ear and landed in the river, where it stuck.

'Sorry,' said Cuddy.

'Tsk, tsk,' said Sergeant Colon.

That was the worst part. It would have been better all round if he'd called the dwarf some names. It would have been better if he'd made it seem that Cuddy was worth an insult.

He turned around and walked off towards Pseudopolis Yard.

They heard his muttered comment.

'What him say?' said Detritus.

'"A fine body of *men*",' said Angua, going red.

Cuddy spat on the ground, which didn't take long on account of its closeness. Then he reached under his cloak and produced, like a conjuror extracting a size 10 rabbit from a size 5 hat, his double-headed battle axe. And started to run.

By the time he reached the virginal target he was a blur. There was a rip and the dummy exploded like a nuclear haystack.

The other two wandered up and inspected the result, as pieces of chaff gently drifted to the ground.

'Yes, all right,' said Angua. 'But he did say you're supposed to be able to ask them questions afterwards.'

'He didn't say they've got to be able to answer them,' said Cuddy grimly.

'Lance-Constable Cuddy, deduct one dollar for target,' said Detritus, who already owed eleven dollars for bows.

'"If it's worth turning up"!' said Cuddy, losing the axe somewhere about his person again. 'Speciesist!'

'I don't think he meant it that way,' said Angua.

'Ho, it's all right for *you*,' said Cuddy.

'Why?'

''cos you a *man*,' said Detritus.

Angua was bright enough to pause for a moment to think this over.

'A woman,' she said.

'Same thing.'

'Only in broad terms. Come on, let's go and have a drink . . .'

The transient moment of camaraderie in adversity completely evaporated.

'Drink with a troll?'

'Drink with a dwarf?'

'All right,' said Angua. 'How about *you* and *you* coming and having a drink with *me*?'

Angua removed her helmet and shook out her hair. Female trolls don't have hair, although the more fortunate ones are able to cultivate a fine growth of lichen, and a female dwarf is more likely to be complimented on the silkiness of her beard than on her scalp. But it was just possible the sight of Angua scraped little sparks off some shared, ancient, cosmic maleness.

'I haven't really had a chance to look around,' she said. 'But I saw a place in Gleam Street.'

Which meant that they had to cross the river, at least two of them trying to indicate to passers-by that they weren't with at least one of the other two. Which meant that, with desperate nonchalance, they were looking around.

Which meant that Cuddy saw the dwarf in the water.

If you could call it water.

If you could still call it a dwarf.

They looked down.

'You know,' said Detritus, after a while, 'that look like that dwarf who make weapons in Rime Street.'

'Bjorn Hammerhock?' said Cuddy.

'That the one, yeah.'

'It looks a *bit* like him,' Cuddy conceded, still talking in a cold flat voice, 'but not *exactly* like him.'

'What d'you mean?' said Angua.

'Because Mr Hammerhock,' said Cuddy, 'didn't have such a great big hole where his chest should be.'

*   *   *

Doesn't he ever sleep? thought Vimes. Doesn't the bloody man ever get his head down? Isn't there a room somewhere with a black dressing gown hanging on the door?

He knocked on the door of the Oblong Office.

'Ah, captain,' said the Patrician, looking up from his paperwork. 'You were commendably quick.'

'Was I?'

'You got my message?' said Lord Vetinari.

'No, sir. I've been . . . occupied.'

'Indeed. And what could occupy you?'

'Someone has killed Mr Hammerhock, sir. A big man in the dwarf community. He's been . . . shot with something, some kind of siege weapon or something, and dumped in the river. We've just fished him out. I was on the way to tell his wife. I think he lives in Treacle Street. And then I thought, since I was passing . . .'

'This is very unfortunate.'

'Certainly it was for Mr Hammerhock,' said Vimes.

The Patrician leaned back and stared at Vimes.

'Tell me,' he said, 'how was he killed?'

'I don't know. I've never seen anything like it . . . there was just a great big hole. But I'm going to find out what it was.'

'Hmm. Did I mention that Dr Cruces came to see me this morning?'

'No, sir.'

'He was very . . . concerned.'

'Yes, sir.'

'I think you upset him.'

'Sir?'

The Patrician seemed to be reaching a decision. His chair thumped forward.

'Captain Vimes—'

'Sir?'

'I know that you are retiring the day after tomorrow and feel, therefore, a little . . . restless. But while you are captain of the Night Watch I am asking you to follow two very specific instructions . . .'

'Sir?'

'You will cease *any* investigations connected with this theft from the Assassins' Guild. Do you understand? It is entirely Guild business.'

'Sir.' Vimes kept his face carefully immobile.

'I'm choosing to believe that the unspoken word in that sentence was a *yes,* captain.'

'Sir.'

'And that one, too. As for the matter of the unfortunate Mr Hammerhock . . . The body was discovered just a short while ago?'

'Yes, sir.'

'Then it's out of your jurisdiction, captain.'

'What? Sir?'

'The Day Watch can deal with it.'

'But we've *never* bothered with that hours-of-daylight jurisdiction stuff!'

'Nevertheless, in the current circumstances I shall instruct Captain Quirke to take over the investigation, if it turns out that one is necessary.'

If one is necessary. If people don't end up with half their chest gone by accident. Meteorite strike, perhaps, thought Vimes.

He took a deep breath and leaned on the Patrician's desk.

'Mayonnaise Quirke couldn't find his arse with an atlas! And he's got no idea about how to talk to dwarfs! He calls them gritsuckers! My men found the body! It's my jurisdiction!'

The Patrician glanced at Vimes' hands. Vimes removed them from the desk as if it had suddenly grown red-hot.

'Night Watch. That's what you are, captain. Your writ runs in the hours of darkness.'

'It's *dwarfs* we're talking about! If we don't get it right, they'll take the law into their own hands! That usually means chopping the head off the nearest troll! And you'll put *Quirke* on this?'

'I've given you an order, captain.'

'But—'

'You may go.'

'You can't—'

'I said you may *go*, Captain Vimes!'

'*Sir.*'

Vimes saluted. Then he turned about, and marched out of the room. He closed the door carefully, so that there was barely a click.

The Patrician heard him thump the wall outside. Vimes wasn't aware, but there were a number of barely perceptible dents in the wall outside the Oblong Office, their depths corresponding to his emotional state at the time.

By the sound of it, this one would need the services of a plasterer.

Lord Vetinari permitted himself a smile, although

there was no humour in it.

The city *operated*. It was a self-regulating college of Guilds linked by the inexorable laws of mutual self-interest, and it *worked*. On average. By and large. Overall. Normally.

The last thing you needed was some Watchman blundering around upsetting things, like a loose . . . a loose . . . a loose siege catapult.

Normally.

Vimes seemed in a suitable emotional state. With any luck, the orders would have the desired effect . . .

There's a bar like it in every big city. It's where the coppers drink.

The Guard seldom drank in Ankh-Morpork's more cheerful taverns when they were off duty. It was too easy to see something that would put them back on duty again.* So they generally went to The Bucket, in Gleam Street. It was small and low-ceilinged, and the presence of city guards tended to discourage other drinkers. But Mr Cheese, the owner, wasn't too worried about this. No one drinks like a copper who has seen too much to stay sober.

Carrot counted out his change on the counter.

'That's three beers, one milk, one molten sulphur on coke with phosphoric acid—'

---

*Suicide, for example. Murder was in fact a fairly uncommon event in Ankh-Morpork, but there were a lot of suicides. Walking in the night-time alleyways of The Shades was suicide. Asking for a short in a dwarf bar was suicide. Saying 'Got rocks in your head?' to a troll was suicide. You could commit suicide very easily, if you weren't careful.

'With umbrella in it,' said Detritus.

'—and A Slow Comfortable Double-Entendre with lemonade.'

'With a fruit salad in it,' said Nobby.

'Woof?'

'And some beer in a bowl,' said Angua.

'That little dog seems to have taken quite a shine to you,' said Carrot.

'Yes,' said Angua. 'I can't think why.'

The drinks were put in front of them. They stared at the drinks. They drank the drinks.

Mr Cheese, who knew coppers, wordlessly re-filled the glasses and Detritus' insulated mug.

They stared at the drinks. They drank the drinks.

'You know,' said Colon, after a while, 'what gets me, what really *gets* me, is they just dumped him in the water. I mean, not even weights. Just dumped him. Like it didn't matter if he was found. You know what I mean?'

'What gets *me*,' said Cuddy, 'is that he was a dwarf.'

'What gets me is that he was murdered,' said Carrot.

Mr Cheese passed along the line again. They stared at the drinks. They drank the drinks.

Because the fact was that, despite all evidence to the contrary, murder was not a commonplace occurrence in Ankh-Morpork. There were, it was true, assassinations. And as aforesaid there were many ways one could inadvertently commit suicide. And there were occasional domestic fracas on a Saturday night as people sought a cheaper alternative to divorce. There were all these things, but at least they had a *reason,* however unreasonable.

'Big man in the dwarfs, was Mr Hammerhock,' said Carrot. 'A good citizen, too. Wasn't always stirring up old trouble like Mr Stronginthearm.'

'He's got a workshop in Rime Street,' said Nobby.

'Had,' said Sergeant Colon.

They stared at the drinks. They drank the drinks.

'What I want to know is,' said Angua, 'what put that hole in him?'

'Never see anything like that,' said Colon.

'Hadn't someone better go and tell Mrs Hammerhock?' said Angua.

'Captain Vimes is doing it,' said Carrot. 'He said he wouldn't ask anyone else to do it.'

'Rather him than me,' said Colon fervently. 'I wouldn't do that for a big clock. They can be fearsome when they're angry, those little buggers.'

Everyone nodded gloomily, including the little bugger and the bigger little bugger by adoption.

They stared at the drinks. They drank the drinks.

'Shouldn't we be finding out who did it?' said Angua.

'Why?' said Nobby.

She opened and shut her mouth once or twice, and finally came out with: 'In case they do it again?'

'It wasn't an assassination, was it?' said Cuddy.

'No,' said Carrot. 'They always leave a note. By law.'

They looked at the drinks. They drank the drinks.

'What a city,' said Angua.

'It all works, that's the funny thing,' said Carrot.

'D'you know, when I first joined the Watch I was so simple I arrested the head of the Thieves' Guild for thieving?'

'Sounds good to me,' said Angua.

'Got into a bit of trouble for that,' said Carrot.

'You see,' said Colon, 'thieves are *organized* here. I mean, it's *official*. They're *allowed* a certain amount of thieving. Not that they do much these days, mind you. If you pay them a little premium every year they give you a card and leave you alone. Saves time and effort all round.'

'And all thieves are members?' said Angua.

'Oh, *yes*,' said Carrot. 'Can't go thieving in Ankh-Morpork without a Guild permit. Not unless you've got a special talent.'

'Why? What happens? What *talent*?' she said.

'Well, like being able to survive being hung upside down from one of the gates with your ears nailed to your knees,' said Carrot.

Then Angua said: 'That's terrible.'

'Yes, I know. But the thing is,' said Carrot, 'the thing is: it works. The whole thing. Guilds and organized crimes and everything. It all seems to work.'

'Didn't work for Mr Hammerhock,' said Sergeant Colon.

They looked at their drinks. Very slowly, like a mighty sequoia beginning the first step towards resurrection as a million Save The Trees leaflets, Detritus toppled backwards with his mug still in his hand. Apart from the 90° change in position, he didn't move a muscle.

'It's the sulphur,' said Cuddy, without looking around. 'It goes right to their heads.'

Carrot thumped his fist on the bar.

'We ought to do something!'

'We could nick his boots,' said Nobby.

'I mean about Mr Hammerhock.'

'Oh, yeah, yeah,' said Nobby. 'You sound like old Vimesy. If we was to worry about every dead body in this town—'

'But not like this!' snapped Carrot. 'Normally it's just . . . well . . . suicide, or Guild fighting, stuff like that. But he was just a dwarf! Pillar of the community! Spent all day making swords and axes and burial weapons and crossbows and torture implements! And then he's in the river with a great big hole in his chest! Who's going to do anything about it, if not us?'

'You been putting anything in your milk?' said Colon. 'Look, the dwarfs can sort it out. It's like Quarry Lane. Don't stick your nose where someone can pull it off and eat it.'

'We're the *City* Watch,' said Carrot. 'That doesn't mean just that part of the city who happens to be over four feet tall and made of flesh!'

'No dwarf did it,' said Cuddy, who was swaying gently. 'No troll, neither.' He tried to tap the side of his nose, and missed. 'The reason being, he still had all his arms and legs on.'

'Captain Vimes'll want it investigated,' said Carrot.

'Captain Vimes is trying to learn to be a civilian,' said Nobby.

'Well, I'm not going to—' Colon began, and got off his stool.

He hopped. He jumped up and down a bit, his mouth opening and shutting. Then the words managed to come out.

'My foot!'

'What about your foot?'

'Something stuck in it!'

He hopped backwards, clutching at one sandal, and fell over Detritus.

'You'd be amazed what can get stuck to your boots in this town,' said Carrot.

'There's something on the bottom of your sandal,' said Angua. 'Stop waving it about, you silly man.'

She drew her dagger.

'Bit of card or something. With a drawing pin in it. You picked it up somewhere. Probably took a while for you to tread it through . . . there.'

'Bit of card?' said Carrot.

'There's something written on it . . .' Angua scraped away the mud.

'GONNE'

'What does that mean?' she said.

'I don't know. Something's gone, I suppose. Perhaps it's Mr Gonne's visiting card, whoever he is,' said Nobby. 'Who cares? Let's have ano—'

Carrot took the card and turned it over and over in his hands.

'Save the pin,' said Cuddy. 'You only get five of them for a penny. My cousin Gimick makes them.'

'This is important,' said Carrot, slowly. 'The captain ought to know about this. I think he was looking for it.'

'What's important about it?' said Sergeant Colon. 'Apart from my foot hurting like blazes.'

'I don't know. The captain'll know,' said Carrot stubbornly.

'You tell him, then,' said Colon. 'He's staying up at her ladyship's now.'

'Learning to be a gentleman,' said Nobby.

'I'm *going* to tell him,' said Carrot.

Angua glanced through the grubby window. The moon would be up soon. That was one trouble with cities. The damn thing could be lurking behind a tower if you weren't careful.

'And I'd better be getting back to my lodgings,' she said.

'I'll accompany you,' said Carrot, quickly. 'I ought to go and find Captain Vimes in any case.'

'It'll be out of your way . . .'

'Honestly, I'd like to.'

She looked at his earnest expression.

'I couldn't put you to the trouble,' she said.

'That's all right. I like walking. It helps me think.'

Angua smiled, despite her desperation.

They stepped out into the softer heat of the

evening. Instinctively, Carrot settled into the policeman's pace.

'Very old street, this,' he said. 'They say there's an underground stream under it. I read that. What do you think?'

'Do you really like walking?' said Angua, falling into step.

'Oh, yes. There are many interesting byways and historical buildings to be seen. I often go for walks on my day off.'

She looked at his face. Ye gods, she thought.

'Why did you join the Watch?' she said.

'My father said it'd make a man of me.'

'It seems to have worked.'

'Yes. It's the best job there is.'

'Really?'

'Oh, yes. Do you know what "policeman" means?'

Angua shrugged. 'No.'

'It means "man of the *polis*". That's an old word for city.'

'Yes?'

'I read it in a book. Man of the city.'

She glanced sideways at him again. His face glowed in the light of a torch on the street corner, but it had some inner glow of its own.

He's *proud*. She remembered the oath.

Proud of being in the damn *Watch*, for gods' sake—

'Why did *you* join?' he said.

'Me? Oh, I . . . I like to eat meals and sleep indoors. Anyway, there isn't that much choice, is there? It was that or become . . . hah . . . a seam-stress.'*

'And you're not very good at sewing?'

Angua's sharp glance saw nothing but honest innocence in his face.

'Yes,' she said, giving up, 'that's right. And then I saw this poster. "The City Watch Needs Men! Be A Man In The City Watche!" So I thought I'd give it a go. After all, I'd only have something to gain.'

She waited to see if he'd fail to pick this one up, too. He did.

'Sergeant Colon wrote the notice,' said Carrot. 'He's a fairly direct thinker.'

He sniffed.

'Can you smell something?' he said. 'Smells like . . . a bit like someone's thrown away an old privy carpet?'

'Oh, thank you very much,' said a voice very low down, somewhere in the darkness. 'Oh, yes. Thank you very much. That's very wossname of you. Old privy carpet. Oh, yes.'

'Can't smell anything,' Angua lied.

'Liar,' said the voice.

'Or hear anything.'

Captain Vimes' boots told him he was in Scoone Avenue. His feet were doing the walking of their own volition; his mind was somewhere else. In fact, some

---

*A survey by the Ankh-Morpork Guild of Merchants of tradespeople in the dock areas of Morpork found 987 women who gave their profession as 'seamstress'. Oh . . . and two needles.

of it was dissolving gently in Jimkin Bearhugger's finest nectar.

If only they hadn't been so damn *polite*! There were a number of things he'd seen in his life which he'd always try, without success, to forget. Up until now he would have put, at the top of the list, looking at the tonsils of a giant dragon as it drew the breath intended to turn him into a small pile of impure charcoal. He still woke up sweating at the memory of the little pilot light. But he dreaded now that it was going to be replaced by the recollection of all those impassive dwarf faces, watching him politely, and the feeling that his words were dropping into a deep pit.

After all, what could he say? 'Sorry he's dead – and that's official. We're putting our worst men on the case'?

The late Bjorn Hammerhock's house had been full of dwarfs – silent, owlish, *polite* dwarfs. The news had got around. He wasn't telling anyone anything they didn't know. Many of them were holding weapons. Mr Stronginthearm was there. Captain Vimes had talked to him before about his speeches on the subject of the need for grinding all trolls in little bits and using them to make roads. But the dwarf wasn't saying anything now. He was just looking smug. There was an air of quiet, *polite* menace, that said: We'll listen to you. Then we'll do what we decide to do.

He hadn't even been sure which one was Mrs Hammerhock. They all looked alike to him. When she was introduced – helmeted, bearded – he'd got polite, noncommittal answers. No, she'd locked his workshop and seemed to have mislaid the key. Thank you.

He'd tried to indicate as subtly as possible that a wholesale march on Quarry Lane would be frowned upon by the guard (probably from a vantage point at a safe distance) but hadn't the face to spell it out. He couldn't say: don't take matters into your own hands for the guard are mightily in pursuit of the wrong-doer, because he didn't have a clue where to start. Had your husband any enemies? Yes, someone put a huge great hole in him, but apart from *that,* did he have any enemies?

So he'd extracted himself with as much dignity as possible, which wasn't very much, and after a battle with himself which he'd lost, he'd picked up half a bottle of Bearhugger's Old Persnickety and wandered into the night.

Carrot and Angua reached the end of Gleam Street.

'Where are you staying?' said Carrot.

'Just down there.' She pointed.

'Elm Street? Not *Mrs Cake's*?'

'Yes. Why not? I just wanted a clean place, reasonably priced. What's wrong with that?'

'Well . . . I mean, I've nothing against Mrs Cake, a lovely woman, one of the best . . . but . . . well . . . you must have noticed . . .'

'Noticed what?'

'Well . . . she's not very . . . you know . . . *choosy.*'

'Sorry. I'm still not with you.'

'You must have seen some of the other guests? I mean, doesn't Reg Shoe still have lodgings there?'

'Oh,' said Angua, 'you mean the zombie.'

'And there's a banshee in the attic.'

'Mr Ixolite. Yes.'

'And there's old Mrs Drull.'

'The ghoul. But she's retired. She does children's party catering now.'

'I mean, doesn't it strike you the place is a bit odd?'

'But the rates are reasonable and the beds are clean.'

'I shouldn't think anyone ever sleeps in them.'

'All *right*! I had to take what I could *get*!'

'Sorry. I know how it is. I was like that myself when I first arrived here. But my advice is to move out as soon as it's polite and find somewhere . . . well . . . more suitable for a young lady, if you know what I mean.'

'Not really. Mr Shoe even tried to help me upstairs with my stuff. Mind you, I had to help him upstairs with his arms afterwards. Bits fall off him all the time, poor soul.'

'But they're not really . . . our kind of people,' said Carrot wretchedly. 'Don't get me wrong. I mean . . . dwarfs? Some of my best friends are dwarfs. My *parents* are dwarfs. Trolls? No problem at *all* with trolls. Salt of the earth. Literally. Wonderful chaps under all that crust. But . . . undead . . . I just wish they'd go back to where they came from, that's all.'

'Most of them came from round here.'

'I just don't like 'em. Sorry.'

'I've got to go,' said Angua, coldly. She paused at the dark entrance of an alley.

'Right. Right,' said Carrot. 'Um. When shall I see you again?'

'Tomorrow. We're in the same job, yes?'

'But maybe when we're off duty we could take a—'

'Got to go!'

Angua turned and ran. The moon's halo was already visible over the rooftops of Unseen University.

'Okay. Well. Right. Tomorrow, then,' Carrot called after her.

Angua could feel the world spinning as she stumbled through the shadows. She shouldn't have left it so long!

She stumbled out into a cross-street with a few people in it and managed to make it to an alley mouth, pawing at her clothes . . .

She was seen by Bundo Prung, recently expelled from the Thieves' Guild for unnecessary enthusiasm and conduct unbecoming in a mugger, and a desperate man. An isolated woman in a dark alley was just about what he felt he could manage.

He glanced around, and followed her in.

Silence followed, for about five seconds. Then Bundo emerged, very fast, and didn't stop running until he reached the docks, where a boat was leaving on the tide. He ran up the gangplank just before it was pulled up, and became a seaman, and died three years later when an armadillo fell on his head in a far-off country, and in all that time never said what he'd seen. But he did scream a bit whenever he saw a dog.

Angua emerged a few seconds later, and trotted away.

Lady Sybil Ramkin opened the door and sniffed the night air.

'Samuel Vimes! You're drunk!'

'Not yet! But I hope to be!' said Vimes, in cheerful tones.

'And you haven't changed out of your uniform!'

Vimes looked down, and then up again.

'That's right!' he said brightly.

'The guests will be here any minute. Go on up to your room. There's a tub drawn and Willikins has laid out a suit for you. Get along with you . . .'

'Jolly good!'

Vimes bathed in lukewarm water and a rosy alcoholic glow. Then he dried himself off as best he could and looked at the suit on the bed.

It had been made for him by the finest tailor in the city. Sybil Ramkin had a generous heart. She was a woman out for all she could give.

The suit was blue and deep purple, with lace on the wrists and at the throat. It was the height of fashion, he had been told. Sybil Ramkin wanted him to go up in the world. She'd never actually said it, but he knew she felt he was far too good to be a copper.

He stared at it in muzzy incomprehension. He'd never really worn a suit before. When he was a kid there'd been whatever rags could be tied on, and later on there'd been the leather knee britches and chainmail of the Watch – comfortable, practical clothes.

There was a hat with the suit. It had pearls on it.

Vimes had never worn any headgear before that hadn't been hammered out of one piece of metal.

The shoes were long and pointy.

He'd always worn sandals in the summer, and the traditional cheap boots in the winter.

Captain Vimes could just about manage to be an officer. He wasn't at all sure how to become a gentleman. Putting on the suit would seem to be part of it . . .

Guests were arriving. He could hear the crunch of carriage wheels on the driveway, and the flip-flop of the sedan-chair carriers.

He glanced out of the window. Scoone Avenue was higher than most of Morpork and offered unrivalled views of the city, if that was your idea of a good time. The Patrician's Palace was a darker shape in the dusk, with one lighted window high up. It was the centre of a well-lit area, which got darker and darker as the view widened and began to take in those parts of the city where you didn't light a candle because that was wasting good food. There was red torchlight around Quarry Lane . . . well, Trolls' New Year, understandable. And a faint glow over the High Energy Magic building at Unseen University; Vimes would arrest all wizards on suspicion of being too bloody clever by half. But more lights than you'd expect to see around Cable and Sheer, the part of the city that people like Captain Quirke referred to as 'tinytown' . . .

'Samuel!'

Vimes adjusted his cravat as best he could.

He'd faced trolls and dwarfs and dragons, but now he was having to meet an entirely new species. The rich.

It was always hard to remember, afterwards, how the world looked when she was *dans une certaine condition,* as her mother had delicately called it.

For example, she *remembered* seeing smells. The actual streets and buildings . . . they were there, of course, but only as a drab monochrome background against which the sounds and, yes, the smells seared like brilliant lines of . . . coloured fire and clouds of . . . well, of coloured smoke.

That was the point. That was where it all broke down. There were no proper words afterwards for what she heard and smelled. If you could see an eighth distinct colour just for a while, and then describe it back in the seven-coloured world, it'd have to be . . . 'something like a sort of greenish-purple'. Experience did not cross over well between species.

Sometimes, although not very often, Angua thought she was very lucky to get to see both worlds. And there was always twenty minutes after a Change when *all* the senses were heightened, so that the world glowed in every sensory spectrum like a rainbow. It was nearly worth it just for that.

There were varieties of werewolf. Some people merely had to shave every hour and wear a hat to cover the ears. They could pass for nearly normal.

But she could recognize them, nevertheless. Werewolves could spot another werewolf across a crowded street. There was something about the eyes. And, of course, if you had time, there were all sorts of other clues. Werewolves tended to live alone and take jobs that didn't bring them into contact with animals. They wore scent or aftershave a lot and tended to be very fastidious about their food. And kept diaries with the phases of the moon carefully marked in red ink.

It was no life, being a werewolf in the country. A stupid chicken went missing and you were a number one suspect. Everyone said it was better in the city.

It was certainly overpowering.

Angua could see several hours of Elm Street all in one go. The mugger's fear was a fading orange line. Carrot's trail was an expanding pale green cloud, with an edge that suggested he was slightly worried; there were additional tones of old leather and armour polish. Other trails, faint or powerful, criss-crossed the street.

There was one that smelled like an old privy carpet.

'Yo, bitch,' said a voice behind her.

She turned her head. Gaspode looked no better through canine vision, except that he was at the centre of a cloud of mixed odours.

'Oh. It's you.'

''S'right,' said Gaspode, feverishly scratching himself. He gave her a hopeful look. 'Just askin', you understand, just gettin' it over with right now, for the look of the thing, for wossname's sake as it might be, but I s'pose there's no chance of me sniffing—'

'None.'

'Just askin'. No offence meant.'

Angua wrinkled her muzzle.

'How come you smell so bad? I mean, you smelled bad enough when I was human, but now—'

Gaspode looked proud.

'Good, innit,' he said. 'It didn't just happen. I had to work at it. If you was a true dog, this'd be like really great aftershave. By the way, you want to get a collar, miss. No one bothers you if you've got a collar.'

'Thanks.'

Gaspode seemed to have something on his mind.

'Er . . . you don't rip hearts out, do you?'

'Not unless I want to,' said Angua.

'Right, right, right,' said Gaspode hurriedly. 'Where're you going?'

He broke into a waddling, bow-legged trot to keep up with her.

'To have a sniff around Hammerhock's place. I didn't ask you to come.'

'Got nothing else to do,' said Gaspode. 'The House of Ribs don't put its rubbish out till midnight.'

'Haven't you got a home to go to?' said Angua, as they trotted under a fish-and-chip stall.

'Home? Me? Home? Yeah. Of course. No problemo. Laughing kids, big kitchen, three meals a day, humorous cat next door to chase, own blanket and spot by the fire, he's an old softy but we love him, ekcetra. No problem there. I just like to get out a bit,' said Gaspode.

'Only, I see *you* haven't got a collar.'

'It fell off.'

'Right?'

'It was the weight of all them rhinestones.'

'I expect it was.'

'They let me do pretty much as I like,' said Gaspode.

'I can see that.'

'Sometimes I don't go home for, oh, days at a time.'

'Right?'

'Weeks, sometimes.'

'Sure.'

'But they're always so glad to see me when I do,' said Gaspode.

'I thought you said you slept up at the University,' said Angua, as they dodged a cart in Rime Street.

For a moment Gaspode smelled uncertain, but he recovered magnificently.

'Yeah, right,' he said. 'We-ell, you know how it is, families . . . All them kids picking you up, giving you biscuits and similar, people pattin' you the whole time. Gets on yer nerves. So I sleeps up there quite often.'

'Right.'

'More often than not, point of fact.'

'Really?'

Gaspode whimpered a little.

'You want to be careful, you know. A young bitch like you can meet real trouble in this dog's city.'

They had reached the wooden jetty behind Hammerhock's workshop.

'How d'you—' Angua paused. There was a mixture of smells here, but the overpowering one was as sharp as a saw.

'Fireworks?'

'And fear,' said Gaspode. 'Lots of fear.'

He sniffed the planks. 'Human fear, not dwarf. You can tell if it's dwarfs. It's the rat diet, see? Phew! Must have been real bad to stay this strong.'

'I smell one male human, one dwarf,' said Angua.

'Yeah. One dead dwarf.'

Gaspode stuck his battered nose along the line of the door, and snuffled noisily.

'There's other stuff,' he said, 'but it's a bugger what with the river so close and everything. There's oil and . . . grease . . . and all sorts – hey, where're you going?'

Gaspode trotted after her as Angua headed back to Rime Street, nose close to the ground.

'Following the trail.'

'What for? He won't thank you, you know.'

'Who won't?'

'Your young man.'

Angua stopped so suddenly that Gaspode ran into her.

'You mean Corporal Carrot? He's not my young man!'

'Yeah? I'm a dog, right? It's all in the nose, right? Smell can't lie. Pheremonies. It's the ole sexual alchemy stuff.'

'I've only known him a couple of nights!'

'Aha!'

'What do you mean, *aha*?'

'Nothing, nothing. Nothing wrong with it, any-way—'

'There isn't any *it* to be wrong!'

'Right, right. Not that it would be,' said Gaspode, adding hurriedly, 'even if there was. Everyone likes Corporal Carrot.'

'They do, don't they,' said Angua, her hackles settling down. 'He's very . . . likeable.'

'Even Big Fido only bit his hand when Carrot tried to pat him.'

'Who's Big Fido?'

'Chief Barker of the Dog Guild.'

'Dogs have got a Guild? Dogs? Pull one of the other ones, it's got bells on—'

'No, straight up. Scavenging rights, sunbathing spots, night-time barking duty, breeding rights, howling rotas . . . the whole bone of rubber.'

'Dog Guild,' snarled Angua sarcastically. 'Oh, yeah.'

'Chase a rat up a pipe in the wrong street and call me a liar. 'S'good job for you I'm around, else you could get into big trouble. There's big trouble for a dog in this town who ain't a Guild member. It's lucky for you,' said Gaspode, 'that you met me.'

'I suppose you're a big ma—dog in the Guild, yes?'

'Ain't a member,' said Gaspode smugly.

'How come you survive, then?'

'I can think on my paws, me. Anyway, Big Fido leaves me alone. I got the Power.'

'What power?'

'Never you mind. Big Fido . . . he's a friend o' mine.'

'Biting a man's arm for patting you doesn't sound very friendly.'

'Yeah? Last man who tried to pat Big Fido, they only ever found his belt buckle.'

'Yes?'

'And that was in a tree.'

'Where are we?'

'Not even a tree near here. What?'

Gaspode sniffed the air. His nose could read the city in a way reminiscent of Captain Vimes' educated soles.

'Junction of Scoone Avenue and Prouts,' he said.

'Trail's dying out. It's mixed up with too much other stuff.'

Angua sniffed around for a while. Someone had come up here, but too many people had crossed the trail. The sharp smell was still there, but only as a suggestion in the welter of conflicting scents.

She was aware of an overwhelming smell of approaching soap. She'd noticed it before, but only as a woman and only as a faint whiff. As a quadruped, it seemed to fill the world.

Corporal Carrot was walking up the road, look-ing thoughtful. He wasn't looking where he was going, however, but he didn't need to. People stood aside for Corporal Carrot.

It was the first time she'd seen him through these eyes. Good grief. How did people not notice it? He walked through the city like a tiger through tall grass, or a hubland bear across the snow, wearing the landscape like a skin—

Gaspode glanced sideways. Angua was sitting on her haunches, staring.

'Yer tongue's hanging out,' he said.

'What? . . . So? So what? That's natural. I'm panting.'

'Har, har.'

Carrot noticed them, and stopped.

'Why, it's the little mongrel dog,' he said.

'Woof, woof,' said Gaspode, his traitor tail wagging.

'I see *you've* got a lady friend, anyway,' said Carrot, patting him on the head and then absent-mindedly wiping his hand on his tunic.

'And, my word, what a splendid bitch,' he said. 'A Ramtop wolfhound, if I'm any judge.' He stroked Angua in a vague friendly way. 'Oh, well,' he said. 'This isn't getting any work done, is it?'

'Woof, whine, give the doggy a biscuit,' said Gaspode.

Carrot stood up and patted his pockets. 'I think I've got a piece of biscuit here – well, I could believe you understand every word I say . . .'

Gaspode begged, and caught the biscuit easily.

'Woof, woof, fawn, fawn,' he said.

Carrot gave Gaspode the slightly puzzled look that people always gave him when he said 'woof' instead of barking, nodded at Angua, and carried on towards Scoone Avenue and Lady Ramkin's house.

'There,' said Gaspode, crunching the stale biscuit noisily, 'goes a very nice boy. Simple, but nice.'

'Yes, he is simple, isn't he?' said Angua. 'That's what I first noticed about him. He's simple. And everything else here is complicated.'

'He was making sheep's eyes at you earlier,' said

Gaspode. 'Not that I've got anything against sheep's eyes, mind you. If they're fresh.'

'You're disgusting.'

'Yeah, but at least I stay the same shape all month, no offence meant.'

'You're asking for a bite.'

'Oh, yeah,' moaned Gaspode. 'Yeah, you'll bite me. Aaargh. Oh, yes, that'll *really* worry me, that will. I mean, think about it. I've got so many dog diseases I'm only alive 'cos the little buggers are too busy fighting among 'emselves. I mean, I've even got Licky End, and you only get that if you're a pregnant sheep. Go on. Bite me. Change my life. Every time there's a full moon, suddenly I grow hair and yellow teeth and have to go around on all fours. Yes, I can see that making a big difference to my ongoing situation. Actually,' he said, 'I'm definitely on a losing streak in the hair department, so maybe a, you know, not the whole bite, maybe just a nibble—'

'Shut up.' At least *you've* got a lady friend, Carrot had said. As if there was something on his mind . . .

'A quick lick, even—'

'Shut up.'

'This unrest is all Vetinari's fault,' said the Duke of Eorle. 'The man has no style! So now, of course, we have a city where grocers have as much influence as barons. He even let the *plumbers* form a Guild! That's against nature, in my humble opinion.'

'It wouldn't be so bad if he set some kind of social example,' said Lady Omnius.

'Or even governed,' said Lady Selachii. 'People seem to be able to get away with anything.'

'I admit that the old kings were not necessarily *our* kind of people, towards the end,' said the Duke of Eorle, 'but at least they stood for something, in my humble opinion. We had a decent city in those days. People were more respectful and knew their place. People put in a decent day's work, they didn't laze around all the time. And we certainly didn't open the gates to whatever riffraff was capable of walking through. And of course we also had law. Isn't that so, captain?'

Captain Samuel Vimes stared glassily at a point somewhere to the left and just above the speaker's left ear.

Cigar smoke hung almost motionless in the air. Vimes was dimly aware that he'd spent several hours eating too much food in the company of people he didn't like.

He longed for the smell of damp streets and the feel of the cobbles under his cardboard soles. A tray of postprandial drinks was orbiting the table, but Vimes hadn't touched it, because it upset Sybil. And she tried not to show it, and that upset him even more.

The Bearhugger's had worn off. He hated being sober. It meant he started to think. One of the thoughts jostling for space was that there was no such thing as a humble opinion.

He hadn't had much experience with the rich and powerful. Coppers didn't, as a rule. It wasn't that they were less prone to commit crimes, it was just that the crimes they committed tended to be so far above the normal level of criminality that they were beyond the reach of men with bad boots and rusting mail. Owning a hundred slum properties wasn't a crime, although living in one was, almost. Being an Assassin – the Guild never actually *said* so, but an important qualification was being the son or daughter of a gentleman – wasn't a crime. If you had enough money, you could hardly commit crimes at all. You just perpetrated amusing little peccadilloes.

'And now everywhere you look it's uppity dwarfs and trolls and rude people,' said Lady Selachii. 'There's more dwarfs in Ankh-Morpork now than there are in any of their own cities, or whatever they call their holes.'

'What do you think, captain?' said the Duke of Eorle.

'Hmm?' Captain Vimes picked up a grape and started turning it over and over in his fingers.

'The current ethnic problem.'

'Are we having one?'

'Well, yes . . . Look at Quarry Lane. There's fighting there every night!'

'And they have absolutely no concept of religion!'

Vimes examined the grape minutely. What he wanted to say was: Of course they fight. They're *trolls*. Of course they bash one another with clubs – trollish is basically body language and, well, they like to shout. In fact, the only one who ever gives anyone any real trouble is that bastard Chrysoprase, and that's only because he apes humans and is a quick learner. As for religion, troll gods were hitting one another with clubs ten thousand years before we'd even stopped trying to eat rocks.

But the memory of the dead dwarf stirred something perverse in his soul.

He put the grape back on his plate.

'Definitely,' he said. 'In my view, the godless bastards should be rounded up and marched out of the city at spearpoint.'

There was a moment's silence.

'It's no more than they deserve,' Vimes added.

'Exactly! They're barely more than animals,' said Lady Omnius. Vimes suspected her first name was Sara.

'Have you noticed how massive their heads are?' said Vimes. 'That's really just rock. Very small brains.'

'And morally, of course . . .' said Lord Eorle.

There was a murmur of vague agreement. Vimes reached for his glass.

'Willikins, I don't think Captain Vimes wants any wine,' said Lady Ramkin.

'Wrong!' said Vimes cheerfully: 'And while we're on the subject, how about the dwarfs?'

'I don't know if anyone's noticed,' said Lord Eorle, 'but you certainly don't see as many dogs about as you used to.'

Vimes stared. It was true about the dogs. There didn't seem to be quite so many mooching around these days, that was a fact. But he'd visited a few dwarf bars with Carrot, and knew that dwarfs would indeed eat dog, but only if they couldn't get rat. And ten thousand dwarfs eating continuously with knife, fork and shovel wouldn't make a dent in Ankh-Morpork's rat population. It was a major feature in dwarfish letters back home: come on, everyone, and bring the ketchup.

'Notice how small their heads are?' he managed. 'Very limited cranial capacity, surely. Fact of measurement.'

'And you never see their women,' said Lady Sara Omnius. 'I find that very . . . suspicious. You know what they say about dwarfs,' she added darkly.

Vimes sighed. He was just about aware that you saw their women all the time, although they looked just like the male dwarfs. Surely *everyone* knew that, who knew anything about dwarfs?

'Cunning little devils too,' said Lady Selachii. 'Sharp as needles.'

'You know,' Vimes shook his head, 'you know, that's what's so damn annoying, isn't it? The way they can be so incapable of any rational thought and so bloody shrewd at the same time.'

Only Vimes saw the look Lady Ramkin flashed him. Lord Eorle stubbed out his cigar.

'They just move in and take over. And work away like ants all the time real people should be getting some sleep. It's not natural.'

Vimes' mind circled the comment and compared it to the earlier one about a decent day's work.

'Well, one of them won't be working so hard,' said Lady Omnius. 'My maid said one of them was found in the river this morning. Probably some tribal war or something.'

'Hah . . . it's a start, anyway,' said Lord Eorle,

laughing. 'Not that anyone will notice one more or less.'

Vimes smiled brightly.

There was a wine bottle near his hand, despite Willikins' tactful best efforts to remove it. The neck looked invitingly grippable—

He was aware of eyes on him. He looked across the table into the face of a man who was watching him intently and whose last contribution to the conversation had been 'Could you be so kind as to pass me the seasonings, captain?' There was nothing remarkable about the face, except for the gaze – which was absolutely calm and mildly amused. It was Dr Cruces. Vimes had the strong impression that his thoughts were being read.

'Samuel!'

Vimes' hand stopped halfway to the bottle. Willikins was standing next to her ladyship.

'Apparently there's a young man at the door asking for you,' said Lady Ramkin. 'Corporal Carrot.'

'Gosh, this is exciting!' said Lord Eorle. 'Has he come to arrest us, do you think? Hahaha.'

'Ha,' said Vimes.

Lord Eorle nudged his partner.

'I expect that somewhere a crime is being committed,' he said.

'Yes,' said Vimes. 'Quite close, I think.'

Carrot was shown in, with his helmet under his arm at a respectful angle.

He gazed at the select company, licked his lips nervously, and saluted. Everyone was looking at him. It was hard not to notice Carrot in a room. There were bigger people than him in the city. He didn't loom. He just seemed, without trying, to distort things around him. Everything became background to Corporal Carrot.

'At ease, corporal,' said Vimes. 'What's up? I mean,' he added quickly, knowing Carrot's erratic approach to colourful language, 'what is the reason for you being here at this time?'

'Got something to show you, sir. Uh. Sir, I think it's from the Assass—'

'We'll just go and talk about it outside, shall we?' said Vimes. Dr Cruces hadn't twitched a muscle.

Lord Eorle sat back. 'Well, I must say I'm impressed,' he said. 'I'd always thought you Watchmen were a pretty ineffective lot, but I see you're pursuing your duty at all times. Always on the alert for the criminal mind, eh?'

'Oh, yes,' said Vimes. 'The criminal mind. Yes.'

The cooler air of the ancestral hallway came as a blessing. He leaned against the wall and squinted at the card.

' "Gonne"?'

'You know you said you saw something in the courtyard—' Carrot began.

'What's a gonne?'

'Maybe something *wasn't* in the Assassins' museum, and they put this sign on it?' said Carrot. 'You know, like "Removed for Cleaning"? They do that in museums.'

'No, I shouldn't think th—What do you know about museums, anyway?'

'Oh, well, sir,' said Carrot. 'I sometimes visit

them on my day off. The one in the University, of course, and Lord Vetinari lets me look around the old Palace one, and then there's the Guild ones, they generally let me in if I ask nicely, and there's the dwarf museum off Rime Street—'

'Is there?' said Vimes, interested despite himself. He'd walked along Rime Street a thousand times.

'Yes, sir, just up Whirligig Alley.'

'Fancy that. What's in it?'

'Many interesting examples of dwarf bread, sir.'

Vimes thought about this for a moment. 'That's not important right now,' he said. 'This isn't how you spell gone, anyway.'

'Yes it is, sir,' said Carrot.

'I meant, it's not how gone is normally spelled.'

He flicked the card back and forth in his fingers.

'A man'd have to be a fool to break into the Assassins' Guild,' he said.

'Yes, sir.'

The anger had burned away the fumes. Once again he felt . . . not, not the thrill, that wasn't the right word . . . the *sense* of something. He still wasn't sure what it was. But it was there, waiting for him—

'Samuel Vimes, what's going on?'

Lady Ramkin shut the dining-room door behind her.

'I was watching you,' she said. 'You were being very rude, Sam.'

'I was trying not to be.'

'Lord Eorle is a very old friend.'

'Is he?'

'Well, I've known him a long time. I can't stand

the man, actually. But you were making him look foolish.'

'He was making himself look foolish. I was merely helping.'

'But I've often heard you being . . . rude about dwarfs and trolls.'

'That's different. I've got a *right*. That idiot wouldn't know a troll if it walked over him.'

'Oh, he would know if a troll walked over him,' said Carrot, helpfully. 'Some of them weigh as much as—'

'What's so important, anyway?' said Lady Ramkin.

'We're . . . looking for whoever killed Chubby,' said Vimes.

Lady Ramkin's expression changed instantly.

'That's different, of course,' she said. 'People like that should be publicly flogged.'

Why did I say that? thought Vimes. Maybe because it's true. The . . . gonne . . . goes missing, next minute there's a little dwarf artificer thrown in the river with a nasty draught where his chest should be. They're linked. Now all I have to do is find the links . . .

'Carrot, can you come back with me to Hammerhock's?'

'Yes, captain. Why?'

'I want to see inside that workshop. And this time I've got a dwarf with me.'

More than that, he added, I've got Corporal Carrot. Everyone *likes* Corporal Carrot.

*   *   *

Vimes listened while the conversation droned on in dwarfish. Carrot seemed to be winning, but it was a near thing. The clan was giving in not because of reason, or in obedience to the law, but because . . . well . . . because it was Carrot who was asking.

Finally, the corporal looked up. He was sitting on a dwarf stool, so his knees practically framed his head.

'You have to understand, you see, that a dwarf's workshop is very important.'

'Right,' said Vimes. 'I understand.'

'And, er . . . you're a bigger.'

'Sorry?'

'A bigger. Bigger than a dwarf.'

'Ah.'

'Er. The inside of a dwarf's workshop is like . . . well, it's like the inside of his clothes, if you know what I mean. They say you can look, if I'm with you. But you mustn't touch anything. Er. They're not very happy about this, captain.'

A dwarf who was possibly Mrs Hammerhock produced a bunch of keys.

'I've always got on well with dwarfs,' said Vimes.

'They're not happy, sir. Um. They don't think we'll do any good.'

'We'll do our best!'

'Um. I didn't translate that properly. Um. They don't think *we're* any good. They don't mean to be offensive, sir. They just don't think we'll be allowed to get anywhere, sir.'

* * *

'Ow!'

'Sorry about that, captain,' said Carrot, who was walking like an inverted L. 'After you. Mind your head on the—'

'Ow!'

'Perhaps it'd be best if you sat down and I'll look around.'

The workshop was long and, of course, low, with another small door at the far end. There was a big workbench under a skylight. On the opposite wall was a forge and a tool rack. And a hole.

A chunk of plaster had fallen away a few feet above the ground, and cracks radiated away from the shattered brickwork underneath.

Vimes pinched the bridge of his nose. He hadn't found time to sleep today. That was another thing. He'd have to get used to sleeping when it was dark. He couldn't remember when he'd last slept at night.

He sniffed.

'I can smell fireworks,' he said.

'Could be from the forge,' said Carrot. 'Anyway, trolls and dwarfs have been letting fireworks off all over the city.'

Vimes nodded.

'All right,' he said, 'so what can we see?'

'Someone thumped the wall pretty hard just here,' said Carrot.

'Could have happened at any time,' said Vimes.

'No, sir, because there's the plaster dust underneath and a dwarf always keeps his workshop clean.'

'Really?'

There were various weapons, some of them half

finished, on racks by the bench. Vimes picked up most of a crossbow.

'He did good work,' he said. 'Very good at mechanisms.'

'Well known for it,' said Carrot, poking around aimlessly on the bench. 'A very delicate hand. He made musical boxes for a hobby. Could never resist a mechanical challenge. Er. What are we looking for *actually*, sir?'

'Not sure. Now *this* is good . . .'

It was a war axe, and so heavy that Vimes' arm sagged. Intricate etched lines covered the blade. It must have represented weeks of work.

'Not your actual Saturday night special, eh?'

'Oh no,' said Carrot, 'that's a burial weapon.'

'I should think it is!'

'I mean, it's made to be buried with a dwarf. Every dwarf is buried with a weapon. You know? To take with him to . . . wherever he's going.'

'But it's fine workmanship! And it's got an edge like — aargh,' Vimes sucked his finger, 'like a razor.'

Carrot looked shocked. 'Of course. It'd be no good him facing them with an *inferior* weapon.'

'What them are you talking about?'

'Anything bad he encounters on his journey after death,' said Carrot, a shade awkwardly.

'Ah.' Vimes hesitated. This was an area in which he did not feel comfortable.

'It's an ancient tradition,' said Carrot.

'I thought dwarfs didn't believe in devils and demons and stuff like that.'

'That's true, but . . . we're not sure if they know.'

'Oh.'

Vimes laid down the axe and picked up something else from the work rack. It was a knight in armour, about nine inches high. There was a key in its back. He turned it, and then nearly dropped the thing when the figure's legs started to move. He put it down, and it began to march stiffly across the floor, waving its sword.

'Moves a bit like Colon, don't it,' said Vimes. 'Clockwork!'

'It's the coming thing,' said Carrot. 'Mr Hammerhock was good at that.'

Vimes nodded. 'We're looking for anything that shouldn't be here,' he said. 'Or something that should be and isn't. Is there anything missing?'

'Hard to say, sir. It isn't here.'

'What?'

'Anything that's missing, sir,' said Carrot conscientiously.

'I mean,' said Vimes, patiently, 'anything not here which you'd expect to find.'

'Well, he's got – he *had* – all the usual tools, sir. Nice ones, too. Shame, really.'

'What is?'

'They'll be melted down, of course.'

Vimes stared at the neat racks of hammers and files.

'Why? Can't some other dwarf use them?'

'What, use another dwarf's actual *tools*?' Carrot's mouth twisted in distaste, as though someone had suggested he wear Corporal Nobbs' old shorts. 'Oh, no, that's not . . . right. I mean, they're . . . part of him. I mean . . . someone else using them, after he's used them all these years, I mean . . . urrgh.'

'Really?'

The clockwork soldier marched under the bench.

'It'd feel . . . wrong,' said Carrot. 'Er. Yukky.'

'Oh.' Vimes stood up.

'Capt—'

'Ow!'

'—mind your head. Sorry.'

Rubbing his head with one hand, Vimes used the other to examine the hole in the plaster.

'There's . . . something in here,' he said. 'Pass me one of those chisels.'

There was silence.

'A chisel, please. If it makes you feel any better, we *are* trying to find out who killed Mr Hammerhock. All right?'

Carrot picked one up, but with considerable reluctance.

'This is Mr Hammerhock's chisel, this is,' he said reproachfully.

'Corporal Carrot, will you stop being a dwarf for two seconds? You're a guard! And give me the damn chisel! It's been a long day! Thank you!'

Vimes prised at the brickwork, and a rough disc of lead dropped into his hand.

'Slingshot?' said Carrot.

'No room in here,' said Vimes. 'Anyway, how the hell could it get this far into the wall?'

He slipped the disc into his pocket.

'That seems about it, then,' he said, straightening up. 'We'd better – ow! – oh, fish out that clockwork soldier, will you? Better leave the place tidy.'

Carrot scrabbled in the darkness under the bench. There was a rustling noise.

'There's a piece of paper under here, sir.'

Carrot emerged, waving a small yellowing sheet. Vimes squinted at it.

'Looks like nonsense to me,' he said, eventually. 'It's not dwarfish, I know that. But these symbols – these things I've seen before. Or something like them.' He passed the paper back to Carrot. 'What can you make of it?'

Carrot frowned. 'I could make a hat,' he said, 'or a boat. Or a sort of chrysanthemum—'

'I mean the symbols. *These* symbols, just here.'

'Dunno, captain. They do look familiar, though. Sort of . . . like alchemists' writing?'

'Oh, no!' Vimes put his hands over his eyes. 'Not the bloody alchemists! Oh, no! Not that bloody gang of mad firework merchants! I can take the Assassins, but not those idiots! No! Please! What time is it?'

Carrot glanced at the hourglass on his belt. 'About half past eleven, captain.'

'Then I'm off to bed. Those clowns can wait until tomorrow. You could make me a happy man by telling me that this paper belonged to Hammerhock.'

'Doubt it, sir.'

'Me too. Come on. Let's go out through the back door.'

Carrot squeezed through.

'Mind your head, sir.'

Vimes, almost on his knees, stopped and stared at the doorframe.

'Well, corporal,' he said eventually, 'we know it wasn't a troll that did it, don't we? Two reasons. One, a troll couldn't get through this door, it's dwarf sized.'

'What's the other reason, sir?'

Vimes carefully pulled something off a splinter on the low door lintel.

'The other reason, Carrot, is that trolls don't have hair.'

The couple of strands that had been caught in the grain of the beam were red and long. Someone had left them there inadvertently. Someone tall. Taller than a dwarf, anyway.

Vimes peered at them. They looked more like threads than hair. Fine red threads. Oh, well. A clue was a clue.

He carefully folded them up in a scrap of paper borrowed from Carrot's notebook, and handed them to the corporal.

'Here. Keep this safe.'

They crawled out into the night. There was a narrow, plank walkway attached to the walls, and beyond that was the river.

Vimes straightened up carefully.

'I don't like this, Carrot,' he said. 'There's something bad underneath all this.'

Carrot looked down.

'I mean, there are hidden things happening,' said Vimes, patiently.

'Yes, sir.'

'Let's get back to the Yard.'

They proceeded to the Brass Bridge, quite slowly, because Carrot cheerfully acknowledged everyone they met. Hard-edged ruffians, whose normal response to a remark from a Watchman would be genteelly paraphrased by a string of symbols generally found on the top row of a typewriter's keyboard, would actually smile awkwardly and mumble something harmless in response to his hearty, 'Good evening, Masher! Mind how you go!'

Vimes stopped halfway across the bridge to light his cigar, striking a match on one of the ornamental hippos. Then he looked down into the turbid waters.

'Carrot?'

'Yes, captain?'

'Do you think there's such a thing as a criminal mind?'

Carrot almost audibly tried to work this out.

'What . . . you mean like . . . Mr Cut-Me-Own-Throat Dibbler, sir?'

'He's not a criminal.'

'You *have* eaten one of his pies, sir?'

'I mean . . . yes . . . but . . . he's just geographically divergent in the financial hemisphere.'

'Sir?'

'I mean he just disagrees with other people about the position of things. Like money. He thinks it should all be in his pocket. No, I meant—' Vimes closed his eyes, and thought about cigar smoke and flowing drink and laconic voices. There were people who'd steal money from people. Fair enough. That was just theft. But there were people who, with one easy word, would steal the humanity from people. That was something else.

The point was . . . well, *he* didn't like dwarfs and trolls. But he didn't like anyone very much. The point was that he moved in their company every day, and he had a right to dislike them. The point was that no fat idiot had the right to say things like that.

He stared at the water. One of the piles of the bridge was right below him; the Ankh sucked and gurgled around it. Debris – baulks of timber, branches, rubbish – had piled up in a sort of sordid floating island. There was even fungus growing on it.

What he could do with right now was a bottle of Bearhugger's. The world swam into focus when you looked at it through the bottom of a bottle.

Something else swam into focus.

Doctrine of signatures, thought Vimes. That's what the herbalists call it. It's like the gods put a 'Use Me' label on plants. If a plant looks like a part of the body, it's good for ailments peculiar to that part. There's teethwort for teeth, spleenwort for . . . spleens, eyebright for eyes . . . there's even a toad-stool called *Phallus impudicus,* and I don't know what *that's* for but Nobby is a big man for mush-room omelettes. Now . . . either that fungus down there is *exactly* the medicine for hands, or . . .

Vimes sighed.

'Carrot, can you go and get a boathook, please?'

Carrot followed his gaze.

'Just to the left of that log, Carrot.'

'Oh, no!'

'I'm afraid so. Haul it out, find out who he was, make out a report for Sergeant Colon.'

The corpse was a clown. Once Carrot had climbed down the pile and moved the debris aside, he floated face up, a big sad grin painted on his face.

'He's dead!'

'Catching, isn't it?'

Vimes looked at the grinning corpse. Don't investigate. Keep out of it. Leave it to the Assassins and bloody Quirke. These are your orders.

'Corporal Carrot?'

'Sir?'

These are your orders . . .

Well, damn that. What did Vetinari think he was? Some kind of clockwork soldier?

'We're going to find out what's been going on here.'

'Yes, sir!'

'Whatever else happens. We're going to find out.'

The river Ankh is probably the only river in the universe on which the investigators can chalk the outline of the corpse.

'Dear Sgt Colon,

'I hope you are well. The weather is Fine. This is a corpse who, we fished out of the river last night but, we don't know who he is except he is a member of the Fools' Guild called Beano. He has been seriously hit on the back of the head and has been stuck under the bridge for some time, he is not a Pretty sight. Captain

Vimes says to find out things. He says he thinks it
is mixed up with the Murder of Mr Hammerhock. He says talk to the Fools. He says Do It.
Also please find attached Piece of Paper. Captain
Vimes says, try it out on the Alchemists—'

Sergeant Colon stopped reading for a while to
curse all alchemists.

'—because it is Puzzling Evidence. Hoping this
finds you in Good Health, Yours Faithfully,
Carrot Ironfoundersson, (Cpl).'

The sergeant scratched his head. What the hell
did that all mean?

Just after breakfast a couple of senior jesters from
the Fools' Guild had come to pick up the corpse.
Corpses in the river . . . well, there was nothing very
unusual about that. But it wasn't the way clowns
died, usually. After all, what did a clown have that
was worth stealing? What sort of danger was a
clown?

As for the alchemists, he was blowed if he was—

Of course, *he* didn't have to. He looked up at the
recruits. They had to be good for something.

'Cuddy and Detritus – *don't salute!* – I've got a
little job for you. Just take this piece of paper to
the Alchemists' Guild, all right? And ask one of the
loonies to tell you what he makes of it.'

'Where's the Alchemists' Guild, sergeant?' said
Cuddy.

'In the Street of Alchemists, of course,' said

Colon, 'at the moment. But I should run, if I was you.'

The Alchemists' Guild is opposite the Gamblers' Guild. Usually. Sometimes it's above it, or below it, or falling in bits around it.

The gamblers are occasionally asked why they continue to maintain an establishment opposite a Guild which accidentally blows up its Guild Hall every few months, and they say: 'Did you read the sign on the door when you came in?'

The troll and the dwarf walked towards it, occasionally barging into each other by deliberate accident.

'Anyway, you so clever, he gave paper to me?'

'Hah! Can you read it, then? Can you?'

'No, I tell you to read it. That called del-eg-ay-shun.'

'Hah! Can't read! Can't count! Stupid troll!'

'Not stupid!'

'Hah! Yes? Everyone knows trolls can't even count up to four!'*

'Eater of rats!'

'How many fingers am I holding up? You tell me, Mr Clever Rocks in the Head.'

---

*In fact, trolls traditionally count like this: one, two, three . . . many, and people assume this means they can have no grasp of higher numbers. They don't realize that many can *be* a number. As in: one, two, three, *many*, many-one, many-two, many-three, *many many*, many-many-one, many-many-two, many-many-three, *many many many*, many-many-many-one, many-many-many-two, many-many-many-three, *LOTS*.

'Many,' Detritus hazarded.

'Har har, no, five. You'll be in *big* trouble on payday. Sergeant Colon'll say, stupid troll, he won't know how many dollars I give him! Hah! How come you read the notice about joining the Watch, anyway? Got someone to read it to you?'

'How come *you* read notice? Get someone to hold you up?'

They walked into the door of the Alchemists' Guild.

'I knock. *My* job!'

'I'll knock!'

When Mr Sendivoge, the Guild secretary, opened the door it was to find a dwarf hanging on the knocker and being swung up and down by a troll. He adjusted his crash helmet.

'Yes?' he said.

Cuddy let go.

Detritus' massive brows knitted.

'Er. You loony bastard, what you make of this?' he said.

Sendivoge stared from Detritus to the paper. Cuddy was struggling to get around the troll, who was almost completely blocking the doorway.

'*What'd you go and call him that for?*'

'*Sergeant Colon, he said—*'

'I could make a hat out of it,' said Sendivoge, 'or a string of dollies, if I could get some scissors—'

'What my . . . colleague means, sir, is can you help us in our inquiries in re the writing on this alleged piece of paper here?' said Cuddy. 'That bloody hurt!'

Sendivoge peered at him.

'Are you Watchmen?' he said.

'I'm Lance-Constable Cuddy and this,' said Cuddy, gesturing upwards, 'is Lance-trying-to-be-Constable Detritus – *don't salu*-oh . . .'

There was a thump, and Detritus slumped sideways.

'Suicide squad, is he?' said the alchemist.

'He'll come round in a minute,' said Cuddy. 'It's the saluting. It's too much for him. You know trolls.'

Sendivoge shrugged and stared at the writing.

'Looks . . . familiar,' he said. 'Seen it somewhere before. Here . . . you're a dwarf, aren't you?'

'It's the nose, isn't it?' said Cuddy. 'It always gives me away.'

'Well, I'm sure we always try to be of help to the community,' said Sendivoge. 'Do come in.'

Cuddy's steel-tipped boots kicked Detritus back into semi-sensibility, and he lumbered after them.

'Why the, er, why the crash helmet, mister?' said Cuddy, as they walked along the corridor. All around them was the sound of hammering. The Guild was usually being rebuilt.

Sendivoge rolled his eyes.

'Balls,' he said, 'billiard balls, in fact.'

'I knew a man who played like that,' said Cuddy.

'Oh, no. Mr Silverfish is a good shot. That tends rather to be the problem, in fact.'

Cuddy looked at the crash helmet again.

'It's the ivory, you see.'

'Ah,' said Cuddy, not seeing, 'elephants?'

'Ivory *without* elephants. Transmuted ivory. Sound commercial venture.'

'I thought you were working on gold.'

'Ah, yes. Of course, you people know all about gold,' said Sendivoge.

'Oh, yes,' said Cuddy, reflecting on the phrase 'you people'.

'The gold,' said Sendivoge, thoughtfully, 'is turning out to be a bit tricky . . .'

'How long have you been trying?'

'Three hundred years.'

'That's a long time.'

'But we've been working on the ivory for only a week and it's going very well!' said the alchemist quickly. 'Except for some side effects which we'll doubtless soon be able to sort out.'

He pushed open a door.

It was a large room, heavily outfitted with the usual badly ventilated furnaces, rows of bubbling crucibles, and one stuffed alligator. Things floated in jars. The air smelled of a limited life expectancy.

A lot of equipment had been moved away, however, to make room for a billiard table. Half a dozen alchemists were standing around it in the manner of men poised to run.

'It's the third this week,' said Sendivoge, gloomily. He nodded to a figure bent over a cue.

'Er, Mr Silverfish—' he began.

'Quiet! Game on!' said the head alchemist, squinting at the white ball.

Sendivoge glanced at the score rail.

'Twenty-one points,' he said. 'My word. Perhaps

we're adding just the right amount of camphor to the nitro-cellulose after all—'

There was a click. The cue ball rolled away, bounced off the cushion—

—and then accelerated. White smoke poured off it as it bore down on an innocent cluster of red balls.

Silverfish shook his head.

'Unstable,' he said. 'Everybody *down*!'

Everyone in the room ducked, except for the two Watchmen, one of whom was in a sense pre-ducked and the other of whom was several minutes behind events.

The black ball took off on a column of flame, whiffled past Detritus' face trailing black smoke and then shattered a window. The green ball was staying in one spot but spinning furiously. The other balls cannoned back and forth, occasionally bursting into flame or caroming off the walls.

A red one hit Detritus between the eyes, curved back on to the table, holed itself in the middle pocket and then blew up.

There was silence, except for the occasional bout of coughing. Silverfish appeared through the oily smoke and, with a shaking hand, moved the score point one notch with the burning end of his cue.

'One,' he said. 'Oh well. Back to the crucible. Someone order another billiard table—'

''Scuse me,' said Cuddy, prodding him in the knee.

'Who's there?'

'Down here!'

Silverfish looked down.

'Oh. Are you a dwarf?'

Cuddy gave him a blank stare.

'Are you a giant?' he said.

'Me? Of course not!'

'Ah. Then I must be a dwarf, yes. And that's a troll behind me,' said Cuddy. Detritus pulled himself into something resembling attention.

'We've come to see if you can tell us what's on this paper,' said Cuddy.

'Yur,' said Detritus.

Silverfish looked at it.

'Oh, yes,' he said, 'some of old Leonard's stuff. Well?'

'Leonard?' said Cuddy. He glared at Detritus. 'Write this down,' he snapped.

'Leonard of Quirm,' said the alchemist.

Cuddy still looked lost.

'Never heard of him?' said Silverfish.

'Can't say I have, sir.'

'I thought everyone knew about Leonard da Quirm. Quite barmy. But a genius, too.'

'Was he an alchemist?'

Write this down, write this down . . . Detritus looked around blearily for a burnt bit of wood and a handy wall.

'Leonard? No. He didn't belong to a Guild. Or he belonged to all the Guilds, I suppose. He got around quite a bit. He *tinkered*, if you know what I mean?'

'No, sir.'

'He painted a bit, and messed about with mechanisms. Any old thing.'

Or a hammer and chisel even, thought Detritus.

'This,' said Silverfish, 'is a formula for . . . oh, well, I might as well tell you, it's hardly a big secret . . . it's a formula for what we called No. 1 Powder. Sulphur, saltpetre and charcoal. You use it in fireworks. Any fool could make it up. But it looks odd because it's written back to front.'

'This sounds important,' hissed Cuddy to the troll.

'Oh, no. He always used to write back to front,' said Silverfish. 'He was odd like that. But very clever all the same. Haven't you seen his portrait of the Mona Ogg?'

'I don't think so.'

Silverfish handed the parchment to Detritus, who squinted at it as if he knew what it meant. Maybe he could write on this, he thought.

'The teeth followed you around the room. Amazing. In fact some people said they followed them *out* of the room and all the way down the street.'

'I think we should talk to Mr da Quirm,' said Cuddy.

'Oh, you could do that, you could do that, certainly,' said Silverfish. 'But he might not be in a position to listen. He disappeared a couple of years ago.'

. . . then when I find something to write with, thought Detritus, I have to find someone teach me how write . . .

'Disappeared? How?' said Cuddy.

'We think,' said Silverfish, leaning closer, 'that he found a way of making himself invisible.'

'Really?'

'Because,' said Silverfish, nodding conspiratorially, '*no one's seen him.*'

'Ah,' said Cuddy. 'Er. This is just off of the top of my head, you understand, but I suppose he couldn't . . . just have gone somewhere where you couldn't see him?'

'Nah, that wouldn't be like old Leonard. He wouldn't disappear. But he might vanish.'

'Oh.'

'He was a bit . . . unhinged, if you know what I mean. Head too full of brains. Ha, I remember he had this idea once of getting lightning out of lemons! Hey, Sendivoge, you remember Leonard and his lightning lemons?'

Sendivoge made little circular motions alongside his head with one finger. 'Oh, yes. "If you stick copper and zinc rods in the lemon, hey presto, you get tame lightning." Man was an idiot!'

'Oh, not an idiot,' said Silverfish, picking up a billiard ball that had miraculously escaped the detonations. 'Just so sharp he kept cutting himself, as my granny used to say. Lightning lemons! Where's the sense in that? It was as bad as his "voices-in-the-sky" machine. I told him: Leonard, I said, what are wizards for, eh? There's perfectly normal magic available for that kind of thing. Lightning lemons? It'll be men with wings next! And you know what he said? You know what he said? He said: Funny you should say that . . . Poor old chap.'

Even Cuddy joined in the laughter.

'And did you try it?' he said, afterwards.

'Try what?' said Silverfish.

'Har. Har. Har,' said Detritus, toiling behind the others.

'Putting the metal rods in the lemons?'

'Don't be a damn fool.'

'What dis letter mean?' said Detritus, pointing at the paper.

They looked.

'Oh, that's not a symbol,' said Silverfish. 'That's just old Leonard's way. He was always doodling in margins. Doodle, doodle, doodle. I told him: you should call yourself Mr Doodle.'

'I thought it was some alchemy thing,' said Cuddy. 'It looks a bit like a crossbow without the bow. And this word Ennogeht. What does that mean?'

'Search me. Sounds barbarian to me. Anyway . . . if that's all, officer . . . we've got some serious research to do,' said Silverfish, tossing the fake ivory ball up in the air and catching it again. 'We're not all daydreamers like poor old Leonard.'

'Ennogeht,' said Cuddy, turning the paper round and round. 'T-h-e-g-o-n-n-e—'

Silverfish missed the ball. Cuddy got behind Detritus just in time.

'I've done this before,' said Sergeant Colon, as he and Nobby approached the Fools' Guild. 'Keep up against the wall when I bangs the knocker, all right?'

It was shaped like a pair of artificial breasts, the sort that are highly amusing to rugby players and anyone whose sense of humour has been surgically removed. Colon gave it a quick rap and then flung himself to safety.

There was a whoop, a few honks on a horn, a little tune that someone somewhere must have thought was very jolly, a small hatch slid aside above the knocker and a custard pie emerged slowly, on the end of a wooden arm. Then the arm snapped and the pie collapsed in a little heap by Colon's foot.

'It's sad, isn't it?' said Nobby.

The door opened awkwardly, but only by a few inches, and a small clown stared up at him.

'I say, I say, I say,' it said, 'why did the fat man knock at the door?'

'I don't know,' said Colon automatically. 'Why *did* the fat man knock at the door?'

They stared at each other, tangled in the punch-line.

'That's what I asked *you*,' said the clown reproachfully. He had a depressed, hopeless voice.

Sergeant Colon struck out towards sanity.

'Sergeant Colon, Night Watch,' he said, 'and this here is Corporal Nobbs. We've come to talk to someone about the man who . . . was found in the river, okay?'

'Oh. Yes. Poor Brother Beano. I suppose you'd better come in, then,' said the clown.

Nobby was about to push at the door when Colon stopped him, and pointed wordlessly upwards.

'There seems to be a bucket of whitewash over the door,' he said.

'Is there?' said the clown. He was very small, with huge boots that made him look like a capital L. His face was plastered with flesh-coloured make-up on which a big frown had been painted. His hair had been made from a couple of old mops, painted red. He wasn't fat, but a sort of hoop in his trousers was supposed to make him look amusingly overweight. A pair of rubber braces, so that his trousers bounced up and down when he walked, were a further component in the overall picture of a complete and utter twerp.

'Yes,' said Colon. 'There is.'

'Sure?'

'Positive.'

'Sorry about that,' said the clown. 'It's stupid, I know, but kind of traditional. Wait a moment.'

There were sounds of a stepladder being lugged into position, and various clankings and swear-words.

'All right, come on in.'

The clown led the way through the gatehouse. There was no sound but the flop-flop of his boots on the cobbles. Then an idea seemed to occur to him.

'It's a long shot, I know, but I suppose neither of you gentlemen'd like a sniff of my buttonhole?'

'No.'

'No.'

'No, I suppose not.' The clown sighed. 'It's not easy, you know. Clowning, I mean. I'm on gate duty 'cos I'm on probation.'

'You are?'

'I keep on forgetting: is it crying on the outside and laughing on the inside? I always get it mixed up.'

'About this Beano—' Colon began.

'We're just holding his funeral,' said the little clown. 'That's why my trousers are at half-mast.'

They stepped out into the sunlight again.

The inner courtyard was lined with clowns and fools. Bells tinkled in the breeze. Sunlight glinted off red noses and the occasional nervous jet of water from a fake buttonhole.

The clown ushered the guards into a line of fools.

'I'm sure Dr Whiteface will talk to you as soon as we've finished,' he said. 'My name's Boffo, by the way.' He held out his hand hopefully.

'Don't shake it,' Colon warned.

Boffo looked crestfallen.

A band struck up, and a procession of Guild members emerged from the chapel. A clown walked a little way ahead, carrying a small urn.

'This is very moving,' said Boffo.

On a dais on the opposite side of the quadrangle was a fat clown in baggy trousers, huge braces, a bow tie that was spinning gently in the breeze, and a top hat. His face had been painted into a picture of misery. He held a bladder on a stick.

The clown with the urn reached the dais, climbed the steps, and waited.

The band fell silent.

The clown in the top hat hit the urn-carrier about the head with the bladder – once, twice, three times . . .

The urn-bearer stepped forward, waggled his wig, took the urn in one hand and the clown's belt in the other and, with great solemnity, poured the ashes

161

of the late Brother Beano into the other clown's trousers.

A sigh went up from the audience. The band struck up the clown anthem 'The March of the Idiots', and the end of the trombone flew off and hit a clown on the back of the head. He turned and swung a punch at the clown behind him, who ducked, causing a third clown to be knocked through the bass drum.

Colon and Nobby looked at one another and shook their heads.

Boffo produced a large red and white handker-chief and blew his nose with a humorous honking sound.

'Classic,' he said. 'It's what he would have wanted.'

'Have you any idea what happened?' said Colon.

'Oh, yes. Brother Grineldi did the old heel-and-toe trick and tipped the urn down—'

'I mean, why did Beano die?'

'Um. We think it was an accident,' said Boffo.

'An accident,' said Colon flatly.

'Yes. That's what Dr Whiteface thinks.' Boffo glanced upwards, briefly. They followed his gaze. The rooftops of the Assassins' Guild adjoined the Fools' Guild. It didn't do to upset neighbours like that, especially when the only weapon you had was a custard pie edged with short-crust pastry.

'That's what Dr Whiteface thinks,' said Boffo again, looking at his enormous shoes.

Sergeant Colon liked a quiet life. And the city could spare a clown or two. In his opinion, the loss of the whole boiling could only make the world a slightly happier place. And yet . . . and yet . . .

honestly, he didn't know what had got into the Watch lately. It was Carrot, that was what it was. Even old Vimes had picked it up. We don't let things lie any more . . .

'Maybe he was cleaning a club, sort of thing, and it accidentally went off,' said Nobby. He'd caught it, too.

'No one'd want to kill young Beano,' said the clown, in a quiet voice. 'He was a friendly soul. Friends everywhere.'

'Almost everywhere,' said Colon.

The funeral was over. The jesters, jokers and clowns were going about their business, getting stuck in doorways on the way. There was much pushing and shoving and honking of noses and falling of prats. It was a scene to make a happy man slit his wrists on a fine spring morning.

'All I know is,' said Boffo, in a low voice, 'that when I saw him yesterday he was looking very . . . odd. I called out to him when he was going through the gates and—'

'How do you mean, odd?' said Colon. I am detectoring, he thought, with a faint touch of pride. People are Helping me with My Inquiries.

'Dunno. Odd. Not quite himself—'

'This was yesterday?'

'Oh, yes. In the morning. I know because the gate rota—'

'*Yesterday* morning?'

'That's what I said, mister. Mind you, we were all a bit nervous after the bang—'

'Brother Boffo!'

'Oh, no—' mumbled the clown.

A figure was striding towards them. A terrible figure.

No clowns were funny. That was the whole purpose of a clown. People laughed at clowns, but only out of nervousness. The point of clowns was that, after watching them, anything else that happened seemed enjoyable. It was nice to know there was someone worse off than you. Someone had to be the butt of the world.

But even clowns are frightened of something, and that is the white-faced clown. The one who never gets in the way of the custard. The one in the shiny white clothes, and the deadpan white make-up. The one with the little pointy hat and the thin mouth and the delicate black eyebrows.

Dr Whiteface.

'Who are these gentlemen?' he demanded.

'Er—' Boffo began.

'Night Watch, sir,' said Colon, saluting.

'And why are you here?'

'Investigating our inquiries as to the fatal demise of the clown Beano, sir,' said Colon.

'I rather think that is Guild business, sergeant. Don't you?'

'Well, sir, he *was* found in the—'

'I am sure it is something we don't need to bother the Watch with,' said Dr Whiteface.

Colon hesitated. He'd prefer to face Dr Cruces than this apparition. At least the Assassins were *supposed* to be unpleasant. Clowns were only one step away from mime artists, too.

'No, sir,' he said. 'It was obviously an accident, right?'

'Quite so. Brother Boffo will show you to the door,' said the head clown. 'And then,' he added, 'he will report to my office. Does he understand?'

'Yes, Dr Whiteface,' mumbled Boffo.

'What'll he do to you?' said Nobby, as they headed for the gate.

'Hat full of whitewash, probably,' said Boffo. 'Pie inna face if I'm lucky.'

He opened the wicket gate.

'A lot of us ain't happy about this,' he whispered. 'I don't see why those buggers should get away with it. We ought to go round to the Assassins and have it out with them.'

'Why the Assassins?' said Colon. 'Why would they kill a clown?'

Boffo looked guilty. 'I never said a thing!'

Colon glared at him. 'There's definitely something odd happening, Mr Boffo.'

Boffo looked around, as if expecting a vengeful custard pie at any moment.

'You find his nose,' he hissed. 'You just find his nose. His poor nose!'

The gate slammed shut.

Sergeant Colon turned to Nobby.

'Did exhibit A have a nose, Nobby?'

'Yes, Fred.'

'Then what was that about?'

'Search me.' Nobby scratched a promising boil. 'P'raps he meant a false nose. You know. Those red ones on elastic? The ones,' said Nobby, grimacing, 'they think are funny. He didn't have one.'

Colon rapped on the door, taking care to stand out of the way of any jolly amusing booby traps.

The hatch slid aside.

'Yes?' hissed Boffo.

'Did you mean his false nose?' said Colon.

'His real one! Now bugger off!'

The hatch snapped back.

'Mental,' said Nobby, firmly.

'Beano *had* a real nose. Did it look wrong to you?' said Colon.

'No. It had a couple of holes in it.'

'Well, I don't know about noses,' said Colon, 'but either Brother Boffo is dead wrong or there's something fishy going on.'

'Like what?'

'Well, Nobby, you're what I might call a career soldier, right?'

''S'right, Fred.'

'How many dishonourable discharges have you had?'

'Lots,' said Nobby, proudly. 'But I always puts a poultice on 'em.'

'You've been on a lot of battlefields, ain't you?'

'Dozens.'

Sergeant Colon nodded.

'So you've seen a lot of corpses, right, when you've been ministering to the fallen—'

Corporal Nobbs nodded. They both knew that 'ministering' meant harvesting any personal jewellery and stealing their boots. In many a faraway battlefield the last thing many a mortally wounded foeman ever saw was Corporal Nobbs heading towards him with a sack, a knife and a calculating expression.

'Shame to let good stuff go to waste,' said Nobby.

'So you've noticed how dead bodies get . . . deader,' said Sergeant Colon.

'Deader than dead?'

'You know. More corpsey,' said Sergeant Colon, forensic expert.

'Goin' stiff and purple and suchlike?'

'Right.'

'And then sort of manky and runny . . .'

'Yes, all right—'

'Makes it easier to get the rings off, mind you—'

'The *point* is, Nobby, that you can tell how old a corpse is. That clown, for e.g. You saw him, same as me. How long, would you say?'

'About 5' 9", I'd say. His boots didn't fit, I know that. Too floppy.'

'I meant how long he'd been dead.'

'Couple of days. You can tell because there's this—'

'So how come Boffo saw him yesterday morning?'

They strolled onwards.

'Bit of a poser, that is,' said Nobby.

'You're right. I expect the captain'll be very interested.'

'Maybe he was a zombie?'

'Shouldn't think so.'

'Never could stand zombies,' Nobby mused.

'Really?'

'It was always so hard to nick their boots.'

Sergeant Colon nodded at a passing beggar. 'You still doing the folk dancing on your nights off, Nobby?'

'Yes, Fred. We're practising "Gathering Sweet Lilacs" this week. There is a very complicated double crossover-step.'

'You're definitely a man of many parts, Nobby.'

'Only if I couldn't cut the rings off, Fred.'

'What I mean is, you presents an intriguing dichotomy.'

Nobby took a kick at a small scruffy dog.

'You been reading books again, Fred?'

'Got to improve my mind, Nobby. It's these new recruits. Carrot's got his nose in a book half the time, Angua knows words I has to look up, even the shortarse is brighter'n me. They keep on extracting the urine. I'm definitely a bit under-endowed in the head department.'

'You're brighter than Detritus,' said Nobby.

'That's what I tell myself. I say, "Fred, whatever happens, you're brighter than Detritus." But then I say, "Fred – so's *yeast*."'

He turned away from the window.

So. The damn Watch!

That damn Vimes! *Exactly* the wrong man in the wrong place. Why didn't people learn from history? Treachery was in his very genes! How could a city run properly with someone like that, *poking* around? That wasn't what a Watch was for. Watchmen were supposed to do what they were told, and see to it that other people did too.

Someone like Vimes could upset things. Not

because he was clever. A clever Watchman was a contradiction in terms. But sheer randomness might cause trouble.

The gonne lay on the table.

'What shall I do about Vimes?'

Kill him.

Angua woke up. It was almost noon, she was in her own bed at Mrs Cake's, and someone was knocking at the door.

'Mmm?' she said.

'Oi don't know. Shall I ask him to go away?' said a voice from around keyhole level.

Angua thought quickly. The other residents had warned her about this. She waited for her cue.

'Oh, thanks, love. Oi was forgetting,' said the voice.

You had to pick your time, with Mrs Cake. It was difficult, living in a house run by someone whose mind was only nominally attached to the present. Mrs Cake was a psychic.

'You've got your precognition switched on again, Mrs Cake,' said Angua, swinging her legs out of bed and rummaging quickly through the pile of clothes on the chair.

'Where'd we got to?' said Mrs Cake, still on the other side of the door.

'You just said, "I don't know, shall I ask him to go away?" Mrs Cake,' said Angua. Clothes! That was always the trouble! At least a male werewolf only had to worry about a pair of shorts and pretend he'd been on a brisk run.

'Right.' Mrs Cake coughed. '"There's a young man downstairs asking for you",' she said.

'"Who is it?",' said Angua.

There was a moment's silence.

'Yes, oi think that's all sorted out,' said Mrs Cake. 'Sorry, dear. Oi get terrible headaches if'n people don't fill in the right bits. Are you human, dear?'*

'You can come in, Mrs Cake.'

It wasn't much of a room. It was mainly brown. Brown oilcloth flooring, brown walls, a picture over the brown bed of a brown stag being attacked by brown dogs on a brown moorland against a sky which, contrary to established meteorological knowledge, was brown. There was a brown wardrobe. Possibly, if you fought your way through the mysterious old coats† hanging in it, you'd break through into a magical fairyland full of talking animals and goblins, but it'd probably not be worth it.

Mrs Cake entered. She was a small fat woman, but made up for her lack of height by wearing a huge black hat; not the pointy witch variety, but one covered with stuffed birds, wax fruit and other assorted decorative items, all painted black. Angua quite liked her. The rooms were clean,‡ the rates were cheap, and Mrs Cake had a very understanding approach to people who lived slightly unusual lives and had, for example, an aversion to garlic. Her daughter was a werewolf and she knew all about the

---

*More usually a landlady would ask 'Are you decent?', but Mrs Cake knew her lodgers.
†Brown.
‡And brown.

need for ground floor windows and doors with long handles that a paw could operate.

'He's got chainmail on,' said Mrs Cake. She was holding a bucket of gravel in either hand. 'He's got soap in his ears, too.'

'Oh. Er. Right.'

'Oi can tell 'im to bugger off if you like,' said Mrs Cake. 'That's what I allus does if the wrong sort comes round. Especially if they've got a stake. I can't be having with that sort of thing, people messing up the hallways, waving torches and stuff.'

'I think I know who it is,' said Angua. 'I'll see to it.'

She tucked in her shirt.

'Pull the door to if you go out,' Mrs Cake called after her as she went out into the hall. 'Oi'm just off to change the dirt in Mr Winkins' coffin, on account of his back giving him trouble.'

'It looks like gravel to me, Mrs Cake.'

'Orthopaedic, see?'

Carrot was standing respectfully on the doorstep with his helmet under his arm and a very embarrassed expression on his face.

'Well?' said Angua, not unkindly.

'Er. Good morning. I thought, you know, perhaps, you not knowing very much about the city, really. I could, if you like, if you don't mind, not having to go on duty for a while . . . show you some of it . . . ?'

For a moment Angua thought she'd contracted prescience from Mrs Cake. Various futures flitted across her imagination.

'I haven't had breakfast,' she said.

'They make a very good breakfast in Gimlet's dwarf delicatessen in Cable Street.'

'It's lunchtime.'

'It's breakfast time for the Night Watch.'

'I'm practically vegetarian.'

'He does a soya rat.'

She gave in. 'I'll fetch my coat.'

'Har, har,' said a voice, full of withering cynicism.

She looked down. Gaspode was sitting behind Carrot, trying to glare while scratching himself furiously.

'Last night we chased a cat up a tree,' said Gaspode. 'You and me, eh? We could make it. Fate has thrown us together, style of fing.'

'Go *away*.'

'Sorry?' said Carrot.

'Not you. That dog.'

Carrot turned.

'Him? Is he bothering you now? He's a nice little chap.'

'Woof, woof, biscuit.'

Carrot automatically patted his pocket.

'See?' said Gaspode. 'This boy is Mister Simple, am I right?'

'Do they let dogs in dwarf shops?' said Angua.

'No,' said Carrot.

'On a hook,' said Gaspode.

'Really? Sounds good to me,' said Angua. 'Let's go.'

'Vegetarian?' mumbled Gaspode, limping after them. 'Oh, my.'

'Shut up.'

'Sorry?' said Carrot.

'I was just thinking aloud.'

Vimes' pillow was cold and hard. He felt it gingerly. It was cold and hard because it was not a pillow but a table. His cheek appeared to be stuck to it, and he was not interested in speculating what with.

He hadn't even managed to take his armour off.

But he did manage to unstick one eye.

He'd been writing in his notebook. Trying to make sense of it all. And then he'd gone to sleep.

What time was it? No time to look back.

He traced out:

Stolen from Afsafsins' Guild: gonne – > Hammer-hock killed.

Smell of fireworks. Lump of lead. Alchymical Symbols. 2nd body in river. A clown. Where was his red nose? Gonne.

He stared at the scrawled notes.

I'm on the path, he thought. I don't have to know where it leads. I just have to follow. There's always a crime, if you look hard enough. And the Assassins are in this somewhere.

Follow every lead. Check every detail. Chip, chip away.

I'm hungry.

He staggered to his feet and looked at his face in the cracked mirror over the basin.

Events of the previous day filtered through the

clogged gauze of memory. Central to all of them was the face of Lord Vetinari. Vimes grew angry just thinking about that. The cool way he'd told Vimes that he mustn't take an interest in the theft from—

Vimes stared at his reflection—

—something stung his ear and smashed the glass.

Vimes stared at the hole in the plaster, surrounded by the remains of a mirror frame. Around him, the mirror glass tinkled to the floor.

Vimes stood stock still for a long moment.

Then his legs, reaching the conclusion that his brain was somewhere else, threw the rest of him to the floor.

There was another tinkle and a half bottle of Bearhugger's exploded on the desk. Vimes couldn't even remember buying it.

He scrambled forward on hands and knees and pulled himself upright alongside the window.

Images flashed through his mind. The dead dwarf. The hole in the wall . . .

A thought seemed to start in the small of his back and spread upwards to his brain. These were lath and plaster walls, and old ones at that; you could push a finger through them with a bit of effort. As for a lump of metal—

He hit the floor at the same time as a *pock* coincided with a hole punched through the wall on one side of the window. Plaster dust puffed into the air.

His crossbow was leaning against the wall. He wasn't an expert but, hells, who was? You pointed it and you fired it. He pulled it towards him, rolled on his back, stuck his foot in the stirrup and hauled on the string until it clicked into place.

Then he rolled back on to one knee and slotted a quarrel into the groove.

A catapult, that's what it was. It had to be. Troll-sized, perhaps. Someone up on the roof of the opera house or somewhere high . . .

Draw their fire, draw their fire . . . he picked up his helmet and balanced it on the end of another quarrel. The thing to do was crouch below the window and . . .

He thought for a moment. Then he shuffled across the floor to the corner, where there was a pole with a hook on the end. Once upon a time it had been used to open the upper windows, now long rusted shut.

He balanced his helmet on the end, wedged himself into the corner, and with a certain amount of effort moved the pole so that the helmet just showed over the window si . . .

Pock.

Splinters flew up from a point on the floor where it would undoubtedly have severely inconvenienced anyone lying on the boards cautiously raising a decoy helmet on a stick.

Vimes smiled. Someone was trying to kill him, and that made him feel more alive than he had done for days.

And they were also slightly less intelligent than he was. This is a quality you should always pray for in your would-be murderer.

He dropped the pole, picked up the crossbow,

spun past the window, fired at an indistinct shape on the opera house roof opposite as if the bow could possibly carry across that range, leapt across the room and wrenched at the door. Something smashed into the doorframe as the door swung to behind him.

Then it was down the back stairs, out of the door, over the privy roof, into Knuckle Passage, up the back steps of Zorgo the Retrophrenologist,* into Zorgo's operating room and over to the window.

Zorgo and his current patient looked at him curiously.

Pugnant's roof was empty. Vimes turned back and met a pair of puzzled gazes.

''Morning, Captain Vimes,' said the retrophrenologist, a hammer still upraised in one massive hand.

Vimes smiled manically.

'Just thought—' he began, and then went on, '—I saw an interesting rare butterfly on the roof over there.'

Troll and patient stared politely past him.

'But there wasn't,' said Vimes.

---

*It works like this. Phrenology, as everyone knows, is a way of reading someone's character, aptitude and abilities by examining the bumps and hollows on their head. Therefore – according to the kind of logical thinking that characterizes the Ankh-Morpork mind – it should be possible to *mould* someone's character by *giving* them carefully graded bumps in all the right places. You can go into a shop and order an artistic temperament with a tendency to introspection and a side order of hysteria. What you actually *get* is hit on the head with a selection of different size mallets, but it creates employment and keeps the money in circulation, and that's the main thing.

He walked back to the door.

'Sorry to have bothered you,' he said, and left.

Zorgo's patient watched him go with interest.

'Didn't he have a crossbow?' he said. 'Bit odd, going after interesting rare butterflies with a crossbow.'

Zorgo readjusted the fit of the grid on his patient's bald head.

'Dunno,' he said, 'I suppose it stops them creating all these damn thunderstorms.' He picked up the mallet again. 'Now, what were we going for today? Decisiveness, yes?'

'Yes. Well, no. Maybe.'

'Right.' Zorgo took aim. 'This,' he said with absolute truth, 'won't hurt a bit.'

It was more than just a delicatessen. It was a sort of dwarf community centre and meeting place. The babble of voices stopped when Angua entered, bending almost double, but started up again with slightly more volume and a few laughs when Carrot followed. He waved cheerfully at the other customers.

Then he carefully removed two chairs. It was just possible to sit upright if you sat on the floor.

'Very . . . nice,' said Angua. 'Ethnic.'

'I come in here quite a lot,' said Carrot. 'The food's good and, of course, it pays to keep your ear to the ground.'

'That'd certainly be easy here,' said Angua, and laughed.

'Pardon?'

'Well, I mean, the ground is . . . so much . . . closer . . .'

She felt a pit opening wider with every word. The noise level had suddenly dropped again.

'Er,' said Carrot, staring fixedly at her. 'How can I put this? People are talking in Dwarfish . . . but they're listening in Human.'

'Sorry.'

Carrot smiled, and then nodded at the cook behind the counter and cleared his throat noisily.

'I think I might have a throat sweet somewhere—' Angua began.

'I was ordering breakfast,' said Carrot.

'You know the menu off by heart?'

'Oh, yes. But it's written on the wall as well.'

Angua turned and looked again at what she'd thought were merely random scratches.

'It's Oggham,' said Carrot. 'An ancient and poetic runic script whose origins are lost in the mists of time but it's thought to have been invented even before the Gods.'

'Gosh. What does it say?'

Carrot really cleared his throat this time.

> 'Soss, egg, beans and rat 12p
> Soss, rat and fried slice 10p
> Cream-cheese rat 9p
> Rat and beans 8p
> Rat and ketchup 7p
> Rat 4p'

'Why does ketchup cost almost as much as the rat?' said Angua.

'Have you tried rat without ketchup?' said

Carrot. Anyway, I ordered you dwarf bread. Have you ever eaten dwarf bread?'

'No.'

'Everyone should try it once,' said Carrot. He appeared to consider this. 'Most people do,' he added.*

Three and a half minutes after waking up, Captain Samuel Vimes, Night Watch, staggered up the last few steps to the roof of the city's opera house, gasped for breath and threw up *allegro ma non troppo.*

Then he leaned against the wall, waving his crossbow vaguely in front of him.

There wasn't anyone else on the roof. There were just the leads, stretching away, drinking up the morning sunlight. It was already almost too hot to move.

When he felt a bit better he poked around among the chimneys and skylight. But there were a dozen ways down, and a thousand places to hide.

He could see right into his room from here.

---

*Rat and cream cheese is only one of the famous Discworld dishes available in cosmopolitan Ankh-Morpork. According to the Guild of Merchants' publication *Wellcome to Ankh-Morpork, Citie of One Thousand Surprises*: 'Also to be bought in its well-stuffed emporia are Slumpie, Jammy Devils, Fikkun haddock, Distressed Pudding, Clooty Dumplings† and, not to be forgotten, the Knuckle Sandwich, made from finest pig knuckles. Not for something is it said, For a True Taste of Ankh-Morpork, Try a Knuckle Sandwich.'
†Not to be confused with the Scottish Clootie Dumpling, which is a kind of suet pudding full of fruit. The Ankh-Morpork version sits on the tongue like finest meringue, and on the stomach like a concrete bowling ball.

Come to that, he could see into the rooms of most of the city.

Catapult . . . no . . .

Oh, well. At least there'd been witnesses.

He walked to the edge of the roof, and peered over.

'Hello, there,' he said. He blinked. It was six storeys down, and not a sight to look at on a recently emptied stomach.

'Er . . . could you come up here, please?' he said.

''Ight oo are.'

Vimes stood back. There was a scrape of stone and a gargoyle pulled itself laboriously over the parapet, moving like a cheap stop-motion animation.

He didn't know much about gargoyles. Carrot had said something once about how marvellous it was, an urban troll species that had evolved a symbiotic relationship with gutters, and he had admired the way they funnelled run-off water into their ears and out through fine sieves in their mouths. They were probably the strangest species on the Disc.* You didn't get many birds nesting on buildings colonized by gargoyles, and bats tended to fly around them.

---

*Wrong. Vimes didn't travel much except on foot, and knew little of the Lancre Suicide Thrush, for example, or the Shadowing Lemma, which exists in only two dimensions and eats mathematicians, or the quantum weather butterfly. But it is possible that the strangest, and possibly saddest, species on Discworld is the hermit elephant. This creature, lacking the thick hide of its near relatives, lives in huts, moving up and building extensions as its size increases. It's not unknown for a traveller on the plains of Howondaland to wake up in the morning in the middle of a village that wasn't there the night before.

'What's your name, friend?'

''ornice-oggerooking-Oardway.'

Vimes' lips moved as he mentally inserted all those sounds unobtainable to a creature whose mouth was stuck permanently open. Cornice-over-looking-Broadway. A gargoyle's personal identity was intimately bound up with its normal location, like a limpet.

'Well now, Cornice,' he said, 'do you know who I am?'

'Oh,' said the gargoyle sullenly.

Vimes nodded. It sits up here in all weather straining gnats through its ears, he thought. People like that don't have a crowded address book. Even whelks get out more.

'I'm Captain Vimes of the Watch.'

The gargoyle pricked up its huge ears.

'Ar. Oo erk or Ister Arrot?'

Vimes worked this one out, too, and blinked.

'You know Corporal Carrot?'

'Oh, *Ess*. Air-ee-un owes Arrot.'

Vimes snorted. I grew up here, he thought, and when I walk down the street everyone says, 'Who's that glum bugger?' Carrot's been here a few months and *everyone* knows him. And he knows everyone. *Everyone* likes him. I'd be annoyed about that, if only he wasn't so likeable.

'You live right up here,' said Vimes, interested despite the more pressing problem on his mind, 'how come you know Arrot . . . Carrot?'

'Ee cuns uk ere um-imes an awks oo ugg.'

'Uz ee?'

'Egg.'

'Did someone else come up here? Just now?'

'Egg.'

'Did you see who it was?'

'Oh. Ee oot izh oot on i ed. Ang et ogg a ire-erk. I or ing un ah-ay a-ong Or-oh-Erns Eet.'

Holofernes Street, Vimes translated. Whoever it was would be well away by now.

'Ee ad a ick,' Cornice volunteered. 'A ire-erk htick.'

'A what?'

'Ire-erk. Oo oh? Ang! Ock! Arks! Ockekts! Ang!'

'Oh, *fireworks*.'

'Egg. Aks ot I ed.'

'A firework stick? Like . . . like a rocket stick?'

'Oh, ih-ee-ot! A htick, oo oint, ik koes ANG!'

'You point it and it goes bang?'

'Egg!'

Vimes scratched his head. Sounded like a wizard's staff. But they didn't go bang.

'Well . . . thanks,' he said. 'You've been . . . eh-ee elkfhull.'

He turned back towards the stairs.

Someone had tried to kill him.

And the Patrician had warned him against investigating the theft from the Assassins' Guild. *Theft*, he said.

Up until then, Vimes hadn't even been certain there *had* been a theft.

And then, of course, there are the laws of chance. They play a far greater role in police procedure than narrative causality would like to admit. For every murder solved by the careful discovery of a vital footprint or a cigarette end, a hundred failed to be resolved because the wind blew some leaves the wrong way or it didn't rain the night before. So many crimes are solved by a happy accident – by the random stopping of a car, by an overheard remark, by someone of the right nationality happening to be within five miles of the scene of the crime without an alibi . . .

Even Vimes knew about the power of chance.

His sandal clinked against something metallic.

'And this,' said Corporal Carrot, 'is the famous commemorative arch celebrating the Battle of Crumhorn. We won it, I think. It's got over ninety statues of famous soldiers. It's something of a landmark.'

'Should have put up a stachoo to the accountants,' said a doggy voice behind Angua. 'First battle in the universe where the enemy were persuaded to sell their weapons.'

'Where is it, then?' said Angua, still ignoring Gaspode.

'Ah. Yes. That's the problem,' said Carrot. 'Excuse me, Mr Scant. This is Mr Scant. Official Keeper of the Monuments. According to ancient tradition, his pay is one dollar a year and a new vest every Hogswatchday.'

There was an old man sitting on a stool at the road junction, with his hat over his eyes. He pushed it up.

'Afternoon, Mr Carrot. You'll be wanting to see the triumphal arch, will you?'

'Yes, please.' Carrot turned back to Angua. 'Unfortunately, the actual practical design was turned over to Bloody Stupid Johnson.'

The old man eventually produced a small cardboard box from a pocket, and reverentially took off the lid.

'Where is it?'

'Just there,' said Carrot. 'Behind that little bit of cotton wool.'

'Oh.'

'I'm afraid that for Mr Johnson accurate measurements were something that happened to other people.'

Mr Scant closed the lid.

'He also did the Quirm Memorial, the Hanging Gardens of Ankh, and the Colossus of Morpork,' said Carrot.

'The Colossus of Morpork?' said Angua.

Mr Scant held up a skinny finger. 'Ah,' he said. 'Don't go away.' He started to pat his pockets. 'Got 'im 'ere somewhere.'

'Didn't the man ever design anything useful?'

'Well, he did design an ornamental cruet set for Mad Lord Snapcase,' said Carrot, as they strolled away.

'He got that right?'

'Not exactly. But here's an interesting fact, four families live in a salt shaker and we use the pepper pot for storing grain.'

Angua smiled. Interesting facts. Carrot was full of interesting facts about Ankh-Morpork. Angua felt she was floating uneasily on a sea of them. Walking along a street with Carrot was like having three guided tours rolled into one.

'Now here,' said Carrot, 'is the Beggars' Guild. They're the oldest of the Guilds. Not many people know that.'

'Is that so?'

'People think it'd be the Fools or the Assassins. Ask anyone. They'll say "the oldest Guild in Ankh-Morpork is certainly the Fools' Guild or the Assassins' Guild". But they aren't. They're quite recent. But there's been a Beggars' Guild for centuries.'

'Really?' said Angua, weakly. In the last hour she'd learned more about Ankh-Morpork than any reasonable person wanted to know. She vaguely suspected that Carrot was trying to court her. But, instead of the usual flowers or chocolate, he seemed to be trying to gift-wrap a city.

And, despite all her better instincts, she was feeling jealous. Of a city! Ye gods, I've known him a couple of days!

It was the way he wore the place. You expected him any moment to break into the kind of song that has suspicious rhymes and phrases like 'my kind of town' and 'I wanna be a part of it' in it; the kind of song where people dance in the street and give the singer apples and join in and a dozen lowly matchgirls suddenly show amazing choreographical ability and everyone acts like cheery lovable citizens instead of the murderous, evil-minded, self-centred individuals they suspect themselves to be. But the point was that if Carrot had erupted into a song and dance, people *would* have joined in. Carrot could have jollied a circle of standing stones to form up behind him and do a rumba.

'There's some very interesting old statuary in the main courtyard,' he said. 'Including a very good one of Jimi, the God of Beggars. I'll show you. They won't mind.'

He rapped on the door.

'You don't have to,' said Angua.

'It's no trouble—'

The door opened.

Angua's nostrils flared. There was a smell . . .

A beggar looked Carrot up and down. His mouth dropped open.

'It's Cumbling Michael, isn't it?' said Carrot, in his cheery way.

The door slammed.

'Well, that wasn't very friendly,' said Carrot.

'Stinks, don't it?' said a nasty little voice from somewhere behind Angua. While she was in no mood to acknowledge Gaspode, she found herself nodding. Although the beggars were an entire cocktail of odours the second biggest one was fear, and the biggest of all was blood. The scent of it made her want to scream.

There was a babble of voices behind the door, and it swung open again.

This time there was a whole crowd of beggars there. They were all staring at Carrot.

'All right, yer honour,' said the one hailed as Cumbling Michael, 'we give in. How did you know?'

'How did we know wh—' Carrot began, but Angua nudged him.

'Someone's been killed here,' she said.

'Who's she?' said Cumbling Michael.

'Lance-Constable Angua is a man of the Watch,' said Carrot.

'Har, har,' said Gaspode.

'I must say you people are getting better,' said Cumbling Michael. 'We only found the poor thing a few minutes ago.'

Angua could *feel* Carrot opening his mouth to say 'Who?' She nudged him again.

'You'd better take us to him,' she said.

He turned out to be—

—for one thing, he turned out to be a she. In a rag-strewn room on the top floor.

Angua knelt beside the body. It was very clearly a body now. It certainly wasn't a person. A person normally had more head on their shoulders.

'Why?' she said. 'Who'd do such a thing?'

Carrot turned to the beggars clustered around the doorway.

'Who was she?'

'Lettice Knibbs,' said Cumbling Michael. 'She was just the lady's maid to Queen Molly.'

Angua glanced up at Carrot.

'Queen?'

'They sometimes call the head beggar king or queen,' said Carrot. He was breathing heavily.

Angua pulled the maid's velvet cloak over the corpse.

'Just the maid,' she muttered.

There was a full-length mirror in the middle of the floor, or at least the frame of one. The glass was scattered like sequins around it.

So was the glass from a window pane.

Carrot kicked aside some shards. There was a groove in the floor, and something metallic embedded in it.

'Cumbling Michael, I need a nail and a length of string,' said Carrot, very slowly and carefully. His eyes never left the speck of metal. It was almost as if he expected it to do something.

'I don't think—' the beggar began.

Carrot reached out without turning his head and picked him up by his grubby collar without apparent effort.

'A length of string,' he repeated, 'and a nail.'

'Yes, Corporal Carrot.'

'And the rest of you, go away,' said Angua.

They goggled at her.

'Do it!' she shouted, clenching her fists. 'And stop staring at her!'

The beggars vanished.

'It'll take a while to get the string,' said Carrot, brushing aside some glass. 'They'll have to beg it off someone, you see.'

He drew his knife and started digging at the floorboards, with care. Eventually he excavated a metal slug, flattened slightly by its passage through the window, the mirror, the floorboards and certain parts of the late Lettice Knibbs that had never been designed to see daylight.

He turned it over and over in his hand.

'Angua?'

'Yes?'

'How did you know there was someone dead in here?'

'I . . . just had a feeling.'

The beggars returned, so unnerved that half a dozen of them were trying to carry one piece of string.

Carrot hammered the nail into the frame under the smashed pane to hold one end of the string. He stuck his knife in the groove and affixed the other end of the string to it. Then he lay down and sighted up the string.

'Good grief.'

'What is it?'

'It must have come from the roof of the opera house.'

'Yes? So?'

'That's more than two hundred yards away.'

'Yes?'

'The . . . thing went an inch into an oak floor.'

'Did you know the girl . . . at all?' said Angua, and felt embarrassed at asking.

'Not really.'

'I thought you knew everyone.'

'She was just someone I'd see around. The city's full of people who you just see around.'

'Why do beggars need servants?'

'*You don't think my hair gets like this by itself, dear, do you?*'

There was an apparition in the doorway. Its face was a mass of sores. There were warts, and *they* had warts, and *they* had hair on. It was possibly female, but it was hard to tell under the layers and layers of rags. The aforementioned hair looked as though it had been permed by a hurricane. With treacle on its fingers.

Then it straightened up.

'Oh. Corporal Carrot. Didn't know it was you.'

The voice was normal now, no trace of whine or wheedle. The figure turned and brought her stick down hard on something in the corridor.

'Naughty boy, Dribbling Sidney! You could have told I it were Corporal Carrot!'

'Arrgh!'

The figure strode into the room.

'And who's your ladyfriend, Mr Carrot?'

'This is Lance-Constable Angua. Angua, this is Queen Molly of the Beggars.'

For once, Angua noted, someone wasn't surprised to find a female in the Watch. Queen Molly nodded at her as one working woman to another. The Beggars' Guild was an equal-opportunity non-employer.

'Good day to you. You couldn't spare I ten thousand dollars for a small mansion, could you?'

'No.'

'Just asking.'

Queen Molly prodded at the gown.

'What was it, corporal?'

'I think it's a new kind of weapon.'

'We heard the glass smash and there she was,' said Molly. 'Why would anyone want to kill her?'

Carrot looked at the velvet cloak.

'Whose room is this?' he said.

'Mine. It's my dressing room.'

'Then whoever did it wasn't after her. He was after you, Molly. "Some in rags, and some in tags, and one in a velvet gown" . . . it's in your Charter, isn't it? Official dress of the chief beggar. She probably couldn't resist seeing what it looked like on her. Right gown, right room. Wrong person.'

Molly put her hand to her mouth, risking instant poisoning.

'Assassination?'

Carrot shook his head. 'That doesn't sound right. They like to do it up close. It's a caring profession,' he added, bitterly.

'What should I do?'

'Burying the poor thing would be a good start.' Carrot turned the metal slug over in his fingers. Then he sniffed it.

'Fireworks,' he said.

'Yes,' said Angua.

'And what are you going to do?' said Queen Molly.

'You're Watchmen, aren't you? What's happening? What are you going to do about it?'

Cuddy and Detritus were proceeding along Phedre Road. It was lined with tanneries and brick kilns and timber yards and was not generally considered a beauty spot which was why, Cuddy suspected, they'd been given it to patrol 'to get to know the city'. It got them out of the way. Sergeant Colon thought they made the place look untidy.

There was no sound but the clink of his boots and the thump of Detritus' knuckles on the ground.

Finally, Cuddy said: 'I just want you to know that I don't like being teamed up with you any more than you like being teamed up with me.'

'Right!'

'But if we're going to have to make the best of it, there'd better be some changes, okay?'

'Like what?'

'Like it's ridiculous you not even being able to count. I know trolls can count. Why can't you?'

'Can count!'

'How many fingers am I holding up, then?'

Detritus squinted.

'Two?'

'Okay. *Now* how many fingers am I holding up?'

'Two . . . and one more . . .'

'So two and one more is . . . ?'

Detritus looked panicky. This was calculus territory.

'Two and one more is three.'

'Two and one more is three.'

'Now how many?'

'Two and two.'

'That's *four*.'

'Four-er.'

'*Now* how many?'

Cuddy tried eight fingers.

'A twofour.'

Cuddy looked surprised. He'd expected 'many', or possibly 'lots'.

'What's a twofour?'

'A two and a two and a two and a two.'

Cuddy put his head on one side.

'Hmm,' he said. 'Okay. A twofour is what we call an *eight*.'

'Ate.'

'You know,' said Cuddy, subjecting the troll to a long critical stare, 'you might not be as stupid as you look. This is not hard. Let's think about this. I mean . . . *I'll* think about this, and you can join in when you know the words.'

Vimes slammed the Watch House door behind him. Sergeant Colon looked up from his desk. He had a pleased expression.

'What's been happening, Fred?'

Colon took a deep breath.

'Interesting stuff, captain. Me and Nobby did some *detectoring* up at the Fools' Guild. I've writ it all down what we found out. It's all here. A proper report.'

'Fine.'

'All written down, look. Properly. Punctuation and everything.'

'Well done.'

'It's got commas and everything, look.'

'I'm sure I shall enjoy it, Fred.'

'And the—and Cuddy and Detritus have found out stuff, too. Cuddy's done a report, too. But it's not got so much punctuation as mine.'

'How long have I been asleep?'

'Six hours.'

Vimes tried to make mental space for all of this, and failed.

'I've got to get something inside me,' he said.

'Some coffee or something. And then the world will somehow be better.'

Anyone strolling along Phedre Road might have seen a troll and a dwarf apparently shouting at one another in excitement.

'A two-thirtytwo, and eight, and a one!'

'See? How many bricks in that pile?'

Pause.

'A sixteen, an eight, a four, a one!'

'Remember what I said about dividing by eight-and-two?'

Longer pause.

'Two-enty-nine . . . ?'

'Right!'

'Right!'

'You can get there!'

'I can get there!'

'You're a natural at counting to two!'

'I'm a nat'ral at counting to two!'

'If you can count to two, you can count to anything!'

'If I can count to two, I can count to anything!'

'And then the world is your mollusc!'

'My mollusc! What's a mollusc?'

Angua had to scurry to keep up with Carrot.

'Aren't we going to look at the opera house?' she said.

'Later. Anyone up there'll be long gone by the time we get there. We must tell the captain.'

'You think she was killed by the same thing as Hammerhock?'

'Yes.'

'There are . . . niner birds.'

'That's right.'

'There are . . . one bridge.'

'Right.'

'There are . . . four-ten boats.'

'All right.'

'There are . . . one tousand. Three hundret. Six-ty. Four bricks.'

'Okay.'

'There are—'

'I should give it a rest now. You don't want to wear everything out by counting—'

'There are – one running man . . .'

'What? Where?'

Sham Harga's coffee was like molten lead, but it had this in its favour: when you'd drunk it, there was this overwhelming feeling of relief that you'd got to the bottom of the cup.

'That,' said Vimes, 'was a bloody awful cup of coffee, Sham.'

'Right,' said Harga.

'I mean I've drunk a lot of bad coffee in my time but that, that was like having a saw dragged across my tongue. How long'd it been boiling?'

'What's today's date?' said Harga, cleaning a glass. He was generally cleaning glasses. No one ever found out what happened to the clean ones.

'August the fifteenth.'

'What year?'

Sham Harga smiled, or at least moved various muscles around his mouth. Sham Harga had run a successful eatery for many years by always smiling, never extending credit, and realizing that most of his customers wanted meals properly balanced between the four food groups: sugar, starch, grease and burnt crunchy bits.

'I'd like a couple of eggs,' said Vimes, 'with the yolks real hard but the whites so runny that they drip like treacle. And I want bacon, that special bacon all covered with bony nodules and dangling bits of fat. And a slice of fried bread. The kind that makes your arteries go clang just by looking at it.'

'Tough order,' said Harga.

'You managed it yesterday. And give me some more coffee. Black as midnight on a moonless night.'

Harga looked surprised. That wasn't like Vimes.

'How black's that, then?' he said.

'Oh, pretty damn black, I should think.'

'Not necessarily.'

'What?'

'You get more stars on a moonless night. Stands to reason. They show up more. It can be quite bright on a moonless night.'

Vimes sighed.

'An *overcast* moonless night?' he said.

Harga looked carefully at his coffee pot.

'Cumulus or cirro-nimbus?'

'I'm sorry? What did you say?'

'You gets city lights reflected off cumulus,

because it's low lying, see. Mind you, you can get high-altitude scatter off the ice crystals in—'

'A moonless night,' said Vimes, in a hollow voice, 'that is as black as that coffee.'

'Right!'

'And a doughnut.' Vimes grabbed Harga's stained vest and pulled him until they were nose to nose. 'A doughnut as doughnutty as a doughnut made of flour, water, one large egg, sugar, a pinch of yeast, cinnamon to taste and a jam, jelly or rat filling depending on national or species preference, Okay? Not as doughnutty as something in any way metaphorical. Just a doughnut. One doughnut.'

'A doughnut.'

'Yes.'

'You only had to say.'

Harga brushed off his vest, gave Vimes a hurt look, and went back into the kitchen.

'*Stop!* In the name of the law!'

'What the law's name, then?'

'How should I know!'

'Why we chasing him?'

'Because he's running away!'

Cuddy had only been a guard for a few days, but already he had absorbed one important and basic fact: it is almost impossible for anyone to be in a street without breaking the law. There are a whole quiverful of offences available to a policeman who wishes to pass the time of day with a citizen, ranging from Loitering with Intent through Obstruction to Lingering While Being the Wrong

Colour/Shape/Species/Sex. It occurred briefly to him that anyone *not* making a dash for it when they saw Detritus knuckling along at high speed behind them was probably guilty of contravening the Being Bloody Stupid Act of 1581. But it was too late to take that into account. Someone was running, and they were chasing. They were chasing because he was running, and he was running because they were chasing.

Vimes sat down with his coffee and looked at the thing he'd picked up from the rooftop.

It looked like a short set of Pan pipes, provided Pan was restricted to six notes, all of them the same. They were made of steel, welded together. There was a strip of serrated metal along one side, like a flattened-out cogwheel, and the whole thing reeked of fireworks.

He laid it carefully beside his plate.

He read Sergeant Colon's report. Fred Colon had spent some time on it, probably with a dictionary. It went as follows:

'Report of Sgt F. Colon. Approx. 10am today, Auguste 15, I proceeded in the company of Corporal, C. W. St. J. Nobbs, to the Guild of Fools and Joculators in God Street, whereupon we conversed with clown Boffo who said, clown Beano, the *corpus derelicti*, was definitely seen by him, clown Boffo, leaving the Guild the previous morning just after the explosion. {This is dead bent in my opinion, the reason being, the stiff was dead at least two days, Cpl C. W. St. J. Nobbs agrees, so someone is telling meat pies, never trust anyone who falls on his arse for a living.} Whereupon Dr Whiteface met us, and, damn near gave us the *derriere velocite* out of the place. It seemed to us, viz, me and Cpl C. W. St. J. Nobbs, that the Fools are worried that it might have been the Assassins, but we don't know why. Also, clown Boffo went on about us looking for Beano's nose, but he had a nose on when we saw him here, so we said to clown Boffo, did he mean a false nose, he said, no, a real one, bugger off. Whereupon we come back here.'

Vimes worked out what *derriere velocite* meant. The whole nose business looked like a conundrum wrapped up in an enigma, or at least in Sergeant Colon's handwriting, which was pretty much the same thing. Why be asked to look for a nose that wasn't lost?

He looked at Cuddy's report, written in the careful angular handwriting of someone more used to runes. And sagas.

'Captain Vimes, this herewith is the chronicle of me, Lance-Constable Cvddy. Bright was the morning and high ovr hearts when we proceeded to the Alchemists Gvild, where events eventvated as I shall now sing. These inclvded exploding balls. As to the qvest vpon which we were sent, we were informed that the attached piece of paper [attached] is in the handwriting of Leonard

---

of Qvirm, who vanished in mysteriovs circvmstances. It is how to make a powder called No. 1 powder, which is vsed in fireworks. Mr Silverfish the alchemist says any alchemists knows it. Also, in the margin of the paper, is a drawing of The Gonne, becavse I asked my covsin Grabpot abovt Leonard and he vsed to sell paints to Leonard and he recognized the writing and said Leonard always wrote backwards becavse he was a genivs. I have copied same herewith.'

Vimes laid the papers down and put the piece of metal on top of them.

Then he reached in his pocket and produced a couple of metal pellets.

A stick, the gargoyle had said.

Vimes looked at the sketch. It looked, as Cuddy had noted, like the stock of a crossbow with a pipe on the top of it. There were a few sketches of strange mechanical devices alongside it, and a couple of the little six-pipe things. The whole drawing looked like a doodle. Someone, possibly this Leonard, had been reading a book about fireworks and had scribbled in the margins.

Fireworks.

Well . . . fireworks? But fireworks weren't a weapon. Crackers went bang. Rockets went up, more or less, but all you could be sure of them hitting was the sky.

Hammerhock was noted for his skill with mechanisms. That wasn't a major dwarfish attribute. People thought it was, but it wasn't. They were skilled with metal all right, and they made good swords and jewellery, but they weren't too *technical* when it came to things like cogwheels and springs. Hammerhock was unusual.

So . . .

Supposing there was a weapon. Supposing there was something about it that was different, strange, terrifying.

No, that couldn't be it. It'd either end up all over the place, or it'd be destroyed. It wouldn't end up in the Assassins' museum. What got put in museums? Things that hadn't worked, or had got lost, or ought to be remembered . . . so where's the sense in putting our firework *on show*?

There had been a lot of locks on the door. So . . . not a museum you just wandered into, then. Maybe you had to be a high-up Assassin, and one day one of the Guild leaders'd take you down there at dead, hah, of night, and say . . . and say . . .

For some reason the face of the Patrician loomed up at this point.

Once again Vimes felt the edge of something, some fundamental central thing . . .

'Where'd he go? Where'd he go?'

There was a maze of alleys around the doors. Cuddy leaned against a wall and fought for breath.

'There he go!' shouted Detritus. 'Along Whalebone Lane!'

He lumbered off in pursuit.

*   *   *

Vimes put down his coffee cup.

Whoever had shot those lead balls at him had been very accurate across several hundred yards, and had got off six shots faster than anyone could fire an arrow . . .

Vimes picked up the pipes. Six little pipes, six shots. And you could carry a pocketful of these things. You could shoot further, faster, more accurately than anyone else with any other kind of weapon . . .

So. A new *type* of weapon. Much, much faster than a bow. The Assassins wouldn't like that. They wouldn't like that *at all*. They weren't even keen on bows. The Assassins preferred to kill up close.

So they'd put the . . . the *gonne* safely under lock and key. The gods alone knew how they'd come by it in the first place. And a few senior Assassins would know about it. They'd pass on the secret: *beware of things like this . . .*

'Down there! He went into Grope Alley!'

'Slow down! Slow down!'

'Why?' said Detritus.

'It's a dead end.'

The two Watchmen lumbered to a halt.

Cuddy knew that he was currently the brains of the partnership, even though Detritus was presently counting, his face beaming with pride, the stones in the wall beside him.

Why had they chased someone halfway across the city? Because they'd run away. *No one* ran away from the Watch. Thieves just flashed their licences.

Unlicensed thieves had nothing to fear from the Watch, since they'd saved up all their fear for the Thieves' Guild. Assassins always obeyed the letter of the law. And honest men didn't run away from the Watch.* Running away from the Watch was downright suspicious.

The origin of Grope Alley's name was fortunately lost in the celebrated mists of time, but it had come to be deserved. It had turned into a kind of tunnel as upper storeys were built out and over it, leaving a few inches of sky.

Cuddy peered around the corner, into the gloom.

Click. Click.

It came from deep in the darkness.

'Detritus?'

'Yeah?'

'Did he have any weapons?'

'Just a stick. One stick.'

'Only . . . I smell fireworks.'

Cuddy pulled his head back, very carefully.

There had been the smell of fireworks in Hammerhock's workshop. And Mr Hammerhock ended up with a big hole in his chest. And a sense of named dread, which is much more specific and terrifying than nameless dread, was stealing over Cuddy. It was similar to the feeling you get when you're playing a high stakes game and your opponent suddenly grins and you realize that you don't know *all* the rules but you *do* know you'll be

---

*The axiom 'Honest men have nothing to fear from the police' is currently under review by the Axioms Appeal Board.

lucky to get out of this with, if you are very fortunate, your shirt.

On the other hand . . . he could picture Sergeant Colon's face. We chased this man into an alley, sarge, and then we came away . . .

He drew his sword.

'Lance-Constable Detritus?'

'Yes, Lance-Constable Cuddy?'

'Follow me.'

Why? The damn thing was made of metal, wasn't it? Ten minutes in a hot crucible and that'd be the end of the problem. Something like that, something dangerous, why not just get rid of it? Why keep it?

But that wasn't human nature, was it? Sometimes things were too fascinating to destroy.

He looked at the strange metal tubes. Six short pipes, welded together, sealed firmly at one end. There was a small hole in the top side of each of the pipes . . .

Vimes slowly picked up one of the lumps of lead . . .

The alley twisted once or twice, but there were no other alleys or doors off it. There was one at the far end. It was larger than a normal door, and heavily constructed.

'Where are we?' whispered Cuddy.

'Don't know,' said Detritus. 'Back of the docks somewhere.'

Cuddy pushed open the door with his sword.

'Cuddy?'

'Yeah?'

'We walked seven-ty-nine steps!'

'That's nice.'

Cold air rushed past them.

'Meat store,' whispered Cuddy. 'Someone picked the lock.'

He slipped through and into a high, gloomy room, as large as a temple, which in some ways it resembled. Faint light crept through the high, ice-covered windows. From rack upon rack, all the way to the ceiling, hung meat carcasses.

They were semi-transparent and so very cold Cuddy's breath turned to crystals in the air.

'Oh, my,' said Detritus. 'I think this the pork futures warehouse in Morpork Road.'

'What?'

'Used to work here,' said the troll. 'Used to work everywhere. Go away, you stupid troll, you too thick,' he added, gloomily.

'Is there any way out?'

'The main door is in Morpork Street. But no one comes in here for months. Till pork exists.'*

---

*Probably no other world in the multiverse has warehouses for things which only exist *in potentia,* but the pork futures warehouse in Ankh-Morpork is a product of the Patrician's rules about baseless metaphors, the literal-mindedness of citizens who assume that everything must exist somewhere, and the general thinness of the fabric of reality around Ankh, which is so thin that it's as thin as a very thin thing. The net result is that trading in pork futures – in pork *that doesn't exist yet* – led to the building of the warehouse to store it in until it does. The extremely low temperatures are caused by the imbalance in the temporal energy flow. At least, that's what the wizards in the High Energy Magic building say. And they've got proper pointy hats and letters after their name, so they know what they're talking about.

Cuddy shivered.

'You in here!' he shouted. 'It's the Watch! Step out now!'

A dark figure appeared from between a couple of pre-pigs.

'Now what we do?' said Detritus.

The distant figure raised what looked like a stick, holding it like a crossbow.

And fired. The first shot zinged off Cuddy's helmet.

A stony hand clamped on to the dwarf's head and Detritus pushed Cuddy behind him, but then the figure was running, running towards them, still firing.

Detritus blinked.

Five more shots, one after another, punctured his breastplate.

And then the running man was through the open door, slamming it behind him.

'Captain Vimes?'

He looked up. It was Captain Quirke of the Day Watch, with a couple of his men behind him.

'Yes?'

'You come with us. And give me your sword.'

'What?'

'I think you heard me, captain.'

'Look, it's *me*, Quirke. Sam Vimes? Don't be a fool.'

'I ain't a fool. I've got men with crossbows. *Men.* It's you that'd be the fool if you resist arrest.'

'Oh? I'm under arrest?'

'Only if you don't come with us . . .'

*　　　*　　　*

The Patrician was in the Oblong Office, staring out of the window. The multi-belled cacophony of five o'clock was just dying away.

Vimes saluted. From the back, Vetinari looked like a carnivorous flamingo.

'Ah, Vimes,' he said, without looking around, 'come here, will you? And tell me what you see.'

Vimes hated guessing games, but he joined the Patrician anyway.

The Oblong Office had a view over half the city, although most of it was rooftops and towers. Vimes' imagination peopled the towers with men holding gonnes. The Patrician would be an easy target.

'What do you see out there, captain?'

'City of Ankh-Morpork, sir,' said Vimes, keeping his expression carefully blank.

'And does it put you in mind of anything, captain?'

Vimes scratched his head. If he was going to play games, he was going to play games . . .

'Well, sir, when I was a kid we owned a cow once, and one day it got sick, and it was always my job to clean out the cowshed, and—'

'It reminds *me* of a clock,' said the Patrician. 'Big wheels, little wheels. All clicking away. The little wheels spin and the big wheels turn, all at different speeds, you see, but the *machine* works. And that is the most important thing. The machine keeps going. Because when the machine breaks down . . .'

He turned suddenly, strode to his desk with his usual predatory stalk, and sat down.

'Or, again, sometimes a piece of grit might get into the wheels, throwing them off balance. One speck of grit.'

Vetinari looked up and flashed Vimes a mirthless smile.

'I won't have that.'

Vimes stared at the wall.

'I believe I told you to forget about certain recent events, captain?'

'Sir.'

'Yet it appears that the Watch have been getting in the wheels.'

'Sir.'

'What am I to do with you?'

'Couldn't say, sir.'

Vimes minutely examined the wall. He wished Carrot was here. The lad might be simple, but he was so simple that sometimes he saw things that the subtle missed. And he kept coming up with simple ideas that stuck in your mind. Policeman, for example. He'd said to Vimes one day, while they were proceeding along the Street of Small Gods: Do you know where 'policeman' comes from, sir? Vimes hadn't. 'Polis' used to mean 'city', said Carrot. That's what policeman means: 'a man for the city'. Not many people know that. The word 'polite' comes from 'polis', too. It used to mean the proper behaviour from someone living *in* a city.

Man of the city . . . Carrot was always throwing out stuff like that. Like 'copper'. Vimes had believed all his life that the Watch were called coppers because they carried copper badges, but no, said

Carrot, it comes from the old word *cappere*, to capture.

Carrot read books in his spare time. Not well. He'd have real difficulty if you cut his index finger off. But continuously. And he wandered around Ankh-Morpork *on his day off.*

'Captain Vimes?'

Vimes blinked.

'Sir?'

'You have no concept of the delicate balance of the city. I'll tell you one more time. This business with the Assassins and the dwarf and this clown . . . you are to cease involving yourself.'

'No, sir. I can't.'

'Give me your badge.'

Vimes looked down at his badge.

He never really thought about it. It was just something he'd always had. It didn't *mean* anything very much . . . really . . . one way or the other. It was just something he'd always had.

'My badge?'

'And your sword.'

Slowly, with fingers that suddenly felt like bananas, and bananas that didn't belong to him at that, Vimes undid his sword belt.

'And your badge.'

'Um. Not my badge.'

'Why not?'

'Um. Because it's my badge.'

'But you're resigning anyway when you get married.'

'Right.'

Their eyes met.

'How much does it mean to you?'

Vimes stared. He couldn't find the right words. It was just that he'd always been a man with a badge. He wasn't sure he could be one without the other.

Finally Lord Vetinari said: 'Very well. I believe you're getting married at noon tomorrow.' His long fingers picked up the gilt-embossed invitation from the desk. 'Yes. You can keep your badge, then. And have an honourable retirement. But I'm keeping the sword. And the Day Watch will be sent down to the Yard shortly to disarm your men. I'm standing the Night Watch down, Captain Vimes. In due course I might appoint another man in charge – at my leisure. Until then, you and your men can consider yourselves on leave.'

'The Day Watch? A bunch of—'

'I'm sorry?'

'Yes, sir.'

'One infraction, however, and the badge is mine. Remember.'

Cuddy opened his eyes.

'You're alive?' said Detritus.

The dwarf gingerly removed his helmet. There was a gouge in the rim, and his head ached.

'It looks like a mild skin abrasion,' said Detritus.

'A what? *Ooooh.*' Cuddy grimaced. 'What about you, anyway?' he said. There was something odd about the troll. It hadn't quite dawned on him what it was, but there was definitely something unfamiliar, quite apart from all the holes.

'I suppose the armour was *some* help,' said Detritus. He pulled at the straps of his breastplate. Five discs of metal slid out at around belt level. 'If it hadn't slowed them down I'd be seriously abraded.'

'What's up with you? Why are you talking like that?'

'Like what, pray?'

'What happened to the "me big troll" talk? No offence meant.'

'I'm not sure I understand.'

Cuddy shivered, and stamped his feet to keep warm.

'Let's get out of here.'

They trotted to the door. It was shut fast.

'Can you knock it down?'

'No. If this place wasn't troll proof, it'd be empty. Sorry.'

'Detritus?'

'Yes?'

'Are you all right? Only there's steam coming off your head.'

'I do feel . . . er . . .'

Detritus blinked. There was a tinkle of falling ice. Odd things were happening in his skull.

Thoughts that normally ambulated sluggishly around his brain were suddenly springing into vibrant, coruscating life. And there seemed to be more and more of them.

'My goodness,' he said, to no one in particular.

This was a sufficiently un-troll-like comment that even Cuddy, whose extremities were already going numb, stared at him.

'I do believe,' said Detritus, 'that I am genuinely cogitating. How very interesting!'

'What do you mean?'

More ice cascaded off Detritus as he rubbed his head.

'Of course!' he said, holding up a giant finger. 'Superconductivity!'

'Wha'?'

'You see? Brain of impure silicon. Problem of heat dissipation. Daytime temperature too hot, processing speed slows down, weather gets hotter, brain stops completely, trolls turn to stone until nightfall, ie, colder-temperature,however,lower-temperature*enough*,brainoperates*faster*and—'

'I think I'm going to freeze to death soon,' said Cuddy.

Detritus looked around.

'There are small glazed apertures up there,' he said.

'Too hi' to rea', e'en if I st' on y'shoulders,' mumbled Cuddy, slumping down further.

'Ah, but my plan involves throwing something through them to attract help,' said Detritus.

'Wha' pla'?'

'I have in fact eventuated twenty-three but this one has a ninety-seven per cent chance of success,' said Detritus, beaming.

'Ha'nt got an'ting t'throw,' said Cuddy.

'*I* have,' said Detritus, scooping him up. 'Do not worry. I can compute your trajectory with astonishing precision. And then all you will need to do is fetch Captain Vimes or Carrot or someone.'

Cuddy's feeble protests described an arc through the freezing air and vanished along with the window glass.

Detritus sat down again. Life was so simple, when you really thought about it. And he was really thinking.

He was seventy-six per cent sure he was going to get at least seven degrees colder.

Mr Cut-Me-Own-Throat Dibbler, Purveyor, Merchant Venturer and all-round salesman, had thought long and hard about going into ethnic food-stuffs. But it was a natural career procession. The old sausage-in-a-bun trade had been falling off lately, while there were all these trolls and dwarfs around with money in their pockets or wherever it was trolls kept their money, and money in the possession of other people had always seemed to Throat to be against the proper natural order of things.

Dwarfs were easy enough to cater for. Rat-on-a-stick was simple enough, although it meant a general improvement in Dibbler's normal catering standards.

On the other hand, trolls were basically, when you got right down to it, no offence meant, speak as you find . . . basically, they were walking rocks.

He'd sought advice about troll food from Chrysoprase, who was also a troll, although you'd hardly know it any more, he'd been around humans so long he wore a suit now and, as he said, had learned all kindsa civilized things, like extortion, money-lending at 300 per cent interest per munf, and stuff like that. Chrysoprase might have been born in a cave above the snowline on some mountain somewhere, but five minutes in Ankh-Morpork and he'd fitted right in. Dibbler liked to think of Chrysoprase as a friend; you'd hate to think of him as an enemy.

Throat had chosen today to give his new approach a try. He pushed his hot food barrow through streets broad and narrow, crying:

'Sausages! Hot sausages! Inna bun! *Meat* pies! Get them while they're hot!'

This was by way of a warm up. The chances of a human eating anything off Dibbler's barrow unless it was stamped flat and pushed under the door after two weeks on a starvation diet was, by now, remote. He looked around conspiratorially – there were always trolls working in the docks – and took the cover off a fresh tray.

Now then, what was it? Oh, yes . . .

'Dolomitic conglomerates! *Get* chore dolomitic conglomerates heeyar! Manganese nodules! Manganese nodules! Get them while they're . . . uh . . . nodule-shaped.' He hesitated a bit, and then rallied. 'Pumice! Pumice! Tufa a dollar! Roast limestones—'

A few trolls wandered up to stare at him.

'You, sir, you look . . . hungry,' said Dibbler, grinning widely at the smallest troll. 'Why not try our shale on a bun? Mmm-mmm! Taste that alluvial deposit, know what I mean?'

C. M. O. T. Dibbler had a number of bad points, but species prejudice was not one of them. He liked anyone who had money, regardless of the colour and shape of the hand that was proffering it. For Dibbler believed in a world where a sapient creature could walk tall, breathe free, pursue life, liberty and happiness, and step out towards the bright new dawn. If they could be persuaded to gobble something off Dibbler's hot-food tray at the same time, this was all to the good.

The troll inspected the tray suspiciously, and lifted up a bun.

'Urrh, yuk,' he said, 'it's got all ammonites in it! Yuk!'

'Pardon?' said Dibbler.

'Dis shale,' said the troll, 'is stale.'

'Lovely and fresh! Just like mother used to hew!'

'Yeah, and there's bloody quartz all through dis granite,' said another troll, towering over Dibbler. 'Clogs the arteries, quartz.'

He slammed the rock back on the tray. The trolls ambled off, occasionally turning around to give Dibbler a suspicious look.

'Stale? *Stale!* How can it be stale? It's *rock*!' shouted Dibbler after them.

He shrugged. Oh, well. The hallmark of a good businessman was knowing when to cut your losses.

He closed the lid of the tray, and opened another one.

'Hole food! Hole food! Rat! Rat! Rat-onna-stick! Rat-in-a-bun! Get them while they're dead! Get chore—'

There was a crash of glass above him, and Lance-Constable Cuddy landed head first in the tray.

'There's no need to rush, plenty for everyone,' said Dibbler.

'Pull me out,' said Cuddy, in a muffled voice. 'Or pass me the ketchup.'

Dibbler hauled on the dwarf's boots. There was ice on them.

'Just come down the mountain, have you?'

'Where's the man with the key to this warehouse?'

'If you liked our rat, then why not try our fine selection of—'

Cuddy's axe appeared almost magically in his hand.

'I'll cut your knees off,' he said.

'GerhardtSockoftheButchers'Guildiswhoyou want.'

'Right.'

'Nowpleasetaketheaxeaway.'

Cuddy's boots skidded on the cobbles as he hurried off.

Dibbler peered at the broken remains of the cart. His lips moved as he calculated.

'Here!' he shouted. 'You owe – hey, you owe me for three rats!'

Lord Vetinari had felt slightly ashamed when he watched the door close behind Captain Vimes. He couldn't work out why. Of course, it was hard on the man, but it was the only way . . .

He took a key from a cabinet by his desk and walked over to the wall. His hands touched a mark on the plaster that was apparently no different from a dozen other marks, but this one caused a section of wall to swing aside on well-oiled hinges.

No one knew all the passages and tunnels hidden in the walls of the Palace; it was said that some of them went a lot further than that. And there were any amount of old cellars under the city. A man with a pick-axe and a sense of direction could go where he liked just by knocking down forgotten walls.

He walked down several narrow flights of steps and along a passage to a door, which he unlocked. It swung back on well-oiled hinges.

It was not, exactly, a dungeon; the room on the other side was quite airy and well lit by several large but high windows. It had a smell of wood shavings and glue.

'Look out!'

The Patrician ducked.

Something batlike clicked and whirred over his head, circled erratically in the middle of the room, and then flew apart into a dozen jerking pieces.

'Oh dear,' said a mild voice. 'Back to the drawing tablet. Good afternoon, your lordship.'

'Good afternoon, Leonard,' said the Patrician. 'What was that?'

'I call it a flapping-wing-flying-device,' said Leonard da Quirm, getting down off his launching stepladder. 'It works by gutta-percha strips twisted tightly together. But not very well, I'm afraid.'

Leonard of Quirm was not, in fact, all that old. He was one of those people who started looking venerable around the age of thirty, and would probably still look about the same at the age of ninety. He wasn't exactly bald, either. His head had just grown up through his hair, rising like a mighty rock dome through heavy forest.

Inspirations sleet through the universe continuously. Their destination, as if they cared, is the right mind in the place at the right time. They hit the right neuron, there's a chain reaction, and a little while later someone is blinking foolishly in the TV lights and wondering how the hell he came up with the idea of pre-sliced bread in the first place.

Leonard of Quirm knew about inspirations. One of his earliest inventions was an earthed metal nightcap, worn in the hope that the damn things would stop leaving their white-hot trails across his tortured imagination. It seldom worked. He knew the shame of waking up to find the sheets covered with nocturnal sketches of unfamiliar siege engines and novel designs for apple-peeling machines.

The da Quirms had been quite rich and young Leonard had been to a great many schools, where he had absorbed a ragbag of information despite his habit of staring out of the window and sketching the flight of birds. Leonard was one of those unfortunate individuals whose fate it was to be fascinated by the world, the taste, shape and movement of it . . .

He fascinated Lord Vetinari as well, which is why he was still alive. Some things are so perfect of their type that they are hard to destroy. One of a kind is always special.

He was a model prisoner. Give him enough wood, wire, paint and above all give him paper and pencils, and he stayed put.

The Patrician moved a stack of drawings and sat down.

'These are good,' he said. 'What are they?'

'My cartoons,' said Leonard.

'This is a good one of the little boy with his kite stuck in a tree,' said Lord Vetinari.

'Thank you. May I make you some tea? I'm afraid I don't see many people these days, apart from the man who oils the hinges.'

'I've come to . . .'

The Patrician stopped and prodded at one of the drawings.

'There's a piece of yellow paper stuck to this one,' he said, suspiciously. He pulled at it. It came away from the drawing with a faint sucking noise, and then stuck to his fingers. On the note, in Leonard's crabby backward script, were the words: 'krow ot smees sihT: omeM'.

'Oh, I'm rather pleased with that,' said Leonard. 'I call it my "Handy-note-scribbling-piece-of-paper-with-glue-that-comes-unstuck-when-you-want".'

The Patrician played with it for a while.

'What's the glue made of?'

'Boiled slugs.'

The Patrician pulled the paper off one hand. It stuck to the other hand.

'Is that what you came to see me about?' said Leonard.

'No. I came to talk to you,' said Lord Vetinari, 'about the gonne.'

'Oh, dear. I'm very sorry.'

'I am afraid it has . . . escaped.'

219

'My goodness. I thought you said you'd done away with it.'

'I gave it to the Assassins to destroy. After all, they pride themselves on the artistic quality of their work. They should be horrified at the idea of *anyone* having that sort of power. But the damn fools did *not* destroy it. They thought they could lock it away. And now they've lost it.'

'They didn't destroy it?'

'Apparently not, the fools.'

'And nor did you. I wonder why?'

'I . . . do you know, I don't know?'

'I should never have made it. It was merely an application of principles. Ballistics, you know. Simple aerodynamics. Chemical power. Some rather good alloying, although I say it myself. And I'm rather proud of the rifling idea. I had to make a quite complicated tool for that, you know. Milk? Sugar?'

'No, thank you.'

'People are searching for it, I trust?'

'The Assassins are. But they won't find it. They don't think the right way.' The Patrician picked up a pile of sketches of the human skeleton. They were extremely good.

'Oh, dear.'

'So I am relying on the Watch.'

'This would be the Captain Vimes you have spoken of.'

Lord Vetinari always enjoyed his occasional conversations with Leonard. The man always referred to the city as if it was another world. 'Yes.'

'I hope you have impressed upon him the importance of the task.'

'In a way. I've absolutely forbidden him to undertake it. Twice.'

Leonard nodded. 'Ah. I . . . think I understand. I hope it works.'

He sighed.

'I suppose I should have dismantled it, but . . . it was so clearly a *made* thing. I had this strange fancy I was merely assembling something that already existed. Sometimes I wonder where I got the whole idea. It seemed . . . I don't know . . . sacrilege, I suppose, to dismantle it. It'd be like dismantling a person. Biscuit?'

'Dismantling a person is sometimes necessary,' said Lord Vetinari.

'This, of course, is a point of view,' said Leonard da Quirm politely.

'You mentioned sacrilege,' said Lord Vetinari. 'Normally that involves gods of some sort, does it not?'

'Did I use the word? I can't imagine there is a god of gonnes.'

'It is quite hard, yes.'

The Patrician shifted uneasily, reached down behind him, and pulled out an object.

'What,' he said, 'is this?'

'Oh, I wondered where that had gone,' said Leonard. 'It's a model of my spinning-up-into-the-air machine.'*

---

*It has probably been gathered that although Leonard da Quirm was absolutely the greatest technological genius of all time, he was a bit of a Detritus when it came to thinking up names.

Lord Vetinari prodded the little rotor.

'Would it work?'

'Oh, yes,' said Leonard. He sighed. 'If you can find one man with the strength of ten men who can turn the handle at about one thousand revolutions a minute.'

The Patrician relaxed, in a way which only then drew gentle attention to the foregoing moment of tension.

'Now there is in this city,' he said, 'a man with a gonne. He has used it successfully once, and almost succeeded a second time. Could anyone have invented the gonne?'

'No,' said Leonard. 'I am a genius.' He said it quite simply. It was a statement of fact.

'Understood. But once a gonne has *been* invented, Leonard, how much of a genius need someone be to make the second one?'

'The rifling technique requires considerable finesse, and the cocking mechanism that slides the bullette assembly is finely balanced, and of course the end of the barrel must be very . . .' Leonard saw the Patrician's expression, and shrugged. 'He must be a clever man,' he said.

'This city is full of clever men,' said the Patrician. 'And dwarfs. Clever men and dwarfs who tinker with things.'

'I am so very sorry.'

'They never *think*.'

'Indeed.'

Lord Vetinari leaned back and stared at the skylight.

'They do things like open the Three Jolly Luck Take-Away Fish Bar on the site of the old temple in Dagon Street on the night of the Winter solstice when it also happens to be a full moon.'

'That's people for you, I'm afraid.'

'I never did find out what happened to Mr Hong.'

'Poor fellow.'

'And then there's the wizards. Tinker, tinker, tinker. Never think twice before grabbing a thread of the fabric of reality and giving it a pull.'

'Shocking.'

'The alchemists? Their idea of civic duty is mixing up things to see what happens.'

'I hear the bangs, even here.'

'And then, of course, along comes someone like you—'

'I really am terribly sorry.'

Lord Vetinari turned the model flying machine over and over in his fingers.

'You dream of flying,' he said.

'Oh, yes. Then men would be truly free. From the air, there are no boundaries. There could be no more war, because the sky is endless. How happy we would be, if we could but fly.'

Vetinari turned the machine over and over in his hands.

'Yes,' he said, 'I daresay we would.'

'I had tried clockwork, you know.'

'I'm sorry? I was thinking about something else.'

'I meant clockwork to power my flying machine. But it won't work.'

'Oh.'

'There's a limit to the power of a spring, no matter how tightly one winds it.'

'Oh, yes. Yes. And you hope that if you wind a spring one way, all its energies will unwind the other way. And sometimes you have to wind the spring as tight as it will go,' said Vetinari, 'and pray it doesn't break.'

His expression changed.

'Oh dear,' he said.

'Pardon?' said Leonard.

'He didn't thump the wall. I may have gone too far.'

Detritus sat and steamed. Now he felt hungry – not for food, but for things to think about. As the temperature sank, the efficiency of his brain increased even more. It needed something to do.

He calculated the number of bricks in the wall, first in twos and then in tens and finally in sixteens. The numbers formed up and marched past his brain in terrified obedience. Division and multiplication were discovered. Algebra was invented and provided an interesting diversion for a minute or two. And then he felt the fog of numbers drift away, and looked up and saw the sparkling, distant mountains of calculus.

Trolls evolved in high, rocky and above all in *cold* places. Their silicon brains were used to operating at low temperatures. But down on the muggy plains the heat build-up slowed them down and made them dull. It wasn't that only stupid trolls came down to the city. Trolls who decided to come down to the city were often quite smart – but they *became* stupid.

Detritus was considered moronic even by city troll standards. But that was simply because his brain was naturally optimized for a temperature seldom reached in Ankh-Morpork even during the coldest winter . . .

Now his brain was nearing its ideal temperature of operation. Unfortunately, this was pretty close to a troll's optimum point of death.

Part of his brain gave some thought to this. There was a high probability of rescue. That meant he'd have to leave. That meant he'd become stupid again, as sure as $10^{-3} (M_e/M_p)\alpha^6 \, \alpha^G - \frac{1}{2}N \approx 10N$.

Better make the most of it, then.

He went back to the world of numbers so complex that they had no meaning, only a transitional point of view. And got on with freezing to death, as well.

Dibbler reached the Butchers' Guild very shortly after Cuddy. The big red doors had been kicked open and a small butcher was sitting just inside them rubbing his nose.

'Which way did he go?'

'Dat way.'

And in the Guild's main hall the master butcher Gerhardt Sock was staggering around in circles. This was because Cuddy's boots were planted on his chest. The dwarf was hanging on to the man's vest like a yachtsman tacking into a gale, and whirling his axe round and round in front of Sock's face.

'You give it to me right now or I'll make you eat your own nose!'

A crowd of apprentice butchers was trying to keep out of the way.

'But—'

'Don't you argue with me! I'm an officer of the Watch, I am!'

'But you—'

'You've got one last chance, mister. Give it to me right now!'

Sock shut his eyes.

'*What is it you want?*'

The crowd waited.

'Ah,' said Cuddy. 'Ahaha. Didn't I say?'

'No!'

'I'm pretty sure I did, you know.'

'You didn't!'

'Oh. Well. It's the key to the pork futures warehouse, if you must know.' Cuddy jumped down.

'Why?'

The axe hovered in front of his nose again.

'I was just asking,' said Sock, in a desperate and distant voice.

'There's a man of the Watch in there freezing to death,' said Cuddy.

There was quite a crowd around them when they finally got the main door open. Lumps of ice clinked on the stones, and there was a rush of supercold air.

Frost covered the floor and the rows of hanging carcasses on their backwards journey through time.

It also covered a Detritus-shaped lump squatting in the middle of the floor.

They carried it out into the sunlight.

'Should his eyes be flashing on and off like that?' said Dibbler.

'Can you hear me?' shouted Cuddy. 'Detritus?'

Detritus blinked. Ice slid off him in the day's heat.

He could feel the cracking up of the marvellous universe of numbers. The rising temperature hit his thoughts like a flamethrower caressing a snowflake.

'Say something!' said Cuddy.

Towers of intellect collapsed as the fire roared through Detritus' brain.

'Hey, look at *this*,' said one of the apprentices. The inner walls of the warehouse were covered with numbers. Equations as complex as a neural network had been scraped in the frost. At some point in the calculation the mathematician had changed from using numbers to using letters, and then letters themselves hadn't been sufficient; brackets like cages enclosed expressions which were to normal mathematics what a city is to a map.

They got simpler as the goal neared – simpler, yet containing in the flowing lines of their simplicity a spartan and wonderful complexity.

Cuddy stared at them. He knew he'd never be able to understand them in a hundred years. The frost crumbled in the warmer air. The equations narrowed as they were carried on down the wall and across the floor to where the troll had been sitting, until they became just a few expressions that appeared to move and sparkle with a life of their own. This was maths without numbers, pure as lightning.

They narrowed to a point, and at the point was just the very simple symbol: '='.

'Equals what?' said Cuddy. 'Equals what?'

The frost collapsed.

Cuddy went outside. Detritus was now sitting in a puddle of water, surrounded by a crowd of human onlookers.

'Can't one of you get him a blanket or something?' he said.

A very fat man said, 'Huh? Who'd use a blanket after it had been on a troll?'

'Hah, yes, good point,' said Cuddy. He glanced at the five holes in Detritus' breastplate. They were at about head height, for a dwarf. 'Could you come over here for a moment, please?'

The man grinned at his friends, and sauntered over.

'I expect you can see the holes in his armour, right?' said Cuddy.

C. M. O. T. Dibbler was a survivor. In the same way that rodents and insects can sense an earthquake ahead of the first tremors, so he could tell if something big was about to go down on the street. Cuddy was being too nice. When a dwarf was nice like that, it meant he was saving up to be nasty later on.

'I'll just, er, go about my business, then,' he said, and backed away.

'I've got nothing against *dwarfs*, mind you,' said the fat man. 'I mean, dwarfs is practically people, in my book. Just shorter humans, almost. But trolls . . . weeeelll . . . they're not the same as us, right?'

''Scuse me, 'scuse me, gangway, gangway,' said Dibbler, achieving with his cart the kind of getaway customarily associated with vehicles that have fluffy dice on the windscreen.

'That's a nice coat you've got there,' said Cuddy. Dibbler's cart went around the corner on one wheel. 'It's a *nice* coat,' said Cuddy. 'You know what you should do with a coat like that?'

The man's forehead wrinkled.

'Take it off right now,' said Cuddy, 'and give it to the troll.'

'Why, you little—'

The man grabbed Cuddy by his shirt and wrenched him upwards.

The dwarf's hand moved very quickly. There was a scrape of metal.

Man and dwarf made an interesting and absolute stationary tableau for a few seconds.

Cuddy had been brought up almost level with the man's face, and watched with interest as the eyes began to water.

'Let me down,' said Cuddy. 'Gently. I make involuntary muscle movements if I'm startled.' The man did so.

'Now take off your coat . . . good . . . just pass it over . . . thank you . . .'

'Your axe . . .' the man murmured.

'Axe? Axe? My axe?' Cuddy looked down. 'Well, well, well. Hardly knew I was holding it there. My axe. Well, there's a thing.'

The man was trying to stand on tiptoe. His eyes were watering.

'The thing about this axe,' said Cuddy, 'the interesting thing, is that it's a throwing axe. I was champion three years running up at Copperhead. I could draw it and split a twig thirty yards away in one second. *Behind* me. *And* I was ill that day. A bilious attack.'

He backed away. The man sank gratefully on to his heels.

Cuddy draped the coat over the troll's shoulders.

'Come on, on your feet,' he said. 'Let's get you home.'

The troll lumbered upright.

'How many fingers am I holding up?' said Cuddy.

Detritus peered.

'Two and one?' he suggested.

'It'll do,' said Cuddy. 'For a start.'

Mr Cheese looked over the bar at Captain Vimes, who hadn't moved for an hour. The Bucket was used to serious drinkers, who drank without pleasure but with a sort of determination never to see sobriety again. But this was something new. This was worrying. He didn't want a death on his hands.

There was no one else in the bar. He hung his apron on a nail and hurried out towards the Watch House, almost colliding with Carrot and Angua in the doorway.

'Oh, I'm glad that's you, Corporal Carrot,' he said. 'You'd better come. It's Captain Vimes.'

'What's happened to him?'

'I don't know. He's drunk an awful lot.'

'I thought he was off the stuff!'

'I think,' said Mr Cheese cautiously, 'that this is not the case any more.'

A scene, somewhere near Quarry Lane:

'Where we going?'

'I'm going to get someone to have a look at you.'

'Not dwarf doctor!'

'There must be someone up here who knows how to slap some quick-drying cement on you, or whatever you do. Should you be oozing like that?'

'Dunno. Never oozed before. Where we?'

'Dunno. Never been down here before.'

The area was on the windward side of the cattle yards and the slaughterhouse district. That meant it was shunned as living space by everyone except trolls, to whom the organic odours were about as relevant and noticeable as the smell of granite would be to humans. The old joke went: the trolls live next to the cattleyard? What about the stench? Oh, the cattle don't mind . . .

Which was daft. Trolls didn't smell, except to other trolls.

There was a slabby look about the buildings here. They had been built for humans but adapted by trolls, which broadly had meant kicking the doorways wider and blocking up the windows. It was still daylight. There weren't any trolls visible.

'Ugh,' said Detritus.

'Come on, big man,' said Cuddy, pushing Detritus along like a tug pushes a tanker.

'Lance-Constable Cuddy?'

'Yes.'

'You a dwarf. This is Quarry Lane. You found here, you in *deep* trouble.'

'We're city guards.'

'Chrysoprase, he not give a coprolith about that stuff.'

Cuddy looked around.

'What do you people use for doctors, anyway?'

A troll face appeared in a doorway. And another. And another.

What Cuddy had thought was a pile of rubble turned out to be a troll.

There were, suddenly, trolls everywhere.

I'm a guard, thought Cuddy. That's what Sergeant Colon said. Stop being a dwarf and start being a Watchman. That's what I am. Not a dwarf. A Watchman. They gave me a badge, shaped like a shield. City Watch, that's me. I carry a badge.

I wish it was a lot bigger.

Vimes was sitting quietly at a table in the corner of The Bucket. There were some pieces of paper and a handful of metal objects in front of him, but he was staring at his fist. It was lying on the table, clenched so tight the knuckles were white.

'Captain Vimes?' said Carrot, waving a hand in front of his eyes. There was no response.

'How much has he had?'

'Two nips of whiskey, that's all.'

'That shouldn't do this to him, even on an empty stomach,' said Carrot.

Angua pointed at the neck of a bottle protruding from Vimes' pocket.

'I don't think he's been drinking on an empty stomach,' she said. 'I think he put some alcohol in it first.'

'Captain Vimes?' said Carrot again.

'What's he holding in his hand?' said Angua.

'I don't know. This is bad, I've never seen him like this before. Come on. You take the stuff. I'll take the captain.'

'He hasn't paid for his drink,' said Mr Cheese.

Angua and Carrot looked at him.

'On the house?' said Mr Cheese.

There was a wall of trolls around Cuddy. It was as good a choice of word as any. Right now their attitude was more of surprise than menace, such as dogs might show if a cat had just sauntered into the kennels. But when they'd finally got used to the idea that he really existed, it was probably only a matter of time before this state of affairs no longer obtained.

Finally, one of them said, 'What dis, then?'

'He a man of the Watch, same as me,' said Detritus.

'Him a dwarf.'

'He a Watchman.'

'Him got bloody cheek, I know that.' A stubby troll finger prodded Cuddy in the back. The trolls crowded in.

'I count to ten,' said Detritus. 'Then any troll not going about that troll's business, he a sorry troll.'

'You Detritus,' said a particularly wide troll.

'Everyone know you stupid troll, you join Watch because stupid troll, you can't count to—'

Wham.

'One,' said Detritus. 'Two . . . Tree. Four-er . . . Five. Six . . .'

The recumbent troll looked up in amazement.

'That Detritus, him *counting*.'

There was a whirring noise and an axe bounced off the wall near Detritus' head.

There were dwarfs coming up the street, with a purposeful and deadly air. The trolls scattered.

Cuddy ran forward.

'What are you lot doing?' he said. 'Are you mad, or something?'

A dwarf pointed a trembling finger at Detritus.

'What's *that*?'

'He's a Watchman.'

'Looks like a troll to me. Get it!'

Cuddy took a step backwards and produced his axe.

'I know you, Strongintthearm,' he said. 'What's this all about?'

'You know, Watch*man*,' said Strongintthearm. 'The Watch say a troll killed Bjorn Hammerhock. They've found the troll!'

'No, that's not—'

There was a sound behind Cuddy. The trolls were back, armed for dwarf. Detritus turned around and waved a finger at them.

'Any troll move,' he said, 'and I start counting.'

'Hammerhock was killed by a man,' said Cuddy. 'Captain Vimes thinks—'

'The Watch have got the troll,' said a dwarf. 'Damn rocks!'

'Gritsuckers!'

'Monoliths!'

'Eaters of rats!'

'Hah, I been a man only hardly any time,' said Detritus, 'and already I fed up with you stupid trolls. What you think humans say, eh? Oh, them ethnic, them don't know how to behave in big city, go around waving clubs at the drop of a thing you wear on head.'

'We're Watchmen,' said Cuddy. 'Our job is to keep the peace.'

'Good,' said Stronginthearm. 'Go and keep it safe somewhere until we need it.'

'This not Koom Valley,' said Detritus.

'That's right!' shouted a dwarf at the back of the crowd. 'This time we can see you!'

Trolls and dwarfs were pouring in at either end of the street.

'What would Corporal Carrot do at a time like this?' whispered Cuddy.

'He say, you bad people, make me angry, you stop toot sweet.'

'And then they'd go away, right?'

'Yeah.'

'What would happen if we tried that?'

'We look in gutter for our heads.'

'I think you're right.'

'You see that alley? It a nice alley. It say, hello. You outnumbered . . . 256+64+8+2+1 to 1. Drop in and see me.'

A club bounced off Detritus' helmet.

'Run!'

The two Watchmen sprinted for the alley. The impromptu armies watched them and then, differences momentarily forgotten, gave chase.

'Where this go?'

'It goes away from the people chasing us!'

'I *like* this alley.'

Behind them the pursuers, suddenly trying to make progress in a gap barely wide enough to accommodate a troll, realized that they were pushing and shoving with their mortal enemies and started to fight one another in the quickest, nastiest and above all *narrowest* battle ever held in the city.

Cuddy waved Detritus to a halt and peered around a corner.

'I think we're safe,' he said. 'All we have to do is get out of the other end of this and get back to the Watch House. OK?'

He turned around, failed to see the troll, took a step forward, and vanished temporarily from the world of men.

'Oh, no,' said Sergeant Colon. 'He promised he wasn't going to touch it any more! Look, he's had a whole bottle!'

'What is it? Bearhugger's?' said Nobby.

'Shouldn't think so, he's still breathing. Come on, help me up with him.'

The Night Watch clustered around. Carrot had deposited Captain Vimes on a chair in the middle of the Watch House floor.

Angua picked out the bottle and looked at the label.

'C. M. O. T. Dibbler's Genuine Authentic Soggy Mountain Dew,' she read. 'He's going to die! It says, "One hundred and fifty per cent proof"!'

'Nah, that's just old Dibbler's advertising,' said Nobby. 'It ain't got no *proof*. Just circumstantial evidence.'

'Why hasn't he got his sword?' said Angua.

Vimes opened his eyes. The first thing he saw was the concerned face of Nobby.

'Aargh!' he said. 'Swor'? Gi' it 'way! Hooray!'

'What?' said Colon.

'No mo' Watsh! All go' . . .'

'I think he's a bit drunk,' said Carrot.

'Drun'? 'm not drun'! You wouldn'dare call m' drun' if I was sober!'

'Get him some coffee,' said Angua.

'I reckon he's beyond *our* coffee,' said Colon. 'Nobby, nip along to Fat Sally's in Squeezebelly Alley and get a jug of their special Klatchian stuff. Not a metal jug, mind.'

Vimes blinked as they manhandled him into a chair.

'All go 'way,' he said. 'Bang! Bang!'

'Lady Sybil's going to be really mad,' said Nobby. 'You know he promised to leave it alone.'

'Captain Vimes?' said Carrot.

'Mm?'

'How many fingers am I holding up?'

'Mm?'

'How many hands, then?'

'Fo'?'

'Blimey, I haven't seen him like this for years,' said Colon. 'Here, let me try something. *Want another drink, captain*?'

'He certainly doesn't need a—'

'Shut up, I know what I'm doing. Another drink, Captain Vimes?'

'Mm?'

'I've never known him not be able to give a loud clear "yes!",' said Colon, standing back. 'I think we'd better get him up to his room.'

'I'll take him, poor chap,' said Carrot. He lifted Vimes easily, and slung him over his shoulder.

'I hate to see him like this,' said Angua, following him into the hallway and up the stairs.

'He only drinks when he gets depressed,' said Carrot.

'Why does he get depressed?'

'Sometimes it's because he hasn't had a drink.'

The house in Pseudopolis Yard had originally been a Ramkin family residence. Now the first floor was occupied by the guards on an ad hoc basis. Carrot had a room. Nobby had rooms consecutively, four so far, moving out when the floor became hard to find. And Vimes had a room.

More or less. It was hard to tell. Even a prisoner in a cell manages to stamp his personality on it some-where, but Angua had never seen such an unlived-in room.

'This is where he lives?' said Angua. 'Good grief.'

'What did you expect?'

'I don't know. Anything. Something. Not *nothing*.'

There was a joyless iron bedstead. The springs and mattress had sagged so that they formed a sort of mould, forcing anyone who got into it to instantly fold into a sleeping position. There was a wash-stand, under a broken mirror. On the stand was a razor, carefully aligned towards the Hub because Vimes shared the folk belief that this kept it sharp. There was a brown wooden chair with the cane seat broken. And a small chest at the foot of the bed.

And that was all.

'I mean, at least a rug,' said Angua. 'A picture on the wall. Something.'

Carrot deposited Vimes on the bed, where he flowed unconsciously into the shape.

'Haven't you got something in your room?' Angua asked.

'Yes. I've got a cutaway diagram of No.5 shaft at home. It's very interesting strata. I helped cut it. And some books and things. Captain Vimes isn't really an indoors kind of person.'

'But there's not even a candle!'

'He finds his way to bed by memory, he says.'

'Or an ornament or *anything*.'

'There's a sheet of cardboard under the bed,' Carrot volunteered. 'I remember I was with him in Filigree Street when he found it. He said "There's a month's soles in this, if I'm any judge". He was very pleased about that.'

'He can't even afford boots?'

'I don't think so. I know Lady Sybil offered to buy him all the new boots he wanted, and he got a bit offended about that. He seems to try to make them last.'

'But you can buy boots, and you get less than him. *And* you send money home. He must drink it all, the idiot.'

'Don't think so. I didn't think he'd touched the stuff for months. Lady Sybil got him on to cigars.'

Vimes snored loudly.

'How can you admire a man like this?' said Angua.

'He's a very fine man.'

Angua raised the lid of the wooden chest with her foot.

'Hey, I don't think you should do that—' said Carrot wretchedly.

'I'm just looking,' said Angua. 'No law against that.'

'In fact, under the Privacy Act of 1467, it *is* an—'

'There's only old boots and stuff. And some paper.' She reached down and picked up a crudely made book. It was merely a wad of irregular shaped bits of paper sandwiched together between card covers.

'That belongs to Captain—'

She opened the book and read a few lines. Her mouth dropped open.

'Will you look at this? No wonder he never has any money!'

'What d'you mean?'

'He spends it on women! You wouldn't think it, would you? Look at this entry. Four in one week!'

Carrot looked over her shoulder. On the bed, Vimes snorted.

There, on the page, in Vimes' curly handwriting, were the words:

Mrs Gaſkin, Mincing St: $5
Mrs Scurrick, Treacle St: $4
Mrs Maroon, Wixon's Alley: $4
Annabel Curry, Lobſneaks: $2

'Annabel Curry couldn't have been much good, for only two dollars,' said Angua.

She was aware of a sudden drop in temperature.

'I shouldn't think so,' said Carrot, slowly. 'She's only nine years old.'

One of his hands gripped her wrist tightly and the other prised the book out of her fingers.

'Hey, let *go*!'

'Sergeant!' shouted Carrot, over his shoulder, 'can you come up here a moment?'

Angua tried to pull away. Carrot's arm was as immovable as an iron bar.

There was the creak of Colon's foot on the stair, and the door swung open.

He was holding a very small cup in a pair of tongs.

'Nobby got the coff—' he began, and stopped.

'Sergeant,' said Carrot, staring into Angua's face, 'Lance-Constable Angua wants to know about Mrs Gaskin.'

'Old Leggy Gaskin's widow? She lives in Mincing Street.'

'And Mrs Scurrick?'

'In Treacle Street? Takes in laundry now.' Sergeant Colon looked from one to the other, trying to get a handle on the situation.

'Mrs Maroon?'

'That's Sergeant Maroon's widow, she sells coal in—'

'How about Annabel Curry?'

'She still goes to the Spiteful Sisters of Seven-Handed Sek Charity School, doesn't she?' Colon smiled nervously at Angua, still not sure of what was happening. 'She's the daughter of Corporal Curry, but of course he was before your time—'

Angua looked up at Carrot's face. His expression was unreadable.

'They're the widows of coppers?' she said.

He nodded. 'And one orphan.'

'It's a tough old life,' said Colon. 'No pensions for widows, see.'

He looked from one to the other.

'Is there something wrong?' he said.

Carrot relaxed his grip, turned, slipped the book into the box, and shut the lid.

'No,' he said.

'Look, I'm sorr—' Angua began. Carrot ignored her and nodded at the sergeant.

'Give him the coffee.'

'But . . . fourteen dollars . . . that's nearly half his pay!'

Carrot picked up Vimes' limp arm and tried to prise his fist open, but even though Vimes was out cold the fingers were locked.

'I mean, half his *pay*!'

'I don't know what he's holding in here,' said Carrot, ignoring her. 'Maybe it's a clue.'

He took the coffee and hauled up Vimes by his collar.

'You just drink this, captain,' he said, 'and everything will look a lot . . . clearer . . .'

Klatchian coffee has an even bigger sobering effect than an unexpected brown envelope from the tax man. In fact, coffee enthusiasts take the precaution of getting thoroughly drunk before touching the stuff, because Klatchian coffee takes you back through sobriety and, if you're not careful, *out the other side*, where the mind of man should not go. The Watch was generally of the opinion that Samuel Vimes was at least two drinks under par, and needed a stiff double even to be sober.

'Careful . . . careful . . .' Carrot let a few drops dribble between Vimes' lips.

'Look, when I said—' Angua began.

'Forget it.' Carrot didn't even look round.

'I was only—'

'I said forget it.'

Vimes opened his eyes, took a look at the world, and screamed.

'Nobby!'

'Yes, sarge?'

'Did you buy the Red Desert Special or the Curly Mountain Straight?'

'Red Desert, sarge, because—'

'You could have said. Better get me—' He glanced at Vimes' grimace of horror '—half a glass of Bearhugger's. We've sent him too far the other way.'

The glass was fetched and administered. Vimes unstiffened as it took effect.

His palm uncurled.

'Oh, my gods,' said Angua. 'Have we got any bandages?'

The sky was a little white circle, high above.

'Where the hell are we, partner?' said Cuddy.

'Cave.'

'No caves under Ankh-Morpork. It's on loam.'

Cuddy had fallen about thirty feet but had cushioned the fall because he landed on Detritus' head. The troll had been sitting, surrounded by rotting woodwork, in . . . well . . . a cave. Or, Cuddy thought, as his eyes grew accustomed to the gloom, a stone-lined tunnel.

'I didn't do nothing,' said Detritus, 'I just stood there, next minute, everything going past upwards.'

Cuddy reached down into the mud underfoot and brought up a piece of wood. It was very thick. It was also very rotten.

'We fell through something into something,' he said. He ran his hand over the curved tunnel wall. 'And this is *good* masonry. *Very* good.'

'How we get out?'

There was no way to climb back. The tunnel roof was much higher than Detritus.

'We walk out, I think,' said Cuddy.

He sniffed the air, which was dank. Dwarfs have a very good sense of direction underground.

'This way,' he added, setting off.

'Cuddy?'

'Yes?'

'No one ever say there tunnels under the city. No one know about them.'

'So . . . ?'

'So there no way out. Because way out is way in, too, and if no one know about tunnels, then it 'cos no way in.'

'But they've got to lead somewhere.'

'Okay.'

Black mud, more or less dry, made a path at the bottom of the tunnel. There was slime on the walls, too, indicating that at some point in the recent past the tunnel had been full of water. Here and there huge patches of fungi, luminous with decay, cast a faint glow over the ancient stone-work.*

Cuddy felt his spirits lift as he plodded through the darkness. Dwarfs always felt happier underground.

'Bound to find a way out,' he said.

'Right.'

'So . . . how come you joined the Watch, then?'

'Hah! My girl Ruby she say, you want get married, you get proper job, I not marry a troll what people say, him no good troll, him thick as a

---

*It didn't need to. Cuddy, belonging to a race that worked underground for preference, and Detritus, a member of a race notoriously nocturnal, had excellent vision in the dark. But mysterious caves and tunnels always have luminous fungi, strangely bright crystals or at a pinch merely an eldritch glow in the air, just in case a human hero comes in and needs to see in the dark. Strange but true.

short plank of wood.' Detritus' voice echoed in the darkness. 'How about you?'

'I got bored. I worked for my brother-in-law, Durance. He's got a good business making fortune rats for dwarf restaurants. But I thought, this isn't a proper job for a dwarf.'

'Sound like easy job to me.'

'I had the devil of a time getting them to swallow the fortunes.'

Cuddy stopped. A change in the air suggested a vaster tunnel up ahead.

And, indeed, the tunnel opened into the side of a much larger one. There was deep mud on the floor, in the middle of which ran a trickle of water. Cuddy fancied he heard rats, or what he hoped were rats, scuttle away into the dark emptiness. He even thought he could hear the sounds of the city – indistinct, intermingled – filtering through the earth.

'It's like a temple,' he said, and his voice boomed away into the distance.

'Writing here on wall,' said Detritus.

Cuddy peered at the letters hacked deeply into the stone.

'"VIA CLOACA",' he said. 'Hmm. Well, now . . . via is an old word for street or way. Cloaca means . . .'

He peered into the gloom.

'This is a sewer,' he said.

'What that?'

'It's like . . . well, where do trolls dump their . . . rubbish?' said Cuddy.

'In street,' said Detritus. 'Hygienic.'

'This is . . . an underground street just for . . . well, for crap,' said Cuddy. 'I never knew Ankh-Morpork had them.'

'Maybe Ankh-Morpork didn't know Ankh-Morpork had them,' said Detritus.

'Right. You're right. This place is *old*. We're in the bowels of the earth.'

'In Ankh-Morpork even the shit have a street to itself,' said Detritus, awe and wonder in his voice. 'Truly, this a land of opportunity.'

'Here's some more writing,' said Cuddy. He scraped away some slime.

'"*Cirone IV me fabricat*",' he read aloud. 'He was one of the early kings, wasn't he? Hey . . . do you know what that means?'

'No one's been down here since yesterday,' said Detritus.

'No! This place . . . this place is more than two thousand years old. We're quite probably the first people to come down here since—'

'Yesterday,' said the troll.

'Yesterday? Yesterday? What's yesterday got to do with it?'

'Footprints still fresh,' said Detritus.

He pointed.

There were footprints in the mud.

'How long have you lived here?' said Cuddy, suddenly feeling very conspicuous in the middle of the tunnel.

'Nine-er years. That is the number of years I have lived here. Nine-er,' said Detritus, proudly. 'It only one of a large . . . number of numbers I can count to.'

'Have you *ever* heard of tunnels under the city?'

'No.'

'Someone knows about them, though.'

'Yes.'

'What shall we do?'

The answer was inevitable. They'd chased a man into the pork futures warehouse, and nearly died. Then they'd ended up in the middle of a small war, and nearly died. Now they were in a mysterious tunnel where there were fresh footprints. If Corporal Carrot or Sergeant Colon said, 'And what did you do then?', neither of them could face up to the thought of saying 'We came back.'

'The footprints go *this* way,' said Cuddy, 'and then they return. But the ones coming back aren't so deep as the ones going. You can see they're later ones because they're over the top of the other ones. So he was heavier *going* than he was coming back, yes?'

'Right,' said Detritus.

'So that means . . . ?'

'He lose weight?'

'He was carrying something, and he left it . . . up ahead somewhere.'

They stared at the darkness.

'So we go and find what it was?' said Detritus.

'I think so. How do you feel?'

'Feel okay.'

Different species though they were, their minds had focused on a single image, involving a muzzle flash and a lead slug singing through the subterranean night.

'He came back,' said Cuddy.

'Yes,' said Detritus.

They looked at the darkness again.

'It has not been a nice day,' said Cuddy.

'That the truth.'

'I'd just like to know something, in case . . . I mean . . . look, what happened in the pork store? You did all that maths! All that counting!'

'I . . . dunno. I saw it all.'

'All what?'

'Just all of it. Everything. All the numbers in the world. I could count them all.'

'What did they equal?'

'Dunno. What does equal mean?'

They trudged on, to see what the future held.

The trail led eventually into a narrower tunnel, barely wide enough for the troll to stand upright. Finally they could go no further. A stone had dropped out of the roof and rubble and mud had percolated through, blocking the tunnel. But that didn't matter because they'd found what they were looking for, even though they hadn't been looking for it.

'Oh dear,' said Detritus.

'Very definitely,' said Cuddy. He looked around vaguely.

'You know,' he said, 'I reckon these tunnels are usually full of water. They're well below the normal river level.'

He looked back to the pathetic discovery.

'There's going to be a lot of trouble about this,' he said.

*　　*　　*

'It's his badge,' said Carrot. 'Good grief. He's holding it so tight it's cut right into his *hand.*'

Technically Ankh-Morpork is built on loam, but what it is mainly built on is Ankh-Morpork; it has been constructed, burned down, silted up, and rebuilt so many times that its foundations are old cellars, buried roads and the fossil bones and middens of earlier cities.

Below these, in the darkness, sat the troll and the dwarf.

'What we doing now?'

'We ought to leave it here and fetch Corporal Carrot. He'll know what to do.'

Detritus looked over his shoulder at the thing behind them.

'I don't like that,' he said. 'It not right to leave it here.'

'Right. Yes, you're right. But you're a troll and I'm a dwarf. What do you think would happen if people saw us carrying that along the streets?'

'*Big* trouble.'

'Correct. Come on. Let's follow the footprints back out.'

'Supposing it gone when we come back?' said Detritus, lumbering to his feet.

'How? And we're following the tracks out, so if whoever it was who put it there comes back, we'll run straight into them.'

'Oh, good. I glad you said that.'

*   *   *

Vimes sat on the edge of his bed while Angua bandaged his hand.

'Captain *Quirke*?' said Carrot. 'But he's . . . not a good choice.'

'Mayonnaise Quirke, we used to call him,' said Colon. 'He's a pillock.'

'Don't tell me,' said Angua. 'He's rich, thick and oily, yes?'

'And smells faintly of eggs,' said Carrot.

'Plumes in his helmet,' said Colon, 'and a breast-plate you can see your face in.'

'Well, Carrot's got one of those too,' said Nobby.

'Yes, but the difference is, Carrot keeps his armour polished because he . . . likes nice clean armour,' said Colon loyally. 'While Quirke keeps his shiny because he's a pillock.'

'But he's wrapped up the case,' said Nobby. 'I heard about it when I went out for the coffee. He's arrested Coalface the troll. You know, captain? The privy cleaner. Someone saw him near Rime Street just before the dwarf got killed.'

'But he's *massive*,' said Carrot. 'He couldn't have got through the door.'

'He's got a motive,' said Nobby.

'Yes?'

'Yes. Hammerhock was a dwarf.'

'That's not a motive.'

'It is for a troll. Anyway, if he didn't do that, he probably did *something*. There's plenty of evidence against him.'

'Like what?' said Angua.

'He's a troll.'

'That's not evidence.'

'It is to Captain Quirke,' said the sergeant.

'He's bound to have done *something*,' Nobby repeated.

In this he was echoing the Patrician's view of crime and punishment. If there was crime, there should be punishment. If the specific criminal should be involved in the punishment process then this was a happy accident, but if not then any criminal would do, and since everyone was undoubtedly guilty of something, the net result was that, *in general terms,* justice was done.

'He's a nasty piece of work, that Coalface,' said Colon. 'A righthand troll for Chrysoprase.'

'Yes, but he couldn't have killed Bjorn,' said Carrot. 'And what about the beggar girl?'

Vimes sat looking at the floor.

'What do *you* think, captain?' said Carrot.

Vimes shrugged.

'Who cares?' he said.

'Well, *you* care,' said Carrot. 'You always care. We can't let even someone like—'

'Listen to me,' said Vimes, in a small voice. 'Supposing we'd found who killed the dwarf and the clown? Or the girl. It wouldn't make any difference. It's all rotten anyway.'

'What is, captain?' said Colon.

'All of it. You might as well try and empty a well with a sieve. Let the Assassins try to sort it out. Or the thieves. He can try the rats next. Why not? We're not the people for this. We ought to have just stayed with ringing our bells and shouting "All's well!"'

'But all isn't well, captain,' said Carrot.

'So what? When has that ever mattered?'

'Oh, dear,' said Angua, under her breath. 'I think perhaps you gave him too much of that coffee . . .'

Vimes said, 'I'm retiring from the Watch tomorrow. Twenty-five years on the streets—'

Nobby started to grin nervously and stopped as the sergeant, without apparently shifting position, grabbed one of his arms and twisted it gently but meaningfully up his back.

'—and what good's it all been? What *good* have I done? I've just worn out a lot of boots. There's no place in Ankh-Morpork for policemen! Who cares what's right or wrong? Assassins and thieves and trolls and dwarfs! Might as well have a bloody king and have done with it!'

The rest of the Night Watch stood looking at their feet in mute embarrassment. Then Carrot said, 'It's better to light a candle than curse the darkness, captain. That's what they say.'

'*What?*' Vimes' sudden rage was like a thunderclap. 'Who says that? When has that ever been true? It's never been true! It's the kind of thing people without power say to make it all seem less bloody awful, but it's just *words,* it never makes any *difference*—'

Someone hammered at the door.

'That'll be Quirke,' said Vimes. 'You're to hand over your weapons. The Night Watch is being stood down for a day. Can't have coppers running around upsetting things, can we? Open the door, Carrot.'

'But—' Carrot began.

'That was an order. I might not be any good for anything else, but I can bloody well order you to open the door, so open the door!'

Quirke was accompanied by half a dozen members of the Day Watch. They had crossbows. In deference to the fact that they were doing a mildly unpleasant job involving fellow officers, they had them pointing slightly downwards. In deference to the fact that they weren't damn fools, they had the safety catches off.

Quirke wasn't actually a *bad* man. He didn't have the imagination. He dealt more in that sort of generalized low-grade unpleasantness which slightly tarnishes the soul of all who come into contact with it.* Many people are in jobs that are a little beyond them, but there are ways of reacting to the situation. Sometimes they're flustered and nice, sometimes they're Quirke. Quirke handled them with the maxim: it doesn't matter if you're right or wrong, so long as you're definite. There was, on the whole, no real *racial* prejudice in Ankh-Morpork; when you've got dwarfs and trolls, the mere colour of other humans is not a major item. But Quirke was the kind of man to whom it comes naturally to pronounce the word negro with two gs.

He had a hat with plumes in it.

'Come in, come in,' said Vimes. 'It wasn't as if we were doing anything.'

'Captain Vimes—'

'It's all right. We know. Give him your weapons,

*Rather like British Rail.

people. That's an order, Carrot. One official issue sword, one pike or halberd, one night stick or truncheon, one crossbow. That's right, isn't it, Sergeant Colon?'

'Yessir.'

Carrot hesitated only a moment.

'Oh, well,' he said. 'My *official* sword is in the rack.'

'What's that one in your belt?'

Carrot said nothing. However, he shifted position slightly. His biceps strained against the leather of his jerkin.

'Official sword. Right,' said Quirke. He turned. He was one of those people who would recoil from an assault on strength, but attack weakness without mercy. 'Where's the gritsucker?' he said. 'And the rock?'

'Ah,' said Vimes, 'you are referring to those representative members of our fellow sapient races who have chosen to throw in their lots with the people of this city?'

'I mean the dwarf and the troll,' said Quirke.

'Haven't the faintest idea,' said Vimes cheerfully. It seemed to Angua that he was drunk again, if people could get drunk on despair.

'We dunno, sir,' said Colon. 'Haven't seen 'em all day.'

'Probably fighting up in Quarry Lane with the rest of them,' said Quirke. 'You can't trust people of their type. You ought to know that.'

And it also seemed to Angua that although words like halfpint and gritsucker were offensive, they were as terms of universal brotherhood compared to words like 'people of their type' in the mouth of men like Quirke. Much to her shock, she found her gaze concentrating on the man's jugular vein.

'Fighting?' said Carrot. 'Why?'

Quirke shrugged.

'Who knows?'

'Let me think now,' said Vimes. 'It could be something to do with a wrongful arrest. It could be something to do with some of the more restless dwarfs just needing any excuse to have a go at the trolls. What do *you* think, Quirke?'

'I don't think, Vimes.'

'Good man. You're just the type the city needs.'

Vimes stood up.

'I'll be going, then,' he said. 'I'll see you all tomorrow. If there is one.'

The door slammed behind him.

This hall was *huge*. It was the size of a city square, with pillars every few yards to support the roof. Tunnels radiated off it in every direction, and at various heights in the walls. Water trickled out of many of them, from small springs and underground streams.

That was the problem. The film of running water over the stone floor of the hall had wiped away traces of the footprints.

A very large tunnel, almost blocked with debris and silt, led off in what Cuddy was pretty sure was the direction of the estuary.

It was almost pleasant. There was no smell, other than a damp, under-a-stone mustiness. And it was cool.

'I've seen big dwarf halls in the mountains,' said Cuddy, 'but I've got to admit this is something else.' His voice echoed back and forth in the chamber.

'Oh, yes,' said Detritus, 'it's got to be something else, because it's not a dwarf hall in the mountains.'

'Can you see any way up?'

'No.'

'We could have passed a dozen ways to the surface and not known it.'

'Yes,' said the troll. 'It's a knotty problem.'

'Detritus?'

'Yes?'

'Did you know you're getting smarter again, down here in the cool?'

'Really?'

'Can you use it to think of a way out?'

'Digging?' the troll suggested.

There were fallen blocks here and there in the tunnels. Not many; the place had been well built . . .

'Nah. Haven't got a shovel,' said Cuddy.

Detritus nodded.

'Give me your breastplate,' he said.

He leaned it up against the wall. His fist pounded into it a few times. He handed it back. It was, more or less, shovel shaped.

'It's a long way up,' Cuddy said doubtfully.

'But we know the way,' said Detritus. 'It's either that, or stay down here eating rat for rest of your life.'

Cuddy hesitated. The idea had a certain appeal . . .

'Without ketchup,' Detritus added.

'I think I saw a fallen stone just a way back there,' said the dwarf.

Captain Quirke looked around the Watch room with the air of one who was doing the scenery a favour by glancing at it.

'Nice place, this,' he said. 'I think we'll move in here. Better than the quarters near the Palace.'

'But *we're* here,' said Sergeant Colon.

'You'll just have to squash up,' said Captain Quirke.

He glanced at Angua. Her stare was getting on his nerves.

'There'll be a few changes, too,' he said. Behind him, the door creaked open. A small, smelly dog limped in.

'But Lord Vetinari hasn't said who's commanding Night Watch,' said Carrot.

'Ho, yes? Seems to me, seems to *me*,' said Quirke, 'that it's not likely to be one of *you* lot, eh? Seems to me it's likely the Watches'll be combined. Seems to me there's too much sloppiness around the place. Seems to me there's a bit too much of a rag-tag.'

He glanced at Angua again. The way she was looking at him was putting him off.

'Seems to me—' Quirke began again, and then noticed the dog. 'Look at this!' he said. 'Dogs in the Watch House!' He kicked Gaspode hard, and grinned as the dog ran yelping under the table.

'What about Lettice Knibbs, the beggar girl?' said Angua. 'No troll killed her. Or the clown.'

'You got to see the big picture,' said Quirke.

'Mister Captain,' said a low voice from under the table, audible at a conscious level only to Angua, 'you got an itchy bottom.'

'What big picture's this, then?' said Sergeant Colon.

'Got to think in terms of the whole city,' said Quirke. He shifted uneasily.

'*Really* itchy,' said the sub-table voice.

'You feeling all right, Captain Quirke?' said Angua.

The captain squirmed.

'Prickle, prickle, prickle,' said the voice.

'I mean, some things are important, some ain't,' said Quirke. 'Aargh!'

'Sorry?'

'Prickle.'

'Can't hang around here talking to you all day,' said Quirke. 'You. Report to me. Tomorrow afternoon—'

'Prickle, prickle, prickle—'

'Abouuut face!'

The Day Watch scurried out, with Quirke hopping and squirming in, as it were, the rear.

'My word, he seemed anxious to get away,' said Carrot.

'Yes,' said Angua. 'Can't think why.'

They looked at one another.

'Is that it?' said Carrot. 'No more Night Watch?'

*   *   *

It's generally very quiet in the Unseen University library. There's perhaps the shuffling of feet as wizards wander between the shelves, the occasional hacking cough to disturb the academic silence, and every once in a while a dying scream as an unwary student fails to treat an old magical book with the caution it deserves.

Consider orang-utans.

In all the worlds graced by their presence, it is suspected that they can talk but choose not to do so in case humans put them to work, possibly in the television industry. In fact they *can* talk. It's just that they talk in Orang-utan. Humans are only capable of listening in Bewilderment.

The Librarian of Unseen University had uni-laterally decided to aid comprehension by producing an Orang-utan/Human Dictionary. He'd been working on it for three months.

It wasn't easy. He'd got as far as 'Oook.'*

He was down in the Stacks, where it was cool.

And suddenly someone was singing.

He took the pen out of his foot and listened.

A human would have decided they couldn't believe their ears. Orangs are more sensible. If you won't believe your own ears, whose ears will you believe?

Someone was singing, underground. Or trying to sing.

---

*Which can mean . . . well . . . meanings include: 'Pardon me, you're hanging from *my* rubber ring, thank you so very much', 'It may be just vital biomass oxygenating the planet to *you,* but it's home to me' and 'I'm sure there was a rain forest around here a moment ago'.

The chthonic voices went something like this:

'Dlog, glod, Dlog, glod—'

'Listen, you . . . troll! It's the simplest song there is. Look, like this "Gold, Gold, Gold, Gold"?'

'Gold, Gold, Gold, Gold—'

'No! That's the *second* verse!'

There was also the rhythmical sound of dirt being shovelled and rubble being moved.

The Librarian considered matters for a while. So . . . a dwarf and a troll. He preferred both species to humans. For one thing, neither of them were great readers. The Librarian was, of course, very much in favour of reading in general, but readers in particular got on his nerves. There was something, well, *sacrilegious* about the way they kept taking books off the shelves and wearing out the words by reading them. He liked people who loved and respected books, and the best way to do that, in the Librarian's opinion, was to leave them on the shelves where Nature intended them to be.

The muffled voices seemed to be getting closer.

'Gold, gold, gold—'

'Now you're singing the chorus!'

On the other hand, there were proper ways of entering a library.

He waddled over to the shelves and selected Humptulip's seminal work *How to Kille Insects*. All 2,000 pages of it.

Vimes felt quite light-hearted as he walked up Scoone Avenue. He was aware that there was an inner Vimes screaming his head off. He ignored him.

You couldn't be a real copper in Ankh-Morpork and stay sane. You had to *care*. And caring in Ankh-Morpork was like opening a tin of meat in the middle of a piranha school.

Everyone dealt with it in their own way. Colon never thought about it, and Nobby didn't worry about it, and the new ones hadn't been in long enough to be worn down by it, and Carrot . . . was just himself.

Hundreds of people died in the city every day, often of suicide. So what did a few more matter?

The Vimes inside hammered on the walls.

There were quite a few coaches outside the Ramkin mansion, and the place seemed to be infested with assorted female relatives and Interchangeable Emmas. They were baking things and polishing things. Vimes strolled through, more or less unregarded.

He found Sybil out in the dragon house, in her rubber boots and protective dragon armour. She was mucking out, apparently blissfully unaware of the controlled uproar in the mansion.

She looked up as the door shut behind Vimes.

'Oh, there you are. You're home early,' she said. 'I couldn't stand the fuss, so I came out here. But I'll have to go and change soon—'

She stopped when she saw his expression. 'There's something wrong, isn't there?'

'I'm not going back,' said Vimes.

'Really? Last week you said you'd do a full watch. You said you were looking forward to it.'

Not much gets past old Sybil, Vimes thought.

She patted his hand.

'I'm glad you're out of it,' she said.

Corporal Nobbs darted into the Watch House and slammed the door behind him.

'Well?' said Carrot.

'It's not good,' said Nobby. 'They say the trolls are planning to march to the Palace to get Coalface out. There's gangs of dwarfs and trolls wandering around looking for trouble. *And* beggars. Lettice was very popular. And there's a lot of Guild people out there, too. The city,' he said, importantly, 'is def'nitely a keg of No.1 Powder.'

'How do you like the idea of camping out on the open plain?' said Colon.

'What's that got to do with it?'

'If anyone puts a match to anything tonight, it's goodbye Ankh,' said the sergeant morosely. 'Usually we can shut the city gates, right? But there's hardly more'n a few feet of water in the river.'

'You flood the city just to put out fires?' said Angua.

'Yep.'

'Another thing,' said Nobby. 'People threw stuff at me!'

Carrot had been staring at the wall. Now he produced a small, battered black book from his pocket, and started to thumb through the pages.

'Tell me,' he said, in a slightly distant voice, 'has there been an irretrievable breakdown of law and order?'

'Yeah. For about five hundred years,' said Colon.

'Irretrievable breakdown of law'n'order is what Ankh-Morpork is all about.'

'No, I mean more than usual. It's important.' Carrot turned a page. His lips moved silently as he read.

'Throwing stuff at me sounds like a breakdown in law and order,' said Nobby.

He was aware of their expressions.

'I don't think we could make that stick,' said Colon.

'It stuck all right,' said Nobby, '*and* some of it went down my shirt.'

'Why throw things at you?' said Angua.

'It's 'cos I was a Watchman,' said Nobby. 'The dwarfs don't like the Watch 'cos of Mr Hammerhock, and the trolls don't like the Watch 'cos of Coalface being arrested, and people don't like the Watch 'cos of all these angry dwarfs and trolls around.'

Someone thumped at the door.

'That's probably an angry mob right now,' said Nobby.

Carrot opened the door.

'It's not an angry mob,' he announced.

'Ook.'

'It's an orang-utan carrying a stunned dwarf followed by a troll. But he is quite angry, if that's any help.'

Lady Ramkin's butler, Willikins, had filled him a big bath. Hah! Tomorrow it'd be his butler, and his bath. And this wasn't one of the old hip bath, drag-it-in-front-of-the-fire jobs, no. The Ramkin mansion collected water off the roof into a big cistern, after straining out the pigeons, and then it was heated by an ancient geyser* and flowed along drumming, groaning lead pipes to a pair of mighty brass taps and then into an enamelled tub. There were things laid out on a fluffy towel beside it – huge scrubbing brushes, three kinds of soap, a loofah.

Willikins was standing patiently beside the bath, like a barely heated towel rail.

'Yes?' said Vimes.

'His lordship . . . that is, her ladyship's father . . . he required to have his back scrubbed,' said Willikins.

'You go and help the old geyser stoke the furnace,' said Vimes firmly.

Left alone, he struggled out of his breastplate and threw it in the corner. The chainmail shirt followed it, and the helmet, and the money pouch, and various leather and cotton oddments that came between a Watchman and the world.

And then he sank, gingerly at first, into the suds.

'Try soap. Soap'll work,' said Detritus.

'Hold still, will you?' said Carrot.

'You're twisting my head off!'

'Go on, soap him head.'

'Soap your own head!'

There was a *thung* noise and Cuddy's helmet came free.

---

*Who stoked the boiler.

Cuddy emerged, blinking, into the light. He focused on the Librarian, and growled.

'He hit me on the *head*!'

'Oook.'

'He says you came up through the floor,' said Carrot.

'That's no reason to hit me on the *head*.'

'Some of the things that come up through the floor at Unseen University don't even have a head,' said Carrot.

'Oook!'

'Or they have hundreds. Why were you digging down there?'

'We weren't digging down. We were digging up . . .'

Carrot sat and listened. He interrupted only twice.

'*Shot* at you?'

'Five time,' said Detritus, happily. 'Have to report damage to breastplate but not to backplate on account of fortunately my body got in way, saving valuable city property worth three dollars.'

Carrot listened some more.

'Sewers?' he said, eventually.

'It's like the whole city, underground. We saw crowns and stuff carved on the walls.'

Carrot's eyes sparkled. 'That means they must date right back to the days when we had kings! And then when we kept on rebuilding the city we forgot they were down there . . .'

'Um. That's not all that's down there,' said Cuddy. 'We . . . found something.'

'Oh?'

'Something bad.'

'You won't like it at all,' said Detritus. 'Bad, bad, bad. Even worse.'

'We thought it would be best to leave it there,' said Cuddy, 'on account of it being Evidence. But you ought to see it.'

'It's going to upset everything,' said the troll, warming to the part.

'What was it?'

'If we tell you, you say, stupid ethnic people, you pulling my leg off,' said Detritus.

'So you'd better come and see,' said Cuddy.

Sergeant Colon looked at the rest of the Watch.

'All of us?' he said, nervously. 'Er. Shouldn't a couple of senior officers stay up here? In case anything happens?'

'Do you mean in case anything happens up here?' said Angua, tartly. 'Or in case anything happens down there?'

'I'll go with Lance-Constable Cuddy and Lance-Constable Detritus,' said Carrot. 'I don't think anyone else ought to come.'

'But it could be dangerous!' said Angua.

'If I find who's been shooting at Watchmen,' said Carrot, 'it will be.'

Samuel Vimes reached up with a big toe and turned on the hot tap.

There was a respectful knock at the door, and Willikins old-retainer'd in.

'Would sir be wanting anything?'

Vimes thought about it.

'Lady Ramkin said you wouldn't be wanting any alcohol,' said Willikins, as if reading his thoughts.

'Did she?'

'Emphatically, sir. But I have here a very fine cigar.'

He winced as Vimes bit the end off and spat it over the side of the bath, but produced some matches and lit it for him.

'Thank you, Willikins. What's your first name?'

'First name, sir?'

'I mean, what do people call you when they've got to know you better?'

'Willikins, sir.'

'Oh. Right, then. Well. You may go, Willikins.'

'Yes, sir.'

Vimes lay back in the warm water. The inner voice was still in there somewhere, but he tried not to pay any attention. About now, it was saying, you'd be proceeding along the Street of Small Gods, just by the bit of old city wall where you could stop and smoke a rollup out of the wind . . .

To drown it out, he started to sing at the top of his voice.

The cavernous sewers under the city echoed with human and near-human voices for the first time in millennia.

'Hi-ho—'

'—hi-ho—'

'Oook oook oook oook ook—'

'You all *stupid*!'

'I can't help it. It's my nearly-dwarfish blood. We just like singing underground. It comes naturally to us.'

'All right, but why *him* singing? Him *ape*.'

'He's a people person.'

They'd brought torches. Shadows jumped among the pillars in the big cavern, and fled along the tunnels. Whatever the possible lurking dangers, Carrot was beside himself with the joy of discovery.

'It's amazing! The Via Cloaca is mentioned in some old book I read, but everyone thought it was a lost street! Superb workmanship. Lucky for you the river was so low. It looks as though these are normally full of water.'

'That's what I said,' said Cuddy. 'Full of water, I said.'

He glanced cautiously at the dancing shadows, which made weird and worrying shapes on the far wall – strange biped animals, eldritch underground things . . .

Carrot sighed.

'Stop making shadow pictures, Detritus.'

'Oook.'

'What him say?'

'He said "Do Deformed Rabbit, it's my favourite",' Carrot translated.

Rats rustled in the darkness. Cuddy peered around. He kept imagining figures, back there, sighting along some kind of pipe . . .

There were a disturbing few moments when he lost sight of the tracks on the wet stone, but he picked them up again near a mould-hung wall. And then, there was the particular pipe. He'd made a scratch on the stones.

'It's not far along,' he said, handing Carrot the torch. Carrot disappeared.

They heard his footsteps in the mud, and then a whistle of surprise, and then silence for a while.

Carrot reappeared.

'My word,' he said. 'You two know who this is?'

'It *looks* like—' Cuddy began.

'It looks like trouble,' said Carrot.

'You see why we didn't bring it back up?' said Cuddy. 'Carrying a human's corpse through the streets right now would not be a good idea, I thought. Especially this one.'

'I thought some of that, too,' Detritus volunteered.

'Right enough,' said Carrot. 'Well done, men. I think we'd better . . . leave it for now, and come back with a sack later on. And . . . don't tell anyone else.'

'Except the sergeant and everyone,' said Cuddy.

'No . . . not even them. It'd make everyone very . . . jumpy.'

'Just as you say, Corporal Carrot.'

'We're dealing with a sick mind here, men.'

Underground light dawned on Cuddy.

'Ah,' he said. 'You suspect Corporal Nobbs, sir?'

'This is worse. Come on, let's get back up.' He looked back towards the big pillar-barred cavern. 'Any idea where we are, Cuddy?'

'Could be under the Palace, sir.'

'That's what I reckoned. Of course, the tunnels go everywhere . . .'

Carrot's worried train of thought faltered away on some distant track.

There was water in the sewers, even in this drought. Springs flowed into them, or water filtered down from far above. Everywhere was the drip and splash of water. And cool, cool air.

It would almost be pleasant were it not for the sad, hunched corpse of someone that looked for all the world like Beano the clown.

Vimes dried himself off. Willikins had also laid out a dressing gown with brocade on the sleeves. He put it on, and wandered into his dressing room.

That was another new thing. The rich even had rooms for dressing in, and clothes to wear while you went into the dressing rooms to get dressed.

Fresh clothes had been laid out for him. Tonight there was something dashing in red and yellow . . .

. . . *about now he'd be patrolling Treacle Mine Road* . . .

. . . and a hat. It had a feather in it.

Vimes dressed himself, and even wore the hat. And he seemed quite normal and composed, until you realized that he avoided meeting his own gaze in the mirror.

The Watch sat around the big table in the guard-room and in deep gloom. They were Off Duty. They'd never really been Off Duty before.

'What say we have a game of cards?' said Nobby, brightly. He produced a greasy pack from somewhere in the noisome recesses of his uniform.

'You won everyone's wages off them yesterday,' said Sergeant Colon.

'Now's the chance to win 'em back, then.'

'Yeah, but there were five kings in your hand, Nobby.'

Nobby shuffled the cards.

''S'funny, that,' he said, 'there's kings everywhere, when you look.'

'There certainly is if you look up *your* sleeve.'

'No, I mean, there's Kings Way in Ankh, and kings in cards, and we get the King's Shilling when we join up,' said Nobby. 'We got kings all over the place except on that gold throne in the Palace. I'll tell you . . . there wouldn't be all this trouble around the place if we had a king.'

Carrot was staring at the ceiling, his eyebrows locked in concentration. Detritus was counting on his fingers.

'Oh, *yes*,' said Sergeant Colon. 'Beer'd be a penny a pint, the trees'd bloom again. Oh, yeah. Every time someone stubs a toe in this town, turns out it wouldn't have happened if there'd been a king. Vimes'd go spare to hear you talk like that.'

'People'd listen to a king, though,' said Nobby.

'Vimes'd say that's the trouble,' said Colon. 'It's like that thing of his about using magic. That stuff makes him angry.'

'How you get king inna first place?' said Detritus.

'Someone sawed up a stone,' said Colon.

'Hah! Anti-siliconism!'

'Nah, someone *pulled* a sword *out* of a stone,' said Nobby.

'How'd he know it was in there, then?' Colon demanded.

'It . . . it was sticking out, wasn't it?'

'Where anyone could've grabbed it? In *this* town?'

'Only the *rightful* king could do it, see,' said Nobby.

'Oh, *right*,' said Colon. 'I *understand*. Oh, *yes*. So what you're saying is, someone'd decided who the rightful king was *before* he pulled it out? Sounds like a fix to me. Prob'ly someone had a fake hollow stone and some dwarf inside hanging on the other end with a pair of pliers until the right guy came along—'

A fly bounced on the window pane for a while, then zigzagged across the room and settled on a beam, where Cuddy's idly thrown axe cut it in half.

'You got no soul, Fred,' said Nobby. 'I wouldn't've minded being a knight in shining armour. That's what a king does if you're useful. He makes you a knight.'

'A night watchman in crappy armour is about your métier,' said Colon, who looked around proudly to see if anyone had noticed the slanty thing over the e. 'Nah, catch me being respectful to some bloke because he just pulled a sword out of a stone. That don't make you a king. Mind you,' he said, 'someone who could shove a sword *into* a stone . . . a man like *that*, now, *he's* a king.'

'A man like that'd be an ace,' said Nobby.

Angua yawned.

Ding-ding a-ding-ding—

'What the hell's that?' said Colon.

Carrot's chair thumped forward. He fumbled in his pocket and pulled out a velvet bag, which he upended on to the table. Out slid a golden disc about three inches across. When he pressed a catch on one side it opened like a clamshell.

The stopped Watch peered at it.

'It's a clock?' said Angua.

'A watch,' said Carrot.

'It's very big.'

'That's because of the clockwork. There has to be room for all the little wheels. The small watches just have those little time demons in and they don't last and anyway they keep rotten time—'

Ding-ding a-ding-ding, ding dingle ding ding . . .

'And it plays a tune!' said Angua.

'Every hour,' said Carrot. 'It's part of the clockwork.'

Ding. Ding. Ding.

'And it chimes the hours afterwards,' said Carrot.

'It's slow, then,' said Sergeant Colon. 'All the others just struck, you couldn't miss 'em.'

'My cousin Jorgen makes ones like these,' said Cuddy. 'They keep better time than demons or water clocks or candles. Or those big pendulum things.'

'There's a spring and wheels,' said Carrot.

'The important bit,' said Cuddy, taking an eye-glass from somewhere in his beard and examining the watch carefully, 'is a little rocking thingummy that stops the wheels from going too fast.'

'How does it know if they're going too fast?' said Angua.

'It's kind of built-in,' said Cuddy. 'Don't understand it much myself. What's this inscription here . . .'

He read it aloud.

'"A Watch From, Your Old Freinds in the Watch"?'

'It's a play on words,' said Carrot.

There was a long, embarrassed silence.

'Um. I chipped in a few dollars each from you new recruits,' he added, blushing. 'I mean . . . you can pay me back when you like. If you want to. I mean . . . you'd be bound to *be* friends. Once you got to know him.'

The rest of the Watch exchanged glances.

He could lead armies, Angua thought. He really could. Some people have inspired whole countries to great deeds because of the power of their vision. And so could he. Not because he dreams about marching hordes, or world domination, or an empire of a thousand years. Just because he thinks that everyone's really decent underneath and would get along just fine if only they made the effort, and he believes that so strongly it burns like a flame which is bigger than he is. He's got a dream and we're all part of it, so that it shapes the world around him. And the weird thing is that no one wants to disappoint him. It'd be like kicking the biggest puppy in the universe. It's a kind of magic.

'The gold's rubbing off,' said Cuddy. 'But it's a good watch,' he added quickly.

'I was hoping we could give it to him tonight,' said Carrot. 'And all go out for a . . . drink . . .'

'Not a good idea,' said Angua.

'Leave it until tomorrow,' said Colon. 'We'll form a guard of honour at the wedding. That's traditional. Everyone holds their swords up in a kind of arch.'

'We've only got one sword between us,' said Carrot glumly.

They all stared at the floor.

'It's not fair,' said Angua. 'I don't care who stole whatever they stole from the Assassins, but he was right to try to find out who killed Mr Hammerhock. And no one cares about Lettice Knibbs.'

'I like to find out who shoot me,' said Detritus.

'Beats me why anyone'd be daft enough to steal from the Assassins,' said Carrot. 'That's what Captain Vimes said. He said you'd have to be a fool to think of breaking into that place.'

They stared at the floor again.

'Like a clown or a jester?' said Detritus.

'Detritus, he didn't mean a cap-and-bells Fool,' said Carrot, in a kindly voice. 'He just meant you'd have to be some sort of idi—'

He stopped. He stared at the ceiling.

'Oh, my,' he said. 'It's as simple as *that*?'

'Simple as what?' said Angua.

Someone hammered at the door. It wasn't a polite knock. It was the thumping of someone who was either going to have the door opened for them or break it down.

A guard stumbled into the room. Half his armour was off and he had a black eye, but he was just recognizable as Skully Muldoon of the Day Watch.

Colon helped him up.

'Been in a fight, Skully?'

Skully looked up at Detritus, and whimpered.

'The buggers attacked the Watch House!'

'Who?'

'Them!'

Carrot patted him on the shoulder.

'This isn't a troll,' he said. 'This is Lance-Constable Detritus – *don't salute*. Trolls attacked the Day Watch?'

'They're chucking cobbles!'

'You can't trust 'em,' said Detritus.

'Who?' said Skully.

'Trolls. Nasty pieces of work in my opinion,' said Detritus, with all the conviction of a troll with a badge. 'They need keeping a eye on.'

'What's happened to Quirke?' said Carrot.

'I don't know! You lot have got to do *something*!'

'We're stood down,' said Colon. 'Official.'

'Don't give me that!'

'Ah,' said Carrot, brightly. He pulled a stub of pencil out of his pocket and made a little tick in his black book. 'You still got that little house in Easy Street, Sergeant Muldoon?'

'What? What? Yes! What about it?'

'Is the rent worth more than a farthing a month?'

Muldoon stared at him with his one operating eye.

'Are you simple or what?'

Carrot gave him a big smile. 'That's right, Sergeant Muldoon. Is it, though? Worth a farthing, would you say?'

'There's dwarfs running around the streets looking for a fight and you want to know about property prices?'

'A farthing?'

'Don't be daft! It's worth at least five dollars a month!'

'Ah,' said Carrot, ticking the book again. 'That'd be inflation, of course. And I expect you've got a cooking pot . . . do you own at least two-and-one-third acres and more than half a cow?'

'All right, all right,' said Muldoon. 'It's some kind of joke, right?'

'I think probably the property qualification can be waived,' said Carrot. 'It says here that it can be waived for a citizen in good standing. Finally, has there been, in your opinion, an irreparable breakdown of law and order in the city?'

'They turned over Throat Dibbler's barrow and made him eat two of his sausages-inna-bun!'

'Oh, I say!' said Colon.

'Without mustard!'

'I think we can call that a Yes,' said Carrot. He ticked the page again, and closed the book with a definite snap.

'We'd better be going,' he said.

'We were told—' Colon began.

'According to the Laws and Ordinances of Ankh-Morpork,' said Carrot, '*any* residents of the city, in times of the irreparable breakdown of law and order, shall, at the requeſt of an officer of the city who is a citizen in good standing – there's a lot of stuff here about property and stuff, and then it goes on – form themſelves into a militia for city defence.'

'What does that mean?' said Angua.

'Militia . . .' mused Sergeant Colon.

'Hang on, you can't do that!' said Muldoon. 'That's nonsense!'

'It's the law. Never been repealed,' said Carrot.

'We've never had a militia! Never needed one!'

'Until now, I think.'

'Now look here,' said Muldoon, 'you come back with me to the Palace. You're men of the Watch—'

'And we're going to defend the city,' said Carrot.

People were streaming past the Watch House. Carrot stopped a couple by the simple expedient of sticking out his hand.

'Mr Poppley, isn't it?' he said. 'How's the grocery business? Hello, Mrs Poppley.'

'Ain't you heard?' said the flustered man. 'The trolls have set fire to the Palace!'

He followed Carrot's gaze up Broadway, to where the Palace stood squat and dark in the early evening light. Ungovernable flames failed to billow from every window.

'My word,' said Carrot.

'And there's dwarfs breaking windows and everything!' said the grocer. 'A dog's not safe!'

'You can't trust 'em,' said Cuddy.

The grocer stared at him. 'Are you a dwarf?' he said.

'Amazing! How *do* people do it,' said Cuddy.

'Well, I'm off! I'm not stopping to see Mrs Poppley ravished by the little devils! You know what they say about dwarfs!'

The Watch watched the couple head off into the crowd again.

'Well, *I* don't,' said Cuddy, to no one in particular. 'What is it they say about dwarfs?'

Carrot fielded a man pushing a barrow.

'Would you mind telling me what's going on, sir?' he said.

'And do you know what it is they say about dwarfs?' said a voice behind him.

'That's not a sir, that's Throat,' said Colon. 'And will you look at the colour of him!'

'Should he be all shiny like that?' said Detritus.

'Feeling fine! Feeling fine!' said Dibbler. 'Hah! So much for people importuning the standard of my merchandise!'

'What's happening, Throat?' said Colon.

'They say—' Dibbler began, green in the face.

'Who says?' said Carrot.

'*They* say,' said Dibbler. 'You know. They. *Everyone.* They say the trolls have killed someone up at Dolly Sisters and the dwarfs have smashed up Chalky the troll's all-night pottery and they've broken down the Brass Bridge and—'

Carrot looked up the road.

'You just came over the Brass Bridge,' he said.

'Yeah, well . . . that's what they say,' said Dibbler.

'Oh, I see.' Carrot straightened up.

'Did they happen to say . . . sort of, in passing . . . anything else about dwarfs?' said Cuddy.

'I think we're going to have to go and have a word with the Day Watch about the arrest of Coalface,' Carrot said.

'We ain't got no weapons,' said Colon.

'I'm certain Coalface has nothing to do with the

murder of Hammerhock,' said Carrot. 'We are armed with the truth. What can harm us if we are armed with the truth?'

'Well, a crossbow bolt can, e.g., go right through your eye and out the back of your head,' said Sergeant Colon.

'All right, sergeant,' said Carrot, 'so where do we get some *more* weapons?'

The bulk of the Armoury loomed against the sunset.

It was strange to find an armoury in a city which relied on deceit, bribery and assimilation to defeat its enemies but, as Sergeant Colon said, once you'd won their weapons off 'em you needed somewhere to store the things.

Carrot rapped on the door. After a while there were footsteps, and a small window slid back. A suspicious voice said: 'Yes?'

'Corporal Carrot, city militia.'

'Never heard of it. Bugger off.'

The hatch snapped back. Carrot heard Nobby snigger.

He thumped on the door again.

'Yes?'

'I'm Corporal Carrot—' The hatch moved, but hit Carrot's truncheon as he rammed it in the hole. '—and I'm here to collect some arms for my men.'

'Yeah? Where's your authority?'

'What? But I'm—'

The truncheon was knocked away and the hatch thudded into place.

''Scuse me,' said Corporal Nobbs, pushing past.

'Let me have a go. I've been here before, sort of thing.'

He kicked the door with his steel capped boots, known and feared wherever men were on the floor and in no position to fight back.

Snap. 'I told you to bug—'

'Auditors,' said Nobby.

There was a moment's silence.

'What?'

'Here to take inventory.'

'Where's your auth—'

'Oh? Oh? He says where's my authority?' Nobby leered at the guards. 'Oh? Keeps me hanging around here while his cronies can nip out the back to bring the stuff back out of hock, eh?'

'I nev—'

'And, and then, yeah, we'll get the old thousand swords trick, yeah? Fifty crates stacked up, turns out the bottom forty are full of rocks?'

'I—'

'What's your name, mister?'

'I—'

'You open this door right now!' The hatch shut. There was the sound of bolts being pulled back by someone who was not at all convinced it was a good idea and would be asking searching questions in a minute.

'Got a piece of paper on you, Fred? Quick!'

'Yes, but—' said Sergeant Colon.

'Any paper! *Now!*'

Colon fumbled in his pocket and handed Nobby his grocery bill just as the door opened.

Nobby swaggered in at high speed, forcing the man inside to walk backwards.

'Don't run off!' he shouted, 'I haven't found anything wrong—'

'I wasn't r—'

'—YET!'

Carrot had time to get an impression of a cavernous place full of complicated shadows. Apart from the man, who was fatter than Colon, there were a couple of trolls who appeared to be operating a grindstone. Current events did not seem to have penetrated the thick walls.

'All right, no one panic, just stop what you're doing, stop what you're doing, please. I'm Corporal Nobbs, Ankh-Morpork City Ordnance Inspection City Audit—' The piece of paper was waved in front of the man's eyes at vision-blurring speed, and Nobby's voice faltered a bit as he contemplated the end of the sentence, '—Bureau . . . Special . . . Audit . . . Inspection. How many people work here?'

'Just me—'

Nobby pointed at the trolls.

'What about them?'

The man spat on the floor.

'Oh, I thought you said *people*.'

Carrot stuck out his hand automatically and it slammed against Detritus' breastplate.

'Okay,' said Nobby, 'let's see what we've got here . . .' He walked fast along the racks, so that everyone else had to run to keep up. 'What's this?'

'Er—'

'Don't know, eh?'

'Sure . . . it's . . . it's . . .'

'A triple-stringed 2,000lb carriage-mounted siege crossbow with the double-action windlass?'

'Right.'

'Isn't this a Klatchian reinforced crossbow with the goat-leg cocking mechanism and the underhaft bayonet?'

'Er . . . yeah?'

Nobby gave it a cursory examination, and then tossed it aside.

The rest of the Night Watch looked on in astonishment. Nobby had never been known to wield any weapon beyond a knife.

'Have you got one of those Hershebian twelve-shot bows with the gravity feed?' he snapped.

'Eh? What you see is what we got, mister.'

Nobby pulled a hunting crossbow from its rack. His skinny arms twanged as he hauled on the cocking lever.

'Sold the bolts for this thing?'

'They're right there!'

Nobby selected one from the shelf and dropped it into its slot. Then he sighted along the shaft. He turned.

'I *like* this inventory,' said Nobby. 'We'll take it all.'

The man looked down the sights at Nobby's eye and, to Angua's horrified admiration, didn't faint.

'That little bow don't scare *me*,' he said.

'This little bow scare you?' said Nobby. 'No. Right. This is a little bow. A little bow like this wouldn't scare a man like you, because it's such a little bow. It'd need a bigger bow than this to scare a man like you.'

Angua would have given a month's pay to see the quartermaster's face from the front. She'd watched as Detritus had lifted down the siege bow, cocked it with one hand and a barely audible grunt, and stepped forward. Now she could imagine the eyeballs swivelling as the coldness of the metal penetrated the back of the armourer's fleshy red neck.

'Now, the one behind you, that's a *big* bow,' said Nobby.

It wasn't as if the six-foot iron arrow was sharp. It was supposed to smash through doorways, not do surgery.

'Can I pull the trigger yet?' Detritus rumbled, into the man's ear.

'You wouldn't dare fire that thing in here! That's a siege weapon! It'd go right through the wall!'

'Eventually,' said Nobby.

'What this bit for?' said Detritus.

'Now, look—'

'I hope you keep that thing maintained,' said Nobby. 'Them things were a bugger for metal fatigue. Especially on the safety catch.'

'What are a safety catch?' said Detritus.

Everything went quiet.

Carrot found his voice, a long way off.

'Corporal Nobbs?'

'Yessir?'

'I'll take over from this point, if you don't mind.'

He gently pushed the siege bow away, but

Detritus hadn't liked the crack about *people* and it kept swinging back again.

'Now,' said Carrot, 'I don't like this element of coercion. We're not here to bully this poor man. He's a city employee, just like us. It's very wrong of you to put him in fear. Why not just ask?'

'Sorry, sir,' said Nobby.

Carrot patted the armourer on the shoulder.

'May we take some weapons?' he said.

'What?'

'Some weapons? For official purposes?'

The armourer looked unable to cope with this.

'You mean I got a choice?' he said.

'Why, certainly. We practise policing by consent in Ankh-Morpork. If you feel unable to agree to our request, you only have to say the word.'

There was a faint *bong* as the tip of the iron arrow once again bounced on the back of the armourer's skull. He sought in vain for something to say, because the only word he could think of right now was 'Fire!'

'Uh,' he said. 'Uh. Yeah. Right. Sure. Take what you want.'

'Fine, fine. And Sergeant Colon will give you a receipt, adding of course that you release the weapons of your own free will.'

'My own free will?'

'You have absolute choice in the matter, of course.'

The man's face screwed up in the effort of desperate cogitation.

'I reckon . . .'

'Yes?'

286

'I reckon it's okay for you to take 'em. Take 'em right away.'

'Good man. Do you have a trolley?'

'And do you happen to know what it is they say about dwarfs?' said Cuddy.

It crept over Angua once again that Carrot had no irony in his soul. He meant every word. If the man had really held out, Carrot would probably have given in. Of course, there was a bit of a gap between *probably* and *certainly*.

Nobby was down the end of the row, occasionally squeaking with delight as he found an interesting war hammer or an especially evil-looking glaive. He was trying to hold everything, all at once.

Then he dropped the lot and ran forward.

'Oh wow! A Klatchian fire engine! This is more *my* meteor!'

They heard him rummaging around in the gloom. He emerged pushing a sort of bin on small squeaky wheels. It had various handles and fat leathery bags, and a nozzle at the front. It looked like a very large kettle.

'The leather's been kept greased, too!'

'What is it?' said Carrot.

'*And* there's oil in the reservoir!' Nobby pumped a handle energetically. 'Last I heard, this thing had been banned in eight countries and three religions said they'd excommunicate any soldiers found using it!* Anyone got a light?'

---

*Five more embraced it as a holy weapon and instructed that it be used on all infidels, heretics, gnostics and people who fidgeted during the sermon.

'Here,' said Carrot, 'but what's—'

'Watch!'

Nobby lit a match, applied it to the tube at the front of the device, and pulled a lever.

They put out the flames eventually.

'Needs a bit of adjustment,' said Nobby, through his mask of soot.

'No,' said Carrot. For the rest of his life he'd remember the jet of fire scorching his face en route to the opposite wall.

'But it's—'

'No. It's too dangerous.'

'It's *meant* to be—'

'I mean it could hurt people.'

'Ah,' said Nobby, 'right. You should have said. We're after weapons that don't hurt people, right?'

'Corporal Nobbs?' said Sergeant Colon, who'd been even closer to the flame than Carrot.

'Yes, sarge?'

'You heard Corporal Carrot. No heathen weapons. Anyway, how come you know so much about all this stuff?'

'Milit'ry service.'

'Really, Nobby?' said Carrot.

'Had a *special* job, sir. Very responsible.'

'And what was that?'

'Quartermaster, sir,' said Nobby, saluting smartly.

'*You* were a quartermaster?' said Carrot. 'In whose army?'

'Duke of Pseudopolis, sir.'

'But Pseudopolis always lost its wars!'

'Ah . . . well . . .'

'Who did you sell the weapons to?'

'That's a slander, that is! They just used to spend a lot of time away for polishing and sharpening.'

'Nobby, this is Carrot talking to you. How much time, approximately?'

'Approximately? Oh. About a hundred per cent, if we're talking *approximately,* sir.'

'Nobby?'

'Sir?'

'You don't have to call me sir.'

'Yessir.'

In the end, Cuddy remained faithful to his axe, but added a couple more as an afterthought; Sergeant Colon chose a pike because the thing about a pike, the important thing, was that everything happened at the other end of it, i.e., a long way off; Lance-Constable Angua selected, without much enthusiasm, a short sword, and Corporal Nobbs—

—Corporal Nobbs was a kind of mechanical porcupine of blades, bows, points and knobbly things on the end of chains.

'You sure, Nobby?' said Carrot. 'There's nothing you want to leave?'

'It's so hard to choose, sir.'

Detritus was hanging on to his huge bow.

'That all you're taking, Detritus?'

'No sir! Taking Flint and Morraine, sir!'

The two trolls who had been working in the armoury had formed up behind Detritus.

'Swore 'em in, sir,' said Detritus. 'Used troll oath.'

Flint saluted amateurishly.

'He said he'd kick our *goohuloog* heads in if we didn't join up and do what we're told, sir,' he said.

'Very old troll oath,' said Detritus. 'Very famous, very traditional.'

'One of 'em could carry the Klatchian fire engine—' Nobby began hopefully.

'*No*, Nobby. Well . . . welcome to the Watch, men.'

'Corporal Carrot?'

'Yes, Cuddy?'

'It's not fair. They're trolls.'

'We need every man we can get, Cuddy.'

Carrot stood back. 'Now, we don't want people to think we're looking for trouble,' he said.

'Oh, dressed like this, sir, we won't have to look for trouble,' said Sergeant Colon despondently.

'Question, *sir*?' said Angua.

'Yes, Lance-Constable Angua?'

'Who's the enemy?'

'Looking like this, we won't have any problem finding enemies,' said Sergeant Colon.

'We're not looking for enemies, we're looking for information,' said Carrot. 'The best weapon we can use right now is the truth, and to start with, we're going to the Fools' Guild to find out why Brother Beano stole the gonne.'

'Did he steal the gonne?'

'I think he may have, yes.'

'But he died before the gonne was stolen!' said Colon.

'Yes,' said Carrot. 'I know that.'

'Now that,' said Colon, 'is what I calls an *alibi*.'

The squad formed up and, after a brief discussion among the trolls as to which was their left foot and which was their right, marched away. Nobby kept looking back longingly to the fire machine.

Sometimes it's better to light a flamethrower than curse the darkness.

Ten minutes later they'd pushed through the crowds and were outside the Guilds.

'See?' Carrot said.

'They back on to each other,' said Nobby. 'So what? There's still a wall between them.'

'I'm not so sure,' said Carrot. 'We'll jolly well find out.'

'Have we got time?' said Angua. 'I thought we were going to see the Day Watch.'

'There's something I must find out first,' said Carrot. 'The Fools haven't told me the *truth*.'

'Hang on a minute, hang on a minute,' said Sergeant Colon. 'This is going altogether just a bit too far by half. Look, I don't want us to kill anyone, right? I happen to be sergeant around here, if anyone's interested. Understand, Carrot? Nobby? No shooting or swordplay. It's bad enough barging into Guild property, but we'll get into really serious trouble if we shoot anyone. Lord Vetinari won't stop at sarcasm. He might use' – Colon swallowed – '*irony*. So that's an order. What do you want to do, anyway?'

'I just want people to tell me things,' said Carrot.

'Well, if they don't, you're not to hurt them,' said Colon. 'Look, you can ask questions, fair enough.

But if Dr Whiteface starts getting difficult, we're to come away, right? Clowns give me the creeps. And he's worst of all. If he won't answer, we're to leave peacefully and, oh, I don't know, think of something else. That's an order, like I said. Are you clear about this? It's an order.'

'If he won't answer my questions,' said Carrot, 'I'm to leave peacefully. Right.'

'So long as that's understood.'

Carrot knocked on the Fools' door, reached up, caught the custard pie as it emerged from the slot and rammed it back hard. Then he kicked the door so that it swung inwards a few inches.

Someone behind it said 'Ow.'

The door opened a bit further to reveal a small clown covered in whitewash and custard.

'You didn't have to do that,' he said.

'I just wanted to get into the spirit of the thing,' said Carrot. 'I'm Corporal Carrot and this is the citizens' militia, and we all enjoy a good laugh.'

''Scuse me—'

'Except for Lance-Constable Cuddy. And Lance-Constable Detritus enjoys a good laugh too, although some minutes after everyone else. And we're here to see Dr Whiteface.'

The clown's hair rose. Water squirted from his buttonhole.

'Have – have you got an appointment?' he said.

'I don't know,' said Carrot. 'Have we got an appointment?'

'I've got an iron ball with spikes on,' Nobby volunteered.

'That's a morningstar, Nobby.'

'Is it?'

'Yes,' said Carrot. 'An appointment is an engagement to see someone, while a morningstar is a large lump of metal used for viciously crushing skulls. It is important not to confuse the two, isn't it, Mr—?' He raised his eyebrows.

'Boffo, sir. But—'

'So if you could perhaps run along and tell Dr Whiteface we're here with an iron ball with spi— What am I saying? I mean, without an appointment to see him? Please? Thank you.'

The clown scuttled off.

'There,' said Carrot. 'Was that all right, sergeant?'

'He's probably going to be *satirical*, even,' said Colon, morosely.

They waited. After a while Lance-Constable Cuddy took a screwdriver from his pocket and inspected the custard-pie-throwing machine bolted to the door. The rest of them shuffled their feet, except for Nobby, who kept dropping things on his.

Boffo reappeared, flanked by two muscular jesters who didn't look as though they had a sense of humour *at all*.

'Dr Whiteface says there's no such thing as a city militia,' he ventured. 'But. Um. Dr Whiteface says, if it's really important he'll see some of you. But not the trolls or the dwarf. We heard there's gangs of trolls and dwarfs terrorizing the city.'

'Dat's what they say,' said Detritus, nodding.

'Incidentally, do you know what it is they—' Cuddy began, but Nobby nudged him into silence.

'You and me, sergeant?' said Carrot. 'And you, Lance-Constable Angua.'

'Oh dear,' said Sergeant Colon.

But they followed Carrot into the sombre buildings and along the gloomy corridors to Dr Whiteface's office. The chief of all the clowns, fools and jesters was standing in the middle of the floor, while a jester tried to sew extra sequins on his coat.

'Well?'

'Evening, doctor,' said Carrot.

'I should like to make it clear that Lord Vetinari will be hearing about this directly,' said Dr Whiteface.

'Oh, yes. I shall tell him,' said Carrot.

'I can't imagine why you're bothering me when there's rioting in the streets.'

'Ah, well . . . we shall deal with that later. But Captain Vimes always told me, sir, that there's big crimes and little crimes. Sometimes the little crimes look big and the big crimes you can hardly see, but the crucial thing is to decide which is which.'

They stared at one another.

'Well?' the clown demanded.

'I should like you to tell me,' said Carrot, 'about events in this Guild House the night before last.'

Dr Whiteface stared at him in silence.

Then he said, 'If I don't?'

'Then,' said Carrot, 'I am afraid I shall, with extreme reluctance, be forced to carry out the order I was given just before entering.'

He glanced at Colon. 'That's right, isn't it, sergeant?'

'What? Eh? Well, yes—'

'I would much prefer not to do so, but I have no choice,' said Carrot.

Dr Whiteface glared at the two of them.

'But this is Guild property! You have no right to ... to ...'

'I don't know about that, I'm only a corporal,' said Carrot. 'But I've never disobeyed a direct order yet, and I am sorry to have to tell you that I will carry out this one fully and to the letter.'

'Now, see here—'

Carrot moved a little closer.

'If it's any comfort, I'll probably be ashamed about it,' he said.

The clown stared into his honest eyes and saw, as did everyone, only simple truth.

'Listen! If I shout,' said Dr Whiteface, going red under his make-up, 'I can have a dozen men in here.'

'Believe me,' said Carrot, 'that will only make it easier for me to obey.'

Dr Whiteface prided himself on his ability to judge character. In Carrot's resolute expression there was nothing but absolute, meticulous honesty. He fiddled with a quill pen and then threw it down in a sudden movement.

'Confound it!' he shouted. 'How did you find out, eh? Who told you?'

'I really couldn't say,' said Carrot. 'But it makes sense anyway. There's only one entrance to each Guild, but the Guild Houses are back to back. Someone just had to cut through the wall.'

'I assure you we didn't know about it,' said the clown.

Sergeant Colon was lost in admiration. He'd seen people bluff on a bad hand, but he'd never seen anyone bluff with no cards.

'We thought it was just a prank,' said the clown. 'We thought young Beano had just done it with humorous intent, and then he turned up dead and we didn't—'

'You'd better show me the hole,' said Carrot.

The rest of the Watch stood to variations on the theme of At Ease in the courtyard.

'Corporal Nobbs?'

'Yes, Lance-Constable Cuddy?'

'What *is* it everyone says about dwarfs?'

'Oh, come on, you're pulling my leg, right? Everyone knows that who knows *anything* about dwarfs,' said Nobby.

Cuddy coughed.

'Dwarfs don't,' he said.

'What do you mean, dwarfs don't?'

'No one's told *us* what everyone knows about dwarfs,' said Cuddy.

'Well . . . I expect they thought you knew,' said Nobby, weakly.

'Not me.'

'Oh, all *right*,' said Nobby. He glanced at the trolls, then leaned across to Cuddy and whispered in the approximate region of his ear.

Cuddy nodded.

'Oh, is that all?'

'Yes. Er . . . is it true?'

'What? Oh, yes. Of course. It's nat'ral for a dwarf.

Some have got more than others, of course.'

'That's the case all round,' said Nobby.

'I myself, for example, have saved more than seventy-eight dollars.'

'*No!* I mean, no. I mean, I don't mean well-endowed with *money*. I mean . . .' Nobby whispered again. Cuddy's expression didn't change.

Nobby waggled his eyebrows. 'True, is it?'

'How should I know? I don't know how much money humans generally have.'

Nobby subsided.

'There's one thing that's true at least,' he said. 'You dwarfs really love gold, don't you?'

'Of course we don't. Don't be silly.'

'Well—'

'We just say that to get it into bed.'

It was in a clown's bedroom. Colon had occasionally wondered what clowns did in private, and it was all here – the overlarge shoe tree, the very wide trouser press, the mirror with all the candles round it, some industrial-sized sticks of make-up . . . and a bed which looked like nothing more complicated than a blanket on the floor, because that's what it was. Clowns and fools weren't encouraged to live the soft life. Humour was a serious business.

There was also a hole in the wall, just big enough to admit a man. A little pile of crumbling bricks was heaped next to it.

There was darkness on the other side.

On the other side, people killed other people for money.

Carrot stuck his head and shoulders through the hole, but Colon tried to pull him back.

'Hang on, lad, you don't know what horrors lie beyond these walls—'

'I'm just having a look to find out.'

'It could be a torture chamber or a dungeon or a hideous pit or anything!'

'It's just a student's bedroom, sergeant.'

'You see?'

Carrot stepped through. They could hear him moving around in the gloom. It was Assassin's gloom, somehow richer and less gloomy than clown's gloom.

He poked his head through again.

'No one's been in here for a while, though,' he said. 'There's dust all over the floor but there's footprints in it. And the door's locked and bolted. On this side.'

The rest of his body followed Carrot.

'I just want to make sure I fully understand this,' he said to Dr Whiteface. 'Beano made a hole into the Assassins' Guild, yes? And then he went and exploded that dragon? And then he came back through this hole? So how did he get killed?'

'By the Assassins, surely,' said Dr Whiteface. 'They'd be within their rights. Trespass on Guild property is a very serious offence, after all.'

'Did anyone see Beano after the explosion?' said Carrot.

'Oh yes. Boffo was on gate duty and he distinctly remembers him going out.'

'He knows it was him?'

Dr Whiteface looked blank.

'Of course.'

'How?'

'How? He recognized him, of course. That's how you know who people are. You look at them and you say . . . that's him. That's called re-cog-nit-ion,' said the clown, with pointed deliberation. 'It was Beano. Boffo said he looked very worried.'

'Ah. Fine. No more questions, doctor. Did Beano have any friends among the Assassins?'

'Well . . . possibly, possibly. We don't discourage visitors.'

Carrot stared at the clown's face. Then he smiled.

'Of course. Well, that about wraps it all up, I think.'

'If only he'd stuck to something, you know, *original*,' said Dr Whiteface.

'Like a bucket of whitewash over the door, or a custard pie?' said Sergeant Colon.

'That's right!'

'Well, we might as well be going,' said Carrot. 'I imagine you don't want to lay a complaint about the Assassins?'

Dr Whiteface tried to look panicky, but this did not work very well under a mouth painted into a wide grin.

'What? No! I mean – if an Assassin broke into *our* Guild, I mean, not on proper business, and stole something, well, we'd definitely consider we were within our rights to, well—'

'Pour jelly into his shirt?' said Angua.

'Hit him around the head with a bladder on a stick?' said Colon.

'Possibly.'

'Each Guild to their own, of course,' said Carrot. 'I suggest we might as well be going, sergeant. Nothing more for us to do here. Sorry to have troubled you, Dr Whiteface. I can see this must have been a great strain on you.'

The clown was limp with relief.

'Don't mention it. Don't mention it. Happy to help. I know you have your job to do.'

He ushered them down the stairs and into the courtyard, bubbling with small talk now. The rest of the Watch clanked to attention.

'Actually . . .' said Carrot, just as he was being ushered out of the gate, 'there is *one* thing you could do.'

'Of course, of course.'

'Um, I know it's a bit cheeky,' said Carrot, 'but I've always been very interested in Guild customs . . . so . . . do you think someone could show me your museum?'

'Sorry? What museum?'

'The clown museum?'

'Oh, you mean the Hall of Faces. That's not a museum. Of course. Nothing secret about it. Boffo, make a note. We'd be happy to show you around any time, corporal.'

'Thank you very much, Dr Whiteface.'

'Any time.'

'I'm just going off duty,' said Carrot. 'Right now would be nice. Since I happen to be here.'

'You can't go off duty when— ow!' said Colon.

'Sorry, sergeant?'

'You kicked me!'

'I accidentally trod on your sandal, sergeant. I'm sorry.'

Colon tried to see a message in Carrot's face. He'd got used to simple Carrot. Complicated Carrot was as unnerving as being savaged by a duck.

'We'll, er, we'll just be going, then, shall we?' he said.

'No point in staying here now *it's all settled*,' said Carrot, mugging furiously. 'May as well take the night off, really.'

He glanced at the rooftops.

'Oh, well, now it's *all settled* we'll be off, right,' said Colon. 'Right, Nobby?'

'Oh, yeah, we'll be off all right, because it's *all settled*,' said Nobby. 'You hear that, Cuddy?'

'What, that it's *all settled*?' said Cuddy. 'Oh, yeah. We might as well be off. Okay, Detritus?'

Detritus was staring moodily at nothing with his knuckles resting on the ground. This was a normal stance for a troll while waiting for the next thought to arrive.

The syllables of his name kicked a neuron into fitful activity.

'What?' he said.

'It's *all settled*.'

'What is?'

'You know – Mr Hammerhock's death and everything.'

'Is it?'

'Yes!'

'Oh.'

Detritus considered this for a while, nodded, and settled back into whatever state of mind he normally occupied.

Another neuron gave a fizzle.

'Right,' he said.

Cuddy watched him for a moment.

'That's about it,' he said, sadly. 'That's all we're getting.'

'I'll be back shortly,' said Carrot. 'Shall we be off . . . Joey, wasn't it? Dr Whiteface?'

'I suppose there's no harm,' said Dr Whiteface. 'Very well. Show Corporal Carrot anything he likes, Boffo.'

'Right, sir,' said the little clown.

'It must be a jolly job, being a clown,' said Carrot.

'Must it?'

'Lots of japes and jokes, I mean.'

Boffo gave Carrot a lopsided look.

'Well . . .' he said. 'It has its moments . . .'

'I bet it does. I bet it does.'

'Are you often on gate duty, Boffo?' said Carrot pleasantly, as they strolled through the Fools' Guild.

'Huh! Just about all the time,' said Boffo.

'So when did that friend of his, you know, the Assassin . . . visit him?'

'Oh, you know about him, then,' said Boffo.

'Oh, yes,' said Carrot.

'About ten days ago,' said Boffo. 'It's through here, past the pie range.'

'He'd forgotten Beano's name, but he did know

the room. He didn't know the number but he went straight to it,' Carrot went on.

'That's right. I expect Dr Whiteface told you,' said Boffo.

'I've spoken to Dr Whiteface,' said Carrot.

Angua felt she was beginning to understand the way Carrot asked questions. He asked them by not asking them. He simply told people what he thought or suspected, and they found themselves filling in the details in an attempt to keep up. And he never, actually, told lies.

Boffo pushed open a door and fussed around lighting a candle.

'Here we are then,' he said. 'I'm in charge of this, when I'm not on the bloody gate.'

'Ye gods,' said Angua, under her breath. 'It's horrible.'

'It's very interesting,' said Carrot.

'It's historical,' said Boffo the clown.

'All those little heads . . .'

They stretched away in the candlelight, shelf on shelf of them, tiny little clown faces – as if a tribe of headhunters had suddenly developed a sophisticated sense of humour and a desire to make the world a better place.

'Eggs,' said Carrot. 'Ordinary hens' eggs. What you do is, you get a hen's egg, and you make a hole in either end and you blow the egg stuff out, and then a clown paints his make-up on the egg and that's his official make-up and no other clown can use it. That's very important. Some faces have been in the same family for generations, you know.

Very valuable thing, a clown's face. Isn't that so, Boffo?'

The clown was staring at him.

'How do you know all that?'

'I read it in a book.'

Angua picked up an ancient egg. There was a label attached to it, and on the label were a dozen names, all crossed out except the last one. The ink on the earlier ones had faded almost to nothing. She put it down and unconsciously wiped her hand on her tunic.

'What happens if a clown wants to use another clown's face?' she said.

'Oh, we compare all the new eggs with the ones on the shelves,' said Boffo. 'It's not allowed.'

They walked between aisles of faces. Angua fancied she could hear the squelch of a million custard-filled trousers and the echoes of a thousand honking noses and a million grins of faces that weren't smiling. About halfway along was a sort of alcove containing a desk and chair, a shelf piled with old ledgers, and a workbench covered with crusted pots of paint, scraps of coloured horsehair, sequins and other odds and ends of the egg-painter's specialized art. Carrot picked up a wisp of coloured horsehair and twiddled it thoughtfully.

'But supposing,' he said, 'that a clown, I mean a clown with his own face . . . supposing he used another clown's face?'

'Pardon?' said Boffo.

'Supposing you used another clown's make-up?' said Angua.

304

'Oh, that happens all the time,' said Boffo. 'People're always borrowing slap off each other—'

'Slap?' said Angua.

'Make-up,' Carrot translated. 'No, I think what the lance-constable is asking, Boffo, is: could a clown make himself up to look like another clown?'

Boffo's brow wrinkled, like someone trying hard to understand an impossible question.

'Pardon?'

'Where's Beano's egg, Boffo?'

'That's here on the desk,' said Boffo. 'You can have a look if you like.'

An egg was handed up. It had a blobby red nose and a red wig. Angua saw Carrot hold it up to the light and produce a couple of red strands from his pocket.

'But,' she said, trying one more time to get Boffo to understand, 'couldn't you wake up one morning and put on make-up so that you looked like a *different* clown?'

He looked at her. It was hard to tell his expression under the permanently downcast mouth, but as far as she could tell she might as well have suggested that he performed a specific sex act with a small chicken.

'How could I do that?' he said. 'Then I wouldn't be *me*.'

'Someone else might do it, though?'

Boffo's buttonhole squirted.

'I don't have to listen to this sort of dirty talk, miss.'

'What you're saying, then,' said Carrot, 'is that

no clown would ever make up his face in another clown's, um, design?'

'You're doing it again!'

'Yes, but perhaps sometimes by accident a young clown might perhaps—'

'Look, we're decent people, all right?'

'Sorry,' said Carrot. 'I think I understand. Now . . . when we found poor Mr Beano, he didn't have his clown wig on, but something like that could easily have got knocked off in the river. But his nose, now . . . you told Sergeant Colon that someone had taken his nose. His *real* nose. Could you,' said Carrot, in the pleasant tones of someone talking to a simpleton, 'point to *your* real nose, Boffo?'

Boffo tapped the big red nose on his face.

'But that's—' Angua began.

'—your *real* nose,' said Carrot. 'Thank you.'

The clown wound down a little.

'I think you'd better go,' he said. 'I don't like this sort of thing. It upsets me.'

'Sorry,' said Carrot again. 'It's just that . . . I think I'm having an idea. I wondered about it before . . . and I'm pretty certain now. I think I know about the person who did it. But I had to see the eggs to be sure.'

'You saying another clown killed him?' said Boffo belligerently. ''cos if you are, I'm going straight to—'

'Not exactly,' said Carrot. 'But I can show you the killer's face.'

He reached down and took something from the debris on the table. Then he turned to Boffo and opened his hand. He had his back to Angua, and she could not quite see what he was holding. But Boffo gave a strangled cry and ran away down the avenue of faces, his big shoes flip-flopping hugely on the stone flags.

'Thank you,' said Carrot, at his retreating back. 'You've been very helpful.'

He folded his hand again.

'Come on,' he said. 'We'd better be going. I don't think we're going to be popular here in a minute or two.'

'What was that you showed him?' Angua asked, as they proceeded with dignity yet speed towards the gate. 'It was something you came here to find, wasn't it? All that stuff about wanting to see the museum—'

'I *did* want to see it. A good copper should always be open to new experiences,' said Carrot.

They made it to the gate. No vengeful pies floated out of the darkness.

Angua leaned against the wall outside. The air smelled sweeter here, which was an unusual thing to say about Ankh-Morpork air. But at least out here people could laugh without getting paid for it.

'You didn't show me what frightened him,' she said.

'I showed him a murderer,' said Carrot. 'I'm sorry. I didn't think he'd take it like that. I suppose they're all a bit wound up right now. And it's like dwarfs and tools. Everyone thinks in their own ways.'

'You found the murderer's face in there?'

'Yes.'

Carrot opened his hand.

It contained a bare egg.

'He looks like this,' he said.

'He didn't have a *face*?'

'No, you're thinking like a clown. I am very simple,' said Carrot, 'but I think what happened was this. Someone in the Assassins wanted a way of getting in and out without being seen. He realized there's only a thin wall between the two Guilds. He had a room. All he had to do was find out who lived on the other side. Later he killed Beano, and he took his wig and his nose. His *real* nose. That's how clowns think. Make-up wouldn't have been hard. You can get that anywhere. He walked into the Guild made up to look like Beano. He cut through the wall. Then he strolled down to the quad outside the museum, only this time he was dressed as an Assassin. He got the . . . the gonne and came back here. He went through the wall again, dressed up as Beano, and strolled away. And then someone killed *him*.'

'Boffo said Beano looked worried,' said Angua.

'And I thought: that's odd, because you'd have to see a clown right up close to know what his real expression was. But you *might* notice if the make-up wasn't on quite right. Like, maybe, if it was put on by someone who wasn't too used to it. But the important thing is that if another clown sees Beano's face go out of the door, he's seen the *person* leave. They can't think about someone else wearing that face. It's not how they think. A clown and his make-up are the same thing. Without his make-up a clown doesn't exist. A clown wouldn't wear another clown's face in the same way a dwarf wouldn't use another dwarfs tools.'

'Sounds risky, though,' said Angua.

'It was. It was very risky.'

'Carrot? What are you going to do now?'

'I think it might be a good idea to find out whose room was on the other side of the hole, don't you? I think it might belong to Beano's little friend.'

'In the Assassins' Guild? Just us?'

'Um. You've got a point.'

Carrot looked so crestfallen that Angua gave in.

'What time is it?' she said.

Carrot very carefully took Captain Vimes' presentation watch out of its cloth case.

'It's—'

—*abing, abing, abong, bong . . . bing . . . bing . . .*

They waited patiently until it had finished.

A quarter to seven,' said Carrot. 'Absolutely accurate, too. I put it right by the big sundial in the University.'

Angua glanced at the sky.

'Okay,' she said. 'I can find out, I think. Leave it to me.'

'How?'

'Er . . . I . . . well, I could get out of uniform, couldn't I, and, oh, talk my way in as a kitchen maid's sister or something . . .'

Carrot looked doubtful.

'You think that'll work?'

'Can you think of anything better?'

'Not right now.'

'Well, then. I'll . . . er . . . look . . . you go back to

309

the rest of the men and . . . I'll find somewhere to change into something more suitable.'

She didn't have to look around to recognize where the snigger came from. Gaspode had a way of turning up silently like a small puff of methane in a crowded room, and with the latter's distressing ability to fill up all available space.

'Where can you get a change of clothes around here?' said Carrot.

'A good Watchman is always ready to improvise,' said Angua.

'That little dog is awfully wheezy,' said Carrot. 'Why does he always follow us around?'

'I really couldn't say.'

'He's got a present for you.'

Angua risked a glance. Gaspode was holding, but only just, a very large bone in his mouth. It was wider than he was long, and might have belonged to something that died in a tar pit. It was green and furry in places.

'How nice,' she said, coldly. 'Look, you go on. Let me see what I can do . . .'

'If you're sure . . .' Carrot began, in a reluctant tone of voice.

'Yes.'

When he'd gone Angua headed for the nearest alley. There were only a few minutes to moonrise.

Sergeant Colon saluted when Carrot came back, frowning in thought.

'We can go home now, sir?' he suggested.

'What? Why?'

310

'Now it's all sorted out?'

'I just said that to waylay suspicion,' said Carrot.

'Ah. Very clever,' said the sergeant quickly. 'That's what I thought. He's saying that to waylay suspicion, I thought.'

'There's still a murderer out there somewhere. Or something worse.'

Carrot ran his gaze over the ill-assorted soldiery.

'But right now I think we're going to have to sort out this business with the Day Watch,' he said.

'Er. People say it's practically a riot up there,' said Colon.

'That's why we've got to sort it out.'

Colon bit his lip. He was not, as such, a coward. Last year the city had been invaded by a dragon and he'd actually stood on a rooftop and fired arrows at it while it was bearing down on him with its mouth open, although admittedly he'd had to change his underwear afterwards. But that had been *simple*. A great big fire-breathing dragon was straightforward. There it was, right in front of you, about to broil you alive. That was all you had to worry about. Admittedly, it was a *lot* to worry about, but it was . . . simple. It wasn't any kind of mystery.

'We're going to have to sort it out?' he said.

'Yes.'

'Oh. Good. I like sorting things out.'

Foul Ole Ron was a Beggars' Guild member in good standing. He was a Mutterer, and a good one. He would walk behind people muttering in his own private language until they gave him money not to.

People thought he was mad, but this was not, technically, the case. It was just that he was in touch with reality on the cosmic level, and had a bit of trouble focusing on things smaller, like other people, walls and soap (although on very small things, such as coins, his eyesight was Grade A).

Therefore he was not surprised when a handsome young woman streaked past him and removed all her clothes. This sort of thing happened all the time, although up until now only on the inner side of his head.

Then he saw what happened next.

He watched as the sleek golden shape streaked away.

'I *told* 'em! I *told* 'em! I *told* 'em!' he said. 'I'll give 'em the wrong end of a ragman's trumpet, so I shall. Bug'r'em. Millennium hand and shrimp! I *told* 'em!'

Gaspode wagged what was technically a tail when Angua re-emerged.

'"Change into fomefing more fuitable",' he said, his voice slightly muffled by the bone. 'Good one. I brung you thif little token—'

He dropped it on the cobbles. It didn't look any better to Angua's lupine eyes.

'What for?' she said.

'Stuffed with nourishin' marrowbone jelly, that bone,' he said accusingly.

'Forget it,' said Angua. 'Now, how do you normally get into the Assassins' Guild?'

'And maybe afterwards we could kind of hang out in the middens along Phedre Road?' said

Gaspode, his stump of a tail still thumping the ground. 'There's rats along there that'll make your hair stand on—No, all right, forget I mentioned it,' he finished quickly, when fire flashed for a moment in Angua's eyes.

He sighed.

'There's a drain by the kitchens,' he said.

'Big enough for a human?'

'Not even for a dwarf. But it won't be worth it. It's spaghetti tonight. You don't get many bones in spaghetti—'

'Come on.'

He limped along.

'That was a good bone,' he said. 'Hardly even started going green. Hah! I bet you wouldn't say no to a box of chocolates from Mr Hunk, though.'

He cringed as she rounded on him.

'What are you talking about?'

'Nothing! Nothing!'

He trailed after her, whining.

Angua wasn't happy, either. It was always a problem, growing hair and fangs every full moon. Just when she thought she'd been lucky before, she'd found that few men are happy in a relationship where their partner grows hair and howls. She'd sworn: no more entanglements like that.

As for Gaspode, he was resigning himself to a life without love, or at least any more than the practical affection experienced so far, which had consisted of an unsuspecting chihuahua and a brief liaison with a postman's leg.

*   *   *

The No. 1 powder slid down the folded paper into the metal tube. Blast Vimes! Who'd have thought he'd actually head for the opera house? He'd lost a set of tubes up there. But there were still three left, packed neatly in the hollow stock. A bag of No. 1 powder and a rudimentary knowledge of lead casting was all a man needed to rule the city . . .

The gonne lay on the table. There was a bluish sheen to the metal. Or, perhaps, not so much a sheen as a glisten. And, of course, that was only the oil. You had to believe it was only the oil. It was clearly a thing of metal. It couldn't possibly be alive.

And yet . . .

And yet . . .

'They say it was only a beggar girl in the Guild.'

Well? What of it? She was a target of opportunity. That was not my fault. That was your fault. I am merely the gonne. Gonnes don't kill people. People kill people.

'You killed Hammerhock! The boy said you fired yourself! And he'd repaired you!'

You expect gratitude? He would have made another gonne.

'Was that a reason to kill him?'

Certainly. You have no understanding.

Was the voice in his head or in the gonne? He couldn't be certain. Edward had said there was a voice . . . it said that everything you wanted, it could give you . . .

Getting into the Guild was easy for Angua, even through the angry crowds. Some of the Assassins, the ones from noble homes that had big floppy dogs around the place in the same way that lesser folk have rugs, had brought a few with them. Besides, Angua was pure pedigree. She drew admiring glances as she trotted through the buildings.

Finding the right corridor was easy, too. She'd remembered the view from the Guild next door, and counted the number of floors. In any case, she didn't have to look hard. The reek of fireworks hung in the air all along the corridor.

There was a crowd of Assassins in the corridor, too. The door of the room had been forced open. As Angua peered around the corner she saw Dr Cruces emerge, his face suffused with rage.

'Mr Downey?'

A white-haired Assassin drew himself to attention.

'Sir?'

'I want him found!'

'Yes, doctor—'

'In fact I want him inhumed! With Extreme Impoliteness! And I'm setting the fee at ten thousand dollars – I shall pay it personally, you understand? Without Guild tax, either.'

Several Assassins nonchalantly strolled away from the crowd. Ten thousand untaxed dollars was good money.

Downey looked uncomfortable. 'Doctor, I think—'

'Think? You're not paid to think! Heaven knows where the idiot has got to. I ordered the Guild searched! Why didn't anyone force the door?'

'Sorry, doctor, Edward left us weeks ago and I didn't think—'

'You didn't *think*? What are you paid for?'

'Never seen *him* in such a temper,' said Gaspode.

There was a cough behind the chief Assassin. Dr Whiteface had emerged from the room.

'Ah, doctor,' said Dr Cruces. 'I think perhaps we'd better go and discuss this further in my study, yes?'

'I really am most terribly sorry, my lord—'

'Don't mention it. The little . . . devil has made us both look like fools. Oh . . . nothing personal, of course. Mr Downey, the Fools and the Assassins will be guarding this hole until we can get some masons in tomorrow. *No one* is to go through, you understand?'

'Yes, doctor.'

'Very well.'

'That's Mr Downey,' said Gaspode, as Dr Cruces and the chief clown disappeared down the corridor. 'Number two in the Assassins.' He scratched his ear. 'He'd knock off old Cruces for tuppence if it wasn't against the rules.'

Angua trotted forward. Downey, who was wiping his forehead with a black handkerchief, looked down.

'Hello, you're new,' he said. He glanced at Gaspode. 'And the mutt's back, I see.'

'Woof, woof,' said Gaspode, his stump of a tail thumping the floor. 'Incident'ly,' he added for Angua's benefit, 'he's often good for a peppermint if you catch him in the right mood. He's poisoned fifteen people this year. He's almost as good with poisons as old Cruces.'

'Do I need to know that?' said Angua. Downey patted her on the head.

'Oh, Assassins shouldn't kill unless they're being paid. It's these little tips that make all the difference.'

Now Angua was in a position to see the door. There was a name written on a piece of card stuck in a metal bracket.

Edward d'Eath.

'Edward d'Eath,' she said.

'There's a name that tolls a bell,' said Gaspode. 'Family used to live up Kingsway. Used to be as rich as Creosote.'

'Who was Creosote?'

'Some foreign bugger who was rich.'

'Oh.'

'But great-grandad had a terrible thirst, and grandad chased anything in a dress, his dress, you understand, and old d'Eath, well, he was sober and clean but lost the rest of the family money on account of having a blind spot when it came to telling the difference between a one and an eleven.'

'I can't see how that loses you money.'

'It does if you think you can play Cripple Mr Onion with the big boys.'

The werewolf and the dog padded back down the corridor.

'Do you know anything about Master Edward?' said Angua.

'Nope. The house was flogged off recently. Family debts. Haven't seen him around.'

'You're certainly a mine of information,' she said.

'I gets around. No one notices dogs.' Gaspode wrinkled his nose. It looked like a withered truffle. 'Blimey. Stinks of gonne, doesn't it.'

'Yes. Something odd about that,' said Angua.

'What?'

'Something not right.'

There were other smells. Unwashed socks, other dogs, Dr Whiteface's greasepaint, yesterday's dinner – the scents filled the air. But the firework smell of what Angua was now automatically thinking of as the gonne wound around everything else, acrid as acid.

'What's not right?'

'Don't know . . . maybe it's the gonne smell . . .'

'Nah. That started off here. The gonne was kept here for years.'

'Right. Okay. Well, we've got a name. It might mean something to Carrot—'

Angua trotted down the stairs.

''Scuse me . . .' said Gaspode.

'Yes?'

'How can you turn back into a woman again?'

'I just get out of the moonlight and . . . concentrate. That's how it works.'

'Cor. That's all?'

'If it's technically full moon I can Change even during the day if I want to. I only *have* to Change when I'm in the moonlight.'

'Get away? What about wolfbane?'

'Wolfbane? It's a plant. A type of aconite, I think. What about it?'

'Don't it kill you?'

318

'Look, you don't have to believe everything you hear about werewolves. We're human, just like everyone else. Most of the time,' she added.

By now they were outside the Guild and heading for the alley, which indeed they reached, but it lacked certain important features that it had included when they were last there. Most notable of these was Angua's uniform, but there was also a world shortage of Foul Ole Ron.

'Damn.'

They looked at the empty patch of mud.

'Got any other clothes?' said Gaspode.

'Yes, but only back in Elm Street. This is my only uniform.'

'You have to put some clothes on when you're human?'

'Yes.'

'Why? I would have thought a nude woman would be at home in any company, no offence meant.'

'I prefer clothes.'

Gaspode sniffed at the dirt.

'Come on, then,' he sighed. 'We'd better catch up Foul Ole Ron before your chainmail becomes a bottle of Bearhugger's, yes?'

Angua looked around. The scent of Foul Ole Ron was practically tangible.

'All right. But let's be quick about it.'

Wolfbane? You didn't need daft old herbs to make your life a problem, if you spent one week every month with two extra legs and four extra nipples.

*   *   *

There were crowds around the Patrician's Palace, and outside the Assassins' Guild. A lot of beggars were in evidence. They looked ugly. Looking ugly is a beggar's stock in trade in any case. These looked uglier than necessary.

The militia peered around a corner.

'There's hundreds of people,' said Colon. 'And loads of trolls outside the Day Watch.'

'Where's the crowd thickest?' said Carrot.

'Anywhere the trolls are,' said Colon. He remembered himself. 'Only joking,' he added.

'Very well,' said Carrot. 'Everyone follow me.'

The babble stopped as the militia marched, lumbered, trotted and knuckled towards the Day Watch House.

A couple of very large trolls blocked the way. The crowd watched in expectant silence.

Any minute now, Colon thought, someone's going to throw something. And then we're all going to die.

He glanced up. Slowly and jerkily, gargoyle heads were appearing along the gutters. No one wanted to miss a good fight.

Carrot nodded at the two trolls.

They'd got lichen all over them, Colon noticed.

'It's Bluejohn and Bauxite, isn't it?' said Carrot.

Bluejohn, despite himself, nodded. Bauxite was tougher, and merely glared.

'You're just the sort I was looking for,' Carrot went on.

Colon gripped his helmet like a size #10 limpet trying to crawl up into a size #1 shell. Bauxite was an avalanche with feet.

'You're conscripted,' said Carrot.

Colon peeked out from under the brim.

'Report to Corporal Nobbs for your weapons. Lance-Constable Detritus will administer the oath.' He stood back. 'Welcome to the Citizens' Watch. Remember, every lance-constable has a fieldmarshal's baton in his knapsack.'

The trolls hadn't moved.

'Ain't gonna be inna Watch,' said Bauxite.

'Officer material if ever I saw it,' said Carrot.

'Hey, you can't put them in the Watch!' shouted a dwarf from the crowd.

'Why, hello, Mr Stronginthearm,' said Carrot. 'Good to see community leaders here. Why can't they be in the militia?'

All the trolls listened intently. Stronginthearm realized that he was suddenly the centre of attention, and hesitated.

'Well . . . you've only got the one dwarf, for one thing . . .' he began.

'*I'm* a dwarf,' said Carrot, 'technically.'

Stronginthearm looked a little nervous. The whole issue of Carrot's keenly embraced dwarfishness was a difficult one for the more politically minded dwarfs.

'You're a bit big,' he said lamely.

'Big? What's size got to do with being a dwarf?' Carrot demanded.

'Um . . . a lot?' whispered Cuddy.

'Good point,' said Carrot. 'That's a good point.' He scanned the faces. 'Right. We need some honest, law-abiding dwarfs . . . you there . . .'

'Me?' said an unwary dwarf.

'Have you got any previous convictions?'

'Well, I dunno . . . I suppose I used to believe very firmly that a penny saved is a penny earned—'

'Good. And I'll take . . . you two . . . and you. Four more dwarfs, yes? Can't complain about that, eh?'

'Ain't gonna be inna Watch,' said Bauxite again, but uncertainty modulated his tone.

'You trolls can't leave now,' said Detritus. 'Otherwise, too many dwarfs. That's *numbers,* that is.'

'I'm not joining any Watch!' said a dwarf.

'Not man enough, eh?' said Cuddy.

'What? I'm as good as any bloody troll any day!'

'Right, that's sorted out then,' said Carrot, rubbing his hands together. 'Acting-Constable Cuddy?'

'Sir?'

'Hey,' said Detritus, 'how come he suddenly full constable?'

'Since he was in charge of the dwarf recruits,' said Carrot. 'And you're in charge of the troll recruits, Acting-Constable Detritus.'

'I full acting-constable in charge of the troll recruits?'

'Of course. Now, if you would step out of the way, Lance-Constable Bauxite—'

Behind Carrot, Detritus drew a big proud breath.

'Ain't gonna—'

'Lance-Constable Bauxite! You horrible big troll! You standing up straight! You saluting right now! You stepping out of the way of Corporal Carrot! You two troll, you come here! Wurn . . . two-er . . . tree . . . four-er! You in the Watch now! Aaargh, I cannot believe it what my eye it seeing! Where you from, Bauxite?'

'Slice Mountain, but—'

'Slice Mountain! *Slice Mountain?* Only . . .' Detritus looked at his fingers for a moment, and rammed them behind his back. 'Only two-er things come from Slice Mountain! Rocks . . . an' . . . an' . . .' he struck out wildly, 'other sortsa rocks! What kind *you*, Bauxite?'

'What the hell's going on here?'

The Watch House door had opened. Captain Quirke emerged, sword in hand.

'*You two horrible troll! You raise your hand right now, you repeat troll oath—*'

'Ah, captain,' said Carrot. 'Can we have a word?'

'You're in real trouble, *Corporal* Carrot,' snarled Quirke. 'Who do you think you are?'

'*I will do what I told—*'

'Don't *wanna* be inna—'

Wham!

'*I will do what I told—*'

'Just the man on the spot, captain,' said Carrot cheerfully.

'Well, man on the spot, I'm the senior officer here, and you can damn well—'

'Interesting point,' said Carrot. He produced his black book. 'I'm relieving you of your command.'

'*—otherwise I get my goohuloog head kicked in.*'

'*—otherwise I get my goohuloog head kicked in.*'

'Wha—? Are you mad?'

'No, sir, but I'm choosing to believe that you are. There are regulations laid down for this eventuality.'

'Where is your authority?' Quirke stared at the crowd. 'Hah! I suppose you'll say this armed mob is your authority, eh?'

Carrot looked shocked.

'No. The Laws and Ordinances of Ankh-Morpork, sir. It's all down here. Can you tell me what evidence you have against the prisoner Coalface?'

'That damn troll? It's a troll!'

'Yes?'

Quirke looked around.

'Look, I don't have to tell you with everyone here—'

'As a matter of fact, according to the rules, you do. That's why it's called evidence. It means "that which is seen".'

'Listen!' hissed Quirke, leaning towards Carrot. 'He's a *troll*. He's as guilty as hell of *something*. They all are!'

Carrot smiled brightly.

Colon had come to know that smile. Carrot's face seemed to go waxy and glisten when he smiled like that.

'And so you locked him up?'

'Right!'

'Oh. I see. I understand now.'

Carrot turned away.

'I don't know what you think you're—' Quirke began.

People hardly saw Carrot move. There was just a blur, a sound like a steak being thumped on a slab, and the captain was flat on the cobbles.

A couple of members of the Day Watch appeared cautiously in the doorway.

Everyone became aware of a rattling noise. Nobby was spinning the morningstar round and round on the end of its chain, except that because the spiky ball was a very heavy spiky ball, and because the difference between Nobby and a dwarf was species rather than height, it was more a case of both of them orbiting around each other. If he let go, it was an even chance that the target would be hit by a spiky ball or an unexploded Corporal Nobbs. Neither prospect pleased.

'Put it down, Nobby,' hissed Colon, 'I don't think they're going to make trouble . . .'

'I can't let go, Fred!'

Carrot sucked his knuckles.

'Do you think that comes under the heading of "minimum necessary force", sergeant?' he asked. He appeared to be genuinely worried.

'Fred! Fred! What'll I do?'

Nobby was a terrified blur. When you are swinging a spiky ball on a chain, the only realistic option is to keep moving. Standing still is an interesting but brief demonstration of a spiral in action.

'Is he still breathing?' said Colon.

'Oh, yes. I pulled the punch.'

'Sounds minimum enough to me, sir,' said Colon loyally.

'*Fredddd!*'

Carrot reached out absent-mindedly as the morningstar rocketed past and caught it by the chain. Then he threw it against the wall, where it stuck.

'You men in there in the Watch House,' he said, 'come out now.'

Five men emerged, edging cautiously around the prone captain.

'Good. Now go and get Coalface.'

'Er . . . he's in a bit of a bad temper, Corporal Carrot.'

'On account of being chained to the floor,' volunteered another guard.

'Well, now,' said Carrot. 'The thing is, he's going to be unchained right now.' The men shuffled their feet nervously, possibly remembering an old proverb that fitted the occasion very well.* Carrot nodded. 'I won't ask *you* to do it, but I might suggest you take some time off,' he said.

'Quirm is very nice at this time of year,' said Sergeant Colon helpfully. 'They've got a floral clock.'

'Er . . . since you mention it . . . I've got some sick leave coming up,' one of them said.

'I should think that's very probable, if you hang around,' said Carrot.

They sidled off as fast as decency allowed. The crowd hardly paid them any attention. There was still a lot more mileage in watching Carrot.

'Right,' said Carrot. 'Detritus, you take some men and go and bring out the prisoner.'

'I don't see why—' a dwarf began.

---

*It runs: 'He who chains down a troll, especially taking advantage of the situation to put the boot in a few times, had better not be the one who unchains it again.'

'You shut up, you horrible man,' said Detritus, drunk with power.

You could have heard a guillotine drop.

In the crowd, a number of different-sized knobbly hands gripped a variety of concealed weapons.

Everyone looked at Carrot.

That was the strange thing, Colon remembered later. Everyone looked at Carrot.

Gaspode sniffed a lamp-post.

'I see Three-legged Shep has been ill again,' he said. 'And old Willy the Pup is back in town.'

To a dog, a well-placed hitching post or lamp is a social calendar.

'Where are we?' said Angua. Foul Ole Ron's trail was hard to follow. There were so many other smells.

'Somewhere in the Shades,' said Gaspode. 'Sweetheart Lane, smells like.' He snuffled across the ground. 'Ah, here he is again, the little . . .'

"ullo, Gaspode . . ."

It was a deep, hoarse voice, a kind of whisper with sand in it. It came from somewhere in an alley.

"o's yer fwiend, Gaspode?"

There was a snigger.

'Ah,' said Gaspode. 'Uh. Hi, guys.'

Two dogs emerged from the alley. They were huge. Their species was indeterminate. One of them was jet black and looked like a pit bull terrier crossed with a mincing machine. The other . . . the other looked like a dog whose name was almost certainly 'Butch'. Both top and bottom set of fangs had grown so large that he appeared to be looking at the world through bars. He was also bow-legged, although it would probably be a bad if not terminal move for anyone to comment on this.

Gaspode's tail vibrated nervously.

'These are my friends Black Roger and—'

'Butch?' suggested Angua.

'How did you know that?'

'A lucky guess,' said Angua.

The two big dogs had moved around so that they were on either side of them.

'Well, well, well,' said Black Roger. 'Who's this, then?'

'Angua,' said Gaspode. 'She's a—'

'—wolfhound,' said Angua.

The two dogs paced around them hungrily.

'Big Fido know about her?' said Black Roger.

'I was just—' Gaspode began.

'Well, now,' said Black Roger, 'I reckon you'd be wanting to come with us. Guild night tonight.'

'Sure, sure,' said Gaspode. 'No problem there.'

I could certainly manage either of them, Angua thought. But not both at once.

Being a werewolf meant having the dexterity and jaw power to instantly rip out a man's jugular. It was a trick of her father's that had always annoyed her mother, especially when he did it just before meals. But Angua had never been able to bring herself to do it. She'd preferred the vegetarian option.

''ullo,' said Butch, in her ear.

'Don't you worry about anything,' moaned Gaspode. 'Me an' Big Fido . . . we're like that.'

'What're you trying to do? Cross your claws? I didn't know dogs could do that.'

'We can't,' said Gaspode miserably.

Other dogs slunk out of the shadows as the two of them were half led, half driven along byways that weren't even alleys any more, just gaps between walls. They opened out eventually into a bare area, nothing more than a large light well for the buildings around it. There was a very large barrel on its side in one corner, with a ragged bit of blanket in it. A variety of dogs were waiting around in front of it, looking expectant; some of them had only one eye, some of them had only one ear, all of them had scars, and all of them had teeth.

'You,' said Black Roger, 'wait here.'

'Do not twy to wun away,' said Butch, ''cos having your intestines chewed often offends.'

Angua lowered her head to Gaspode level. The little dog was shaking.

'What have you got me into?' she growled. 'This is the dog Guild, right? A pack of strays?'

'Shssssh! Don't say that! These aren't *strays*. Oh, blimey.' Gaspode glanced around. 'You don't just get *any* hound in the Guild. Oh, dear me, no. These are dogs that have been . . .' he lowered his voice, '. . . er . . . bad dogs.'

'Bad dogs?'

'Bad dogs. You naughty boy. Give him a smack. You bad dog,' muttered Gaspode, like some horrible litany. 'Every dog you see here, right, every dog . . . run away. Run away from his or her actual owner.'

'Is that all?'

'All? *All?* Well. Of course. You ain't exactly a dog. You wouldn't understand. You wouldn't know what it was like. But Big Fido . . . he told 'em. Throw off your choke chains, he said. Bite the hand that feeds you. Rise up and howl. He gave 'em pride,' said Gaspode, his voice a mixture of fear and fascination. 'He told 'em. Any dog he finds not bein' a free spirit – that dog is a dead dog. He killed a Dobermann last week, just for wagging his tail when a human went past.'

Angua looked at some of the other dogs. They were all unkempt. They were also, in a strange way, un-doglike. There was a small and rather dainty white poodle that still just about had the overgrown remains of its poodle cut, and a lapdog with the tattered remains of a tartan jacket still hanging from its shoulder. But they weren't milling around, or squabbling. They had a uniform intent look that she'd seen before, although never on dogs.

Gaspode was clearly trembling now. Angua slunk over to the poodle. It still had a diamante collar visible under the crusty fur.

'This Big Fido,' she said, 'is he some kind of wolf, or what?'

'Spiritually, all dogs are wolves,' said the poodle, 'but cynically and cruelly severed from their true destiny by the manipulations of so-called humanity.'

It sounded like a quote. 'Big Fido said that?' Angua hazarded.

The poodle turned its head. For the first time she saw its eyes. They were red, and as mad as hell. Anything with eyes like that could kill anything it wanted because madness, true madness, can drive a fist through a plank.

'Yes,' said Big Fido.

He had been a normal dog. He'd begged, and rolled over, and heeled, and fetched. Every night he'd been taken for a walk.

There was no flash of light when It happened. He'd just been lying in his basket one night and he'd thought about his name, which was Fido, and the name on the basket, which was Fido. And he thought about his blanket with Fido on it, and his bowl with Fido on it, and above all he brooded on the collar with Fido on it, and something somewhere deep in his brain had gone 'click' and he'd eaten his blanket, savaged his owner and dived out through the kitchen window. In the street outside a labrador four times the size of Fido had sniggered at the collar, and thirty seconds later had fled, whimpering.

That had just been the start.

The dog hierarchy was a simple matter. Fido had simply asked around, generally in a muffled voice because he had someone's leg in his jaws, until he located the leader of the largest gang of feral dogs in the city. People – that is, dogs – still talked about the fight between Fido and Barking Mad Arthur, a rottweiler with one eye and a very bad temper. But most animals don't fight to the death, only to the defeat, and Fido was impossible to defeat; he was simply a very small fast killing streak with a collar. He'd hung on to bits of Barking Mad Arthur until Barking Mad Arthur had given in, and then to his amazement Fido had killed him. There was something inexplicably determined about the dog – you could have sandblasted him for five minutes and what was left still wouldn't have given up and *you'd better not turn your back on it.*

Because Big Fido had a dream.

'Is there a problem?' said Carrot.

'That *troll* insulted that *dwarf*,' said Strongin-thearm the dwarf.

'I heard Acting-Constable Detritus give an order to Lance-Constable . . . Hrolf Pyjama,' said Carrot. 'What about it?'

'He's a *troll*!'

'Well?'

'He insulted a dwarf!'

'Actually, it's a technical milit'ry term—' said Sergeant Colon.

'That damn troll just happened to save my life today,' shouted Cuddy.

'What for?'

'What for? *What for?* 'cos it was my life, that's what for! I happen to be very attached to it!'

'I didn't mean—'

'You just shut up, Abba Stronginthearm! What do you know about anything, you civilian! Why're you so stupid? Aargh! I'm too short for this shit!'

A shadow loomed in the doorway. Coalface was a basically horizontal shape, a dark mass of fracture lines and sheer surfaces. His eyes gleamed red and suspicious.

'Now you're letting it go!' moaned a dwarf.

'This is because we have no reason to keep him locked up,' said Carrot. 'Whoever killed Mr Hammerhock was small enough to get through a dwarf's doorway. A troll his size couldn't manage that.'

'But everyone knows he's a *bad* troll!' shouted Stronginthearm.

'I never done nuffin,' said Coalface.

'You can't turn him loose now, sir,' hissed Colon. 'They'll set on him!'

'I never done nuffin.'

'Good point, sergeant. Acting-Constable Detritus!'

'Sir?'

'Volunteer him.'

'I never done nuffin.'

'You can't do that!' shouted the dwarf.

'Ain't gonna be in no Watch,' growled Coalface.

Carrot leaned towards him. 'There's a hundred dwarfs over there. With great big axes,' he whispered.

Coalface blinked.

'I'll join.'

'Swear him in, acting-constable.'

'Permission to enrol another dwarf, sir? To maintain parity?'

'Go ahead, Acting-Constable Cuddy.'

Carrot removed his helmet and wiped his forehead.

'I think that's about it, then,' he said.

The crowd stared at him.

He smiled brightly.

'No one has to stay here unless they want to,' he said.

'I never done nuffin.'

'Yes . . . but . . . look,' said Stronginthearm. 'If he didn't kill old Hammerhock, who did?'

'I never done nuffin.'

'Our inquiries are proceeding.'

'You don't know!'

'But I'm finding out.'

'Oh, yes? And when, pray, will you *know*?'

'Tomorrow.'

The dwarf hesitated.

'All right, then,' he said, with extreme reluctance. 'Tomorrow. But it had better *be* tomorrow.'

'All right,' said Carrot.

The crowd dispersed, or at least spread out a bit. Trolls, dwarfs and humans alike, an Ankh-Morpork citizen is never keen on moving on if there's some street theatre left.

Acting-Constable Detritus, his chest so swollen with pride and pomposity that his knuckles barely touched the ground, reviewed his troops.

'You listen up, you horrible trolls!'

He paused, while the next thoughts shuffled into position.

'You listen up good right now! You in the Watch, boy! It a job with opportunity!' said Detritus. 'I only been doin' it ten minute and already I get promoted! Also got education and training for a good job in Civilian Street!

'This your club with a nail in it. You will eat it. You will sleep on it! When Detritus say Jump, you say . . . what colour! We goin' to do this by the numbers! And I got lotsa numbers!'

'I never done nuffin.'

'You Coalface, you smarten up, you got a field-marshal's button in your knapsack!'

'Never took nuffin, neither.'

'You get down now and give me thirty-two! No! Make it sixty-four!'

Sergeant Colon pinched the bridge of his nose. We're alive, he thought. A troll insulted a dwarf in front of a lot of other dwarfs. Coalface . . . I mean, *Coalface*, I mean, Detritus is Mr Clean by comparison . . . is free and now he's a guard. Carrot laid out Mayonnaise. Carrot's said we'll sort it all out by tomorrow, and it's dark already. But we're alive.

Corporal Carrot is a crazy man.

Hark at them dogs. Everyone's on edge, in this heat.

Angua listened to the other dogs howling, and thought about wolves.

She'd run with the pack a few times, and knew about wolves. These dogs *weren't* wolves. Wolves were peaceful creatures, on the whole, and fairly simple. Come to think of it, the leader of the pack had been rather like Carrot. Carrot fitted into the city in the same way *he'd* fitted into the high forests.

Dogs were brighter than wolves. Wolves didn't *need* intelligence. They had other things. But dogs . . . they'd been given intelligence by humans. Whether they wanted it or not. They were certainly more vicious than wolves. They'd got that from humans, too.

Big Fido was forging his band of strays into what

the ignorant thought a wolf pack was. A kind of furry killing machine.

She looked around.

Big dogs, little dogs, fat dogs, skinny dogs. They were all watching, bright-eyed, as the poodle talked.

About Destiny.

About Discipline.

About the Natural Superiority of the Canine Race.

About Wolves. Only Big Fido's vision of wolves weren't wolves as Angua knew them. They were bigger, fiercer, wiser, the wolves of Big Fido's dream. They were Kings of the Forest, Terrors of the Night. They had names like Quickfang and Silverback. They were what every dog should aspire to.

Big Fido had approved of Angua. She looked very much like a wolf, he said.

They all listened, totally entranced, to a small dog who farted nervously while he talked and told them that the natural shape for a dog was a whole lot bigger. Angua would have laughed, were it not for the fact that she doubted very much if she'd get out of there alive.

And then she watched what happened to a small rat-like mongrel which was dragged into the centre of the circle by a couple of terriers and accused of fetching a stick. Not even wolves did *that* to other wolves. There was no code of wolf behaviour. There didn't need to be. Wolves didn't need rules about being wolves.

When the execution was over, she found Gaspode sitting in a corner and trying to be unobtrusive.

'Will they chase us if we sneak off now?' she said.

'Don't think so. Meeting's over, see?'

'Come on, then.'

They sauntered into an alley and, when they were sure they hadn't been noticed, ran like hell.

'Good grief,' said Angua, when they had put several streets between them and the crowd of dogs. 'He's mad, isn't he?'

'No, mad's when you froth at the mouf,' said Gaspode. 'He's insane. That's when you froth at the brain.'

'All that stuff about wolves—'

'I suppose a dog's got a right to dream,' said Gaspode.

'But wolves aren't like that! They don't even have names!'

'Everyone's got a *name*.'

'Wolves haven't. Why should they? They know who they are, and they know who the rest of the pack are. It's all . . . an image. Smell and feel and shape. Wolves don't even have a word for wolves! It's not *like* that. Names are human things.'

'Dogs have got names. *I've* got a name. Gaspode. 'S'my name,' said Gaspode, a shade sullenly.

'Well . . . I can't explain why,' said Angua. 'But wolves don't have names.'

The moon was high now, in a sky as black as a cup of coffee that wasn't very black at all.

Its light turned the city into a network of silver lines and shadows.

Once upon a time the Tower of Art had been the

centre of the city, but cities tend to migrate gently with time and Ankh-Morpork's centre was now several hundred yards away. The tower still dominated the city, though; its black shape reared against the evening sky, contriving to look blacker than mere shadows would suggest.

Hardly anyone ever looked at the Tower of Art, because it was always there. It was just a thing. People hardly ever look at familiar things.

There was a very faint *clink* of metal on stone. For a moment, anyone close to the tower and looking in exactly the right place might have fancied that a patch of even blacker darkness was slowly but inexorably moving towards the top.

For a moment, the moonlight caught a slim metal tube, slung across the figure's back. Then it swung into shadow again as it climbed onwards.

The window was resolutely shut.

'But she always leaves it open,' Angua whined.

'Must have shut it tonight,' said Gaspode. 'There's a lot of strange people about.'

'But she *knows* about strange people,' said Angua. 'Most of them live in her house!'

'You'll just have to change back to human and smash the window.'

'I can't do that! I'd be naked!'

'Well, you're naked now, ain't you?'

'But I'm a wolf! That's different!'

'I've never worn anything in my whole life. It's never bothered *me*.'

'The Watch House,' muttered Angua. 'There'll be

something at the Watch House. Spare chainmail, at least. A sheet or something. And the door doesn't shut properly. Come on.'

She trotted off along the street, with Gaspode whimpering along behind her.

Someone was singing.

'Blimey,' said Gaspode, 'look at that.'

Four Watchmen slogged past. Two dwarfs, two trolls. Angua recognized Detritus.

'Hut, hut, hut! You without doubt the horriblest recruits I ever see! Pick up them feet!'

'I never done nuffin!'

'Now you doin somefin for the first time in your horrible life, Lance-Constable Coalface! It a man life in the Watch!'

The squad rounded the corner.

'What's been going on?' said Angua.

'Search me. I might know more if one of 'em stops for a widdle.'

There was a small crowd around the Watch House in Pseudopolis Yard. They seemed to be Watchmen, too. Sergeant Colon was standing under a flickering lamp, scribbling on his clipboard and talking to a small man with a large moustache.

'And your name, mister?'

'SILAS! CUMBERBATCH!'

'Didn't you used to be town crier?'

'THAT'S RIGHT!'

'Right. Give him his shilling. Acting-Constable Cuddy? One for your squad.'

'WHO'S ACTING-CONSTABLE CUDDY?' said Cumberbatch.

'Down here, mister.'

The man looked down.

'BUT YOU'RE! A DWARF! I NEVER—'

'Stand to attention when you're talking to a superierierior officer!' Cuddy bellowed.

'Ain't no dwarfs or trolls or humans in the Watch, see,' said Colon. 'Just Watchmen, see? That's what Corporal Carrot says. Of course, if you'd like to be in Acting-Constable Detritus' squad—'

'I LIKE DWARFS,' said Cumberbatch, hurriedly. 'ALWAYS HAVE. NOT THAT THERE ARE ANY IN THE WATCH, MIND,' he added, after barely a second's thought.

'You learn quick. You'll go a long way in this man's army,' said Cuddy. 'You could have a field-marshal's bottom in your napkin any day now. AAAAaabbbb-wut tn! Hut, hut, hut—'

'Fifth volunteer so far,' said Colon to Corporal Nobbs, as Cuddy and his new recruit pounded off into the darkness. 'Even the Dean at the University tried to join. Amazing.'

Angua looked at Gaspode, who shrugged.

'Detritus is certainly clubbing 'em into line,' said Colon. 'After ten minutes they're putty in his hands. Mind you,' he added, 'after ten minutes anything's putty in them hands. Reminds me of the drill sergeant we had when I was first in the army.'

'Tough, was he?' said Nobby, lighting a cigarette.

'Tough? Tough? Blimey! Thirteen weeks of pure misery, that was! Ten-mile run every morning, up to our necks in muck half the time, and him yelling a blue streak and cussin' us every living moment! One time he made me stay up all night cleaning the lavvies with a toothbrush! He'd hit us with a spiky stick to get us out of bed! We had to jump through hoops for that man, we hated his damn guts, we'd have stuck one on him if any of us had the nerve but, of course, none of us did. He put us through three months of living death. But . . . y'know . . . after the passing-out parade . . . us looking at ourselves all in our new uniforms an' all, real soldiers at last, seein' what we'd become . . . well, we saw him in the bar and, well . . . I don't mind telling you . . .' The dogs watched Colon wipe away the suspicion of a tear.

'. . . Me and Tonker Jackson and Hoggy Spuds waited for him in the alley and beat seven kinds of hell out of him, it took three days for my knuckles to heal.' Colon blew his nose. 'Happy days . . . Fancy a boiled sweet, Nobby?'

'Don't mind if I do, Fred.'

'Give one to the little dog,' said Gaspode. Colon did, and then wondered why.

'See?' said Gaspode, crunching it up in his dreadful teeth. 'I'm brilliant. *Brilliant.*'

'You'd better pray Big Fido doesn't find out,' said Angua.

'Nah. He won't touch me. I worry him. I've got the Power.' He scratched an ear vigorously. 'Look, you don't have to go back in there, we could go and—'

'No.'

'Story of my life,' said Gaspode. 'There's Gaspode. Give him a kick.'

'I thought you had this big happy family to

go back to,' said Angua, as she pushed open the door.

'Eh? Oh, yes. Right,' said Gaspode hurriedly. 'Yes. But I like my, sort of, independence. I could stroll back home like a shot, any time I wanted.'

Angua bounded up the stairs, and clawed open the nearest door.

It was Carrot's bedroom. The smell of him, a kind of golden-pink colour, filled it from edge to edge.

There was a drawing of a dwarf mine carefully pinned to one wall. Another held a large sheet of cheap paper on which had been drawn, in careful pencil line, with many crossings-out and smudges, a map of the city.

In front of the window, where a conscientious person would put it to take as much advantage as possible of the available light so's not to have to waste too many of the city's candles, was a small table. There was some paper on it, and a jar of pencils. There was an old chair, too; a piece of paper had been folded up and wedged under a wobbly leg.

And that, apart from a clothes chest, was it. It reminded her of Vimes' room. This was a place where someone came to sleep, not to live.

Angua wondered if there was ever a time when anyone in the Watch was *ever*, really, off duty. She couldn't imagine Sergeant Colon in civilian clothes. When you were a Watchman, you were a Watchman *all the time*, which was a bit of a bargain for the city since it only paid you to be a Watchman for ten hours of every day.

'All right,' she said. 'I can use a sheet off the bed. You shut your eyes.'

'Why?' said Gaspode.

'For decency's sake!'

Gaspode looked blank. Then he said, 'Oh, I get it. Yes, I can see your point, def'nitely. Dear me, you can't have me looking at a naked woman, oh no. Oggling. Gettin' ideas. Deary deary me.'

'You know what I mean!'

'Can't say I do. Can't say I do. Clothing has never been what you might call a thingy of dog wossname.' Gaspode scratched his ear. 'Two meta-syntactic variables there. Sorry.'

'It's different with you. You know what I am. Anyway, dogs are naturally naked.'

'So're humans—'

Angua changed.

Gaspode's ear flattened against his head. Despite himself, he whimpered.

Angua stretched.

'You know the worst bit?' she said. 'It's my hair. You can hardly get the tangles out. And my feet are *covered* in mud.'

She tugged a sheet off the bed and draped it around herself as a makeshift toga.

'There,' she said, 'you see worse on the street every day. Gaspode?'

'What?'

'You can open your eyes now.'

Gaspode blinked. Angua in both shapes was okay to look at, but the second or two in between, as the morphic signal hunted between stations, was not a sight you wished to see on a full stomach.

'I thought you rolled around on the floor grunting and growing hair and stretching,' he whimpered.

Angua peered at her hair in the mirror while her night vision lasted.

'Whatever for?'

'Does . . . all that stuff . . . hurt?'

'It's a bit like a whole-body sneeze. You'd think he'd have a comb, wouldn't you? I mean, a *comb*? Everyone's got a comb . . .'

'A really . . . big . . . sneeze?'

'Even a clothes brush would be something.'

They froze as the door creaked open.

Carrot walked in. He didn't notice them in the gloom, but trudged to the table. There was a flare and a reek of sulphur as he lit first a match and then a candle.

He removed his helmet, and then sagged as if he'd finally allowed a weight to drop on his shoulders.

They heard him say: 'It can't be right!'

'What can't?' said Angua.

Carrot spun around.

'What're you doing here?'

'Your uniform got stolen while you were spying in the Assassins' Guild,' Gaspode prompted.

'My uniform got stolen,' said Angua, 'while I was in the Assassins' Guild. Spying.' Carrot was still staring at her. 'There was some old bloke who kept muttering all the time,' she went on desperately.

'Buggrit? Millennium hand and shrimp?'

'Yes, that's right—'

'Foul Ole Ron.' Carrot sighed. 'Probably sold it

for a drink. I know where he lives, though. Remind me to go and have a word with him when I've got time.'

'You don't want to ask her what she was wearing when she was *in* the Guild,' said Gaspode, who had crept under the bed.

'Shut up!' said Angua.

'What?' said Carrot.

'I found out about the room,' said Angua quickly. 'Someone called—'

'Edward d'Eath?' said Carrot, sitting down on the bed. The ancient springs went *groing-groing-grink.*

'How did you know that?'

'I think d'Eath stole the gonne. I think he killed Beano. But . . . Assassins killing without being paid? It's worse than dwarfs and tools. It's worse than clowns and faces. I hear Cruces is really upset. He's got Assassins looking for the boy all over the city.'

'Oh. Well. I'd hate to be in Edward's shoes when they find him.'

'I'd hate to be in his shoes now. And I know where they are, you see. They're on his poor feet. And *they're* dead.'

'The Assassins have found him, then?'

'No. Someone else did. And then Cuddy and Detritus did. If I'm any judge, he's been dead for several days. You see? That can't be right! But I rubbed the Beano make-up off and took off the red nose, and it was definitely him. And the wig's the right kind of red hair. He must have gone straight to Hammerhock.'

'But . . . someone shot at Detritus. *And* killed the beggar girl.'

'Yes.'

Angua sat down beside him.

'And it couldn't have been Edward . . .'

'Hah!' Carrot undid his breastplate and pulled off his mail shirt.

'So we're looking for someone else. A third man.'

'But there's no clues! There's just some man with a gonne! Somewhere in the city! Anywhere! And I'm tired!'

The springs went *glink* again as Carrot stood up and staggered over to the chair and table. He sat down, pulled a piece of paper towards him, inspected a pencil, sharpened it on his sword and, after a moment's thought, began to write.

Angua watched him in silence. Carrot had a short-sleeved leather vest under his mail. There was a birthmark at the top of his left arm. It was crown-shaped.

'Are you writing it all down, like Captain Vimes did?' she said, after a while.

'No.'

'What *are* you doing, then?'

'I'm writing to my mum and dad.'

'Really?'

'I always write to my mum and dad. I promised them. Anyway, it helps me think. I always write letters home when I'm thinking. My dad sends me lots of good advice, too.'

There was a wooden box in front of Carrot. Letters were stacked in it. Carrot's father had been in the habit of replying to Carrot on the back of Carrot's own letters, because paper was hard to come by at the bottom of a dwarf mine.

'What kind of good advice?'

'About mining, usually. Moving rocks. You know. Propping and shoring. You can't get things wrong in a mine. You have to do things right.'

His pencil scritched on the paper.

The door was still ajar, but there was a tentative tap on it which said, in a kind of metaphorical morse code, that the tapper could see very well that Carrot was in his room with a scantily clad woman and was trying to knock without actually being heard.

Sergeant Colon coughed. The cough had a leer in it.

'Yes, sergeant?' said Carrot, without looking around.

'What do you want me to do next, sir?'

'Send them out in squads, sergeant. At least one human, one dwarf and one troll in each.'

'Yessir. What'll they be doing, sir?'

'They'll be being visible, sergeant.'

'Right, sir. Sir? One of the volunteers just now . . . it's Mr Bleakley, sir. From Elm Street? He's a vampire, well, technic'ly, but he works up at the slaughterhouse so it's not really—'

'Thank him very much and send him home, sergeant.'

Colon glanced at Angua.

'Yessir. Right,' he said reluctantly. 'But he's not a problem, it's just that he needs these extra homo-goblins in his blo—'

'No!'

'Right. Fine. I'll, er, I'll tell him to go away, then.'

Colon shut the door. The *hinge* leered.

'They call you sir,' said Angua. 'Do you notice that?'

'I know. It's not right. People ought to think for themselves, Captain Vimes says. The problem is, people only think for themselves if you tell them to. How do you spell "eventuality"?'

'I don't.'

'Okay.' Carrot still didn't look around. 'We'll hold the city together through the rest of the night, I think. Everyone's seen sense.'

No they haven't, said Angua in the privacy of her own head. They've seen you. It's like hypnotism.

People live your vision. You dream, just like Big Fido, only he dreamed a nightmare and you dream for everyone. You really think everyone is basically nice. Just for a moment, while they are near you, everyone else believes it too.

From somewhere outside came the sound of marching knuckles. Detritus' troop was making another circuit.

Oh, well. He's got to know sooner or later . . .

'Carrot?'

'Hmm?'

'You know . . . when Cuddy and the troll and me joined the Watch – well, you know why it was us three, don't you?'

'Of course. Minority group representation. One troll, one dwarf, one woman.'

'Ah.' Angua hesitated. It was still moonlight outside. She could tell him, run downstairs, Change and be well outside the city by dawn. She'd have to do it. She was an expert at running away from cities.

'It wasn't exactly like that,' she said. 'You see, there's a lot of undead in the city and the Patrician insisted that—'

'Give her a kiss,' said Gaspode, from under the bed.

Angua froze. Carrot's face took on the usual vaguely puzzled look of someone whose ears have just heard what their brain is programmed to believe doesn't exist. He began to blush.

'Gaspode!' snapped Angua, dropping into Canine.

'I know what I'm doin'. A Man, a Woman. It is Fate,' said Gaspode.

Angua stood up. Carrot shot up too, so fast that his chair fell over.

'I must be going,' she said.

'Um. Don't go—'

'Now you just reach out,' said Gaspode.

It'd never work, Angua told herself. It never does. Werewolves have to hang around with other werewolves, they're the only ones who *understand* . . .

But . . .

On the other hand . . . since she'd have to run anyway . . .

She held up a finger.

'Just one moment,' she said brightly and, in one movement, reached under the bed and pulled out Gaspode by the scruff of his neck.

'You need me!' the dog whimpered, as he was carried to the door. 'I mean, what does he know? His idea of a good time is showing you the Colossus of Morpork! Put me—'

The door slammed. Angua leaned on it.

It'll end up just like it did in Pseudopolis and Quirm and—

'Angua?' said Carrot.

She turned.

'Don't say anything,' she said. 'And it might be all right.'

After a while the bedsprings went *glink*.

And shortly after that, for Corporal Carrot, the Discworld moved. And didn't even bother to stop to cancel the bread and newspapers.

Corporal Carrot awoke around four a.m., that secret hour known only to the night people, such as criminals, policemen and other misfits. He lay on his half of the narrow bed and stared at the wall.

It had *definitely* been an interesting night.

Although he was indeed simple, he wasn't stupid, and he'd always been aware of what might be called the *mechanics*. He'd been acquainted with several young ladies, and had taken them on many invigorating walks to see fascinating ironwork and interesting civic buildings until they'd unaccountably lost interest. He'd patrolled the Whore Pits often enough, although Mrs Palm and the Guild of Seamstresses were trying to persuade the Patrician to rename the area The Street of Negotiable Affection. But he'd never seen them in relation to himself, had never been quite sure, as it were, where he fitted in.

This was probably not something he was going to

write to his parents about. They almost certainly knew.

He slid out of bed. The room was stifling hot with the curtains drawn.

Behind him, he heard Angua roll over into the hollow left by his body.

Then, with both hands, and considerable vigour, he threw open the curtains and let in the round, white light of the full moon.

Behind him, he thought he heard Angua sigh in her sleep.

There were thunderstorms out on the plain. Carrot could see lightning flashes stitching the horizon, and he could smell rain. But the air of the city was still and baking, all the hotter for the distant prospect of storms.

The University's Tower of Art loomed in front of him. He saw it every day. It dominated half the city.

Behind him, the bed went *glink*.

'I think there's going to be—' he began, and turned.

As he turned away, he missed the glint of moonlight on metal from the top of the tower.

Sergeant Colon sat on the bench outside the baking air of the Watch House.

There was a hammering noise from somewhere inside. Cuddy had come in ten minutes before with a bag of tools, a couple of helmets and a determined expression. Colon was damned if he knew what the little devil was working on.

He counted again, very slowly, ticking off names on his clipboard.

No doubt about it. The Night Watch had almost twenty members now. Maybe more. Detritus had gone critical, and had sworn in a further two men, another troll and a wooden dummy from outside Corksock's Natty Clothing Co.* If this went on they'd be able to open up the old Watch Houses near the main gates, just like the old days.

He couldn't *remember* when the Watch last had twenty men.

It had all seemed a good idea at the time. It was certainly keeping the lid on things. But in the morning the Patrician was going to get to hear about it, and demand to see the superior officer.

Now, Sergeant Colon was not entirely clear in his own mind who *was* the superior officer at the moment. He felt that it should be either Captain Vimes or, in some way he couldn't quite define, Corporal Carrot. But the captain wasn't around and Corporal Carrot was only a corporal, and Fred Colon

---

*And was the origin, long after the events chronicled here were over, of an Ankh-Morpork folk song scored for tin whistle and nasal passage:

'As I was a-walking along Lower Broadway,
The recruiting party came picking up people by their ankles and
    saying they were going to volunteer to join the Watch unless they
    wanted their goohuloog heads kicked in.
So I went via Peach Pie Street and Holofernes instead,
Singing: Too-ra-li, etc.'

It never really caught on.

had a dreadful apprehension that when Lord Vetinari summoned someone in order to be ironical at them and say things like 'Who's going to pay their wages, pray?' it would be him, Fred Colon, well and truly up the Ankh without a paddle.

They were also running out of ranks. There were only four ranks below the rank of sergeant. Nobby was getting stroppy about anyone else being pro- moted to corporal, so there was a certain amount of career congestion taking place. Besides, some of the Watch had got it into their heads that the way you got promoted was to conscript half a dozen other guards. At Detritus' current rate of progress, he was going to be High Supreme Major General by the end of the month.

And what made it all strange was that Carrot was still only a—

Colon looked up when he heard the tinkle of broken glass. Something golden and indistinct crashed through an upper window, landed in the shadows and fled before he could make out what it was.

The Watch House door slammed open and Carrot emerged, sword in hand.

'Where'd it go? Where'd it go?'

'Dunno. What the hell was it?'

Carrot stopped.

'Uh. Not sure,' he said.

'Carrot?'

'Sarge?'

'I should put some clothes on if I was you, lad.'

Carrot stayed looking into the pre-dawn gloom.

'I mean, I turned around and there it was, and—'

He looked down at the sword in his hand as if he hadn't realized that he was carrying it.

'Oh, damn!' he said.

He ran back to his room and grabbed his britches. As he struggled into them, he was suddenly aware of a thought in his head, clear as ice.

You are a pillock, what are you? Picked up the sword automatically, didn't you? Did it all wrong! Now she's run off and you'll never see her again!

He turned. A small grey dog was watching him intently from the doorway.

Shock like that, she might never Change back again, said his thoughts. Who cares if she's a werewolf? That didn't bother you until you knew! Incident'ly, any biscuits about your person could be usefully thrown to the small dog in the doorway, although come to think of it the chances of having a biscuit on you right now are very small, so forget you ever thought it. Blimey, you really messed that up, right?

. . . thought Carrot.

'Woof woof,' said the dog.

Carrot's forehead wrinkled.

'It's you, isn't it?' he said, pointing his sword.

'Me? Dogs don't talk,' said Gaspode, hurriedly. 'Listen, I should know. I *am* one.'

'You tell me where she's gone. Right now! Or . . .'

'Yeah? Look,' said Gaspode gloomily, 'the first thing I remember in my life, right, the first thing, was being thrown into the river in a sack. With a brick. Me. I mean, I had wobbly legs and a humorously inside-out ear, I mean, I was *fluffy*. Okay, right, so it was the Ankh. Okay, so I could walk ashore. But that was the start, and it ain't never got much better. I mean, I walked ashore *inside* the sack, dragging the brick. It took me three days to chew my way out. Go on. Threaten me.'

'Please?' said Carrot.

Gaspode scratched his ear.

'Maybe I could track her down,' said Gaspode. 'Given the right, you know, encouragement.'

He waggled his eyebrows encouragingly.

'If you find her, I'll give you anything you want,' said Carrot.

'Oh, *well*. *If*. Right. Oh, yes. That's all very well, is *if*. What about something up front? Look at these paws, hey? Wear and tear. And this nose doesn't smell by itself. It is a finely tuned instrument.'

'If you don't start looking right away,' said Carrot, 'I will personally—' He hesitated. He'd never been cruel to an animal in his life.

'I'll turn the matter over to Corporal Nobbs,' he said.

'That's what I like,' said Gaspode bitterly. 'Incentive.'

He pressed his blotchy nose to the ground. It was all show, anyway. Angua's scent hung in the air like a rainbow.

'You can really talk?' said Carrot.

Gaspode rolled his eyes.

''Course not,' he said.

*   *   *

The figure had reached the top of the tower.

Lamps and candles were alight all over the city. It was spread out below him. Ten thousand little earthbound stars . . . and he could turn off any one he wanted, just like that. It was like being a god.

It was amazing how sounds were so audible up here. It was like being a god. He could hear the howl of dogs, the sound of voices. Occasionally one would be louder than the rest, rising up into the night sky.

This was power. The power he had below, the power to say: do this, do that . . . that was just something human, but this . . . this was like being a god.

He pulled the gonne into position, clicked a rack of six bullets into position, and sighted at random on a light. And then on another one. And another one.

He really shouldn't have let it shoot that beggar girl. That wasn't the plan. Guild leaders, that was poor little Edward's plan. Guild leaders, to start with. Leave the city leaderless and in turmoil, and then confront his silly candidate and say: Go forth and rule, it is your destiny.

That was an *old* disease, that kind of thinking. You caught it from crowns, and silly stories. You believed . . . hah . . . you believed that some trick like, like pulling a sword from a stone was somehow a qualification for kingly office. A sword from a stone? The gonne was more magical than *that.*

He lay down, stroked the gonne, and waited.

*   *   *

Day broke.

'I never touched nuffin,' said Coalface, and turned over on his slab.

Detritus hit him over the head with his club.

'Up you get, soldiers! Hand off rock and on with sock! It another beautiful day inna Watch! Lance-Constable Coalface, on your feet, you horrible little man!'

Twenty minutes later a bleary-eyed Sergeant Colon surveyed the troops. They were slumped on the benches, except for Acting-Constable Detritus, who was sitting bolt upright with an air of official helpfulness.

'Right, men,' Colon began, 'now, as you—'

'You men, you listen up good right now!' Detritus boomed.

'Thank you, Acting-Constable Detritus,' said Colon wearily. 'Captain Vimes is getting married today. We're going to provide a guard of honour. That's what we always used to do in the old days when a Watchman got wed. So I want helmets and breastplates bright and shiny. And cohorts gleaming. Not a speck of muck . . . where's Corporal Nobbs?'

There was a *dink* as Acting-Constable Detritus' hand bounced off his new helmet.

'Hasn't been seen for hours, sir!' he reported.

Colon rolled his eyes.

'And some of you will . . . Where's Lance-Constable Angua?'

Dink. 'No one's seen her since last night, sir.'

'All right. We got through the night, we're going

to get through the day. Corporal Carrot says we're to look sharp.'

Dink. 'Yes, sir!'

'Acting-Constable Detritus?'

'Sir?'

'What's that you've got on your head?'

Dink. 'Acting-Constable Cuddy made it for me, sir. Special clockwork thinking helmet.'

Cuddy coughed. 'These big bits are cooling fins, see? Painted black. I glommed a clockwork engine off my cousin, and this fan here blows air over—' He stopped when he saw Colon's expression.

'That's what you've been working on all night, is it?'

'Yes, because I reckon troll brains get too—'

The sergeant waved him into silence.

'So we've got a clockwork soldier, have we?' said Colon. 'We're a real model army, we are.'

Gaspode was geographically embarrassed. He knew where he was, more or less. He was somewhere beyond the Shades, in the network of dock basins and cattle-yards. Even though he thought of the whole city as belonging to him, this wasn't his territory. There were rats here almost as big as he was, and he was basically a sort of terrier shape, and Ankh-Morpork rats were intelligent enough to recognize it. He'd also been kicked by two horses and almost run over by a cart. And he'd lost the scent. She'd doubled back and forth and used rooftops and crossed the river a few times. Werewolves were instinctively good at avoiding pursuit; after all, the surviving ones were descendants of those who could outrun an angry mob. Those who *couldn't* outwit a mob never had descendants, or even graves.

Several times the scent petered out at a wall or a low-roofed hut, and Gaspode would limp around in circles until he found it again.

Random thoughts wavered in his schizophrenic doggy mind.

'Clever Dog Saves The Day,' he muttered. 'Everyone Says, Good Doggy. No they don't, I'm only doing it 'cos I was threatened. The Marvellous Nose. I didn't want to do this. You Shall Have A Bone. I'm just flotsam on the sea of life, me. Who's a Good Boy? Shut up.'

The sun toiled up the sky. Down below, Gaspode toiled on.

Willikins opened the curtains. Sunlight poured in. Vimes groaned and sat up slowly in what remained of his bed.

'Good grief, man,' he mumbled. 'What sort of time d'you call this?'

'Almost nine in the morning, sir,' said the butler.

'Nine in the *morning*? What sort of time is *that* to get up? I don't normally get up until the afternoon's got the shine worn off!'

'But sir is not at work any more, sir.'

Vimes looked down at the tangle of sheets and blankets. They were wrapped around his legs and knotted together. Then he remembered the dream.

He'd been walking around the city.

Well, maybe not so much a dream as a memory.

After all, he walked the city every night. Some part of him wasn't giving up; some part of Vimes was learning to be a civilian, but an old part was marching, no, *proceeding* to a different beat. He'd *thought* the place seemed deserted and harder to walk through than usual.

'Does sir wish me to shave him or will sir do it himself?'

'I get nervous if people hold blades near my face,' said Vimes. 'But if you harness the horse and cart I'll try and get to the other end of the bathroom.'

'Very amusing, sir.'

Vimes had another bath, just for the novelty of it. He was aware from a general background noise that the mansion was busily humming towards W-hour. Lady Sybil was devoting to her wedding all the directness of thought she'd normally apply to breeding out a tendency towards floppy ears in swamp dragons. Half a dozen cooks had been busy in the kitchens for three days. They were roasting a whole ox and doing amazing stuff with rare fruit. Hitherto Sam Vimes' idea of a good meal was liver without tubes. *Haute cuisine* had been bits of cheese on sticks stuck into half a grapefruit.

He was vaguely aware that prospective grooms were not supposed to see putative brides on the morning of the wedding, possibly in case they took to their heels. That was unfortunate. He'd have liked to have talked to someone. If he could talk to someone, it might all make sense.

He picked up the razor, and looked in the mirror at the face of Captain Samuel Vimes.

*   *   *

Colon saluted, and then peered at Carrot.

'You all right, sir? You look like you could do with some sleep.'

Ten o'clock, or various attempts thereof, began to boom around the city. Carrot turned away from the window.

'I've been out looking,' he said.

'Three more recruits this morning already,' said Colon. They'd asked to join 'Mr Carrot's army'. He was slightly worried about that.

'Good.'

'Detritus is giving 'em very basic training,' said Colon. 'It works, too. After an hour of him shouting in their ear, they do anything I tell 'em.'

'I want all the men we can spare up on the rooftops between the Palace and the University,' said Carrot.

'There's Assassins up there already,' said Colon. 'And the Thieves' Guild have got men up there, too.'

'They're Thieves and Assassins. We're not. Make sure someone's up on the Tower of Art as well—'

'Sir?'

'Yes, sergeant?'

'We've been talking . . . me and the lads . . . and, well . . .'

'Yes?'

'It'd save a lot of trouble if we went to the wizards and asked them—'

'Captain Vimes never had any truck with magic.'

'No, but . . .'

'No magic, sergeant.'

'Yes, sir.'

'Guard of honour all sorted out?'

'Yes, sir. Their cohorts all gleaming in purple and gold, sir.'

'Really?'

'Very important, sir, good clean cohorts. Frighten the life out the enemy.'

'Good.'

'But I can't find Corporal Nobbs, sir.'

'Is that a problem?'

'Well, it means the honour guard'll be a bit smarter, sir.'

'I've sent him on a special errand.'

'Er . . . can't find Lance-Constable Angua, either.'

'Sergeant?'

Colon braced himself. Outside, the bells were dying away.

'Did *you* know she was a werewolf?'

'Um . . . Captain Vimes kind of hinted, sir . . .'

'How did he hint?'

Colon took a step back.

'He sort of said, "Fred, she's a damn werewolf. I don't like it any more than you do, but Vetinari says we've got to take one of them as well, and a werewolf's better than a vampire or a zombie, and that's all there is to it." That's what he hinted.'

'I *see*.'

'Er . . . sorry about that, sir.'

'Just let's get through the day, Fred. That's all—'

—abing, abing, a-bing-bong—

'We never even presented the captain with his watch,' said Carrot, taking it out of his pocket. 'He must have gone off thinking we didn't care. He was probably looking forward to getting a watch. I know it always used to be a tradition.'

'It's been a busy few days, sir. Anyway, we can give it to him after the wedding.'

Carrot slipped the watch back into its bag.

'I suppose so. Well, let's get organized, sergeant.'

Corporal Nobbs toiled through the darkness under the city. His eyes had got accustomed to the gloom now. He was dying for a smoke, but Carrot had warned him about that. Just take the sack, follow the trail, bring back the body. And don't nick any jewellery.

People were already filing into the Great Hall of Unseen University.

Vimes had been firm about this. It was the only thing he'd held out for. He wasn't exactly an atheist, because atheism was a non-survival trait on a world with several thousand gods. He just didn't like any of them very much, and didn't see what business it was of theirs that he was getting married. He'd turned down any of the temples and churches, but the Great Hall had a sufficiently churchy look, which is what people always feel is mandatory on these occasions. It's not actually essential for any gods to drop in, but they should feel at home if they do.

Vimes strolled down there early, because there's nothing more useless in the world than a groom just before the wedding. Interchangeable Emmas had taken over the house.

There were already a couple of ushers in place, ready to ask guests whose side they were on.

And there were a number of senior wizards hanging around. They were automatically guests at such a society wedding, and certainly at the reception afterwards. Probably one roast ox wouldn't be enough.

Despite his deep distrust of magic, he quite liked the wizards. They didn't cause trouble. At least, they didn't cause *his* kind of trouble. True, occasionally they fractured the time/space continuum or took the canoe of reality too close to the white waters of chaos, but they never broke the actual *law*.

'Good morning, Archchancellor,' he said.

Archchancellor Mustrum Ridcully, supreme leader of all the wizards in Ankh-Morpork whenever they could be bothered, gave him a cheery nod.

'Good morning, captain,' he said. 'I must say you've got a nice day for it!'

'Hahaha, a nice day for it!' leered the Bursar.

'Oh dear,' said Ridcully, 'he's off again. Can't understand the man. Anyone got the dried frog pills?'

It was a complete mystery to Mustrum Ridcully, a man designed by Nature to live outdoors and happily slaughter anything that coughed in the bushes, why the Bursar (a man designed by Nature to sit in a small room somewhere, adding up figures) was so nervous. He'd tried all sorts of things to, as he put it, buck him up. These included practical jokes, surprise early morning runs, and leaping out at him from behind doors while wearing Willie the Vampire masks in order, he said, to take him out of himself.

The service itself was going to be performed by the Dean, who had carefully made one up; there was no official civil marriage service in Ankh-Morpork, other than something approximating to 'Oh, all right then, if you really must.' He nodded enthusiastically at Vimes.

'We've cleaned our organ especially for the occasion,' he said.

'Hahaha, organ!' said the Bursar.

'And a mighty one it is, as organs go—' Ridcully stopped, and signalled to a couple of student wizards. 'Just take the Bursar away and make him lie down for a while, will you?' he said. 'I think someone's been feeding him meat again.'

There was a hiss from the far end of the Great Hall, and then a strangled squeak. Vimes stared at the monstrous array of pipes.

'Got eight students pumping the bellows,' said Ridcully, to a background of wheezes. 'It's got three keyboards and a hundred extra knobs, including twelve with "?" on them.'

'Sounds impossible for a man to play,' said Vimes politely.

'Ah. We had a stroke of luck there—'

There was a moment of sound so loud that the aural nerves shut down. When they opened again, somewhere around the pain threshold, they could just make out the opening and extremely bent bars of Fondel's 'Wedding March', being played with gusto by someone who'd discovered that the instrument didn't just have three keyboards but a whole range of special acoustic effects, ranging from

Flatulence to Humorous Chicken Squawk. The occasional 'oook!' of appreciation could be heard amidst the sonic explosion.

Somewhere under the table, Vimes screamed at Ridcully: 'Amazing! Who built it!'

'I don't know! But it's got the name B.S. Johnson on the keyboard cover!'

There was a descending wail, one last Hurdy-Gurdy Effect, and then silence.

'Twenty minutes those lads were pumping up the reservoirs,' said Ridcully, dusting himself off as he stood up. 'Go easy on the Vox Dei stop, there's a good chap!'

'Ook!'

The Archchancellor turned back to Vimes, who was wearing the standard waxen pre-nuptial grimace. The hall was filling up quite well now.

'I'm not an expert on this stuff,' he said, 'but you've got the ring, have you?'

'Yes.'

'Who's giving away the bride?'

'Her Uncle Lofthouse. He's a bit gaga, but she insisted.'

'And the best man?'

'What?'

'The best man. You know? He hands you the ring and has to marry the bride if you run away and so on. The Dean's been reading up on it, haven't you, Dean?'

'Oh, yes,' said the Dean, who'd spent all the previous day with *Lady Deirdre Waggon's Book of Etiquette*. 'She's got to marry *someone* once she's turned up. You can't have unmarried brides flapping around the place, being a danger to society.'

'I completely forgot about a best man!' said Vimes.

The Librarian, who'd given up on the organ until it had some more puff, brightened up.

'Ook?'

'Well, go and find one,' said Ridcully. 'You've got nearly half an hour.'

'It's not as easy as that, is it? They don't grow on trees!'

'Oook?'

'I can't think who to ask!'

'*Oook.*'

The Librarian liked being best man. You were allowed to kiss bridesmaids, and they weren't allowed to run away. He was really disappointed when Vimes ignored him.

Acting-Constable Cuddy climbed laboriously up the steps inside the Tower of Art, grumbling to himself. He knew he couldn't complain. They'd drawn lots because, Carrot said, you shouldn't ask the men to do anything you wouldn't do yourself. And he'd drawn the short straw, harhar, which meant the tallest building. That meant if there was any trouble, he'd miss it.

He paid no attention to the thin rope dangling from the trapdoor far above. Even if he'd thought about it . . . so what? It was just a rope.

* * *

Gaspode looked up into the shadows.

There was a growl from somewhere in the darkness. It was no ordinary dog growl. Early man had heard sounds like that in deep caves.

Gaspode sat down. His tail thumped uncertainly.

'Knew I'd find you sooner or later,' he said. 'The old nose, eh? Finest instrument known to dog.'

There was another growl. Gaspode whimpered a bit.

'The thing is,' he said, 'the thing is . . . the actual thing is, see . . . the thing what I've been sent to do . . .'

Late man heard sounds like that, too. Just before he became late.

'I can see you . . . don't want to talk right now,' said Gaspode. 'But the thing is . . . now, I know what you're thinking, is this *Gaspode* obeyin' orders from a *human?*'

Gaspode looked conspiratorially over his shoulder, as if there could be anything worse than what was in front of him.

'That's the whole mess about being a dog, see?' he said. 'That's the thing what Big Fido can't get his mind around, see? You looked at the dogs in the Guild, right? You heard 'em howl. Oh, yes, Death To The Humans, All *Right*. But under all that there's the *fear*. There's the voice sayin': Bad Dog. And it don't come from anywhere but inside, right from inside the bones, 'cos humans made dogs. I knows this. I wish I didn't, but there it is. That's the Power, knowin'. I've read books, I have. Well, chewed books.'

The darkness was silent.

'And you're a wolf and human at the same time, right? Tricky, that. I can see that. Bit of a dichotomy, sort of thing. Makes you kind of like a dog. 'cos that's what a dog is, really. Half a wolf and half a human. You were right about that. We've even got names. Hah! So our bodies tell us one thing, our heads tell us another. It's a dog's life, being a dog. And I bet *you* can't run away from *him*. Not really. He's your master.'

The darkness was more silent. Gaspode thought he heard movement.

'He wants you to come back. The thing is, if he finds you, that's it. He'll speak, and you'll have to obey. But if you goes back of your own accord, then it's *your* decision. You'd be happier as a human. I mean, what can I offer you except rats and a choice of fleas? I mean, I don't know, I don't see it as much of a problem, you just have to stay indoors six or seven nights every month—'

Angua howled.

The hairs that still remained on Gaspode's back stood on end. He tried to remember which was his jugular vein.

'I don't want to have to come in there and get you,' he said. Truth rang on every word.

'The thing is . . . the actual *thing* is . . . I will, though,' he added, trembling. 'It's a bugger, bein' a dog.'

He thought some more, and sighed.

'Oh, I remember. It's the one in the throat,' he said.

*   *   *

Vimes stepped out into the sunlight, except that there wasn't much of it. Clouds were blowing in from the Hub. And—

'Detritus?'

Dink. 'Captain Vimes, *sah*!'

'Who're all these people?'

'Watchmen, sir.'

Vimes stared in puzzlement at the half-dozen assorted guards.

'Who're you?'

'Lance-Constable Hrolf Pyjama, sir.'

'And y— *Coalface*?'

'I never done nuffin.'

'I never done nuffin, *sah*!' yelled Detritus.

'*Coalface*? In the *Watch*?'

Dink. 'Corporal Carrot says there's some good buried somewhere in everyone,' said Detritus.

'And what's your job, Detritus.'

Dink. 'Engineer in charge of deep mining operations, sah!'

Vimes scratched his head.

'That was very nearly a joke, wasn't it?' he said.

'It this new helmet my mate Cuddy made me, sir. Hah! People can't say, there go stupid troll. They have to say, who that goodlooking military troll there, acting-constable already, great future behind him, he got Destiny written all over him like writing.'

Vimes digested this. Detritus beamed at him.

'And where is Sergeant Colon?'

'Here, Captain Vimes.'

'I need a best man, Fred.'

370

'Right, sir. I'll get Corporal Carrot. He's just checking the roofs—'

'Fred! I've known you more than twenty years! Good grief, all you have to do is stand there. Fred, you're *good* at that!'

Carrot appeared at the trot.

'Sorry I'm late. Captain Vimes. Er. We really wanted this to be a surprise—'

'What? What sort of surprise?'

Carrot fished in his pouch. 'Well, captain . . . on behalf of the Watch . . . that is, most of the Watch—'

'Hold on a minute,' said Colon, 'here comes his lordship.'

The clop of hooves and the rattle of harness signalled the approach of Lord Vetinari's carriage.

Carrot glanced around at it. Then he looked at it again. And looked up.

There was a glint of metal, on the roof of the Tower.

'Sergeant, who's on the Tower?' he said.

'Cuddy, sir.'

'Oh. Right.' He coughed. 'Anyway, captain . . . we all clubbed together and—' He paused. 'Acting-Constable Cuddy, right?'

'Yeah. He's reliable.'

The Patrician's carriage was halfway towards Sator Square now. Carrot could see the thin dark figure in the back seat.

He glanced up at the great grey bulk of the tower. He started to run.

'What's up?' said Colon. Vimes started to run, too.

Detritus' knuckles hit the ground as he swung after the others.

And then it hit Colon – a sort of frantic tingle, as though someone had blown on his naked brain.

'Oh, shit,' he said, under his breath.

Claws scrabbled on the dirt.

'He drew his sword!'

'What did you expect? One minute the lad is on top of the world, he's got a whole new interest in his life, something probably even better than goin' for walks, and then he turns round and what he sees is, basically, a wolf. You could of hinted. It's that time of the month, that sort of thing. You can't blame him for being surprised, really.'

Gaspode got to his feet. 'Now, are you going to come on out or have I got to come in there and be brutally savaged?'

Lord Vetinari stood up as he saw the Watch running towards him. That was why the first shot went through his thigh, instead of his chest.

Then Carrot cleared the door of the carriage and flung himself across the man, which is why the next shot went through Carrot.

Angua slunk out.

Gaspode relaxed slightly.

'I can't go back,' said Angua. 'I—'

She froze. Her ears twitched.

'What? What?'

'He's been hurt!'

Angua sprang away.

'Here! Wait for me!' barked Gaspode. 'That's the Shades that way!'

A third shot knocked a chip out of Detritus, who slammed into the carriage, knocking it on its side and severing the traces. The horses scrambled away. The coachman had already made a lightning comparison between current job conditions and his rates of pay and had vanished into the crowd.

Vimes slid to a halt behind the overturned carriage. Another shot spanged off the cobbles near his arm.

'Detritus?'

'Sir?'

'How are you?'

'Oozing a bit, sir.'

A shot hit the carriage wheel above Vimes' head, making it spin.

'Carrot?'

'Right through my shoulder, sir.'

Vimes eased himself along on his elbows.

'Good morning, your lordship,' he said, manically. He leaned back and pulled out a mangled cigar. 'Got a light?'

The Patrician opened his eyes.

'Ah, Captain Vimes. And what happens now?'

Vimes grinned. Funny, he thought, how I never feel really alive until someone tries to kill me. That's when you notice that the sky is blue. Actually, not very blue right now. There's big clouds up there. But I'm noticing them.

'We wait for one more shot,' he said. 'And then we run for proper cover.'

'I appear . . . to be losing a lot of blood,' said Lord Vetinari.

'Who would have thought you had it in you,' said Vimes, with the frankness of those probably about to die. 'What about you, Carrot?'

'I can move my hand. Hurts like . . . heck, sir. But you look worse.'

Vimes looked down.

There was blood all over his coat.

'A bit of stone must have caught me,' he said. 'I didn't even feel it!'

He tried to form a mental picture of the gonne.

Six tubes, all in a line. Each one with its lead slug and charge of No. 1 powder, delivered into the gonne like crossbow bolts. He wondered how long it'd take to put in another six . . .

But we've got him where we want him! There's only one way down out of the Tower!

Yep, we might be sitting out here in the open with him shooting lead pellets at us, but we've got him just where we want him!

Wheezing and farting nervously, Gaspode moved at a shambling run through the Shades and saw, with a heart that sank even further, a knot of dogs ahead of him.

He pushed and squirmed through the tangle of legs.

Angua was at bay in a ring of teeth.

The barking stopped. A couple of large dogs

moved aside, and Big Fido stepped delicately forward.

'So,' he said, 'what we have here is not a dog at all. A spy, perhaps? There's always an enemy. Everywhere. They look like dogs but, inside, they're not dogs. What were you doing?'

Angua growled.

Oh lor', thought Gaspode. She could probably take down a few of 'em, but these are *street* dogs.

He wriggled under a couple of bodies and emerged in the circle. Big Fido turned his red-eyed gaze on him.

'And Gaspode, too,' said the poodle. 'I might have known.'

'You leave her alone,' said Gaspode.

'Oh? You'll fight us all for her, will you?' said Big Fido.

'I got the Power,' said Gaspode. 'You know that. I'll do it. I'll use it.'

'There's no time for this!' snarled Angua.

'You won't do it,' said Big Fido.

'I'll do it.'

'Every dog's paw'll be turned against you—'

'I got the Power, me. You back off, all of you.'

'What power?' said Butch. He was drooling.

'Big Fido knows,' said Gaspode. 'He's *studied*. Now, me an' her are going to walk out of here, right? Nice and slow.'

The dogs looked at Big Fido.

'Get them,' he said.

Angua bared her teeth.

The dogs hesitated.

'A wolf's got a jaw four times stronger'n any dog,' said Gaspode. 'And that's just a *ordinary* wolf—'

'What are you all?' snapped Big Fido. 'You're the pack! No mercy! *Get them!*'

But a pack doesn't act like that, Angua had said. A pack is an association of free individuals. A pack doesn't leap because it's told – a pack leaps because every individual, all at once, decides to leap.

A couple of the bigger dogs crouched . . .

Angua moved her head from side to side, waiting for the first assault . . .

A dog scraped the ground with its paw . . .

Gaspode took a deep breath and adjusted his jaw. Dogs leapt.

'SIT!' said Gaspode, in passable Human.

The command bounced back and forth around the alley, and fifty per cent of the animals obeyed. In most cases, it was the hind fifty per cent. Dogs in mid-spring found their treacherous legs coiling under them—

'BAD DOG!'

—and this was followed by an overpowering sense of racial shame that made them cringe automatically, a bad move in mid-air.

Gaspode glanced up at Angua as bewildered dogs rained around them.

'I said I got the Power, didn't I?' he said. '*Now* run!'

Dogs are not like cats, who amusingly tolerate humans only until someone comes up with a tin opener that can be operated with a paw. Men made dogs, they took wolves and gave them human things

– unnecessary intelligence, names, a desire to belong, and a twitching inferiority complex. All dogs dream wolf dreams, and know they're dreaming of biting their Maker. Every dog knows, deep in his heart, that he is a Bad Dog . . .

But Big Fido's furious yapping broke the spell.

'Get them!'

Angua galloped over the cobbles. There was a cart at the other end of the alley. And, beyond the cart, a wall.

'Not that way!' whined Gaspode.

Dogs were piling along behind them. Angua leapt on to the cart.

'I can't get up there!' said Gaspode. 'Not with my leg!'

She jumped down, picked him up by the scruff of his neck, and leapt back. There was a shed roof behind the cart, a ledge above that and – a few tiles slid under her paws and tumbled into the alley – a house.

'I feel sick!'

'Futupf!'

Angua ran along the ridge of the roof and jumped the alley on the other side, landing heavily in some ancient thatch.

'Aargh!'

'Futupf!'

But the dogs were following them. It wasn't as though the alleys of the Shades were very wide.

Another narrow alley passed below.

Gaspode swung perilously from the werewolf's jaws.

'They're still behind us!'

Gaspode shut his eyes as Angua bunched her muscles.

'Oh, no! Not Treacle Mine Road!'

There was a burst of acceleration followed by a moment of calmness. Gaspode shut his eyes . . .

. . . Angua landed. Her paws scrabbled on the wet roof for a moment. Slates cascaded off into the street, and then she was bounding up to the ridge.

'You can put me down right now,' said Gaspode. 'Right now this minute! Here they come!'

The leading dogs arrived on the opposite roof, saw the gap, and tried to turn. Claws slid on the tiles.

Angua turned, fighting for breath. She'd tried to avoid breathing, during that first mad dash. She'd have breathed Gaspode.

They heard Big Fido's irate yapping.

'Cowards! That's not twenty feet across! That's nothing to a wolf!'

The dogs measured the distance doubtfully. Sometimes a dog has to get right down and ask himself: what species am I?

'It's easy! I'll show you! Look!'

Big Fido ran back a little way, paused, turned, ran . . . and leapt.

There was hardly a curve to the trajectory. The little poodle accelerated out into space, powered less by muscles than by whatever it was that burned in his soul.

His forepaws touched the slates, clawed for a moment on the slick surface, and found no hold. In silence he skidded backwards down the roof, over the edge—

—and hung.

He turned his eyes upwards, to the dog that was gripping him.

'Gaspode? Is that you?'

'Yeff,' said Gaspode, his mouth full.

There was hardly any weight to the poodle but, then, there was hardly any weight to Gaspode. He'd darted forward and braced his legs to take the strain, but there was nothing much to brace them against. He slid down inexorably until his front legs were in the gutter, which began to creak.

Gaspode had an amazingly clear view of the street, three storeys down.

'Oh, *hell*!' said Gaspode.

Jaws gripped his tail.

'Let him go,' said Angua indistinctly.

Gaspode tried to shake his head.

'Stop ftruggling!' he said, out of the corner of his mouth. 'Brave Dog Faves the Day! Valiant Hound in Wooftop Wefcue! No!'

The gutter creaked again.

It's going to go, he thought. Story of my life . . .

Big Fido struggled around.

'What are you holding me up by?'

'Yer collar,' said Gaspode, through his teeth.

'What? To hell with *that*!'

The poodle tried to twist, flailing viciously at the air.

'Ftop it, you daft fbugger! You'll haf uff all off!' Gaspode growled. On the opposite roof, the dog pack watched in horror. The gutter creaked again.

Angua's claws scored white lines on the slates.

Big Fido wrenched and spun, fighting the grip of the collar.

Which, finally, snapped.

The dog turned in the air, hanging for a moment before gravity took hold.

'Free!'

And then he fell.

Gaspode shot backwards as Angua's paws slipped from under her, and landed further up the roof, legs spinning. Both of them made it to the crest and hung there, panting.

Then Angua bounded away, clearing the next alley before Gaspode had stopped seeing a red mist in front of his eyes.

He spat out Big Fido's collar, which slid down the roof and vanished over the edge.

'Oh, thank you!' he shouted. 'Thank you very much! Yes! Leave me here, that's right! Me with only three good legs! Don't you worry about me! If I'm lucky I'll fall off before I starve! Oh yes! Story of my life! You and me, kid! Together! We could have made it!'

He turned and looked at the dogs lining the roofs on the other side of the street.

'You lot! Go home! BAD DOG!' he barked.

He slithered down the other side of the roof. There was an alley there, but it was a sheer drop. He crept along the roof to the adjoining building, but there was no way down. There was a balcony a storey below, though.

'Lat'ral thinking,' he muttered. 'That's the stuff. Now, a wolf, your basic wolf, he'd jump, and if he couldn't jump, he'd be stuck. Whereas me, on account of superior intelligence, can assess the whole wossname and arrive at a solution through application of mental processes.'

He nudged the gargoyle squatting on the angle of the gutter.

'Ot oo oo ont?'

'If you don't help me down to that balcony, I'll widdle in your ear.'

BIG FIDO?

'Yes?'

HEEL.

There were, eventually, two theories about the end of Big Fido.

The one put forward by the dog Gaspode, based on observational evidence, was that his remains were picked up by Foul Ole Ron and sold within five minutes to a furrier, and that Big Fido eventually saw the light of day again as a set of ear muffs and a pair of fleecy gloves.

The one believed by every other dog, based on what might tentatively be called the truth of the heart, was that he survived his fall, fled the city, and eventually led a huge pack of mountain wolves who nightly struck terror into isolated farmsteads. It made digging in the middens and hanging around back doors for scraps seem . . . well, more bearable. They were, after all, only doing it until Big Fido came back.

His collar was kept in a secret place and visited regularly by dogs until they forgot about it.

Sergeant Colon pushed open the door with the end of his pike.

The Tower had floors, a long time ago. Now it was hollow all the way up, criss-crossed by golden shafts of light from ancient window embrasures.

One of them, filled with glittering motes of dust, lanced down on what, not long before, had been Acting-Constable Cuddy.

Colon gave the body a cautious prod. It didn't move. Nothing looking like that should move. A twisted axe lay beside it.

'Oh, no,' he breathed.

There was a thin rope, the sort the Assassins used, hanging down from the heights. It was twitching. Colon looked up at the haze, and drew his sword.

He could see all the way to the top, and there was no one on the rope. Which meant—

He didn't even look around, which saved his life.

His dive for the floor and the explosion of the gonne behind him happened at exactly the same time. He swore afterwards that he felt the wind of the slug as it passed over his head.

Then a figure stepped through the smoke and hit him very hard before escaping through the open door, into the rain.

ACTING-CONSTABLE CUDDY?

Cuddy brushed *himself* off.

'Oh,' he said. 'I see. I didn't think I was going to survive that. Not after the first hundred feet.'

YOU WERE CORRECT.

The unreal world of the living was already fading, but Cuddy glared at the twisted remains of his axe. It seemed to worry him far more than the twisted remains of Cuddy.

'And will you look at that?' he said. 'My dad made that axe for me! A fine weapon to take into the afterlife, I don't think!'

IS THAT SOME KIND OF BURIAL CUSTOM?

'Don't you know? You *are* Death, aren't you?'

THAT DOESN'T MEAN I HAVE TO KNOW ABOUT BURIAL CUSTOMS. GENERALLY, I MEET PEOPLE *BEFORE* THEY'RE BURIED. THE ONES I MEET AFTER THEY'VE BEEN BURIED TEND TO BE A BIT OVER-EXCITED AND DISINCLINED TO DISCUSS THINGS.

Cuddy folded his arms.

'If I'm not going to be properly buried,' he said, 'I ain't going. My tortured soul will walk the world in torment.'

IT DOESN'T HAVE TO.

'It can if it *wants* to,' snapped the ghost of Cuddy.

'Detritus! You haven't got *time* to ooze! Get over to the Tower! Take some people with you!'

Vimes reached the doorway of the Great Hall with the Patrician over his shoulder and Carrot stumbling along behind him. The wizards were clustered around the door. Big heavy drops of rain were beginning to fall, hissing on the hot stones.

Ridcully rolled up his sleeves.

'Hell's bells! What did that to his leg?'

'That's the gonne for you! Sort him out! And Corporal Carrot too!'

'There's no need,' said Vetinari, trying to smile and stand up. 'It's just a flesh—'

The leg collapsed under him.

Vimes blinked. He'd never expected this. The Patrician was the man who always had the answers, who was never surprised. Vimes had a sense that history was flapping loose . . .

'We can handle it, sir,' said Carrot. 'I've got men on the roofs, and—'

'Shut up! Stay here! That's an order!' Vimes fumbled in his pouch and hung his badge on his torn jacket. 'Hey, you . . . Pyjama! I need a sword!'

Pyjama looked sullen.

'I only take orders from Corporal Carrot—'

'Give me a sword right now, you horrible little man! Right! Thank you! Now let's get to the Tow—'

A shadow appeared in the doorway.

Detritus walked in.

They looked at the limp shape in his hands.

He laid it carefully on a bench, without saying a word, and went and sat in a corner. While the others gathered round the mortal remains of Acting-Constable Cuddy, the troll removed his homemade cooling helmet and sat staring at it, turning it over and over in his hands.

'He was on the floor,' said Sergeant Colon, leaning against the doorframe. 'He must have been pushed off the stairs right at the top. Someone else was in there, too. Must've shinned down a rope and caught me a right bang on the side of the head.'

'Being pushed down the Tower's not worth it for a shilling,' said Carrot, vaguely.

It was better when the dragon came, thought Vimes. After it'd killed someone it was at least still a dragon. It went somewhere else but you could say: that's a dragon, that is. It couldn't nip over a wall and become just another person. You always knew what you were fighting. You didn't have to—

'What's that in Cuddy's hand?' he said. He realized he'd been staring at it without seeing it for some time.

He tugged at it. It was a strip of black cloth.

'Assassins wear that,' said Colon blankly.

'So do lots of other people,' said Ridcully. 'Black's black.'

'You're right,' said Vimes. 'Taking any action on the basis of this would be premature. You know, it'd probably get me fired.'

He waved the cloth in front of Lord Vetinari.

'Assassins everywhere,' he said, 'on *guard*. Seems they didn't notice anything, eh? You gave them the bloody gonne because you thought they were the best to guard it! You never thought of giving it to the guards!'

'Aren't we going to give chase, Corporal Carrot?' said Pyjama.

'Chase who? Chase where?' said Vimes. 'He hit old Fred on the head and did a runner. He could trot around a corner, chuck the gonne over a wall, and who'd know? We don't know who we're looking for!'

'I do,' said Carrot.

He stood up, holding his shoulder.

'It's easy to run,' he said. 'We've done a lot of running. But that's not how you hunt. You hunt by sitting still in the right place. Captain, I want the sergeant to go out there and tell people we've got the killer.'

'What?'

'His name is Edward d'Eath. Say we've got him in custody. Say he was caught and badly injured, but he's alive.'

'But we haven't—'

'He's an Assassin.'

'We haven't—'

'Yes, captain. I don't like telling lies. But it might be worth it. Anyway, it's not your problem, sir.'

'It isn't? Why not?'

'You're retiring in less than an hour.'

'I'm still captain right now, corporal. So you have to tell me what's going on. That's how things work.'

'We haven't got time, sir. Do it, Sergeant Colon.'

'Carrot, *I* still run the Watch! I'm the one supposed to give the orders.'

Carrot hung his head.

'Sorry, captain.'

'Right. So long as that's understood. Sergeant Colon?'

'Sir?'

'Put out the news that we've arrested Edward d'Eath. Whoever he is.'

'Yessir.'

'And your next move, Mr Carrot?' said Vimes.

Carrot looked at the assembled wizards.

'Excuse me, sir?'

'Ook?'

'First, we need to get into the library—'

'*First*,' said Vimes, 'someone can lend me a helmet. I don't feel I'm at work without a helmet. Thanks, Fred. Right . . . helmet . . . sword . . . badge. *Now* . . .'

There was sound under the city. It filtered down by all sorts of routes, but it was indistinct, a hive noise.

And there was the faintest of glows. The waters of the Ankh, to use the element in its broadest sense, had washed, to bend the definition to its limit, these tunnels for centuries.

Now there was an extra sound. Footsteps padded over the silt, barely perceptible unless ears had become accustomed to the background noise. And an indistinct shape moved through the gloom, paused at a circle of darkness leading to a smaller tunnel . . .

'How do you feel, your lordship?' said Corporal Nobbs, the upwardly mobile.

'Who are you?'

'Corporal Nobbs, sir!' said Nobby, saluting.

'Do we employ you?'

'Yessir!'

'Ah. You're the dwarf, are you?'

'Nossir. That was the late Cuddy, sir! I'm one of the human beings, sir!'

'You're not employed as the result of any . . . special hiring procedures?'

'Nossir,' said Nobby, proudly.

'My word,' said the Patrician. He was feeling a little light-headed from loss of blood. The Archchancellor had also given him a long drink of something he said was a marvellous remedy, although he'd been unspecific as to what it cured. Verticality, apparently. It was wise to remain sitting upright, though. It was a good idea to be seen to be alive. A lot of inquisitive people were peering around the door. It was important to ensure that rumours of his death were greatly exaggerated.

Corporal self-proclaimed-human Nobbs and some other guards had closed in around the Patrician, on Captain Vimes' orders. Some of them were a lot bulkier than he rather muzzily remembered.

'You there, my man. Have you taken the King's Shilling?' he inquired of one.

'I never took nuffin.'

'Capital, well done.'

And then the crowds scattered. Something golden and vaguely dog-like burst through, growling, its nose close to the ground. And was gone again, covering the ground to the library in long, easy strides. The Patrician was aware of conversation.

'Fred?'

'Yes, Nobby?'

'Did that look a bit familiar to you?'

'I know what you mean.'

Nobby fidgeted awkwardly.

'You should've bawled her out for not being in uniform,' he said.

'Bit tricky, that.'

'If *I'd* run through here without me clothes on, you'd fine me a half a dollar for being improperly dressed—'

'Here's half a dollar, Nobby. Now shut up.'

Lord Vetinari beamed at them. Then there was the guard in the corner, another of the big lumpy ones—

'Still all right, your lordship?' said Nobby.

'Who's that gentleman?'

He followed the Patrician's gaze.

'That's Detritus the troll, sir.'

'Why is he sitting like that?'

'He's thinking, sir.'

'He hasn't moved for some time.'

'He thinks slow, sir.'

Detritus stood up. There was something about the way he did it, some hint of a mighty continent beginning a tectonic movement that would end in the fearsome creation of some unscalable mountain range, which made people stop and look. Not one of the watchers was familiar with the experience of watching mountain building, but now they had some vague idea of what it was like: it was like Detritus standing up, with Cuddy's twisted axe in his hand.

'But deep, sometimes,' said Nobby, eyeing various possible escape routes.

The troll stared at the crowd as if wondering what they were doing there. Then, arms swinging, he began to walk forward.

'Acting-Constable Detritus . . . er . . . as you were . . .' Colon ventured.

Detritus ignored him. He was moving quite fast now, in the deceptive way that lava does.

He reached the wall, and punched it out of the way.

'Has anyone been giving him sulphur?' said Nobby.

Colon looked around at the guard. 'Lance-Constable Bauxite! Lance-Constable Coalface! Apprehend Acting-Constable Detritus!'

The two trolls looked first at the retreating form of Detritus, then at one another, and finally at Sergeant Colon.

Bauxite managed a salute.

'Permission for leave to attend grandmother's funeral, sir?'

'Why?'

'It her or me, sarge.'

'We get our goohuloog heads kicked in,' said Coalface, the less circuitous thinker.

A match flared. In the sewers, its light was like a nova.

Vimes lit first his cigar, and then a lamp.

'Dr Cruces?' he said.

The chief of Assassins froze.

'Corporal Carrot here has a crossbow too,' he said. 'I'm not sure if he'd use it. He's a good man. He thinks everyone else is a good man. I'm not. I'm mean, nasty and tired. And now, doctor, you've had time to think, you're an intelligent man . . . What were you doing down here, please? It can't be to look for the mortal remains of young Edward, because our Corporal Nobbs has taken him off to the Watch morgue this morning, probably nicking any small items of personal jewellery he had on him, but that's just Nobby's way. He's got a criminal mind, has our Nobby. But I'll say this for him: he hasn't got a criminal soul.

'I hope he's cleaned the clown make-up off the poor chap. Dear me. You used him, didn't you? He killed poor old Beano, and then he got the gonne, and he was there when it killed Hammerhock, he even left a bit of his Beano wig in the timbers, and just when he could have done with some good advice, such as to turn himself in, you killed him. The point, the interesting point, is that young Edward couldn't have been the man on the Tower a little while ago. Not with the stab wound in his heart and everything. I know that being dead isn't always a barrier to quiet enjoyment in this city, but I don't think young Edward has been up and about much. The piece of cloth was a nice touch. But, you know, I've never believed in that stuff – footprints in the flower bed, telltale buttons, stuff like that. People think that stuff's policing. It's not. Policing's luck and slog, most of the time. But lots of people'd believe it. I mean, he's been dead . . . what . . . not two days, and it's nice and cool down here . . . you could haul him up, I daresay you could fool people who didn't look too close once he was on a slab, and you'd have got the man who shot the Patrician. Mind you, half the city would be fighting the other half by then, I daresay. Some more deaths would be involved. I wonder if you'd care.' He paused. 'You still haven't said anything.'

'You have no understanding,' said Cruces.

'Yes?'

'D'Eath was right. He was mad, but he was right.'

'About what, Dr Cruces?' said Vimes.

And then the Assassin was gone, diving into a shadow.

'Oh, no,' said Vimes.

A whisper echoed around the man-made cavern.

'Captain Vimes? One thing a good Assassin learns is—'

There was a thunderous explosion, and the lamp disintegrated.

'—never stand near the light.'

Vimes hit the floor and rolled. Another shot hit a foot away, and he felt the splash of cold water.

There was water under him, too.

The Ankh was rising and, in accordance with laws older than those of the city, the water was finding its way back up the tunnels.

'Carrot,' Vimes whispered.

'Yes?' The voice came from somewhere in the pitch blackness to his right.

'I can't see a thing. I lost my night vision lighting that damn lamp.'

'I can feel water coming in.'

'We—' Vimes began, and stopped as he formed a mental picture of the hidden Cruces aiming at a patch of sound.

I should have shot him first, he thought. He's an Assassin!

He had to raise himself slightly to keep his face out of the rising water.

Then he heard a gentle splashing. Cruces was walking towards them.

There was a scratching noise, and then light. Cruces had lit a torch, and Vimes looked up to see the skinny shape in the glow. His other hand was steadying the gonne.

Something Vimes had learned as a young guard drifted up from memory. If you *have* to look along the shaft of an arrow from the wrong end, if a man has you entirely at his mercy, then hope like hell that man is an evil man. Because the evil like power, power over people, and they want to see you in fear. They want you to *know* you're going to die. So they'll talk. They'll gloat.

They'll watch you *squirm*. They'll put off the moment of murder like another man will put off a good cigar.

So hope like hell your captor is an evil man. A good man will kill you with hardly a word.

Then, to his everlasting horror, he heard Carrot stand up.

'Dr Cruces, I arrest you for the murder of Bjorn Hammerhock, Edward d'Eath, Beano the clown, Lettice Knibbs and Acting-Constable Cuddy of the City Watch.'

'Dear me, all those? I'm afraid Edward killed Brother Beano. That was his own idea, the little fool. He *said* he hadn't meant to. And I understand that Hammerhock was killed accidentally. A freak accident. He poked around and the charge fired and the slug bounced off his anvil and killed him. That's what Edward said. He came to see me afterwards. He was very upset. Made a clean breast of the whole thing, you know. So I killed him. Well, what else could I do? He was quite mad. There's no dealing with that sort of person. May I suggest you step back, sire? I'd prefer not to shoot you. No! Not unless I have to!'

It seemed to Vimes that Cruces was arguing with himself. The gonne swung violently.

'He was babbling,' said Cruces. 'He said the gonne killed Hammerhock. I said, it was an accident? And he said no, no accident, the gonne killed Hammerhock.'

Carrot took another step forward. Cruces seemed to be in his own world now.

'No! The gonne killed the beggar girl, too. It wasn't me! Why should I do a thing like that?'

Cruces took a step back, but the gonne swung up towards Carrot. It looked to Vimes as though it moved of its own accord, like an animal sniffing the air . . .

'Get down!' Vimes hissed. He reached out and tried to find his crossbow.

'He said the gonne was jealous! Hammerhock would have made more gonnes! Stop where you are!'

Carrot took another step.

'I had to kill Edward! He was a romantic, he would have got it wrong! But Ankh-Morpork needs a king!'

The gun jerked and fired at the same moment as Carrot leapt sideways.

*　　*　　*

The tunnels were brilliant with smells, mostly the acrid yellows and earthy oranges of ancient drains. And there were hardly any air currents to disturb things; the line that was Cruces snaked through the heavy air. And there was the smell of the gonne, as vivid as a wound.

I smelled gonne in the Guild, she thought, just after Cruces walked past. And Gaspode said that was all right, because the gonne had been in the Guild – but it hadn't been *fired* in the Guild. I smelled it because someone there had fired the thing.

She splashed through the water into the big cavern and saw, with her nose, the three of them – the indistinct figure that smelled of Vimes, the falling figure that was Carrot, the turning shape with the gonne . . .

And then she stopped thinking with her head and let her body take over. Wolf muscle drove her forward and up into a leap, water droplets flying from her mane, her eyes fixed on Cruces' neck.

The gonne fired, four times. It didn't miss once.

She hit the man heavily, knocking him backwards.

Vimes rose in an explosion of spray.

'Six shots! That's six shots, you bastard! I've got you now!'

Cruces turned as Vimes waded towards him, and scurried towards a tunnel, throwing up more spray.

Vimes snatched the bow from Carrot, aimed desperately and pulled the trigger. Nothing happened.

'Carrot! You idiot! You never cocked the damn thing!'

Vimes turned.

'Come on, man! We can't let him get away!'

'It's Angua, captain.'

'What?'

'She's dead!'

'Carrot! *Listen.* Can you find the way out in this stuff? *No!* So come with me!'

'I . . . can't leave her here. I—'

'*Corporal Carrot! Follow me!*'

Vimes half ran, half waded through the rising water towards the tunnel that had swallowed Cruces. It was up a slope; he could feel the water dropping as he ran.

Never give the quarry time to rest. He'd learned that on his first day in the Watch. If you *had* to chase, then stay with it. Give the pursued time to stop and think and you'd go round a corner to find a sock full of sand coming the other way.

The walls and ceiling were closing in.

There were other tunnels here. Carrot had been right. Hundreds of people must have worked for years to build this. What Ankh-Morpork was built on was Ankh-Morpork.

Vimes stopped.

There was no sound of splashing, and tunnel mouths all around.

Then there was a flash of light, up a side tunnel.

Vimes scrambled towards it, and saw a pair of legs in a shaft of light from an open trapdoor.

He launched himself at them, and caught a boot just as it was disappearing into the room above. It kicked at him, and he heard Cruces hit the floor.

Vimes grabbed the edge of the hatchway and struggled through it.

This wasn't a tunnel. It looked like a cellar. He slipped on mud and hit a wall clammy with slime. What was Ankh-Morpork built on? Right . . .

Cruces was only a few yards away, scrambling and slipping up a flight of steps. There had been a door at the top but it had long ago rotted.

There were more steps, and more rooms. Fire and flood, flood and rebuilding. Rooms had become cellars, cellars had become foundations. It wasn't an elegant pursuit; both men slithered and fell, clambered up again, fought their way through hanging curtains of slime. Cruces had left candles here and there. They gave just enough light to make Vimes wish they didn't.

And then there was dry stone underfoot and *this* wasn't a door, but a hole knocked through a wall. And there were barrels, and sticks of furniture, ancient stuff that had been locked up and forgotten.

Cruces was lying a few feet away, fighting for breath and hammering another rack of pipes into the gonne. Vimes managed to pull himself up on to his hands and knees, and gulped air. There was a candle wedged into the wall nearby.

'Got . . . you,' he panted.

Cruces tried to get to his feet, still clutching the gonne.

'You're . . . too old . . . to run . . .' Vimes managed.

Cruces made it up upright, and lurched away.

Vimes thought about it. '*I'm* too old to run,' he added, and leapt.

The two men rolled in the dust, the gonne between them. It struck Vimes much later that the last thing any man of sense would do was fight an Assassin. They had concealed weapons everywhere. But Cruces wasn't going to let go of the gonne. He held it grimly in both hands, trying to hit Vimes with the barrel or the butt.

Curiously enough, Assassins learned hardly any unarmed combat. They were generally good enough at armed combat not to need it. Gentlemen bore arms; only the lower classes used their hands.

'I've *got* you,' Vimes panted. 'You're under *arrest. Be* under arrest, will you?'

But Cruces wouldn't let go. Vimes didn't *dare* let go; the gonne would be twisted out of his grip. It was pulled backwards and forwards between them in desperate, grunting concentration.

The gonne exploded.

There was a tongue of red fire, a firework stink and a *zing-zing* noise from three walls. Something struck Vimes' helmet and *zinged* away towards the ceiling.

Vimes stared at Cruces' contorted features. Then he lowered his head and yanked the gonne hard.

The Assassin screamed and let go, clutching at his nose. Vimes rolled back, gonne in both hands.

It moved. Suddenly the stock was against his shoulder and his finger was on the trigger.

You're mine.

We don't need him any more.

The shock of the voice was so great that he cried out.

He swore afterwards that he didn't pull the trigger. It moved of its own accord, pulling his finger with it. The gonne slammed into his shoulder and a six-inch hole appeared in the wall by the Assassin's head, spraying him with plaster.

Vimes was vaguely aware, through the red mist rising around his vision, of Cruces staggering to a door and lurching through it, slamming it behind him.

All that you hate, all that is wrong – I can put it right.

Vimes reached the door, and tried the handle. It was locked.

He brought the gonne around, not aware of thinking, and let the trigger pull his finger again. A large area of the door and frame became a splinter-bordered hole.

Vimes kicked the rest of it away and followed the gonne.

He was in a passageway. A dozen young men were looking at him in astonishment from half-open doors. They were all wearing black.

He was inside the Assassins' Guild.

A trainee Assassin looked at Vimes with his nostrils.

'Who are you, pray?'

The gonne swung towards him. Vimes managed to haul the barrel upwards just as it fired, and the shot took away a lot of ceiling.

'The *law*, you *sons* of *bitches*!' he shouted.

They stared at him.

Shoot them all. Clean up the world.

'Shut up!' Vimes, a red-eyed, dust-coated, slime-dripping thing from out of the earth, glared at the quaking student.

'Where did Cruces go?' The mist rolled around his head. His hand creaked with the effort of not firing.

The young man jerked a finger urgently towards a flight of stairs. He'd been standing very close when the gonne fired. Plaster dust draped him like devil's dandruff.

The gonne sped away again, dragging Vimes past the boys and up the stairs, where black mud still trailed. There was another corridor there. Doors were opening. Doors closed again after the gonne fired again, smashing a chandelier.

The corridor gave out on to a wide landing at the top of a much more impressive flight of stairs and, opposite, a big oaken door.

Vimes shot the lock off, kicked at the door and then fought the gonne long enough to duck. A cross-bow bolt whirred over his head and hit someone, far down the corridor.

Shoot him! SHOOT HIM!

Cruces was standing by his desk, feverishly trying to slot another bolt into his bow—

Vimes tried to silence the singing in his ears.

But . . . why not? Why not fire? Who was this man? He'd always wanted to make the city a cleaner place, and he might as well start here. And then people would find out what the law was . . .

Clean up the world.

Noon started.

The cracked bronze bell in the Teachers' Guild began the chime, and had midday all to itself for at least seven clangs before the Guild of Bakers' clock, running fast, caught up with it.

Cruces straightened up, and began to edge towards the cover of one of the stone pillars.

'You can't shoot me,' he said, watching the gonne. 'I know the law. And so do you. You're a guard. You can't shoot me in cold blood.'

Vimes squinted along the barrel.

It'd be so easy. The trigger tugged at his finger.

A third bell began chiming.

'You can't just kill me. That's the law. And you're a guard,' Dr Cruces repeated. He licked his dry lips.

The barrel lowered a little. Cruces almost relaxed.

'Yes. I am a guard.'

The barrel rose again, pointed at Cruces' forehead.

'But when the bells stop,' said Vimes, quietly, 'I won't be a guard any more.'

Shoot him! SHOOT HIM!

Vimes forced the butt under his arm, so that he had one hand free.

'We'll do it by the rules,' he said. 'By the rules. Got to do it by the rules.'

Without looking down, he tugged his badge off the remains of his jacket. Even through the mud, it still had a gleam. He'd always kept it polished. When he spun it once or twice, like a coin, the copper caught the light.

Cruces watched it like a cat.

The bells were slackening. Most of the towers had stopped. Now there was only the sound of the gong on the Temple of Small Gods, and the bells of the Assassins' Guild, which were always fashionably late.

The gong stopped.

Dr Cruces put the crossbow, neatly and meticulously, on the desk beside him.

'There! I've put it down!'

'Ah,' said Vimes. 'But I want to make sure you don't pick it up again.'

The black bell of the Assassins' Guild hammered its way to noon.

And stopped.

Silence slammed in like a thunderclap.

The little metallic sound as Vimes' badge bounced on the floor filled it from edge to edge.

He raised the gonne and, gently, let the tension ease out of his hand.

A bell started.

It was a tinny, jolly little tune, barely to be heard at all except in this pool of silence . . .

Cling, bing, a-bing, bong . . .

. . . but much more accurate than hourglasses, water-clocks and pendulums.

'Put down the gonne, captain,' said Carrot, climbing slowly up the stairs.

He held his sword in one hand, and the presentation watch in the other.

. . . *bing, bing, a-bing, cling* . . .

Vimes didn't move.

'Put it down. Put it down now, captain.'

'I can wait out another bell,' said Vimes.

... *a-bing, a-bing* ...

'Can't let you do that, captain. It'd be murder.'

... *clong, a-bing* ...

'You'll stop me, will you?'

'Yes.'

... *bing* ... *bing* ...

Vimes turned his head slightly.

'He killed Angua. Doesn't that mean anything to you?'

... *bing* ... *bing* ... *bing* ... *bing* ...

Carrot nodded.

'Yes. But personal isn't the same as important.'

Vimes looked along his arm. The face of Dr Cruces, mouth open in terror, pivoted on the tip of the barrel.

... *bing* ... *bing* ... *bing* ... *bing* ... *bing* ...

'Captain Vimes?'

... *bing.*

'Captain? Badge 177, captain. It's never had more than dirt on it.'

The pounding spirit of the gonne flowing up Vimes' arms met the armies of sheer stone-headed Vimesness surging the other way.

'I should put it down, captain. You don't need it,' said Carrot, like someone speaking to a child.

Vimes stared at the thing in his hands. The screaming was muted now.

'Put that down now, Watchman! That's an order!'

The gonne hit the floor. Vimes saluted, and then realized what he was doing. He blinked at Carrot.

'Personal isn't the same as *important*?' he said.

'Listen,' Cruces said, 'I'm sorry about the . . . the girl, that was an accident, but I only wanted—There's evidence! There's a—'

Cruces was hardly paying any attention to the Watchmen. He pulled a leather satchel off the table and waved it at them.

'It's here! All of it, sire! Evidence! Edward was stupid, he thought it was all crowns and ceremony, he had no idea what he'd found! And then, last night, it was as if—'

'I'm not interested,' mumbled Vimes.

'The city needs a king!'

'It does not need murderers,' said Carrot.

'But—'

And then Cruces dived for the gonne and scooped it up.

One moment Vimes was trying to reassemble his thoughts, and the next they were fleeing to far corners of his consciousness. He was looking into the mouth of the gonne. It grinned at him.

Cruces slumped against the pillar, but the gonne remained steady, pointing *itself* at Vimes.

'It's all there, sire,' he said. 'Everything written down. The whole thing. Birthmarks and prophecies and genealogy and everything. Even your sword. It's *the* sword!'

'Really?' said Carrot. 'May I see?'

Carrot lowered his sword and, to Vimes' horror, walked over to the desk and pulled the bundle of documents out of the case. Cruces nodded approvingly, as if rewarding a good boy.

Carrot read a page, and turned to the next one.

'This *is* interesting,' he said.

'Exactly. But now we must remove this annoying policeman,' said Cruces.

Vimes felt that he could see all the way along the tube, to the little slug of metal that was soon to launch itself at him . . .

'It's a shame,' said Cruces, 'if only you had—'

Carrot stepped in front of the gonne. His arm moved in a blur. There was hardly a sound.

Pray you never face a good man, Vimes thought. He'll kill you with hardly a word.

Cruces looked down. There was blood on his shirt. He raised a hand to the sword hilt protruding from his chest, and looked back up into Carrot's eyes.

'But why? You could have been—'

And he died. The gonne fell from his hands, and fired at the floor.

There was silence.

Carrot grasped the hilt of his sword and pulled it back. The body slumped.

Vimes leaned on the table and fought to get his breath back.

'Damn . . . his . . . hide,' he panted.

'Sir?'

'He . . . he called you *sire*,' he said. 'What was in that—'

'You're late, captain,' said Carrot.

'Late? Late? What do you mean?' Vimes fought to prevent his brain parting company with reality.

'You were supposed to have been married—'

Carrot looked at the watch, then snapped it shut and handed it to Vimes. '—two minutes ago.'

'Yes, yes. But he called you *sire*, I heard him—'

'Just a trick of the echo, I expect, Mr Vimes.'

A thought broke through to Vimes' attention. Carrot's sword was a couple of feet long. He'd run Cruces clean through. But Cruces had been standing with his back to—

Vimes looked at the pillar. It was granite, and a foot thick. There was no cracking. There was just a blade-shaped hole, front to back.

'Carrot—' he began.

'And you look a mess, sir. Got to get you cleaned up.'

Carrot pulled the leather satchel towards him and slung it over his shoulder.

'*Carrot*—'

'Sir?'

'I *order* you to give—'

'No, sir. You can't order me. Because you are now, sir, no offence meant, a civilian. It's a new life.'

'A *civilian*?'

Vimes rubbed his forehead. It was all colliding in his brain now – the gonne, the sewers, Carrot and the fact that he'd been operating on pure adrenalin, which soon presents its bill and does not give credit. He sagged.

'But this *is* my life. Carrot! This is my *job*.'

'A hot bath and a drink, sir. That's what you need,' said Carrot. 'Do you a world of good. Let's go.'

Vimes' gaze took in the fallen body of Cruces

and, then, the gonne. He went to pick it up, and stopped himself in time.

Not even the wizards had something like this. One burst from a staff and they had to go and lie down.

No wonder no one had destroyed it. You couldn't destroy something as perfect as this. It called out to something deep in the soul. Hold it in your hand, and you had *power*. More power than any bow or spear – they just stored up your own muscles' power, when you thought about it. But the gonne gave you power from outside. You didn't use it, it used you. Cruces had probably been a good man. He'd probably listened kindly enough to Edward, and then he'd taken the gonne, and he'd belonged to it as well.

'Captain Vimes? I think we'd better get that out of here,' said Carrot, reaching down.

'Whatever you do, don't touch it!' Vimes warned.

'Why not? It's only a device,' said Carrot. He picked up the gonne by the barrel, regarded it for a moment, and then smashed it against the wall. Bits of metal pin-wheeled away.

'One of a kind,' he said. 'One of a kind is always special, my father used to say. Let's be going.'

He opened the door.

He shut the door.

'There's about a hundred Assassins at the bottom of the stairs,' he said.

'How many bolts have you got for your bow?' said Vimes. He was still staring at the twisted gonne.

'One.'

'Then it's a good thing you won't have any chance to reload anyway.'

There was a polite knock at the door.

Carrot glanced at Vimes, who shrugged. He opened the door.

It was Downey. He raised an empty hand.

'You can put down your weapons. I assure you they will not be necessary. Where is Dr Cruces?'

Carrot pointed.

'Ah.' He glanced up at the two Watchmen.

'Would you, please, leave his body with us? We will inhume him in our crypt.'

Vimes pointed at the body.

'He *killed*—'

'And now he is dead. And now I must ask you to leave.'

Downey opened the door. Assassins lined the wide stairs. There wasn't a weapon in sight. But, with Assassins, there didn't need to be.

At the bottom lay the body of Angua. The Watchmen walked down slowly, and Carrot knelt and picked it up.

He nodded to Downey.

'Shortly we will be sending someone to collect the body of Dr Cruces,' he said.

'But I thought we had agreed that—'

'No. It must be seen that he is dead. Things must be seen. Things mustn't happen in the dark, or behind closed doors.'

'I am afraid I cannot accede to your request,' said the Assassin firmly.

'It wasn't a request, sir.'

Scores of Assassins watched them walk across the courtyard.

The black gates were shut.

No one seemed about to open them.

'I agree with you, but perhaps you should have put that another way,' said Vimes. 'They don't look at all happy—'

The doors shattered. A six-foot iron arrow passed Carrot and Vimes and removed a large section of wall on the far side of the courtyard.

A couple of blows removed the rest of the gates, and Detritus stepped through. He looked around at the assembled Assassins, a red glow in his eyes. And growled.

It dawned on the smarter Assassins that there was nothing in their armoury that could kill a troll. They had fine stiletto knives, but they needed sledge-hammers.

They had darts armed with exquisite poisons, none of which worked on a troll. No one had ever thought trolls were important enough to be assassinated. Suddenly, Detritus was very important indeed. He had Cuddy's axe in one hand and his mighty crossbow in the other.

Some of the brighter Assassins turned and ran for it. Some were not as bright. A couple of arrows bounced off Detritus. Their owners saw his face as he turned towards them, and dropped their bows.

Detritus hefted his club.

'*Acting-Constable Detritus!*'

The words rang out across the courtyard.

'*Acting-Constable Detritus! Atten-shun!*'

Detritus very slowly raised his hand.

Dink.

'You *listen* to me, Acting-Constable Detritus,' said Carrot. 'If there's a heaven for Watchmen, and gods I hope there is, then Acting-Constable Cuddy is there right now, drunk as a bloody monkey, with a rat in one hand and a pint of Bearhugger's in the other, and he's looking up* at us right now and he's saying: my friend Acting-Constable Detritus won't forget he's a guard. Not Detritus.'

There was a long dangerous moment, and then another *dink.*

'Thank you, Acting-Constable. You'll escort Mr Vimes to the University.' Carrot looked around at the Assassins. 'Good afternoon, gentlemen. We may be back.'

The three Watchmen stepped over the wreckage.

Vimes said nothing until they were well out in the street, and then he turned to Carrot.

'*Why* did he call you—'

'If you'll excuse me, I'll take her back to the Watch House.'

Vimes looked down at Angua's corpse and felt a train of thought derail itself. Some things were too hard to think about. He wanted a nice quiet hour somewhere to put it all together. *Personal isn't the same as important.* What sort of person could think like that? And it dawned on him that while Ankh in the past had had its share of evil rulers, and simply bad rulers, it had never yet come under the heel of a

---

*To trolls, heaven is below.

good ruler. That might be the most terrifying prospect of all.

'Sir?' said Carrot, politely.

'Uh. We'll bury her up at Small Gods, how about that?' said Vimes. 'It's sort of a Watch tradition . . .'

'Yes, sir. You go off with Detritus. He's all right when you give him orders. If you don't mind, I don't think I'll be along to the wedding. You know how it is . . .'

'Yes. Yes, of course. Um. Carrot?' Vimes blinked, to drive away suspicions that clamoured for consideration. 'We shouldn't be too hard on Cruces. I hated the bastard like hell, so I want to be fair to him. I know what the gonne does to people. We're all the same, to the gonne. I'd have been just like him.'

'No, captain. *You* put it down.'

Vimes smiled wanly.

'They call me *Mister* Vimes,' he said.

Carrot walked back to the Watch House, and laid the body of Angua on the slab in the makeshift morgue. Rigor mortis was already setting in.

He fetched some water and cleaned her fur as best he could.

What he did next would have surprised, say, a troll or a dwarf or anyone who didn't know about the human mind's reaction to stressful circumstances.

He wrote his report. He swept the main room's floor; there was a rota, and it was his turn. He had a wash. He changed his shirt, and dressed the wound on his shoulder, and cleaned his armour, rubbing with wire wool and a graded series of cloths until he could, once again, see his face in it.

He heard, far off, Fondel's 'Wedding March' scored for Monstrous Organ with Miscellaneous Farmyard Noises accompaniment. He fished out a half bottle of rum from what Sergeant Colon thought was his secure hiding place, poured himself a very small amount, and drank a toast to the sound, saying, 'Here's to Mr Vimes and Lady Ramkin!' in a clear, sincere voice which would have severely embarrassed anyone who had heard it.

There was a scratching at the door. He let Gaspode in. The little dog slunk under the table, saying nothing.

Then Carrot went up to his room, and sat in his chair and looked out of the window.

The afternoon wore on. The rain stopped around teatime.

Lights came on, all over the city.

Presently, the moon rose.

The door opened. Angua entered, walking softly.

Carrot turned, and smiled.

'I wasn't certain,' he said. 'But I thought, well, isn't it only silver that kills them? I just had to hope.'

It was two days later. The rain had set in. It didn't pour, it slouched out of the grey clouds, running in rivulets through the mud. It filled the Ankh, which slurped once again through its underground kingdom. It poured from the mouths of gargoyles. It hit the ground so hard there was a sort of mist of ricochets.

It drummed off the gravestones in the cemetery behind the Temple of Small Gods, and into the small pit dug for Acting-Constable Cuddy.

There were always only guards at a guard's funeral, Vimes told himself. Oh, sometimes there were relatives, like Lady Ramkin and Detritus' Ruby here today, but you never got *crowds*. Perhaps Carrot was right. When you became a guard, you stopped being everything else.

Although there *were* other people today, standing silently at the railings around the cemetery. They weren't *at* the funeral, but they were watching it.

There was a small priest who gave the generic fill-in-deceased's-name-here service, designed to be vaguely satisfactory to any gods who might be listening. Then Detritus lowered the coffin into the grave, and the priest threw a ceremonial handful of dirt on to the coffin, except that instead of the rattle of soil there was a very final *splat*.

And Carrot, to Vimes' surprise, made a speech. It echoed across the soggy ground to the rain-dripping trees. It was really based around the only text you could use on this occasion: he was my friend, he was one of us, he was a good copper.

He was a good copper. That had got said at every guard funeral Vimes had ever attended. It'd probably be said even at Corporal Nobbs' funeral, although everyone would have their fingers crossed behind their backs. It was what you had to say.

Vimes stared at the coffin. And then a strange feeling came creeping over him, as insidiously as the rain trickling down the back of his neck. It wasn't exactly a suspicion. If it stayed in his mind long enough it would be a suspicion, but right now it was only a faint tingle of a hunch.

He had to ask. He'd never stop thinking about it if he didn't at least *ask*.

So as they were walking away from the grave he said, 'Corporal?'

'Yessir?'

'No one's found the gonne, then?'

'No, sir.'

'Someone said you had it last.'

'I must have put it down somewhere. You know how busy it all was.'

'Yes. Oh, yes. I'm pretty sure I saw you carry most of it out of the Guild . . .'

'Must have done, sir.'

'Yes. Er. I hope you put it somewhere safe, then. Do you, er, do you think you left it somewhere safe?'

Behind them, the gravedigger began to shovel the wet, clinging loam of Ankh-Morpork into the hole.

'I think I must have done, sir. Don't you? Seeing as no one has found it. I mean, we'd soon know if anyone'd found it!'

'Maybe it's all for the best, Corporal Carrot.'

'I certainly hope so.'

'He was a good copper.'

'Yes, sir.'

Vimes went for broke.

'And . . . it seemed to me, as we were carrying that little coffin . . . slightly heavier . . . ?'

'Really, sir? I really couldn't say I noticed.'

'But at least he's got a proper dwarf burial.'

'Oh, yes. I saw to that, sir,' said Carrot.

The rain gurgled off the roofs of the Palace. The gargoyles had taken up their stations at every corner, straining gnats and flies via their ears.

Corporal Carrot shook the drops off his leather rain cape and exchanged salutes with the troll on guard. He strolled through the clerks in the outer rooms and knocked respectfully on the door of the Oblong Office.

'Come.'

Carrot entered, marched to the desk, saluted and stood at ease.

Lord Vetinari tensed, very slightly.

'Oh, yes,' he said. 'Corporal Carrot. I was expecting . . . something like this. I'm sure you've come to ask me for . . . something?'

Carrot unfolded a piece of grubby paper, and cleared his throat.

'Well, sir . . . we could do with a new dartboard. You know. For when we're off duty?'

The Patrician blinked. It was not often that he blinked.

'I beg your pardon?'

'A new dartboard, sir. It helps the men relax after their shift, sir.'

Vetinari recovered a little.

'*Another* one? But you had one only last year!'

'It's the Librarian, sir. Nobby lets him play and he just leans a bit and hammers the darts in with his

415

fist. It ruins the board. Anyway, Detritus threw one through it. Through the wall behind it, too.'

'Very well. And?'

'Well . . . Acting-Constable Detritus needs to be let off having to pay for five holes in his breastplate.'

'Granted. Tell him not to do it again.'

'Yes, sir. Well, I think that's about it. Except for a new kettle.'

The Patrician's hand moved in front of his lips. He was trying not to smile.

'Dear me. Another kettle as well? What happened to the old one?'

'Oh, we still use it, sir, we still use it. But we're going to need another because of the new arrangements.'

'I'm sorry? *What* new arrangements?'

Carrot unfolded a second, and rather larger, piece of paper.

'The Watch to be brought up to an establishment strength of fifty-six; the old Watch Houses at the River Gate, the Deosil Gate and the Hubwards Gate to be reopened and manned on a twenty-four hour basis—'

The Patrician's smile remained, but his face seemed to pull away from it, leaving it stranded and all alone in the world.

'—a department for, well, we haven't got a name for it yet, but for looking at clues and things like dead bodies, e.g., how long they've been dead, and to start with we'll need an alchemist and possibly a ghoul provided they promise not to take anything home and eat it; a special unit using dogs, which could be very useful, and Lance-Constable Angua can deal with that since she can, um, be her own handler a lot of the time; a request here from Corporal Nobbs that Watchmen be allowed all the weapons they can carry, although I'd be obliged if you said no to that; a—'

Lord Vetinari waved a hand.

'All right, all right,' he said. 'I can see how this is going. And supposing I say no?'

There was another of those long, long pauses, wherein may be seen the possibilities of several different futures.

'Do you know, sir, I never even *considered* that you'd say no?'

'You didn't?'

'No, sir.'

'I'm intrigued. Why not?'

'It's all for the good of the city, sir. Do you know where the word "policeman" comes from? It means "man of the city", sir. From the old word *polis*.'

'Yes. I do know.'

The Patrician looked at Carrot. He seemed to be shuffling futures in his head. Then:

'Yes. I accede to all the requests, except the one involving Corporal Nobbs. And you, I think, should be promoted to Captain.'

'Ye-es. I agree, sir. That would be a good thing for Ankh-Morpork. But I will not command the Watch, if that's what you mean.'

'Why not?'

'Because I *could* command the Watch. Because . . . people should do things because an officer tells them. They shouldn't do it just because Corporal Carrot says so. Just because Corporal Carrot is . . . good at being obeyed.' Carrot's face was carefully blank.

'An interesting point.'

'But there used to be a rank, in the old days. Commander of the Watch. I suggest Samuel Vimes.'

The Patrician leaned back. 'Oh, yes,' he said. 'Commander of the Watch. Of course, that became a rather unpopular job, after all that business with Lorenzo the Kind. It was a Vimes who held the post in those days. I've never liked to ask him if he was an ancestor.'

'He was, sir. I looked it up.'

'Would he accept?'

'Is the High Priest an Offlian? Does a dragon explode in the woods?'

The Patrician steepled his fingers and looked at Carrot over the top of them. It was a mannerism that had unnerved many.

'But, you see, captain, the trouble with Sam Vimes is that he upsets a lot of important people. And I think that a Commander of the Watch would have to move in very exalted circles, attend Guild functions . . .'

They exchanged glances. The Patrician got the best of the bargain, since Carrot's face was bigger. Both of them were trying not to grin.

'An excellent choice, in fact,' said the Patrician.

'I'd taken the liberty, sir, of drafting a letter to the cap— to Mr Vimes on your behalf. Just to save you trouble, sir. Perhaps you'd care to have a look?'

'You think of everything, don't you?'

'I hope so, sir.'

Lord Vetinari read the letter. He smiled once or twice. Then he picked up his pen, signed at the bottom, and handed it back.

'And is that the last of your dema— requests?'

Carrot scratched his ear.

'There is one, actually. I need a home for a small dog. It must have a large garden, a warm spot by the fire, and happy laughing children.'

'Good heavens. Really? Well, I suppose we can find one.'

'Thank you, sir. That's all, I think.'

The Patrician stood up and limped over to the window. It was dusk. Lights were being lit all over the city.

With his back to Carrot he said, 'Tell me, captain . . . this business about there being an heir to the throne . . . What do you think about it?'

'I don't think about it, sir. That's all sword-in-a-stone nonsense. Kings don't come out of nowhere, waving a sword and putting everything right. Everyone knows that.'

'But there was some talk of . . . *evidence*?'

'No one seems to know where it is, sir.'

'When I spoke to Captain . . . to Commander Vimes he said you'd got it.'

'Then I must have put it down somewhere. I'm sure I couldn't say where, sir.'

'My word, I hope you absent-mindedly put it down somewhere safe.'

'I'm sure it's . . . well guarded, sir.'

'I think you've learned a *lot* from Cap— *Commander* Vimes, captain.'

'Sir. My father always said I was a quick learner, sir.'

'Perhaps the city does *need* a king, though. Have you considered that?'

'Like a fish needs a . . . er . . . a thing that doesn't work underwater, sir.'

'Yet a king can appeal to the emotions of his subjects, captain. In . . . very much the same way as you did recently, I understand.'

'Yes, sir. But what will he do next day? You can't treat people like puppet dolls. No, sir. Mr Vimes always said a man has got to know his limitations. If there was a king, then the best thing he could do would be to get on with a decent day's work—'

'Indeed.'

'*But* if there was some pressing need . . . then perhaps he'd think again.' Carrot brightened up. 'It's a bit like being a guard, really. When you need us, you really need us. And when you don't . . . well, best if we just walk around the streets and shout All's Well. Providing all *is* well, of course.'

'Captain Carrot,' said Lord Vetinari, 'because we understand one another so well, and I think we *do* understand one another . . . there is something I'd like to show you. Come this way.'

He led the way into the throne room, which was empty at this time of day. As he hobbled across the wide floor he pointed ahead of him.

'I expect you know what that is, captain?'

'Oh, yes. The golden throne of Ankh-Morpork.'

'And no one has sat in it for many hundreds of years. Have you ever wondered about it?'

'Exactly what do you mean, sir?'

'So much gold, when even the brass has been stripped off the Brass Bridge? Take a look *behind* the throne, will you?'

Carrot mounted the steps.

'Good grief!'

The Patrician looked over his shoulder.

'It's just gold foil over wood . . .'

'Quite so.'

It was hardly even wood any more. Rot and worms had fought one another to a standstill over the last biodegradable fragment. Carrot prodded it with his sword, and part of it drifted gently away in a puff of dust.

'What do you think about this, captain?'

Carrot stood up.

'On the whole, sir, it's probably just as well that people don't know.'

'So I have always thought. Well, I will not keep you. I'm sure you have a lot to organize.'

Carrot saluted.

'Thank you, sir.'

'I gather that you and, er, Constable Angua are getting along well?'

'We have a very good Understanding, sir. Of course, there will be minor difficulties,' said Carrot, 'but, to look on the positive side, I've got someone who's always ready for a walk around the city.'

As Carrot had his hand on the door handle Lord Vetinari called out to him.

'Yes, sir?'

Carrot looked back at the tall thin man, standing in the big bare room beside the golden throne filled with decay.

'You're a man interested in words, captain. I'd just invite you to consider something your predecessor never fully grasped.'

'Sir?'

'Have you ever wondered where the word "politician" comes from?' said the Patrician.

'And then there's the committee of the Sunshine Sanctuary,' said Lady Ramkin, from her side of the dining table. 'We must get you on that. And the Country Landowners' Association. And the Friendly Flamethrowers' League. Cheer up. You'll find your time will just fill up like nobody's business.'

'Yes, dear,' said Vimes. The days stretched ahead of him, just filling up like nobody's business with committees and good works and . . . nobody's business. It was probably better than walking the streets. Lady Sybil and Mr Vimes.

He sighed.

Sybil Vimes, *née* Ramkin, looked at him with an expression of faint concern. For as long as she'd known him, Sam Vimes had been vibrating with the internal anger of a man who wants to arrest the gods for not doing it right, and then he'd handed in his badge and he was . . . well, not exactly Sam Vimes any more.

The clock in the corner chimed eight o'clock. Vimes pulled out his presentation watch and opened it.

'That clock's five minutes fast,' he said, above the tinkling chimes. He snapped the lid shut, and read again the words on it: A Watch From, Your Old Freinds In The Watch'.

Carrot had been behind that, sure enough. Vimes had grown to recognize that blindness to the position of 'i's and 'e's and that wanton cruelty to the common comma.

They said goodbye to you, they took you out of the measure of your days, and they gave you a watch . . .

'Excuse me, m'lady?'

'Yes, Willikins?'

'There is a Watchman at the door, m'lady. The tradesman's entrance.'

'You sent a Watchman to the tradesman's entrance?' said Lady Sybil.

'No, m'lady. That's the one he came to. It's Captain Carrot.'

Vimes put his hand over his eyes. 'He's been made captain and he comes to the back door,' he said. 'That's Carrot, that is. Bring him on in.'

It was barely noticeable, except to Vimes, but the butler glanced at Lady Ramkin for her approval.

'Do as your master says,' she said, gallantly.

'I'm no one's mas—' Vimes began.

'Now, Sam,' said Lady Ramkin.

'Well, I'm not,' said Vimes sullenly.

Carrot marched in, and stood to attention. As usual the room subtly became a mere background to him.

'It's all right, lad,' said Vimes, as nicely as he could manage. 'You don't need to salute.'

'Yes I do, sir,' said Carrot. He handed Vimes an envelope. It had the seal of the Patrician on it.

Vimes picked up a knife and broke the seal.

'Probably charging me five dollars for unnecessary wear and tear on my chainmail,' he said.

His lips moved as he read.

'Blimey,' he said eventually. 'Fifty-six?'

'Yes, sir. Detritus is looking forward to breaking them in.'

'Including undead? It says here open to all, regardless of species or mortal status—'

'Yes, sir,' said Carrot, firmly. 'They're all citizens.'

'You mean you could have *vampires* in the Watch?'

'Very good on night duty, sir. And aerial surveillance.'

'And always useful if you want to stake out somewhere.'

'Yes, sir?'

Vimes watched the feeble pun go right through Carrot's head without triggering his brain. He turned back to the paper.

'Hmm. Pensions for widows, I see.'

'Yessir.'

'Re-opening the old Watch Houses?'

'That's what he says, sir.'

Vimes read on:

We *consider particularly that, this enlarged Watch will need an expereinced man in charge who, is held in Esteem by all parts of soceity and, we are convinced that you should fulfil this Roll. You will*

*therefore take up your Duties immediately as,
Commander of the Ankh-Morpork City Watch.
This post traditionally carreis with it the rank of
Knight which, we are minded to resurrect on this
one occasion.*

*Hoping this finds you in good health, Yrs.
faithfully*

Havelock Vetinari (*Patrician*)

Vimes read it again.

He drummed his fingers on the table. There was
no doubt that the signature was genuine. But . . .

'Corp— Captain Carrot?'

'Sah!' Carrot stared straight ahead of him with
the glistening air of one busting with duty and
efficiency and an absolute resolve to duck and dodge
any direct questions put to him.

'I—' Vimes picked up the paper again, put it
down, picked it up, and then passed it over to Sybil.

'My word!' she said. 'A knighthood? Not a moment too soon, either!'

'Oh, no! Not me! You know what I think about
the so-called aristocrats in *this* city – apart from you,
Sybil, of course.'

'Perhaps it's about time the general stock was
improved, then,' said Lady Ramkin.

'His lordship did say,' said Carrot, 'that no part
of the package was negotiable, sir. I mean, it's all or
nothing, if you understand me.'

'All . . . ?'

'Yessir.'

'. . . or nothing.'

'Yessir.'

Vimes drummed his fingers on the table.

'You've won, haven't you?' he said. 'You've *won*.'

'Sir? Don't understand, sir,' said Carrot, radiating honest ignorance.

There was another dangerous silence.

'But, of course,' said Vimes, 'there's no possible way I could oversee this sort of thing.'

'What do you mean, sir?' said Carrot.

Vimes pulled the candelabra towards him and thumped the paper with a finger.

'Well, look what it says here. I mean, opening those old Watch Houses? On the gates? What's the point in that? Right out there on the edge?'

'Oh, I'm sure matters of organization detail can be changed, sir,' said Carrot.

'Keep a general gate guard, *yes*, but if you're going to have any kind of finger on the pulse of . . . look, you'd need one along Elm Street somewhere, close to the Shades and the docks, and another one halfway up Short Street, and maybe a smaller one in Kingsway. Somewhere up there, anyway. You've got to think about population centres. How many men based per Watch House?'

'I thought ten, sir. Allowing for shifts.'

'No, can't do that. Use six at most. A corporal, say, and one other per shift. The *rest* you'll move around on, oh, a monthly rota. You want to keep everyone on their toes, yes? And that way everyone gets to walk every street. That's very important. And . . . wish I had a map here . . . oh . . . thank you, dear. Right. Now, see here. You've got a strength of fixty-six, nominal, okay? But you're taking over day watch too, plus you've got to allow for days off, two grandmother's funerals per year per man – gods know how your undead'll sort out *that* one, maybe they get time off to go to their *own* funerals – and then there's sickness and so on. So . . . we want four shifts, staggered around the city. Got a light? Thanks. We don't want the whole guard changing shift at once. On the other hand, you've got to allow each Watch House officer a certain amount of initiative. But we should maintain a special squad in Pseudopolis Yard for emergencies . . . look, give me that pencil. Now give me that notebook. Right . . .'

Cigar smoke filled the room. The little presentation watch played every quarter of an hour, entirely unheeded.

Lady Sybil smiled and shut the door behind her, and went to feed the dragons.

'Dearest Mumm and Dad,

Well here is Amazing news for, I am now Captain!! It has been a very busy and vareid Week all round as, I shall now recount . . .'

And only one thing more . . .

There was a large house in one of the nicer areas of Ankh, with a spacious garden with a children's treehouse in it and, quite probably, a warm spot by the fire.

And a window, breaking . . .

Gaspode landed on the lawn, and ran like hell

towards the fence. Flower-scented bubbles streamed off his coat. He was wearing a ribbon with a bow on it, and carrying in his mouth a bowl labelled MR HUGGY.

He dug his way frantically under the fence and squirmed into the road.

A fresh pile of horse droppings took care of the floral smell, and five minutes of scratching removed the bow.

'Not a bloody flea left,' he moaned, dropping the bowl. 'An' I had nearly the complete set. Whee-ooo! I'm well out of *that*. Huh!'

Gaspode brightened up. It was Tuesday. That meant steak-and-suspicious-organs pie at the Thieves' Guild, and the head cook there was known to be susceptible to a thumping tail and a penetrating stare. And holding an empty bowl in your mouth and looking pathetic was a sure-fire winner, if Gaspode was any judge. It shouldn't take too long to claw off MR HUGGY.

Perhaps this wasn't the way it ought to be. But it was the way it was.

On the whole, he reflected, it could have been a lot worse.

THE END

INTERESTING TIMES

Terry Pratchett

'Funny, delightfully inventive and refuses to lie
down in its genre'
Observer

'*A foot in the neck is nine points of the law.*'

THERE are many who say that the art of diplomacy is
an intricate and complex dance between two
informed partners, determined by an elaborate set of
elegant and unwritten rules. There are others who
maintain that it's merely a matter of who carries the
biggest stick. Like when a large, heavily fortified and
armoured empire makes a faintly menacing request of a
much smaller, infinitely more cowardly neighbour. It
would be churlish, if not extremely dangerous, not to
comply – particularly if all they want is a wizard, and
they don't specify whether competence is an issue...

'Imagine a collision between Jonathan Swift at his
most scatological and J.R.R. Tolkien on speed...
This is the joyous outcome'
Daily Telegraph

'Like Dickens, much of Pratchett's appeal lies in his
humanism, both in a sentimental regard for his
characters' good fortune, and in that his writing is
generous-spirited and inclusive'
Guardian

9780552153218

MASKERADE
Terry Pratchett

'As funny as Wodehouse and as witty as Waugh'
Independent

'I thought: opera, how hard can it be? Songs. Pretty girls dancing. Nice scenery. Lots of people handing over cash. Got to be better than the cut-throat world of yoghurt, I thought. Now everywhere I go there's...'

DEATH, to be precise. And plenty of it. In unpleasant variations. This isn't real life. This isn't even cheesemongering. It's opera. Where the music matters and where an opera house is being terrorised by a man in evening dress with a white mask, lurking in the shadows, occasionally killing people, and most worryingly, sending little notes, writing maniacal laughter with five exclamation marks. Opera can do that to a man. In such circumstances, life has obviously reached that desperate point where the wrong thing to do **has** to be the right thing to do...

'Cracking dialogue, compelling illogic and unchained whimsy...Pratchett has a subject and a style that is very much his own'
Sunday Times

'Entertaining and gloriously funny'
Chicago Tribune

9780552153232

FEET OF CLAY
Terry Pratchett

'The work of a prolific humorist at his best'
Observer

'Sorry?' said Carrot. 'If it's just a thing, how can it commit murder? A sword is a thing' – *he drew out his own sword; it made an almost silken sound* – *'and of course you can't blame a sword if someone thrust it at you, sir.'*

For members of the City Watch, life consists of troubling times, linked together by periods of torpid inactivity. Now is one such troubling time. People are being murdered, but there's no trace of anything alive having been at the crime scene. Is there ever a circumstance in which you can blame the weapon not the murderer? Such philosophical questions are not the usual domain of the city's police, but they're going to have to start learning fast…

'Like most true originals, Pratchett defies categorization… Deliciously and amiably dotty… Driven by Swiftian logic and equally intellectually inventive'
The Times

'Fantastical, inventive and finally serious… It's enjoyable as crime fiction, but the real attraction is the laughter waiting to be uncovered on every page'
Observer

'An explosion of imaginative lunacy'
Daily Express

9780552153256

Visit

www.**terrypratchett**.co.uk

to discover everything you need to know
about Terry Pratchett and his writing, plus all
manner of other things you may find interesting, such as
videos, competitions, character profiles and games.

 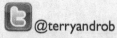